# INFERNA

# SHUTTERCLIQUE #2

INFERNA

WRITTEN BY

# DAVE NEAL

## NOSETOUCH PRESS
### CHICAGO · PITTSBURGH

ISBN-13: ISBN: 978-1-944286-42-2
PAPERBACK EDITION

PUBLISHED BY NOSETOUCH PRESS
WWW.NOSETOUCHPRESS.COM

FOR MORE INFORMATION, CONTACT NOSETOUCH PRESS:
INFO@NOSETOUCHPRESS.COM

CATALOGING-IN-PUBLICATION DATA

NAME: NEAL, DAVE, AUTHOR.
TITLE: INFERNA
DESCRIPTION: CHICAGO, IL : NOSETOUCH PRESS [2025]
IDENTIFIERS: ISBN: 9781944286422 (PAPERBACK)
SUBJECTS: LCSH: SUPER HEROES—FICTION.
GSAFD: FANTASY FICTION.
BISAC: FICTION / FANTASY / URBAN.

COVER & INTERIOR DESIGNED BY CHRISTINE M. SCOTT
WWW.CLEVERCROW.COM

THE SHUTTERCLIQUE #2
# INFERNA

## PREVIOUSLY...

BEREFT OVER THE APPARENT LOSS OF HIS SU-PERHERO GIRLFRIEND, ANNA VICTOR (AKA, VICTORIANA), WHO FLEW INTO THE SUN FOR REASONS UNKNOWN, MITCH PAULSEN (AKA, CAMERAMAN), THROWS HIMSELF INTO SOLO CRIMEFIGHTING. WHEN HE'S APPROACHED BY DECIBELLE, AN ACTIVE MEMBER OF THE SUPERHERO TEAM, THE AFFILIATES, MITCH IS OFFERED A CHANCE TO INVESTIGATE THE VIGILANTE ACTIONS OF ANOTHER AFFILIATE, BRIGHTEYES. IN THE COURSE OF HIS INVES-TIGATING, MITCH BECOMES AWARE OF A COVERT PLOT THAT APPEARS TO IMPLICATE THE AFFILIATES WITH THE NOTORIOUS CRIME LEAGUE, AND THE INVOLVEMENT OF MINDER, WHO IS THE CHAIRMAN OF THE SUPERHERO TEAM.

MITCH FINDS HIS LIFE INCREASINGLY SPIRALING OUT OF CONTROL AS HE RUNS AFOUL OF MINDER AND HIS OPERATIVES, WHO ARE LOOKING TO STOP CAMERAMAN FROM EXPOSING THE CORRUPTION WITHIN THE AFFIL-IATES. WORKING WITH HIS FRIEND, SHANE GREY (AKA, THE KNACK), AND THE UNDERWORLD INVESTIGATOR, IN-FERNA, MITCH PUTS TOGETHER A TEAM OF HEROES TO HELP HIM AGAINST MINDER AND THE AFFILIATES. THIS TEAM, LATER CALLED "THE SHUTTERCLIQUE"—SUC-CESSFULLY BEATS BACK THE AFFILIATES AND THEIR PARTNERS, AND MINDER'S WRONGDOING IS EXPOSED IN THE MEDIA, THANKS TO CAMERAMAN RELEASING IN-CRIMINATING FOOTAGE.

HOWEVER, IN A PRESS CONFERENCE ADDRESSING THIS FOOTAGE AND CAMERAMAN'S INVOLVEMENT IN IT, MINDER IS ASSASSINATED BY UNKNOWN PARTIES, AND MITCH IS FORCED TO OFFER AN ALIBI FOR WHERE HE WAS WHEN MINDER WAS MURDERED. WHILE DEFEND-ING HIMSELF, MITCH DISCOVERS THAT ANNA MAY STILL BE ALIVE—A REVELATION THAT CHANGES EVERYTHING HE THOUGHT HE KNEW....

**I'M MAN ENOUGH TO ADMIT THAT** I basically passed out when I'd seen that metal marble in the bowl. It was one of Anna's, and, no, I hadn't missed the damned thing. I'm not a neat freak, but I am fastidious. And I have a photographic memory, remember? I don't miss things when I'm paying attention to them.

With Tag and Rollergirl hovering over me, I composed myself, got my footing. And I didn't care who knew—I picked the marble up and held it out for them to see.

"Yeah?" Tag Team asked, looking flummoxed in his black and orange costume. "So what, Mitch?"

"It's *hers*," I said. "It's a sign. Anna's *alive*."

They just stared at me, and I know they probably thought I'd lost my, well, marbles. But I hadn't; I'd found them. Just one. *She'd* been here. I don't know how, but she had.

"Mitch, Anna's gone," Tag said.

"Nope," I said, brandishing it like some sacred relic.

"Well, that aside, we need to account for your day," Tag said. "We have to know where you were today. *All day*."

My head was spinning, and I was trying to get my bearings. Christ, the puns never stopped, did they?

*Anna was alive.*

"I didn't shoot Minder," I said. "If I had to spitball a suspect, I'd recommend you locate Deadpan, aka, Sureshot. That seems far more his kind of jam."

Tag Team and Rollergirl exchanged looks. They weren't bad at hero work. They were more support class like I was, so we spoke the same language.

"Somebody took out Minder," I said, cursing my bad luck. To clear my own name, even just anecdotally, I'd have to find out who had murdered Minder—the very guy who'd made my superheroic life hellish for the past few years. Minder was the Number One suspect in what the Knack referred to as "the rot" afflicting the Affiliates. Minder was at the center of the conspiratorial web, and now he was dead.

I jotted down my schedule for the day, careful not to include that I'd actually been at the shooting of Minder—I'd filmed the whole thing. I'd only gotten back here because Inferna had teleported me back, bless her heart. If it hadn't been for her, I'd have been locked up already.

*Anna was alive.*

That revelation slammed around in my head, threatening to upend everything. I broke down my necessary to-do items so I could just work through them and get after finding out where Anna was:

*1. GET TAG TEAM AND ROLLERGIRL OUT OF MY APARTMENT (AND PALEFACE, WHO WAS LURKING OUTSIDE, SINCE I HADN'T INVITED THAT BLOODSUCKER INTO MY PLACE).*

*2. SECURE ALL OF THE FOOTAGE OF MINDER'S ASSASSINATION, WHICH INVOLVED ALSO STUDYING IT FOR CLUES.*

*3. CLEAR MY NAME IN CASE IT WAS GETTING DRAGGED THROUGH THE MUD.*

*4. FIND ANNA.*

She was, of course, tops on my actual list, but those other items would be intruding in my efforts to find Anna, so I had to deal with them to get them out of my way.

"Look, what more do you want?" I asked. Tag looked uncomfortable, and I could only wonder what Rollergirl had by way of an expression, as she was hidden within her powersuit.

"We'd like to take you to Central for questioning," Tag said. "You have no witnesses for being here all day. We can't just take this list you gave us on credit, Mitch."

I caught the brimstone stink before I heard Inferna, who had appeared from my living room, wearing her black leather overcoat and black fedora with a red brim.

She was not alone this time, standing with this wild-looking bald devil-woman with glowing skin and a floating golden diadem-like crown, in a white leather one-piece suit with thigh boots and open-fingered kid gloves and a ragged crimson cape with a hood, radiating hellish heat. She wore the hood with her crown hovering over it.

"*We* can vouch for Mitch being here," Inferna said. "This is Hellmaiden, one of my teammates in the newly-formed netherworldly team, Hell's Belles."

"What?" I said, looking at Inferna and this Hellmaiden, who was looking right at me with these glowing white eyes, staring me down with a look that would melt mountains. She had a logo hanging from a white choker she wore—a white "HM" surrounded by a red fireball on a kind of golden medallion.

I didn't even know what the hell Hell's Belles even was, beyond what Inferna had just said about them. Netherworldly? Huh?

"What?" Tag and Rollergirl said, looking at each other, and at Inferna and her, what, sidekick? Teammate?

Tag composed himself and spoke up.

"We, uh, don't consider you a credible witness, Inferna," he said. "Or your friend."

"Foolish mortal," Inferna said. "Hell's Belles is a celestially-sanctioned supergroup. We're authorized to operate across dimensions by the Trans-Dimensional Incursion Authority."

"The what?" Tag Team asked.

She produced a scroll with arcane script upon it, brandishing it in Tag Team's face, who looked properly befuddled. So much so that he dialed up Shane on his Affilicom, put it on speaker.

"Shane, we're here with Mitch," Tag said. "He's claiming he was here all day. And, ehh, he has witnesses in the form of, well, Inferna and somebody called Hellmaiden. Part of Hell's Belles, whatever that is."

Shane thankfully rolled with it. He was the one who gave me the warning right when the assassination happened, and I know you're probably thinking he had something to do with it, but his warning had given me time to get the hell out of there by way of Inferna.

"That's good enough for me," Shane said. "If Mitch provided his schedule and his witnesses back him up, you can go back to Central, Tag Team. Stand down."

Tag Team acknowledged that and hung up.

"Okay, Mitch," Tag said. "Sorry to have bothered you. It's been a crazy day. Just don't leave town, alright? We may have more questions."

"Fine," I said, walking them out, while Inferna and Hellmaiden watched them go. "I'll call you if I come across anything."

Glancing at the television, I saw they were playing legacy interviews of Minder, which just pissed me off all over again. An asshole didn't become a saint just because he was assassinated, did he?

"You see that? They're making that son of a bitch into some kind of martyr-hero," I said. "But enough of that."

I held up the metal marble, showing it to Inferna with a shaky grin.

"Anna's *alive*, Inferna," I said. "She left me a sign."

Inferna studied the marble, cocking an eyebrow, while Hellmaiden surveyed it from afar, being more occupied with casing my place. I'd never known Inferna to work with a team, but who knew how things worked in Hell.

"Did she?" Inferna asked.

"Hell, yeah, she did," I said. "She *knew* this would be significant to me. That I'd notice it."

I held it to my chest, then pocketed it. I didn't want to put it in the vase with the others, but I showed them to Inferna and her gal pal.

"This was just a silly thing we did," I said. "She knew, though. She *knew* I'd notice."

Inferna smiled, glancing at Hellmaiden, who smiled back awkwardly, even warily. Devils had disarming smiles—they were all-knowing and sly, radiated a kind of worldly carnality and cosmopolitan smugness. I tried to get my head together.

"Why are you here, Inferna?" I asked. "I didn't call you. And what's with this Hell's Belles business?"

"Shane thought you might need my help," Inferna said. "You're in a lot of trouble, Mitch. Maybe more than you know. And regarding Hell's Belles, why can't I have my own team? With all the work I do for you and others, I feel like I could use the help. Right now, we're a power trio—myself, Hellmaiden, and She-Devil. We're to be underworld infernal investigators."

I was secretly amused that Inferna had put together her own team. It hit my funny bone—what the hell would Hell's Belles do? Underworld infernal investigations?

"You know, I think there's an AC/DC cover band with that name," I said. Inferna sighed.

"We're superheroes," Inferna said. "Or antiheroes, at any rate, right, Hellmaiden?"

Hellmaiden nodded her agreement solemnly.

I took a seat on my couch, taking a breather, while Inferna and Hellmaiden lurked.

"It's going to get around that you vouched for me, Fern," I said. It was a nickname I had for her. Just an in-joke between us since ferns didn't grow in Hell, as Inferna had once gravely intoned to me years ago: "There are no ferns in Hell."

"Is that going to be a problem for you, Mitch?" Inferna asked. "We don't want to add to your troubles. Not like the way you keep adding to your tab."

I sighed, trying to organize my mind. I got up and went to my databoard, snatching a stylus, queuing up the original files I had when I'd brainstormed with the Knack about it. I drew an "X" through Minder. It felt bizarre to do that. I also added Hell's Belles, Inferna, Hellmaiden, and She-Devil to the board.

"Who killed Minder?" I asked. "I thought he was at the center of it all, like the puppet master, but he was clearly just part of someone else's plan."

I studied the matrix of information on the databoard (*what was described in detail in BRIGHTEYES, Chapter 20—the editors*). Inferna and Hellmaiden studied it a moment, their devilish eyes appearing to take it all in.

"One of Minder's allies didn't want him talking," I said. "Or else they wanted to pin it all on me in some fashion to cover up what they were really up to."

Hellmaiden was throwing off a lot of heat, so much that I was sweating. Inferna smiled at her sidekick.

"Apologies, Mitch," she said. "Hellmaiden's a hot one. She forgets herself sometimes, how fragile you mortals are."

Hellmaiden backed away, raising her hands in protest. Her glowing hellish radiance made her hard to look at directly for more than a few moments. Her skin was like a fiery black opal shade, constantly roiling and moving in an almost mesmeric fashion.

Then I saw the broadcast news displaying still shots of Cameraman. I turned off the mute.

"Cameraman is a person of interest in the assassination of the Affiliates leader known as Minder, now identified as Rex Traynor," the newswoman said. "The Affiliates are investigating. We go live to hear what Shane Grey, known as the Knack, and now team leader of the Affiliates, has to say on the matter."

That's all well and good when you're at home on the couch, nursing some jasmine tea and watching your boyfriend make dinner. It's one of those luxurious inquiries that might rattle around in your head like...like a marble. Yeah.

But when you're standing on the Sun, half-blinded by the churning plasma, feeling the heat on your heels—who am I kidding? Across your entire naked body—it's another matter entirely.

This isn't one of those "whoopsie" kind of moments from adolescence, where you might find yourself somewhere you ought not to have been, without a clear memory how you got there. No, I'm in a real jam, here, because I'm walking on the Sun.

And I'm not dead.

My costume burned off, as did my hair, but holy crap, I'm not actually dead. The blur of how I got here remains burned in my fractured memory.

*I'm Victoriana.*

*I'm Anna Victor.*

*That's who I am.*

They have to think I'm dead, because that's what Minder did to me. He *made* me do it. Stupid of me, honestly. Innocent?

Naïve? Inexperienced? Overconfident? I was warned, and I didn't listen. I paid the price for it.

What's the right thing to say? I'm from Pittsburgh. I grew up in Mount Lebanon. Happy family. Two older siblings (Lane, my big brother, who became a lawyer; and Blake, the middle sibling, who joined the Navy). My mom and dad were good parents (both doctors—Mom's a neurologist, Dad's a neuro-surgeon—they're a great team, work together in the same clinical practice). *Are* good parents. They're not dead, yet.

I had a happy childhood, and, at least until puberty, a normal childhood, before my powers manifested. Before my hair turned green. What a scandal that caused. Can you imagine? Mom thought I was insane, like I'd dyed my hair green. Dad had me in therapy after I told them that I had no idea how it happened. They loved me. They wanted the best for me. My brothers laughed about it, joked that I'd taken my love of Green Day to the next level. I *do* love Green Day. I won't apologize for it, or for them. Their perky punky pop was part of my adolescent anthem. They mattered to me.

But the green hair and my inability to explain how I got it, oh, the ripples did it cause. My mom took me to Salon Lebanon, where the beauticians tried to dye my hair, tried to bleach it, and tried to cut it. They couldn't do it. Nothing could touch it.

"Anna, what on earth did you do?" Mom asked.

"Nothing, Ma," I said. "I just woke up with it this way."

"Don't lie to me, Anna," Mom said. "Where did you get the dye? Who gave it to you? Was it those friends of yours?"

I think I look like Mom more than Dad—we have similar features. I got her upturned nose, what she'd call our "pixie noses" back in the day, when I was a little girl. And I got her bone structure, like my cheekbones and chin. Dad gave me his grey eyes and thick hair.

Mom actually tried to cut my hair herself when the beauticians couldn't. She took out clippers and broke them trying to cut my hair. I mean that poor pair of clippers whined and sparked and Mom just strained until the clippers broke apart, and she stood there, cursing.

"What is *wrong* with you, Anna?" Mom asked.

"Nothing's wrong with me," I said. "I feel fine. If anything, I feel better than I ever have."

I could see in her eyes, the worry. Mom's smart. She understood.

"Okay," she said, with Dad beside her, the two of them shining penlights into my eyes, taking my temperature, listening to my heart with stethoscopes. Being the doctors that they were. "You're going through some changes, Anna."

"Big changes," Dad said. The medical journals talked about superheroism, the incident rates among the general population. They knew what this meant.

"What can you do, Sweetie?" Mom asked, which was a funny question to ask a teenager. I was an adolescent; I could do anything.

"I don't know," I said. "I don't know what I can do."

It was an honest statement. Nobody in my situation plans on becoming superpowered. It just happens. Mom and Dad debated it between them, right in front of me, wondering where it had come from. They'd done so many ordinary things in their lives, had carefully played by society's unspoken rules. Something like me wasn't supposed to happen.

My brothers thought it was funny, at least at first.

"Little Miss Special," Blake said, throwing a football at me, which I caught. Being the baby sister to two older brothers in Pittsburgh, I knew how to throw footballs, baseballs, basketballs, frisbees, rocks, insults, fists, etc. I knew the mechanics of manhood even as a girl.

I threw the football back to Blake, and he caught it in his chest with a gasp, falling to the ground wheezing. All I'd done was throw it.

"Christ, Anna," he said, getting back to his feet, shaking it off with an unsteady laugh. "What the hell kind of toss was that?"

He threw another one, and I ran to catch it, got there, caught it. It was easy, like zipping across our backyard to nab it. I threw another one back at him, a high lob to try to make it easier for him to maybe catch. Even at the start, I understood I had to be careful. Blake went long and caught it, and we were well apart from each other in the yard. I'd thrown it far.

The powers came with the hair, which sounds stupid to say it, but the hair was the signifier. Whatever had happened to me had manifested with the hair.

Blake looked at me speculatively a moment, then ran toward me with the ball. It was like every other pick-up game we'd play as kids, with me on the receiving end of what brotherly punishment he could inflict on me. Only today was different.

Of my brothers, Blake was the jock, and Lane was the brain. That's what we called him—Lane the Brain. I was the mascot. Or that's what I was supposed to be. Mom and Dad had told my brothers about what had happened, and that they shouldn't tell anybody about it. It was like it was something to be ashamed of. My brothers took it differently—Lane just asked questions, while Blake paced around, unable to comprehend why their little sister had superpowers and *he* did not.

"Better watch it, Anna Montana," Blake said, looking to run me down. He was charging hard, heading right for me. Mom had told them to treat me the same, to not act like anything was any different between us. Blake ran, nostrils flaring, eyes set on me, his high-topped fade barely moving in the wind he generated as he ran. "Try to stop me if you can."

We connected in the latter third of the yard toward the imaginary goal line, his big strong body against my own meager frame, and in that moment when we collided, Blake actually bounced back, hitting the autumn backyard grass with the wind knocked out of him, even fumbling the ball, which bounced away like it was leaving a crime scene against the laws of nature.

I grabbed the ball and tucked it under my arm, proud that I'd stood my ground with Blake. In years past, I'd had to run from him or take shelter behind Lane. Blake curled up in a ball on the lawn, getting his breath back. He refused my out-stretched hand, got back to his feet, looking at me like I was a monster.

"Damn, Anna," he said. "That's messed up."

"Sorry not-sorry, Blake," I said. "*You* ran into *me.*"

Lane had been watching from the back deck, busy reading one of his ever-present books. With my enhanced eyes, I could make out *Man and Superman* by George Bernard Shaw, despite Lane's habit of hiding the titles of what he read.

"You reaped the whirlwind, Blake," Lane said, calling to us with the most blasé of tones he could muster. Lane was always like that.

"This is just wrong, Lanestain," Blake said. "You should try throwing a few with her."

We joined Lane on the deck, while sycamore leaves fell across the yard, moving lazily, like they had all the time in the world.

"No, thanks," Lane said, looking us both over the rims of his tortoise shell glasses. "I know when I'm beaten."

I set the ball on the table and sat next to Lane, while Blake fumed, flexing his arms, recovering himself.

"Blake's never come up against a wall he couldn't break down before, Anna," Lane said, closing his book and patting the back of my hand. "Give him time."

I looked at both of them, smirking. As the youngest, it was nice to have something like that. Blake sat across from me, bull that he was, slamming his elbow on the table, hand out-stretched, fingers extended.

"Blake, come on," I said. Lane chuckled, shaking his head.

"How much humiliation can you handle in one day, Blake?" Lane asked. Blake had arm-wrestled me a half-dozen times since my hair had turned, and he'd lost every time.

"It's just not possible, Lane," Blake said. "Come on, Sugar-puff. Challenge!"

I looked at Lane, who just sighed.

"You get to be ref," I said to Lane, then took Blake's beefy hands in my dainty ones. I was fifteen, Blake was seventeen, and Lane was nineteen. Blake gripped my hand tightly, but I barely felt it. If he'd been trying to squeeze my hand, I hardly felt it.

"It's impossible," Blake said. "The physics, man. Not. Possible. Her skinny little hands, Lane."

He strained against my arm, his face going red, veins and arteries pulsing in his arms and forehead as he tried to move me. Even then, as a girl who'd only just gotten her powers, I was unstoppable, immoveable. His eyes flashed as he fought to beat me fair and square, then grabbed my hand with his other hand and put every ounce of his strength to bear against me, cursing as he fought to move my arm an inch.

Some part of me—the Nice Girl part of me—thought about just faking letting him beat me, if only to put an end to these endless confrontations and competitions. I just wanted him to just see me as his little sister again, versus an opponent to be bested.

However, another part of me—the super part of me—knew that if I gave ground to Blake in that moment and humored his wounded ego, that I'd *never* live that down. That it would shape my world and my horizon in unfathomable ways.

Lane watched us with thoughtful amusement, like he was taking stock for the memoirs he'd be writing one day.

"You can't beat her, Blake," Lane said.

"I can," Blake said. "Will and way, man."

He couldn't move me, and as much as I wanted to bring his arm to the table, with how much force he was throwing at me, I might have broken his arm. I couldn't break my brother's arm. The compromise was that I'd just hold my arm there while he flailed against it.

"Stop it," Blake said, through gritted teeth.

"Stop what?" I asked.

"You know what," he said, although he wouldn't admit it.

"Is this what you want, Blake?" I asked, moving my arm an inch from neutral toward his side. And then another. And another, until we were at about a thirty-degree angle in my favor, and more veins were bulging from his red-faced forehead.

"I'm not going to be beaten yet again by my little sister," Blake said. "I'll have to hand in my Man Card if this happens."

Lane rested his chin in his raised hand, laughing at his brother.

"She's already beaten you like a half-dozen times, Blake," Lane said. "I think your Man Card is definitely retired by now."

"Shut up, Stain," Blake said. I took another inch from Blake, about thirty-five degrees, and held him there.

"I don't want to hurt you, Blake," I said.

"Don't worry about me, Anna Banana," Blake said. Even new to it, less than a month into being what I'd become, I knew there was no way he'd ever be able to beat me again. Not at this, not at anything. I was amazed at Blake's refusal to give in, to concede defeat. I released his grip, and he didn't want to let go, but he couldn't stop me from letting go, even as he panted, shaking out his hand.

"Anna wins again," Lane said, holding up my hand, which I let him take. Blake stomped and cursed around the deck, shaking out his arm. "Don't let Mom see you challenging Anna like that in public, Blake. The neighbors might get to talking."

I smiled at both of my brothers, pretending for a moment that it was normal, just another day. My normal days were past me, though. My folks voiced a desire to send me away to a private school, where my powers could be discreetly hidden away. It had been a weird discussion.

"Anna, they'll take you away from us," she said. "The government (and others) look for supers. You can't let *anyone* know what you can do."

Supers were everywhere. I'd see them on the news. Especially the Affiliates, saving the world, time and again. Or showing up at public events. I liked Tantrum best, with her yellow and black costume and punky black hair, cut short. Her power was telekinesis, and she was badass, moving stuff with her mind. She was *strong*. I dug that.

"Okay," I said. "At least until I'm eighteen."

"No, Baby," Mom said. "Never. People will want to use you."

"Your mother's right," Dad said. "You don't want that kind of hassle."

"Or try out for sports," Blake said. "You could easily be an Olympian."

"Blake, that's a bad idea," Dad said. "It wouldn't be fair."

"Besides, I think the moment they tried to do a blood test on Anna, the secret would be out," Lane said. "And then Anna would be at the center of a super-scandal for trying to pass as normal at a sporting event."

Mom agreed with Lane wholeheartedly, and I agreed, mostly because I didn't want to be a sports figure; I wanted to be an actual superhero, using my powers to help people who needed it. Idealistic, yeah, but I was fifteen.

"There are all sorts of ways to make a contribution to society," Dad said. "You're smart, Anna. You'll go to college and get a job and make a difference in meaningful ways."

To hear Mom and Dad basically blowing off my superpowers was hurtful, I'll admit. It was like they didn't believe in me. That's how I saw it back then. I understood that they were just trying to protect me, but they also didn't want my powers disrupting their lives. They had very successful, comfortable lives. They had provided for us, and we'd wanted for nothing.

However, just as with Blake's pointless arm-wrestling, Mom and Dad's worrying about people learning about my powers becoming known was a thing. I don't know what I'd have been if they'd been supportive of me instead of fearing me as the family secret. It went all over the place with me.

"Anna, you should quit the field hockey team," she said. "Can you imagine what might happen if you injured one of the other girls or killed them?"

"Jesus, Ma," I said. "I'm not a maniac."

She approached and cupped my face in her hands, which felt impossibly soft against my cheek, fragile, even. The look in her eyes was worry and fear. I could see it all too clearly with my enhanced senses.

"I know you're not, Sweetie," she said. "But the rules changed the moment this happened. Everything's changed.

You can't do what you did before, you can't be who you used to be. And you can't let *anybody* know your secret."

"I don't even know what I can do," I said. "How can I know what's right for me if I don't learn who I am?"

Very teen drama, I know. I left in a huff, Mom calling after me as I flew—yeah, totally, literally—flew off. You might think that would be one of those anguish-ridden discoveries, fraught and full of falls and mishaps. However, I took to flying so naturally. It was weirdly easy—I just thought about flying and I could fly.

Lane told me it was impossible, that there was no physical way I could just fly without some apparent form of propulsion, but I didn't listen to him.

And when I flew, my head would clear. I told myself maybe I was like Tantrum, who could use her telekinesis to make herself fly. That was how I made it work in my head how I was doing it. However it happened, I just soared around Mount Lebanon, above the canopy of old trees, out of sight.

Most often, I'd fly at night, where I could do it without people seeing me as easily as in the day. The night flights were the best, the way the neighborhood was illuminated, the way Pittsburgh glowed at night.

And with my enhanced senses, everything was phantasmagoric. It was like being high, I imagined. My powers kicked in before my friends got their hands on drugs, and I couldn't take them. I was immune to intoxication. That sucked, because while they were all getting wasted or baked, I was stone sober. I was THE designated driver every time. Goody Two-Shoes.

But flying, what a trip that was. Silent in the sky, I would fly, remembering Lane's admonishment that I stay below radar level.

"You don't want to get to radar level," he said. "That'll give them fits at the airport. They'll think you're a UFO."

I thought that was funny, but I was mindful of it, trying to fly no higher than the skyscrapers downtown. Although part of me wanted to really see how high I could fly, and how fast.

One night, I took off and just put some distance between home and myself, and I went skyward. What can I say? I went up, up, and away.

And it was wild. I just went ever higher, picking up speed, until I actually spooked myself when I'd seen how high I'd gotten. I was out there. I could see the curvature of the planet. Since it was night, I could see the expanse of black and the city lights in clusters—Pittsburgh, Youngstown, Cleveland, Akron, Canton, Columbus, even Toledo, Dayton, Cincinnati, and Steubenville. It was an island chain of lights in a sea of darkness.

In that moment up there in the cold, I realized that I wasn't breathing, or that I didn't need to breathe. Talk about a mind ride! I put my hands to my chest and could feel myself just hanging out up there, in the vacuum of space, seeing satellites sparkling and shooting by, and the radioactivity washing over the electromagnetic field protecting the planet. It didn't hurt me. Even the orbital trash swirling around there at incredible velocity didn't hurt me.

How small and delicate the world seemed, and then I went back down, and (oopsie!) burned off all my clothes from the friction of reentry. I tried to take it slowly. But moving from absence of air-to-air resistance put me through my paces. I was mortified to be up there like that, flying naked through the night's sky, like a witch.

Was that what I was? It felt like witchcraft, if only in that it was forbidden fun that my parents would have freaked over and would have had people praying for me and my parents, dealing with their doubtlessly demon-led daughter.

I made my way back down, trying to keep my bearings, because when you're up there and out there, it's easy to get lost. Things get small and insignificant so quickly when you're spacing out. But I'd been in Girl Scouts as a kid and didn't lose my way.

No, I made it back home, chagrined that I'd fried my clothes. I snuck back in, grabbing my favorite flannel pajamas and slipping them on, nobody at home the wiser about what I'd been up to.

With all the supers out there, I wasn't the first one to fly over the city, I was sure. But I'm willing to bet I was the first person in Pittsburgh to fly into space unassisted, and very likely the first to fly naked over the city.

That night, I didn't have to dream about flying, but I did, anyway.

**3**

although his suit still bore Minder's blood. The cameras were flashing as he quieted the room. His handsome face, his white hair and noble profile commanded attention. The steadiness of his gaze. He looked positively presidential.

"We're all still dealing with this incredible loss for the team," Shane said, which made me scoff. "Rex had been a member of the Affiliates for a dozen years. His loss will affect us all for some time."

There was a cacophony of voices until Shane called on one of them.

"Go ahead, Caryn," Shane said.

"Caryn Underwood of Innermedia," she said. Caryn Underwood hated me. Not me personally. Cameraman. She had this whole deal with Cameraman. "Is there any truth to the rumors that Cameraman might be responsible for this heinous act?"

Shane handled the question calmly. He handled *everything* calmly. He'd be a good chairman for the Affiliates. In fact, given that he'd brought Anna and me into the Affiliates to try to root out the corruption he claimed was in the team, I could hopefully count on him as Chairman to keep the Affiliates off my back.

"I've known Cameraman a long time," Shane said. "He's never shot or killed anyone. He shoots pictures, not people."

Inferna chuckled at that. "Good line."

"Memorable," Hellmaiden said in a sinister whisper.

"Ah, she talks," I said, glancing at the glowing devil-woman sidekick, who put a hand on her hip as she regarded me, the radiance of which caught my eye before Shane's press conference drew my attention again, as Underwood spoke up again.

"I have sources that say there was bad blood between Minder and Cameraman," Underwood said. "Can you confirm or deny this?"

"I have worked with both men for years," Shane said. "I wasn't aware of any bad blood."

"It's just curious to me that Mr. Traynor was executed right before revealing Cameraman's secret identity," Underwood said. "Don't you find that unusual, Mr. Grey?"

"Rex had known Cameraman's secret identity for three years," Shane said. "Why he might have threatened to reveal it is a mystery to me."

Other reporters tried to speak up, but Underwood got one more zinger in.

"Mr. Traynor referred to Cameraman as an 'info-terrorist' —do you care to elaborate on that?" Underwood asked. "As well as the scandalous revelations Cameraman shared out to various media organizations? Those are some hefty accusations."

"We're looking into all of it," Shane said. "I know Cameraman to be a man of great personal integrity, and we are investigating the assertions made in those files he released. Lynn Credible will be running a separate press conference about the specifics of those accusations."

I couldn't resist speaking up then.

"She was Rex's right hand," I said. "She's going to throw me right under the bus."

"Do you want us to do something about her, Mitch?" Inferna asked.

"Whoa, no," I said. "Seriously, I can handle this. I appreciate what you've done, Fern, but I can take care of this."

Inferna glanced at Hellmaiden, who shook her head, crossed her arms.

"We're going to help you whether you want us to or not, Mitch," Inferna said. "How about this—if you chafe at adding to your already prodigious tab, how about you help Hell's Belles work a few cases, and we'll lend a hand with this mess you're in?"

When some devil-women offer to lend a hand, Gentle Reader, you have to proceed with considerable caution. However, I'd seen what Inferna could do in a fight, and Hellmaiden didn't look like a slouch, either.

"What kind of cases?" I asked. I could only imagine what Hell's Belles might view as appropriate casework.

Inferna seemed well-pleased that I'd help them out, although I doubted I'd be able to do much. She waved her hands and created little illusions of the targets of her cases.

"Yo-Yo Duncan, a rising gangster operating here in Chicago, under the tutelage of a devil named Lord Ruthven. A Philadelphia serial arsonist who calls himself Hellbringer—and who may be under demonic influence. And a drug dealer named Theo Strong, operating out of Cincinnati, working with a Duchess of Hell named Lethalia," Inferna said.

"Lethalia," I said. "Friend of yours, Fern? Family?"

She made the illusions vanish with a wave of her hands.

"Perceptive as ever, Mitch," she said. "Not a friend, but, instead, a major problem."

It was interesting seeing how Inferna's evasive, hellish mind worked. I wondered how helping her out would net out in the netherworld. Would it strengthen or weaken her ties to the underworld? I didn't know. She seemed to sense my confusion.

"I'm out to stop bad people in your world," she said. "I'm working against the underworld in these efforts. Hellmaiden, She-Devil, and I are fighting to help make your world a better place, Mitch. Powerful players in my dimension are working hard to forge greater links between our dimension and yours. I'm working to sever those links as much as I can."

I ushered them into my workroom, where I played back the footage I'd taken of the Minder getting murdered.

"Nothing in here leaves this room, right?" I said, pointing to both Inferna and Hellmaiden. "Except maybe you, Hellmaiden—you're emitting a lot of light and heat. Can you wait in the other room?"

Hellmaiden looked chagrined but nodded.

"Sure," she said, backing into the other room, closing the door behind her. I wasn't trying to be a dick; lighting just always matters with production work. And the heatwaves she was throwing off could have damaged my tapes and files. Climate control matters with production.

"Sorry about that, Mitch," Inferna said. "Hellmaiden's still finding her way."

"What's with the crown?" I asked.

"It's magical," Inferna said.

"Of course it is," I said, rolling the footage I had of the assassination. My headcams had a built-in steadiness to them, which ensured smooth footage, even if I was running around. Seeing the assassination again this way, through the footage brought it back, even clashing with my memories of what happened.

Three shots, fired in close succession. All head shots. I played them back slowly, watching Minder's head explode and come back together, back ands forth.

"He was dead from the first shot," I said. "Those are explosive high-velocity rounds. See the way they detonate on impact? Not big explosions, but enough to guarantee fatality. Nobody wanted to take any chances."

Inferna took a seat next to me and watched.

"One shooter," she said. "You can see from the ballistic trajectory."

I advanced the footage to when I'd turned to look where the shots came from, to the rooftop area I'd seen. The shooter was wearing adaptive camouflage and was literally cloaked.

Zooming in, I tried to enhance the image, which looked like a kind of camouflaged wraith.

"You can see the hood they were wearing," I said. "They're in a poncho."

I again tried to get closer, but the pixels got too pronounced when I did so. Still, I printed up a couple of copies of it, and sent one to Shane.

*This is the shooter,* I wrote in the note I sent to him.

"Not a lot to go on," I said, "But the smart money's on Deadpan."

I jotted another note to Shane.

*I'm betting it's Deadpan,* I wrote. *Find out where he was.*

*Will do,* Shane wrote back.

The door opened again, and Hellmaiden reappeared.

"Sorry," she whispered. "I'd just rather be in here than out there."

I decided to be less of a production prick about it, nodded.

"Just don't lean against the tapes on those shelves," I said. "I don't want anything melting."

Inferna glanced back at Hellmaiden.

"Would you like me to send you back?" she asked.

"Hell, no," Hellmaiden said, putting her hand on her hip and glaring at Inferna. I could detect some tension between the two devil-women.

Out of curiosity, I turned a thermographic camera on Hellmaiden, and saw that her body temperature was incredible, blinding white through the viewfinder—like around 10,000 degrees Fahrenheit. Somehow, the hellish clothes she wore contained her heat, but the waves of heat radiated off of her exposed fire-opalescent skin, like her arms, shoulders, and head. I worried that she might set off my fire alarms but was grateful she'd kept her hood-shroud on, since that seemed to mediate the heat and light she threw off.

"Hmm," I said. "Somebody gave White Arrow my address. Somebody bumped off Minder. Something else is at work here."

"Crime League," Hellmaiden said.

"Could be, could be," I replied. "One thing Minder had said was how he and the Crime League were working together. That means his points of contact would have to be Dr. Crime, Crimebot, and the Instigator. But Tag Team put Instigator away, so it's got to be either Dr. Crime or Crimebot. They wouldn't accept anyone else being in charge."

I went to my workroom computer (yes, they were networked throughout the building, thank you for noticing), and drew up last known locations for Dr. Crime and Crimebot. Dr. Crime was last seen in London, while Crimebot had been last seen operating in Houston.

Whistling while I worked, I punched up the active Crime League roster. That might help with figuring out what was going on.

### THE CRIME LEAGUE

- **DR. CRIME:** *LEADER, CRIMINAL MASTERMIND*
- **THE INSTIGATOR:** *LEADER, ESPIONAGE AND SABOTAGE*
- **CRIMEBOT:** *LEADER, CRIMINAL MASTERMIND*
- **DEATHCLOWN:** *DEVIL-CLOWN*
- **JACK RABBIT:** *MASTER THIEF AND TECHNOGUY*
- **QUICK CHICK:** *SPEEDSTER*
- **DOLLFACE:** *CREEPY KILLER CLOWN GIRL, POSSIBLE AUTOMATON OR POSSESSED PROTÉGÉ OF DEATHCLOWN*
- **SPARKLER:** *ELECTRICAL SUPERHUMAN*
- **ICE QUEEN:** *ICE-POWERED SUPERHUMAN*
- **SCENESTER:** *TELEPORTER*
- **SERPENTINA:** *SUPER-STRONG SNAKE WOMAN*
- **STRONGARM:** *BULKY SUPER-BRUISER*
- **MS. FORTUNE:** *PRECOG*
- **JOHNNY RUBICON:** *ANOTHER PRECOG (WEIRD, RIGHT? TWO PRECOGS?)*
- **STILETTO:** *SKILLS CHARACTER, MISTRESS OF ASSASSINS*
- **SHUTTERBUG:** *THE EVIL EQUIVALENT OF ME*

"Those are the active/official members," I said. "However, I'd be inclined to include Paleface and Deadpan as auxiliaries, since those two had associations with the League, and I don't believe that Minder actually rehabilitated them."

Looking at that roster, I could see a possible lineup of members who might be able to carry out what had been going on:

### DR. CRIME/CRIMEBOT: LEADERS
- **MS. FORTUNE AND/OR JOHNNY RUBICON:** *LOGISTICS AND STRATEGY*
- **SCENESTER:** *OPERATIONS/TROUBLESHOOTING AND TRANSPORTATION*
- **STILETTO:** *OPERATIONS/ASSASSINATION*
- **SHUTTERBUG:** *OPERATIONS/PUBLIC RELATIONS*

This was just my own brainstorming, but this lineup made sense.

"Okay," I said. "I'm thinking Dr. Crime and/or Crimebot hatched this plan to attack and/or undermine the Affiliates, possibly leaning on their precogs to hash out what might work best, with Stiletto to carry out the necessary wetwork, Scenester to assist, with Shutterbug to gather intel and/or disseminate mis- and disinformation."

Inferna and Hellmaiden didn't object, so I took that as tacit agreement.

"Scenester already dipped his toes in with Minder," I said. "He's a bit of a smoking gun, as far as the Crime League is concerned."

"How will we stop them?" Inferna asked.

That was the key question. I'd have to go toe-to-toe with Shutterbug to try to offset the messaging damage she would be applying. Not glamorous, I know, but it was a factor. Information warfare was hell.

"I need to figure that out," I said. "I need to talk to Shane and just see what's been going on."

aware of how skeeved out my parents were about it, I decided the easiest thing to do until I could get out on my own was to play the alter ego game as best as I could—to masquerade as normal to blend in, just to keep the heat off me, and to research superheroes in the real world. When I was sixteen, I just started scrapbooking and journaling, like seeing who was out there, what they were doing. In a way, I was living vicariously through them, studying them, learning how they did what they did.

There were the big-ticket ones like Tantrum, Tandem, Rad Lad, and Ephemera. I thought it was cool that she led the Affiliates. Her costume was fab, with this purple facemask that was linked to her cape, and this black sheer bodysuit she wore. Her logo was this stylized "E" in black, surrounded by a purple cloud, which she wore as a sort of brooch. It wasn't the most visible of logos, but to my adolescent self, it was awesome. And I thought it was neat that a woman led the Affiliates, the greatest hero team in the world. Ephemera looked like a ghost, and her phasing powers were neat, in that she could control her density, like to either be intangible or to become super dense and invulnerable. She made it look easy.

The Knack was interesting, too, and strange—he was this devastatingly handsome white-haired youngish man, radiating style, charisma, grace, and poise far beyond his years. And he was always opening new care centers and donating to worthy causes, speaking out on things that mattered. The term "philanthropist" gets tossed out pretty readily, but the Knack clearly walked his talk. He had a strange moral authority that came through in his media appearances, and when he joined the Affiliates, it seemed both fated and also strangely contrary, given how open he seemed, and how secretive they were as an organization.

The Affiliates hogged the headlines, but there was another hero who intrigued me, just because he was so weirdly enigmatic: Cameraman.

The early stories about him referred to him as "The Cameraman"—and I thought that was funny. It made him like an urban legend. He'd get ink, usually buried in the newspapers Dad would read, but I'd see them:

### Mysterious "Camera-Man" Exposes Municipal Corruption

### City Councilman Embroiled in "Cameraman" Case

### Traxxon CEO Caught Up in "Camera-Man" Scandal

### Entire Board of Directors at Econiconsortium Ousted After "Cameraman" Revelations

### "Camera-Man" Secret Footage Scandalizes Factory Farm Industry

### Senator Effingham Resigns Amid "Cameraman" Exposé

### "Camera-Man" Claims Responsibility for Scuttling Gangster-Led Casino Deal

### Three Congressmen Expelled in Disgrace by "Camera-Man" Fiasco

### Government Officials Seek Out "Cameraman" in Conspiracy Trial

"This 'Camera-Man' seems like trouble," Dad said. "There are proper ways of going about things, respecting our institutions. He's just a headline-grabbing troublemaker. A pot-stirrer."

I was hooked. This invisible man out there, working from the shadows. There weren't even any pictures of him. He was like a ghost, and I *loved* ghosts.

Don't get me wrong: I loved watching the other superheroes doing their thing, but Cameraman was doing this newspaper ninja thing, breaking stories that would lead to bigwigs getting busted.

Not that I was obsessive. It was an adolescent crush, and for someone like me, who had superpowers but couldn't go out and be super (not yet, anyway), he was doing what I wanted to be doing. I'd make sketches of him, what I thought he might look like, which was funny because how did you draw an invisible man?

Totes went on an Invisible Man bender—read the book, would watch all those old movies, bore my friends about it. I did my own sleuthing, like to figure out where he might be based. I sequenced the stories, the first ones that mentioned him, to mark his first known appearance. Chicago news covered him first, that's where he broke.

It was simple math—he was in Chicago. Or that was where he was based. And when the time came, I'd get there, and I'd find him. Or he'd find me.

Meanwhile, I dropped out of field hockey and joined Art Club and took photography classes, which Mom and Dad deemed "safe" enough for me to do without my superpowers being apparent. I worked on the yearbook, taking pictures, walking around with my camera, and, yes, I was trying to understand Cameraman when I was doing that. If I couldn't find him or know him, I could at least see some of the world the way he did, with his camera.

The biggest thing I got out of camerawork was how framing something gave it importance and relevance you'd never notice without the frame. Like if you just looked at something normally, it was there. The moment you framed it through a camera's viewfinder, however, it suddenly became significant. Literally anything could be transformed that way. The act of looking *made* it matter. Like it was magic.

I started a photoblog and an Instagram feed of my pictures. Just stupid, artsy shots. Pensive black and white, psychedelic color composition pieces. It was a hobby for me, an outlet for my obsession with that mystery man out there, and a way of passing time pretending to be normal.

Life intruded on my fantasy world, and I won't go through all of that. I went to University of Pennsylvania after high school, where I majored in Philosophy, just to give my parents fits. That was my act of rebellion, my payback for them forcing me to keep my super-self in check. Take that, Mom and Dad—I'm majoring in Philosophy! It was a funny moment for me in retrospect because they knew that if they pushed me too hard on it, I might literally fly away.

"I just don't think you've given your future enough consideration, Sweetie," Mom said.

"They have a stellar neuroscience program, Anna," Dad said. "You could be great at that."

Lane understood, and I think he even halfway approved. Blake made fun of it.

"Philosophy's dead, Anna Banana," he said, while we played catch in the back, throwing a baseball back and forth. "Nobody cares about what people think anymore, or why."

I held back, the ball smacking safely from glove to glove. To anyone looking at us, it looked normal. I was bursting at the seams, however. Every night I had gone out and practiced my powers, flexed my muscles. I might even have fought crime covertly. Seriously, shhhh!

My first almost-boyfriend, Devon Green, was a punk poet. That's how he saw himself, anyway. He'd *loved* my green hair, had thought I'd done it because of him. I'd met up with him and his friends at the Pizzacade, where they were busy being badass between slices and turns playing PUNCH-OUT!! on a vintage arcade game in the pizzeria that had somehow managed to survive, right next to a Carousel circus pinball machine.

They (Devon, punk rock grrl Swizzle, and Doug Sims) made fun of my hair, because it was still long, despite being green.

"Whoa," Devon said, running a hand through his picture-perfect black pompadour. He was wearing a green army jacket and carefree blue jeans and red Chuckies. "Now that's something I *never* thought I'd see."

The three of them half-assed their way as a punk power trio, The Angry Disasters, with Devon as lead singer/guitarist, Swizzle on bass, and Doug Sims on drums. They'd play in Devon's garage, mostly doing Hüsker Dü, Jawbreaker, and Blink-182 covers when they weren't skateboarding, smoking, and drinking purloined beer. Devon and Doug were often called "D&D" at school, as they were pretty much inseparable, and had been gamer geeks before they'd gone all punk.

Swizzle, who had burgundy hair with shaved sides and wore white makeup, had ghoulishly big black eyes and wore a dizzying array of safety pins on her wayward Riot Grrl-on-acid get up, open-mouth sneered at me while eating breadsticks. She had a fantastic black leather jacket that was well-worn and wonderful, covered with band pins across it. She went to a different school.

"Too much by half, Victor," she said. Swizzle (real name, Tina Olivieri) despised me. Devon just reached out and touched my hair with a finger-gloved hand, toying with and tugging it. I didn't even feel it. I didn't mind him pawing me. Swizzle hated it, though; I could see that in her eyes.

"I like it," he said. "It represents. I'll bet your mom lost her mind."

"Yeah," I said, looking sheepish. I suppose I was trying to find normalcy by hanging out with my abnormal friendoids.

Devon, who wore eyeliner, brought himself close to me, close enough that I could smell the cigarettes on his breath.

"Seriously," he said. "You should cut it."

"I can't," I said. Back then, I didn't know how.

"You can't?" Swizzle said, slurping on her frozen Coke. "More like you *won't*, Poseur."

She just stared me down defiantly, and I held her gaze. I was wearing one of my Green Day tees (my "Kerplunk!" tee, my favorite), my army green cargo pants and Doc Martens.

"What?" she said. "Did I hit a nerve, rich girl?"

"Hey," Devon said, chuckling nervously. "We're *all* rich kids, Swiz. Don't *you* have a trust fund?"

Swizzle shrugged like it didn't matter.

"I had to work for it," she said.

"Never trust a trust fund baby," I said, daring Swizzle to take a swing at me. She raised a ringed fist to deck me, and I all but led with my chin. "Take your shot, Tina."

Doug, who'd been playing the pinball game, actually stopped to take a look. He was scarecrow-gangly and brainless, dyed his hair jet black and was overly fond of striped shirts and natty jeans and a denim vest smothered with buttons and patches. He worshipped Glenn Danzig. Nothing got guys' attention quite like the prospect of two girls fighting.

"Yinz know da rules—no fighting in here," Louis the Owner said. He was this Swedish meatball of a man with a wrinkly bald face locked into a perpetual squint beneath his white sailor hat he always paired with a white apron. He had old tattoos on his arms, mermaids mangled by muscle and time well-spent somewhere in the South Pacific.

"You heard him, Sicko Vicko," Swizzle said. "You want to dance? How about this—if I beat you, I get to shave that head of yours."

"And what if I win?" I asked.

"You won't," Swizzle said.

"If I win, I get your leather jacket," I said, which made Swizzle snort.

"You won't," she said again, while Devon and Doug sauntered out to join us, mesmerized by this bizarre moment. Seeing them looking at her, Swizzle didn't want to be seen as backing down, so she stuck out her jaw and nodded. "Fine, Bitch."

This wasn't how I had seen it going, exactly. I'd just wanted to get away from my parents' funny vibe and had thought maybe hanging with my peers might make it better. Instead, I was watching Swizzle circle me, ornamented fists raised, while Devon and Doug clapped and cheered. Even Louis squinted out at us, likely ready to shoo us off the parking lot if we caused too much trouble, but maybe a little curious how it might turn out.

Swizzle took a hard swing at me, harder than I would have imagined she might have otherwise done, but she and I had a rivalry over Devon that went on for a while. She caught me right on the chin and cried out, shaking her hand out as she struck me.

"My turn," I said, while she jumped up and down, cursing and nursing her hand. I brought up my fist, my studded bracelet on my arm, glinting in the sunlight.

"I give up," Swizzle said, taking off her leather jacket and holding it out with her unwounded hand, like some kind of sacrificial offering. "Fuck you, Freakette, take it, take it."

If I hadn't been a teen at the time, I'd have shown mercy, but I so took it, because Swizzle had it coming. It would be worth the hatred, honestly. I slipped her leather jacket on, which looked fabulous on me, while Swizzle seared me with her hateful eyes. I'd take her stink off of it with my own favored perfume.

"Looks like shit on you," she said. "And I'll get another one just like this."

She snapped her fingers on her unhurt hand, although she looked like she was about to cry, flipping up her skateboard and taking off, flipping us off with her good hand as she went.

"You *just* broke our bassist," Doug said.

"Totes," Devon said.

"She'll be fine," I said. "I think."

"Are you kidding?" Devon said. "She'll run to Daddy and tell him you stole her jacket. Her dad's a city councilman. I smell a scandal. Cops at your door. Megaphones. Journalists. Maybe Cameraman will turn up to film it."

Devon knew I dug Cameraman, and that kind of stung, I'll admit. Although I also loved to imagine that Cameraman might actually show up. Doug got up, his plank under his arm, studied my face.

"Not even a bruise, Devo," he said. Devon did the same, looking me over.

"Damn, Anna," he said. "Since when did you get so hardcore?"

"Punk's an attitude, Dev," I said. And I had to resist the urge to take to the skies right then, leave them slack-jawed. Instead, we skated to one of the bird sanctuary parks and just dicked around the rest of the day. Devon treated us to a poem he wrote, inspired by the half-fight, jotted into his well-worn red notebook he perpetually back-pocketed:

### Anna Wrecks It

*Hasty words and flying fists*
*Swizzle stuck halfway between*
*Sucked and fucked, one might say, yay!*
*But the truth is that Anna*
*Must pay to play on this day.*

Doug didn't give a shit about Devon's poems, but I kind of liked it, gave him some claps, even though I thought maybe he was having a joke at my expense. You never knew with Devon, who lit a joint and smoked it without a care in the world, his blue eyes boring into me. I couldn't tell if he could tell that I'd changed, and I couldn't tell if he even cared. In that silly exchange with Swizzle, I knew that what I'd been, whatever I'd been to them, was long gone. She'd thrown hands at me and come away broken.

Me? I was just fine.

"Wonders never cease, Dougster. Lady Green Day *somehow* managed to slay Duchess Dickless today," Devon said, shaking his head. "Who knew?"

"To the Victor go the spoils," I said, grinning wickedly at them both, stopping them in their tracks.

And I kept the jacket, no matter what anybody said. I *still* have it.

**5**

THANKFULLY, SHANE TOOK MY CALL while I paced around my living room, with no sign of Inferna or Hellmaiden, who were chasing down leads on one of the cases they were working. The idea that Inferna was even working cases still tickled me. I don't know what I imagined her doing when she wasn't here, but chasing down supernatural baddies wasn't necessarily top on my list.

I told Shane my suspicions, and, to his credit, he listened before speaking.

"Your exposure of Minder's likely involvement in Ephemera's mental breakdown has resonance, but since he's dead, it's—no pun intended—a dead end. The Polygon Program is likely the area that's got higher-ups particularly worried."

Press organizations had been calling my Cameraman hotline since the stories broke, and I'd kept them dangling for now, especially in the wake of the Anna thing—although part of me wondered if someone had planted that there knowing it would throw me off. I'm just saying, if Anna was back, where the hell was she? Was she hurt?

"What about Credible?" I asked. "At the very least, she was in thick with Minder. She has to be part of the scheme with the League."

"I fired her," Shane said. "Right before her press conference."

Wow, I imagine that shocked her. I didn't think Shane had that level of corporate gangster in him. Me? I totally would have done it. Especially after she'd tried to kill or at least maim me (*BRIGHTEYES, Chapter 26—the editors*).

"Nice," I said. "I'm sure she was pissed."

"She wasn't happy, no," Shane said. "We're doing damage control with the Crime League assertions you made—basically pinning the corruption on Minder and Credible, since the others are claiming they didn't know anything about it."

"Do you believe them?" I asked.

"I don't know," Shane said.

"How about this: reinstate me for membership in the Affiliates," I said. "With your chairman position, you can grant me access to the files. Let me go through them. *I'll* find every smoking gun. Faster if you let AFFILIA help me."

AFFILIA (Advanced Forensic File Interface Liminal Intelligence Advocate) was the resident AI for the Affiliates, linking the branches and serving as a computational aide. The AI had come online after I'd quit the team, so I'd missed out on working with her (they gave her a female voice, hence "her"), although I'd heard enough about AFFILIA coming online in meetings to at least be aware that she was available to the Affiliates.

There was no reason for Shane to avoid granting me that kind of file access.

"Here's the thing, Shane," I said. "Either Minder's last words were true—that I'm an info-terrorist out to ruin the Affiliates, or he was a corrupt bastard who misused his position of power to collude with the Crime League and contravene the pursuit of superheroic justice. But both stories can't be true. Let the Affiliates come out in my favor and I'll chase down the corruption wherever it leads. That's what the League *doesn't* want. I expect they'll go into full character assassination mode with me, just to make sure I don't gain access to the data. Get ahead of it before that happens. Timing is everything, remember?"

"I remember," Shane said. "I can't unilaterally add you back to the team, especially the way things are going. Let me talk to the others and get back with you."

"Okay," I said. "But work quickly, because if they can't character assassinate me, they're going to literally assassinate me."

"Are you okay?" Shane asked. "Do you need someone there?"

"Inferna's got my back," I said. "She's formed her own power trio, after all. Maybe we inspired her."

"Not exactly the company you want to keep in the court of public opinion," Shane said.

"Are you playing devil's advocate, Shane?" I asked, and we shared a nervous laugh. "You be careful."

"Please," Shane said. "*You* be careful, Mitch."

I hung up, feeling pretty good about the call. The simplest thing was reinstating me—the fact was that despite Minder slandering me, and whatever drek Credible might hurl, I was clean. I hadn't done anything wrong but expose wrongdoing within the greatest superhero team in the world. Did *that* make me a bad person?

Still, it paid to be cautious. I went to my voicemail and checked the messages. There were a dozen requests for interview, across media companies. Was it the right time for Cameraman to make an appearance like that? Or maybe I would just go viral and do something on social media and let them chase after that. That alone would draw attention. Yeah, that was the way to go. At least it would be on my terms. I barely used my social media channels, treating them as the garnish to the main course of my own highly secretive life, with just periodic postings of footage to keep people's eyes on where I wanted them to go.

I went to my authenticated social media channels and saw the flood of responses from lovers and haters and sighed. There were plenty of people who supported my exposing what Minder had done, just as there were plenty who slagged me as an "info-terrorist" and whatever else they'd been told I was in media channels.

It seemed absurd, but I was steeped in absurdity. I put on my costume and set up my camera. If nothing else, Cameraman needed to chime in. I started recording and hoped it might make a dent.

"Hey, all," I said. "This is Cameraman. I'm sure you're wondering what the hell is going on with the Affiliates. First off, I stand behind everything I accused Minder of. He was a bad guy, and I categorically deny any involvement in his murder. In fact, I think the likeliest suspects for his murder include the criminal elements he'd been conspiring with. Do I need to name names? Dr. Crime and Crimebot, I'm calling you both out. I don't (yet) know how you managed to work your deal with Minder, but you both benefited from having an inside man with Minder. I'm assuming you offed him because, what? His usefulness had expired? Or was this just your way of getting after me? To try to shut me up and shut me down? It's *not* going to work. I'm going to expose everything you've been doing, and I'm going to get you both locked away where you can't hurt anybody ever again. Minder's deal with you, his willingness to look the other way? That died with him."

I paused recording, thought about that. Sometimes it helped to talk things out. Why did they kill Minder? As ever, I went back to Motive, Means, and Opportunity. Motive mattered. Motive *always* mattered. Why did they kill him? He was their ace inside man. What did the League have to gain by doing this?

Not wanting to delay, I uploaded that clip to my social media, so at least that could be out there, regardless of what might happen to me.

I combed the feeds to see where things might be going. There were hit pieces on Inferna and Hellmaiden, including clips of them taking down Yo-Yo Duncan and Lord Ruthven, his patron. Whoever shot that footage did a good job, as it showed the two devil-women diving in and kicking gangster ass with the ferocious fury they were able to bring—Inferna with her fiery sword in one hand and whip in the other, and Hellmaiden flying around and bashing baddies, firing off beams of high-energy plasma hellfire (?) that sent them running. Lord Ruthven looked perfectly satanic in his black high-collared suit, his red face and trimmed goatee beard making him look particularly villainous.

"Your hour is at hand, Ruthven," Inferna said, but he only laughed.

"I've only just begun, Inferna," Ruthven said, only to curse when Hellmaiden flew into him, socking him in the jaw, knocking him on his ass. I laughed. Seeing that made me miss Anna. Hellmaiden grabbed Ruthven by his lapels and snarled into his face, and I could see where she touched him with her glowing fingers, his clothing burst into flame.

"No," Hellmaiden said, snarling. "*You're* finished."

She knocked Ruthven out cold with a couple of hammer-blows, which was probably the first time I'd ever seen footage of a devil getting knocked out cold, even as hellfire burned across his nice suit. Hellmaiden tossed him aside and turned her glowing eyes to Yo-Yo Duncan, who was already on his hands and knees, pleading with Inferna to be spared.

"You made your deal with that devil," Inferna said. "I'm taking you both back where you belong."

Inferna then snagged him with her fiery whip, dragging him across the warehouse floor, where she picked up Ruthven.

She said something I couldn't hear to Hellmaiden, and then vanished in a poof, leaving Hellmaiden alone in the warehouse a moment, where she used her plasma beams to torch all of the drugs and drug manufacturing equipment, before taking flight, melting through one of the warehouse windows.

Once gone, the videographer turned the camera on herself, and I was shocked to see Shutterbug there, in her strange bee-tle-like costume, which was several shades of grey, with big, bulbous bug-seeming eyes that I was all but certain contained HUD displays.

"The devil's getting his due, seems to me," Shutterbug said. "And while we're on topic, who the hell is Hellmaiden? Seems like Inferna's got herself a new sidekick. Or is there more here than meets the eye? Stay tuned as I track these soul-stealing devils."

The feed cut out, and I was wondering why Shutterbug might have been tracking Inferna. I'd have to ask both of them, if the opportunity presented itself. Shutterbug was always so elusive.

Then my proximity alert went off, and I saw that Hellmaiden was at the roof of my brownstone. I toggled my intercom.

"Hello, Hellmaiden," I said. "Can I help you?"

"Can you let me in?" she asked.

I buzzed her in, and she flew on in, reached my workroom all too quickly for my liking, since I liked to think my place was a labyrinth of mystery and intrigue. She came in, and that wave of heat flowed ahead of her, almost breathtaking.

"I just saw you take down Duncan and Lord Ruthven," I said.

She looked surprised—I actually saw it in her blinding white eyes going wider. Her skin looked like living fire opal, constantly swirling, radiating colors. I actually put a protective filter up with my visor so I could look at her without hurting my eyes.

"You saw?" she said.

"Yeah," I said. "You two have a tail—Shutterbug was spying on you. In fact, if she was tailing you there, she may have followed you here."

"Oh, hell," she said, whipping her hooded head around. "I'm so sorry. Inferna just said I should keep an eye on you."

"She did?" I said, laughing. "She thinks I'm in danger?"

"We both do," Hellmaiden said.

"Well, congratulations on kicking those gangsters' asses," I said. "That was impressive as hell."

Sorry/not-sorry for the hell puns. When in hell, do as the devils do. Hellmaiden actually smiled at my stupid pun, which seemed like a win.

"Who is Shutterbug, anyway?" she asked.

"She's like the anti-me," I said. "My arch enemy."

"I thought White Arrow was your arch enemy," Hellmaiden asked.

"Ah, good point," I said. "My *other* arch enemy. Arrow was just a thwarted rival. Shutterbug represents the evil application of audiovisual technology and surveillance."

Hellmaiden actually laughed, itself a weird sort of sound, like a raspy thing that spoke of tortured landscapes and endless desolation. I don't know how I felt that, but I did.

"Meaning?"

"Oh, well, like how I expose wrongdoers who think they can get away with it," I said. "Shutterbug blackmails and extorts people, using incriminating and/or damning footage she's collected to get them to pay her to keep quiet about the secrets she's uncovered."

"Weird," Hellmaiden said. "She makes money like that?"

"There's good money in extortion and blackmail, if you're good at getting the scoop," I said, feeling bizarre that I was schooling a satanic sidekick on extortion. "This should be baseline for you devilish types, right? I mean, you wrote the book on extortion schemes."

She laughed nervously. "I'm still learning, I guess."

"Inferna's a great teacher," I said. "She knows all the ropes. I didn't even know they had, what, internships in Hell?"

Hellmaiden scoffed, folding her arms, her glowing fingertips drumming on her forearms.

"I'm not an intern," she said. "I'm a freelancer. I was contracted to help Inferna with these three cases."

"Ah," I said. "A freelance crimefighter? Love it. What happens when you fulfill your contract?"

"I'm free," Hellmaiden said. "Free to do and be what I want."

I could hear the hint of unexpressed agony in her tone, which was a weird kind of voice, like it carried a feeling that called to mind crackling flame. What did a devil-woman even want? Was their path forged in iron for them?

"What do you want?" I asked.

"To be here," she said. "Away from all of that underworld stuff. It's a horrible place."

Now I was the one to laugh, and hearing me laugh, she laughed, too. FML, sharing a laugh with a devil-woman.

"By definition, yes? I mean, table stakes, when you get down to it," I said.

"It's awful," she said.

"I really should let Inferna take me there properly one day," I said. "I could shoot a documentary."

Hellmaiden laughed again, wagging a luminous finger at me.

"You would *not* want to do that," she said.

"No, I'm totally doing that," I said. "I'll add it to my TBD list. Hey, something else occurred to me: maybe I can help you with your remaining cases, and you can help me find this woman."

I held up my phone and showed her a picture of Anna. Seeing her smile, photographically frozen, made my heart ache all the more. Hellmaiden trained her glowing eyes on it, then glanced at me.

"Who is she?" she asked.

"Anna Victor," I said. "Victoriana. My girlfriend. I thought she was dead, but then I got this sign, and I think maybe she's not dead."

I held up the marble, which Hellmaiden eyed a moment, before returning her gaze to me.

"She's pretty," Hellmaiden said. "You love her?"

"Oh, yeah," I said. "Absolutely."

I felt very uncomfortable opening up to a devil. Their whole thing was getting people to do that so they could use that against them.

"I'll help you find her," Hellmaiden said.

"Awesome," I said. "I've got so much going on right now, every bit of help I can get would be great. Minder made her fly into the Sun. I thought she was dead, because, you know, who survives that?"

"But she's tough," Hellmaiden said.

"Super-tough," I said. "Minder's such a bastard. He got into her head and messed her up."

"Telepaths," she said. "The worst."

"That's exactly what I said!" I laughed again. Talking to her like that, I could almost ignore the waves of heat that flowed off of her. My suit protected me from some of it, but it was still wild. Like standing near a blast furnace.

The social media feeds were popping with reactions to my posts, which again were about one-quarter people ripping on me as a superhero, one-quarter disagreeing with what I said, one-quarter agreeing with me, and one-quarter saying stupid stuff that barely related to anything I'd posted.

Shutterbug's post had a similar reaction, perhaps with more sexual comments and fire emoji because it was Inferna and Hellmaiden sexily fighting crime.

"You're a hit," I said, holding up my phone. "'Hellmaiden is HOT!' already has like 3005 likes."

She chuckled again, shaking her head.

"People are so stupid," she said.

"They really are," I said. "Hey, you want to go take down that serial arsonist? I feel like I could benefit from getting out of town. Just promise me you won't melt my van."

"I could meet you there if you can't take my heat," she said.

"That works," I said. I went to my computer and dredged up Hellbringer's dossier:

**ALIAS: HELLBRINGER**

*REAL/ASSUMED NAME: DESMOND "FIRE" DRAKE*
*HAIR: BROWN*
*EYES: BROWN*
*HEIGHT: 5'11"*
*WEIGHT: 190 LBS.*

**POWERS:** *HELLBRINGER POSSESSES FIRE-RELATED SUPERPOWERS, INCLUDING:*

•**FIRE GENERATION:** *HELLBRINGER CAN SPONTANEOUSLY CONJURE UP HELLFIRE, WHICH BURNS AS LONG AS HE WILLS IT TO.*

•**PYROKINESIS:** *HELLBRINGER CAN CONTROL ANY FIRE, WHICH INCLUDES MAKING IT BURN MORE FIERCELY, SNUFF-ING IT OUT, MAKING IT MOVE WHERE HE WILLS IT TO, AND EVEN CREATING FIRE STRUCTURES AND MONSTERS.*

•**IMMUNITY TO FIRE:** *HELLBRINGER IS IMPERVIOUS TO DAM-AGE FROM FIRE.*

**THREAT LEVEL: 7/10**

She studied it a moment, glancing furtively at me.

"You keep dossiers on everybody," she said.

"I do," I said.

"Do you have one on me?" she asked.

"We've only just met," I said. "But you can be sure I will, once we've worked a case or two."

She smiled at this notion, almost to herself, except that I'd noticed it. Inferna often had that sly smile of hers, but I think Hellmaiden was the first time I made a devil smile. In my weird life, that counted as a victory.

"Alright," she said. "I'll meet you in Philadelphia."

"Oh, wait," I said. "That's like at least an eleven-hour drive. I'll need Inferna to teleport me or something. Inferna?"

At the mention of her name, Inferna appeared, smirking at us while wearing a crimson raincoat with a black beret that had a gold pitchfork brooch pinned to it. She was wearing back slacks and red combat knee boots and a black blouse.

"What are you two getting up to?" Inferna asked.

"Hellbringer," Hellmaiden said, her demeanor turned to all-business the moment Inferna appeared. I wondered what relationship those two had.

"Since you two jumped ahead and took out Yo-Yo, I'm going to help you with your Philadelphia arsonist guy." I said. "Getting out of town and trading Chicago winds for fiery Philadelphia."

Inferna looked at both of us a moment, cocking her head as she contemplated it.

"You want me to teleport you there," she said. "Is that all I am to you, Mitch? There are no free rides, you know. You're trying to work down your tab, not add to it."

"It's an eleven-hour drive," Hellmaiden said. "And I can't fly him all that way in a timely fashion without killing him at the speeds I'd have to fly."

"Yeah," Inferna said. "We can't have that. Fine. But this is a Hell's Belles gig, Mitch. We simply *must* pick up She-Devil, or she'll never forgive us."

**EVERYONE WANTS TO FEEL SPECIAL.** That's at the heart
of the human condition. However, to actually *be* special—to be
endowed with superhuman powers—it was a real head scram-
bler. Especially when I was committed to keeping it a secret
for the sake of my family's privacy and preoccupations.

A lot of people talk about the double lives that superheroes
lead. All true. College happened, I was a legal adult, and I remembered that I'd wanted to go out and be a superhero, and
nobody could stop me.

But I pushed my debut back until I could get my graduate
degree, if only because I didn't want to drop out of college. In
retrospect, it was so stupid—I wasn't Victoriana, yet—but I
had those powers. What did a college degree matter to a superhuman? A graduate degree, even? Nothing.

Do you see the irony of it? The paradox? College degrees
were for norms.

I had the power. And, in secret, I used it. I put what art
and design skills I had to work designing my own costume, my
superhero identity. I liked red and white, and sewed myself a
costume with that, hearkening back to Ephemera's cool costume, but with my own take. I liked capes, made myself a cool
red cape. The one thing I didn't have was a name or a logo.
That was the hardest part. The feel had to be right. I doodled
designs in my notebooks, in the margins, imaginary slugfests

with known supervillains. Then it came to me in a bit of day-dreaming (and, yes, how old was I?) I had jotted;

*Anna Victor + Cameraman*

In my notebook, feeling stupid and silly. Ideas take hold of you, though, and the idea of something—or someone—can surpass the reality, if you've never experienced that reality. Not knowing who he was made him intoxicating to me, this photographic phantom. I practiced my signature, toying with curls and flourishes...

*Anna Victor.*
*Anna Victor!*
*Anna Victor?*
*Anna Victor...*

*Victor, Anna.*

Then it hit me like a thunderbolt:

Victoriana!

It was perfect! Soooo on the nose!

My family, with their whole fretting over secrecy, respect-ability, all of that. I'd throw that right on its head by making my alias incorporate my name. Seeing it like that, I smiled. I wrote it out heroically, with a big emphasis on the "V"—V for Victor. V for Victory. It was perfect. I had my logo. And it was just too funny, given what "victoriana" meant.

I sewed a golden "V" on my suit, made it a Victorian type of V. It was just too funny. It's like I was mocking the hypocriti-cal, stuffy, and prudish Victorian values that held me back by wearing them on my chest and on the back of my cape. It felt meta.

Victoriana.

That's who I was. Now, I just had to stage my superheroic debut, once I'd graduated from college, gotten into grad school to placate my parents, who were still horrified by my Philosophy major. Yeah, it would be perfect. A debutante ball for Victoriana, something *nobody* would see coming. And, yes, I wore my green hair proudly as Victoriana. Mom and Dad would freak out, and maybe that was part of the point. Baby had to stretch her wings and fly, and they'd just have to deal with it. I could already see them sweating and fretting.

I still studied the other superheroes, the ones who worked on teams, the ones who were soloists, how they did what they did, what their respective styles and missions were. Sound & Fury worked out of the South, focusing on human trafficking. Some of them went after the gangs (Thee Souldier, Bitchqueen, Truth & Consequences), and others went after white supremacists and fascists (Red Baron, Fisticuffs & Browbeat, Praxis).

I also still tracked what Cameraman was up to, and used to play a little game when I was dating—like viewing boyfriends through my own detective lens, seeing how they were or were not like Cameraman, or at least how I imagined Cameraman to be. I jokingly called it my "Parallax View"—how near or far a guy came to my fantasy conception of Cameraman.

Who could possibly compete with a conception? They did their best. I tried not to crush them between my thighs. They always came up short, and that wasn't fair to them, but was I really expected to settle into a life I wasn't made for? Meanwhile, the headlines kept coming...

### "Cameraman" Foils Drug Kingpin With Industry Ties
### Who is Cameraman? A Study in Surveillance
### First Photo of Mysterious "Cameraman" Sources Say

That last one caught my eye, this blurry photograph of the mysterious man. He was a shadow among shadows, finally photographed, and I looked at who had photographed him: Caryn Underwood.

She was a photographer who worked in the Chicagoland area. You know I looked her up, to see what her deal was. She was well-represented in digital media and photographed well: big brown eyes, dark eyes. Pointy little chin. Pointy nose. Pixie-cut bleached blonde hair. Cute in this edgy sort of way. Journalism degree from Columbia. Award-winning photography exhibitions. I watched some digital clips of her, talking about Cameraman:

"Who is he?" Underwood asked. "I'm just not comfortable with someone snooping around people's dirty laundry, are you? I think he's an intrusive menace. And why doesn't he just come out in the open? Why does he have to hide? Who is he hiding from, and why? What are you so afraid of, Cameraman?"

Her voice was as sharp as her chin. I didn't like her. I didn't like her going after Cameraman. Not one bit.

**WITH EVERYTHING GOING ON IN MY LIFE,** working with some satanic *Charlie's Angels* wasn't entirely the gig I had envisioned for myself.

But with Shane doing whatever backroom negotiating he needed to be doing with the Affiliates, and Shutterbug prowling out there somewhere, the social media skirmishes raging around whether I was a hero, antihero, or villain, it only made sense that I get out there and do a little do-gooder type work.

I opted to use my Firecam suit, which couldn't hurt when dealing with an arsonist. Hellmaiden watched me put it on with great amusement.

"You look cute in it," she said, which made me blush despite trying to be all serious about it. This suit had saved my life in the past. "You used that against Pyroclastic Flo."

"How'd you know that?" I asked.

She tapped her forehead with a luminescent finger. "We do have televisions in Hell, you know."

"Hellavision?" I asked, which made her giggle. "Now I really do need to do that documentary. Maybe you can give me the guided tour."

"You'll be just like Dante," she said, and we shared a laugh while I finished suiting up.

However, before I go into how it went with Hellbringer, I absolutely have to introduce you to the third leg on the diabolical stool that was Hell's Belles: She-Devil. Also known as Tamara Sorrows, occult librarian.

**ALIAS: SHE-DEVIL**

*REAL/ASSUMED NAME: TAMARA SORROWS*
*HAIR: BROWN / BLACK*
*EYES: BROWN / RED*
*HEIGHT: 5'3" / 6'6"*
*WEIGHT: 105 LBS. / 400 LBS.*

**POWERS:** *SHE-DEVIL POSSESSES SUPERPOWERS, INCLUDING:*

• **SUPER-STRENGTH:** *SHE-DEVIL IS SUPERHUMANLY STRONG, EASILY ABLE TO LIFT EIGHTY-FIVE TONS.*

• **INVULNERABILITY:** *SHE-DEVIL IS IMMUNE TO ANY FIRE DAMAGE, AS WELL AS POISON, AND IS RESISTANT TO COLD AND NORMAL INJURY.*

• **HORNS:** *SHE-DEVIL'S HORNS, IN ADDITION TO BEING DEADLY WEAPONS, CAN (ONCE PER DAY) FIRE A BOLT OF ENERGY, LIGHTNING, HELLFIRE, ACID, OR ICE, DEPENDING ON HER INCLINATION. THESE ATTACKS TAKE A FEW MINUTES TO BUILD BEFORE THEY CAN BE USED.*

• **INFRARED VISION:** *SHE-DEVIL IS ABLE TO SEE CLEARLY IN THE DARK.*

• **VULNERABILITIES:** *SHE-DEVIL IS VULNERABLE TO SILVER AND HOLY WATER.*

**THREAT LEVEL: 8/10**

Tamara Sorrows worked as the head librarian of the Augenblick Foundation Library of Occult History, located on the Near West Side of Chicago, in an old Victorian mansion that had been turned into a lending library by the Foundation. It contained a wealth of arcana, with books, tomes, grimoires, scrolls, talismans, and other assorted items of occult interest.

I had little need of the Occult Library, but my association with Inferna meant that I was at least aware of it. When we turned up by means of Inferna's teleportation, Tamara merely looked up from a book she was reading behind her desk, her round-rimmed spectacles sliding down her nose as she regarded us. She fixed them with a pointed push of a finger. She was more than a little Creole and Seminole and had brought that arcane knowledge gleaned from the bayou up here to Chicago.

"We're closed," she said. "Oh, wait, Inferna. Yeah."

"We're on," Inferna said. "Right now. We even brought Cameraman."

I could feel Tamara's brown eyes slide over me with a kind of sardonic disapproval.

"You know, he's all over the news, Inferna," she said. "Is this one of those high-profile kinds of jobs?"

"We're taking down Hellbringer," Inferna said. "Get your better half fired up and we'll bounce to Philadelphia."

She-Devil came about because Tamara had come across an incantation in one of the books in the library, one that had bound her to a devil named Ossifier, who had been trapped in the tome as a prisoner and could only find release by means of the incantation Tamara had invoked.

However, instead of simply taking over Tamara's body and life, Ossifier had to time-share with her, the two of them working out an alter-ego timetable that allowed them equal time to do what they enjoyed doing. For Ossifier, that meant pounding opponents with his fists. For Tamara, it meant holding down a steady job without infernal interference.

She-Devil was the result of their diabolical détente. Tamara carefully set down her eyeglasses and invoked her alter-ego, as Ossifier manifested within her, causing her diminutive frame to burst and swell into a hulking devil-woman whose shoulder was at nose-level to me. Contrasted with Inferna's own sleek and stylish horns, Ossifier's were these great Baroque, black winding spires on her forehead, twin tines that crackled with energy between them.

"Did you catch that, Cameraman?" She-Devil said, her voice a guttural growl.

"Oh, was I supposed to be rolling?" I asked (I totally did catch it).

Inferna produced a Tarot card that carried upon it the image of Hellbringer, who looked like this fiery apparition, gleefully dancing in a bonfire, with shadows lurking behind him. She tossed it to the ground and began her incantational efforts.

Hellmaiden looked at She-Devil, who just glowered back at her, while Inferna prepared herself to teleport all of us to Philadelphia.

And then her spell took effect, and we found ourselves in my hometown. In my years living in Chicago, I'd mostly left Philly in the back burner of my brain. I grew up in Old City, but that's not something I needed to dwell on, because there was no way in hell I was showing up at my parents' place with this crew with me.

As such, we had appeared in Strawberry Mansion, guided at least somewhat by whatever Inferna's Tarot card had drawn us to. The neighborhood was one of the most crime-ridden in the area, and it at least made some sense that Hellbringer might have targeted it for his arson activities.

"Hellmaiden, take to the skies," Inferna said. "I'll join you shortly. She-Devil, you and Cameraman keep to the rooftops."

I did not relish jumping rooftop to rooftop in one of the most dangerous neighborhoods in Philadelphia, so I just toggled my stealth mode (full invisibility) and began recording.

"This is Cameraman," I said. "I'm here with the Hell's Belles, the premier occult investigators the underworld has to offer. We're hunting down a serial arsonist who calls himself the Hellbringer, who's been a very nasty sort of baddie, taking to torching homes and businesses in this area. I'm here with She-Devil, one of the founding members of the Belles."

"Quiet, Cameraman," She-Devil said, cupping a pointed ear. "He's close."

"Overhead, we have Inferna and Hellmaiden," I said, aiming my headcam upward, which revealed them both—fiery Inferna and her bat wings, while Hellmaiden's luminosity was almost shooting starlike. At distance, safe from the heat, they were both bizarrely beautiful to behold.

I felt the whoosh of the fire before I'd seen it, coming from another rooftop, carrying with it the cackle of Hellbringer, who had been firing at She-Devil, although when the fiery blast hit us, my own silhouette was visible in the conflagration. I didn't know if he'd spotted me or not, but I was very grateful I'd been wearing my Firecam suit.

"Hellbringer sees you, sister She-Devil," Hellbringer yelled, brandishing hellfire in his outstretched hands, which were black against the firelight. Underlit by his own flame, he looked particularly menacing, his eyes wide. He wore a black, orange, and red costume—mostly soot black with the highlights in the other colors, with a big smiling fireball in the center of his chest.

Protected as I was by my suit, I kept the shot going, adjusting for the contrast in lighting between the fire and Hellbringer, trying to capture both She-Devil and him. I also wasn't going to dwell on the fact that this was magical hellfire burning on my suit, which meant that it would burn as long as Hellbringer wanted it to, which might mean I would burn through even the protective armor I wore. I didn't know how long my suit would honestly last against sustained hellfire. I tried not to dwell on it.

"Folks, this is Hellbringer," I said, finding some comfort in the narration as I did. "He seems to have discovered us."

She-Devil sprang from her fiery perch to land near Hellbringer, missing the mark and passing with a crash through the roof of the building where Hellbringer had been standing.

Hellmaiden streamed down to Hellbringer in a flash, tackling him and knocking him from the rooftop, where he tumbled groundward, breaking his fall with some jets of fire that didn't quite get him flying, but slowed his descent to a manageable level.

As he landed, Inferna swooped down on him, her burning whip at the ready, snagging him on the leg and jerking him off his feet.

Hellmaiden paused by the fire I was attempting to escape, flicking her cape at me.

"Grab on, Cameraman," she said. "I'll help you to the ground."

"Thanks," I said, jumping and clawed at her ragged crimson cape, as she gently lowered me to the ground in a save worthy of Victoriana, which made me miss her even more.

"You're welcome," she said, even as she was seized by this massive fire talon fist that manifested out of nowhere, powered by the mad pyrokinetic power of Hellbringer's mind. Of course, I captured all of it with my POV helmet cam.

Inferna whipped Hellbringer across his back, which only had him chortling, just as She-Devil came crashing out of the building she'd been in, still burning with the hellfire that he'd hit her with. I was still burning, too, I noticed, to my growing dismay. Alarms would sound once my armor had been depleted, although I suspected I'd feel it well before the armor failed.

She-Devil ran for Hellbringer in this amazing animal stride, her face a toothy leer as she raced for Hellbringer.

Hellmaiden flashed bright in the sky, her strange plasma energy repelling the hellfire, actually snuffing it out in some manner I couldn't fathom. She then flew for Hellbringer, who was driven to a cackling panic by the Hell's Belles, who were attacking him from three sides at once—Hellmaiden blasted him with her energy beams, She-Devil nailed him with a freeze ray fired from between her horns, and Inferna whipped him several times.

Then something happened which I was so glad I caught. It was the kind of footage someone like me prays for in their professional life (don't judge me for what you're about to see).

Overwhelmed as he was by the Belles, Hellbringer let out a caterwaul and a fireball that blasted away from him in an incendiary shockwave that knocked back all three of the Belles. Even from where I was, even protected in my suit, I could feel the force of it. Illuminated in the center of the blaze of his own making, Hellbringer burst—which is to say, he split apart bloodily and, emerging within him was the demon patron that Inferna had suspected was there all along.

You can watch the footage as often as you like, and it'll still be incredible, but from within him came this thing that arose out of Hellbringer's own destruction—a baptism of boiling blood and burning bone, this fiery figure appeared, growing larger by the moment. It was gigantic, jet black, but riven by orange-red rivulets, with great eyes of fire and massive obsid-ian fangs, a crown of fire around its head.

"Behold, Volcanis!" bellowed the being, each utterance spewing fiery cinders which landed on the ground and ignited whatever they touched. "Demon Lord of Desolation, Destruc-tion, and Doom!"

"Whoa," I said, having caught all of it. In the night's sky, Volcanis was mesmerizing, and residents of Strawberry Man-sion were crying out at the sight of this growing monster in their midst.

Inferna called out to the Belles, who resumed their attack. She-Devil dove for one of the massive legs of Volcanis, swinging as hard as she was able, while Inferna took to the air with her bat wings. Her own hellfire would be useless against something like Volcanis, I surmised, but I could see her taking stock of the surroundings. I tossed the one dronecam I had airborne, going online and remote-piloting it at what I felt was a safe distance.

Hellmaiden took flight and landed an astounding, booming aerial uppercut—basically flying directly up at Volcanis and catching him on the chin with such force that he was knocked back, nearly falling over. The blast of it alone was like a mas-sive cannon firing. I could feel the impact from where I stood.

But, mindful of the terrified civilian onlookers, Hellmaiden grabbed Volcanis by the chin and hurled him into the Schuylkill River, which was a sight in itself and I was grateful I could catch it—this massive black burning figure going airborne, landing with a hissing splash into the river that displaced great waves. My dronecam caught all of it, like the massive piles of steam as the enraged Volcanis splashed around in the river, cursing out the Hell's Belles.

Luminous as a meteorite, Hellmaiden flew after the demon lord, while She-Devil leaped after it, and Inferna swept down to scoop me up.

"Incredible," I said. "Unbelievable."

"You caught that, did you?" she said.

"Oh, hell, yeah," I said. "Hellmaiden's amazing."

"She sure is," Inferna said. "Try not to get killed, Cam."

She set me down on the east bank of the river and went to help her compatriots, who were duking it out with Volcanis, who was throwing these fiery swings with fists the size of skyscrapers.

My headphone rang, and it was Shane.

"Mitch," he said. "What's going on in Philadelphia?"

"No worries, Shane," I said. "Just a demon invasion. Somebody named Volcanis. Not up on my demonology but seems he had possessed that Hellbringer fella."

"Who's fighting him?" Shane asked.

"Inferna, She-Devil, and Hellmaiden," I said. "And, you know, me."

"Right," Shane said. "I'm sending Tandem and Wingman. They're on their way."

"Right," I said, watching Volcanis breathe hellfire at his attackers, the flames lighting up the riverbank. Even amid that firestorm, I could still make out the gleam of Hellmaiden, who was like this firefly next to the massive Volcanis, at least until she fired her plasma blasts at him or struck him—each strike created a thunderous boom.

"Is the situation under control?" Shane asked.

"Getting there," I said. "Gotta go."

Volcanis gestured, and the river water around him began to bubble and steam anew, and I could see the demon lord was conjuring a volcano beneath his feet—a volcanic cone that was gushing lava like from an open wound in the Earth itself.

"All will succumb to my unholy fire," Volcanis roared, even as Hellmaiden smashed him in his obsidian teeth with a powerful punch that shattered them, raining slabs of jagged obsidian that fell earthward, impaling themselves in the mud of the riverbank, each one bigger than a vending machine.

"Enough of this," Hellmaiden said, grabbing Volcanis by the scruff of his neck and flying upward with him, leaving torrents of magma flowing from him to the ground in incandescent splashes. They looked like some hellacious rocket ship, flying into space—the blinding luminosity of Hellmaiden and the chthonic fury of Volcanis as they went skyward. I sent my camdrone after them, trying to keep up, but she just flew too quickly.

"Breaking contact with the Earth seems to have shorted out the volcanic manifestation of Volcanis," I said, panning down to catch the waning of the ad hoc volcano, which was quickly being filled by river water, which explosively contacted the conjured lava. Tilting back upward, I could only make out the starlike light of Hellmaiden.

Then Tandem flew in, followed by Wingman in an Affilijet, shining lights on the area of the battle, while Inferna was putting out the hellfire with snaps of her fingers.

I brought my dronecam back down, while Tandem flew upward with a sonic boom. The city was full of the sound of sirens, as people were trying to deal with the fires that had broken out.

Then there was a great flash in the sky, and I looked back up instinctively, catching it with my headcam.

"There seems to have been an explosion," I said. "Not sure what we're seeing, here. No, wait, I see Hellmaiden heading back down. You can see the luminous spot in the sky, like a shooting star. That's her. I don't, however, see Volcanis. Looks like Tandem's flying up to meet Hellmaiden, and I see Wingman flying around, making sure everyone's okay. I'd say we're definitely seeing a resolution to Hellbringer's efforts to burn the city. From how it looked, I'm thinking Hellbringer is dead. I'll have to talk to Hellmaiden and see what happened up there. This is Cameraman, signing off for now."

I cut my feed, already confident this footage would keep me going for a long time. Hellmaiden did a pass overhead, her luminescent body visible even from that height, as she swung by a couple of times.

Without hesitating, I started my recording again.

"Looks like she's alright," I said. "Hellmaiden's headed this way."

She landed near me, glowing brightly in the night light.

"Hellmaiden, what happened up there?" I asked.

"I gave Volcanis hell," she said, smiling at me.

MY FIRST BIG FIGHT, like the one where it was me against another super, took place in Pittsburgh, when I was on Thanksgiving break, visiting my family. It was a local villain, a muscle-bound bruiser who called himself The Stealer.

Honestly, not much imagination. He was a total Yinzer, with a heavy Pittsburgh accent and wearing a black and yellow costume that had this yellow hand logo on his chest, like an outstretched hand that was reaching for something. He wore a black and yellow football helmet that had his logo on it.

Stealer had literally knocked over an armored truck, had torn the doors off it and was taking the bags of money while the security were firing their guns at him, the bullets bouncing off his impervious skin. I didn't know where his powers had come from, nor did I particularly care.

"Ha, ya slippy jagoffs!" Stealer yelled. "Yinz can't do a thing to me with yer guns n'at! My skin's like arn! Do yer worst!"

He was loading the stolen money into a pickup truck driven by Sister Sludge, his sidekick and partner. Sludge wore a wild costume that had this rainbow color that looked like what oil looks like on water. She could transform into a gooey liquid and propel herself around, being alternatively sticky or slippery, depending on how she needed to be in that moment. She sprayed her sludge on the security guys and cop cars, and the two of them were able to flee the scene with the stolen money, with Sludge driving and the Stealer in the back. Police had attempted to pursue, but Sludge coated the roads with her slippy sludge (her words for it) and made them spin out.

It looked like it would've been a clean getaway, but I was flying overhead, and decided I would stop them.

Was I nervous? Yes. Definitely. It was one thing to sneak out at night and fly around, quietly intervening here and there. But this was the real deal, and I had the element of surprise on them, because Stealer was occupied with yelling insults at the police, and Sludge was driving hard for the barricade they were speeding toward.

I figured subtlety wasn't the order of the day, so I swooped in and grabbed Stealer by the chin, hurling him into the Allegheny River. And I mean I grabbed him and threw him *hard*, so hard that he actually skipped across the river like a stone, crashing into the shore on the other side, embedded in the riverbank.

Then I gave their pickup truck a two-legged piledriver kind of stomp, which shattered its rear axle and sent Sludge right into the windshield, her gooey self splashing on it as she cursed.

She oozed from the ruined truck, and I landed near her, taking another hard swing, only to see my fist pass through her liquefied form and to have her glue onto me and flip me, hurling me hard to the ground.

"Hah, no match for my scungy sludge," she said, her voice strange to my ears. "Who're you? Superbitch?"

Sister Sludge threw herself at me, smothering me, her syrupy voice in my ears.

"I'm going to drown you, Superbitch," she said, squeezing hard. It was wild, being enveloped by her silvery liquid form, unable to see or hear anything but her voice. But while my fist had passed through her, she was far from being immune to my attacks.

I began spinning like a top, moving so quickly that Sludge began flinging off of me by the force of, well, centrifugal force. Sludge splattered off of me in one of those camera-ready takedowns that was caught by some of the cops at the barricade. It looked impressive, like me spinning and this rainbow-silvery goo flinging off of me in noisy splatters. My actions led Sludge to being captured when Hazardous Materials teams came up and gathered all of the sloppy remnants of her in sealable biohazard-emblazoned containers.

Having taken that action, I went airborne and quickly chased down Stealer, who was recovering himself on the riverbank, cursing me as he saw me approaching. He looked laughably muddy. I felt like a fighter jet, hurtling toward him. To his credit, he didn't try to run away, but, instead, threw a punch at me right as I went for him, and the two of us collided, creating a deafening detonation upon impact that could be heard at least a mile away, like a kind of thunderclap.

I don't want to be insulting, but I knew from that moment of impact that I was stronger than Stealer. Far stronger.

"Who da hell are you, ya nebby jag?" Stealer asked, throwing another haymaker which I simply took, watching him curse and shake out his hand. He'd hurt himself punching me, and I was sure that this wasn't something he'd experienced before.

"I'm Victoriana," I said, treating him to an uppercut that sent him skyward. I did not knock him into orbit, but I did knock him out cold, and had a few seconds to compose myself as he came back down. Just in case, I hit him again, and as he flew across the skyline, I flew after him and fetched him, bringing him back to the crime scene where they were mopping up Sister Sludge. I made sure Stealer was out cold, which he was.

"Who are you?" the cops asked, as I set Stealer down on the stretch of road.

"I'm Victoriana," I said, practicing my delivery of my superhero alias with the proper authority. "Happy to help!"

And off I flew, before they could ask me anything else, because I was actually a little shy and shocked at how well it had gone. I don't know what I'd expected, but it had gone incredibly smoothly. I also didn't want to give any interviews or anything, because my family would see and know it was me. Plus, I didn't really want to be caught on camera being awkward, just in case Cameraman might see me. I would die.

The news got out there, anyway, and the police cameras had captured the bits of me battling Sister Sludge and Stealer. People loved it, loved me:

### New Kid on the Block: Victoriana Bests Stealer and Sister Sludge in Bank-Robbing Bid

### She's Got the Beat: Victoriana Takes Down Stealer and Sludge in Riverside Battle

### Pittsburgh's Protector? Victoriana Belts Stealer and Sister Sludge in One-Sided Fight

### V is for Victory: Superheroine Sends Stealer and Sister Sludge Packing

### Two Turkeys Bagged for Thanksgiving by Victorious Vixen

I was ecstatic, adding the clips to my scrapbooks, and my parents were calling me while I was coming down, with Mom particularly losing it.

"Sweetheart, we saw you on the news," Mom said. "We can't figure out what on earth you might be thinking."

"I'm a superhero, Ma," I said. "I stopped a bank robbery."

"That's the job of the police," Dad said. "Not you."

"I'm *making* it my job," I said. "And you can't stop me from doing it."

"You can't just go out there like that," Mom said. "You should have consulted with us first, Anna. You think people aren't going to make an association between your green hair and, well, this strange identity you're assuming?"

I knew they wouldn't understand. Their entire lives were grounded in a way that would prevent their understanding who I was.

"I like my green hair," I said. "That's part of who I am."

"You're being very selfish, Anna," Mom said. "And, in practical terms, what can you possibly hope to accomplish? You're better than this, Sweetie."

"The government's going to come for you," Dad said. "They're going to seek you out. At least talk to Lane. Let him represent you if you need legal representation. Do you need a lawyer?"

They were hopelessly mired in the mechanics of the mundane. I don't know if that's something with all parents, or just them. I didn't want them to worry, but I also wasn't going to let them hold me back. I could not sit on that.

I participated in a handful of other regionally high-profile super-brawls while in town—Admiral Alchemy in Cleveland (thwarting his bid to poison Lake Erie, which was almost redundant), taking down Dr. Darkness in Pittsburgh (whose scheme seemed to be bringing a dome of darkness to Pittsburgh forever—don't ask me why), ruining the schemes of Haymaker, Right Cross, and the Jabber outside of Akron (they were a supervillain team that called themselves the Rubber City Ringleaders, being a trio of superpowered boxers who had teamed up after being tired of working simply as hired muscle).

From those local battles had come my biggest profile-raiser, when Doctor Fist had set his sights on Pittsburgh, where he'd actually challenged me to a fight. Doctor Fist was an A-list villain, he considered himself the strongest supervillain out there.

He was almost unbelievably overbuilt, being this muscle-bound man-monster of around seven feet in height. Fist wore a costume of white and blue (blue boots, white costume, blue speedo, no gloves), wore this kind of gladiator-type blue helmet with a crest on it, and had a white fist logo in the center of his broad chest. He had a well-trimmed black beard, and had appeared downtown, yelling threats to any who'd listen.

"Where is the vaunted maiden, this Victoriana, who seeks to flex in the androgenic arena of superheroic might?" he yelled, breaking windows with the power of his voice.

"I'm here," I said, flying down slowly to face this man-mountain. He actually smiled at the sight of me.

"Ah, such a wee slip of a woman you are," he said. "*This* is the Terror of the Tri-State?"

I'll admit that Doctor Fist intimidated me. He had battled the Affiliates to a standstill a dozen times. He'd knocked out

Rad Lad in Long Beach and had fought Tandem to a stalemate in Miami, having punched Tandem so hard that he'd actually split Tandem into two, leaving Fusillad and Lassitude stunned and reeling, plucked from harm's way only by Tantrum's timely telekinesis. If it hadn't been for Ephemera intervening and phasing into him in her intangible form and driving him off, who knows what Fist might've done?

"We shouldn't be fighting downtown, Doctor," I said, making him laugh.

"They're all roaches, Victoriana," he said. "Made for crunching underfoot."

He was circling me, leaning forward, readying himself for attack. I refused to let myself be captive to my intimidation. Fist threw a jab at me, which I dodged. Not because I didn't think I could take it, but because I didn't want him setting the terms of our fight.

"Quick," he said. "Quick is good. Not enough, but good."

When he came at me again, he did so without hesitation, supremely confident in his superiority. This was a man who'd fought the strongest heroes and come out on top. The arrogance of power flowed through his veins.

I let him hit me. Was that arrogance or innocence? He caught me in the jaw, and it made my head whip, actually made my ears ring from the force of the blow. It was the hardest hit I'd yet taken, and if he hadn't badly underestimated me, I might have been flattened by that blow.

It took me back to something I remembered Blake and Lane talking about, when those two were boxing in our basement, while they let me ring the bell and time their fight.

"It's not the punches you throw that make a warrior out of you," Lane said, blocking Blake's attacks. "It's the ones you can take. That's the truest measure of a fighter. Anyone can take a swing; not everyone can take a punch."

Blake promptly pounded Lane in the face, and he took it, counterpunching Blake in the stomach, knocking the wind out of him, before finishing him with a combination to the face that left Blake spinning, reeling, tumbling to the floor. I counted him out, amazed that Lane had beaten him.

I took the punch, grateful that my head hadn't come flying off. And in that intimate moment, the martial intimacy of a fistfight, I could see his ice blue eyes widening that I'd actually taken that blow from him. He brought his other fist around, determined to drop me like that, deciding to bring more power to his punches, since that first punch, that test punch, hadn't been enough.

As much as I would have enjoyed a downtown slugfest with Doctor Fist, I couldn't avoid thinking about all of the civilians around us, the ordinary people watching in fascination, awe, and terror, fearful for their lives, what might happen to them as much as which of us might prevail in that fight. How much damage would the city take if Fist and I were to really duke it out?

All of this flew through my ringing head from that blow he struck, as I ducked below his follow-up punch, which cut the air over my head, and then I delivered the uppercut of uppercuts. It was such a gorgeous punch, I still relish seeing the photographs of it that people took that day.

That moment my fist caught the underside of his chin—and I had to use a whisker of my flight to reach him, because he was so tall—and the moment I struck him, there was a wave of force that shattered what windows hadn't been broken by his yelling, like in a few hundred yards around us.

I saw his eyes close as he winced, feeling it, and up he went. We're talking straight up. Doctor Fist—who couldn't fly—was flying. He shot upward and broke the sound barrier several times in his ascent. I know because I chased after him, flying right at him, being there for him once the force of my blow eventually petered out. He just kept accelerating, but I wasn't content to let him hit the ground.

No, I caught up to him, grabbed him by his centurion helmet, and hurled him into space. The way it looked on the ground, the way the story went was that I'd knocked Doctor Fist into orbit. I'm confessing that I knocked him into the sky, but to launch him into orbit, I had to grab him and throw him there. I *did* put him into orbit; just not with one punch. It would be something Fist would say again and again, because it would come up constantly after I'd done that to him. As much as my own reputation benefited from it, so his suffered from it, and he worked extra-hard over the years to try to recover from that single punch I'd thrown.

In retrospect, I know I could have actually done it, but at the time, I didn't realize just how strong I was. I do know that once the adrenaline rush faded, I realized that I'd broken my hand. It healed almost as quickly as the damage had been done, but I'd broken my damned hand taking out Doctor Fist. That's how tough he was.

He glared at me as I put him into orbit, nursing a broken jaw. I'd broken his jaw as surely as I'd broken my hand. We watched each other a moment, our super-healing factors mending the injuries sustained up in orbit.

I'd flown back downtown, going slowly this time, so I didn't burn up my clothes, and by the time I got back down, my hand had healed, and nobody was the wiser for it. The media was there, people taking pictures, cheering young Victoriana for her triumph. The headlines ran, the social media stirred. I'd made the A-list of solo superheroes in that marvelous moment:

**Punching Above Her Weight: Victoriana
Knocks Doctor Fist Into Orbit**

**Fist's Flying: Victoriana Launches Doctor Fist Into Space**

**Knuckle Sandwich? Doctor Fist Pounded
by Victoriana the Amateur Amazon**

**Punch for Lunch—Victoriana Saves
Midday Downtown from Doctor Fist**

**Fist Fight: Victoriana Gets the Upper Hand on Doctor Fist**

People ran clips of the fight on social media, and it was all over the place, like people obsessing over my alter ego. Lane had texted me about it:

*Nice job, Slugger.*

That meant a lot to me. Mom and Dad were both petrified and proud, with Dad offering some of his half-handed praise so Mom didn't have to.

"Great job, Sweetheart. We're proud of you and we are terrified," Dad said. "But did you *really* have to take that shot from him?"

That "Fist-fight" made me. People reached out to me, tried to find me. Media people. Agents. Other supers. And, most importantly, the Knack. The Knack actually came to me a few weeks later, after I'd taken out Mister Mayhem in Manhattan, who'd wanted to destroy the Met for some reason.

He'd just showed up while I was making sure Mayhem wasn't getting back up anytime soon.

"Hey," he said, getting out of this gorgeous grey Jaguar coupe. "I'm the Knack."

"I know who you are," I said. "What's up?"

He smiled to himself, showing off his perfect teeth. He was wearing a white sport coat, grey shirt, black pants and black leather loafers.

"Victoriana, what do you think about the Affiliates?" he asked.

People were all around us, cordoned off by the police, who'd done crowd control when I'd been taking on Mister Mayhem, who was still out cold from the drubbing I'd given him.

"Are you asking me if I like them or what?" I asked.

"Sure," he said. "Maybe we can go somewhere and talk?"

The idea of going for a car ride with the Knack when I could fly anywhere I liked was almost quaint.

"Yeah, okay," I said, flying over to his car, glancing back at Mayhem. The Knack just shook his head, still smiling.

"Don't worry about Mayhem," he said. "We're sending a team to deal with him. Great work in that fight, by the way."

He drove us out of there, and sitting in his car, which smelled of cedar and sandalwood, I felt comfortable, at ease, even, despite the post-fight rush. I always felt a rush after a scrap.

"The Affiliates could use someone like you," Shane said. It might feel presumptuous calling him that, but he was the one with the public identity.

"Could they?" I replied. He nodded, driving us so smoothly through the city, you would have been surprised to know we were in Manhattan. He was expertly navigating a maze that would have left anyone else hopelessly lost and/or mired in traffic, exasperated hands in the air.

"Yes," Shane said. "What's more, I need your help, so I'll speak plainly. There's rot in the Affiliates. I can't isolate it, but it's there. I need someone like you to help me deal with it. Someone who's strong, has the power to do something about it. Someone who isn't afraid to take on some bad guys. Someone with a good heart and a ton of courage."

"Wow," I said. "I'm honored."

"First thing, though," he said. "We need to get you a proper costume."

"What's wrong with my costume?" I asked, feeling mortified. Had something ripped while I'd been fighting Mayhem? I mentally processed the fight and couldn't isolate any wardrobe fails. Had my ass been hanging out? Cleavage? I circumspectly ran my hands across me, trying to appear nonchalant.

"Nothing," Shane said. "But it's not strong enough for you. You need something at least as strong as you."

He directed me to a box in the back seat, a grey box wrapped with black ribbon. I took it, opened it, saw a replica of my own costume in it, wrapped in white tissue paper.

"It's made from Zetacloth," Shane said. "Highly indestructible. It'll let you be your super-self without, you know, problems. Everybody on the team uses it for their costumes."

"Wow, thanks," I said. I toyed with the costume, which felt silky in my hands. "It's beautiful."

The Knack smiled, getting us out of Manhattan.

"Where are we going?" I asked.

"The Hamptons," he said. "I have a place there. You don't have to be anywhere right now, do you?"

I didn't, and the prospect of a two-hour drive to the Hamptons with the Knack was a journey I was eager to take. He was so incredibly chill, so cool, as he told me about the Affiliates, about his own heroic journey, and he asked me about mine, but not in an intrusive way. It was more conversational.

I felt like an idiot, just blathering to him, mindful of my secret identity.

"I'm not sure I'd want to be on the east coast," I said.

"Sure," Shane said. "It's not for everyone. I bounce from coast to coast, depending on where I'm needed."

"I mean, I'd go anywhere I needed to, but I'm from Pittsburgh," I said. "New York feels like a world away."

The Knack nodded.

"Where would you be if you could be anywhere?" he asked.

"Chicago," I said, and he smiled to himself.

"Really? Why?" he asked.

I steeled myself before speaking. I didn't want to sound like some goofy fangirl. Shane glanced at me, his expression affably unreadable.

"I want to meet Cameraman," I said, and he chuckled.

"Yeah?" he said. I nodded. He shook his head. "You know, I *know* Cameraman."

"You do?" I asked, entirely too eagerly.

"Yeah," Shane said. "I've known him from when he started. We teamed up against the Fearsome Frogmen about eight years ago."

"No way," I said, not owning up that I had scrapbooked that fight, which had featured the Knack with the beaten Frogmen, but no sign of Cameraman. My head was swimming with that knowledge. Naturally, the Knack would know Cameraman. It only made sense. Superheroes always knew each other. They were part of this elite club of supers.

"Totally," Shane said. "He doesn't think much of me. Or any of us, really. Supers."

I laughed. "Why not?"

"Oh, I think it's his sense of social justice," Shane said. "The power principle vexes him. The unfairness of it all, those of us with powers, versus the majority without."

"Wait, he *doesn't* have, like, invisibility superpowers?" I asked. Shane shook his head.

"Get out of here," I said. "He does all of that stuff he does *without* powers?"

Shane nodded, giving me a sidelong look.

"I've helped him out over the years since that first battle," he said. "He's needed some funding, and I've done my part to lend a hand. He's got a good heart, although he pretends he's beyond all of that."

My mind reeled at the idea that Cameraman wasn't super-powered. I had just assumed he was. Why would someone without powers do what he did? At least in my situation, my powers compelled me to take that path. But that he was doing it out of what? Revenge? Some obsessive quest for justice? Was he crazy?

"I'm amazed," I said. "I *have* to meet him."

Shane laughed again, drumming his fingers on the steering wheel. "Go to Chicago, you'll find him sooner or later. Just look for trouble and you'll find him there, or he'll find you, more likely. I could give you his number, if you wanted to call him, but I *wouldn't* recommend cold-calling him. He's likely to think the worst of you if you did that. At the very least, he'll wonder why you're calling him, and who gave you his number."

"Wow," I said, acutely aware of how many times I'd already said "Wow" in the company of the Knack. It had started raining, and the rain on the windshield was soothing.

"No, I'll find him," I said.

"You like him?" Shane asked.

"I *love* him," I said. "I kept a scrapbook of all of his busts. He's not old, is he?"

Shane laughed again.

"Depends on what you consider old," Shane said. "He's twenty-nine years old."

Being twenty-six at that time, I was fine with twenty-nine. It was the right kind of mature. He wasn't some man-boy finding himself, and he wasn't some old man starting to fall apart. I know that sounds terrible, but it was a consideration. Nobody could keep up with me, but there was an acceptable margin where somebody might have a hope of trying. Then again, it also meant that Cameraman had been doing his superheroic thing since he was eighteen years old, which was sort of incredible. Who even did that?

"How old are you?" I asked.

"I'm thirty-one," Shane said. "Old."

"Hardly," I said. "You don't look that old."

Shane laughed to himself.

"That's because it's *not* old," he said. "But I've been who I am since I was a teen. I've been at it for around fifteen years, now."

He told me about his origin, which I already knew, because it had been published in the past, interviews he'd given. He'd been very open about it.

"It's sad that you lost your parents," I said. "That you couldn't save them."

"Yeah," Shane said. "It was a long time ago."

I couldn't have imagined not having my parents around. If anything, they'd kept me out of superheroing by at least a decade by paying for my college and grad school and getting me a condo in Pittsburgh. What was I going to do, turn them down? They *wanted* to help in the way they thought might help.

"It's easier if you're alone," I said, watching the rain dance on the windows of his car. "Nobody to worry about but yourself."

I told him about how my family had me hide my abilities, how afraid they'd been for anyone to discover who I was.

"That had to have been tough," Shane said. "But their concern is understandable. They don't want you to get hurt. It'll happen in this business. Pain and suffering. Death."

"I guess," I said. "Mostly I just think they don't want me disrupting their very comfortable lives."

"What you can do, what you must do, it's beyond their experience," Shane said. "People in their position historically can't relate to that. It's not their fault. I've seen the footage of what you've done. It's impressive."

I blushed, flattered that the Knack might compliment my heroic handiwork. It was like having a movie star compliment your acting.

We reached his place in the Hamptons, which was this beautiful house that even the rain couldn't obscure, and I wondered why the Knack had taken me all of this way out of the city. Part of me wondered if he was maybe planning to hook up with me. That put me in a place, because if the Knack came onto me, I am sure I would have, you know, gone wherever that took me in that precise moment. He, however, snapped me back to the here and now.

"You have incredible promise, but you're not entirely ready for the Affiliates," Shane said. "Not yet. You remembered me telling you about the rot?"

"Yeah," I said.

"I can't in good conscience send you in unprepared," Shane said, disabling the alarm to his place and letting me in. The place smelled of fine wood and polish. There were beautiful things in it—paintings that had to have cost a fortune, and statues. The place was beyond modern—it was ultramodern.

"Shaundra, are you here?" Shane asked.

"Who?" I asked, but the Knack walked away, turning on lights, and, unsure what else to do, I put on that Zetacloth supersuit the Knack had gifted me. It was incredible, felt like a super second skin. It made my own homemade costume feel amateurish and shoddy by comparison. This was next-level, and I spun around in it, looking at myself in a full-length mirror down the hall.

I was admiring myself when an apparition emerged from the mirror, floating there, gazing at me intangibly. My heart jumped in my chest the moment I recognized her.

"Ohmigod! Ephemera," I said. Ephemera just stared at me, then reached out for me with her arms. She was in her iconic purple and black costume, and I was afraid as I felt her hands pass through me, into me, the way I tingled where we'd touched.

I backed away from her instinctively, actually flying backward, while Ephemera glided toward me.

"Shane?" I said, and he appeared, glancing at Ephemera and me.

"Shaundra, this is a friend," he said. "This is Victoriana. She's here to help."

Ephemera floated there, watching me, her mask making her face unreadable, except for the eyes, which glowed white.

I knew about the news stories about her, about her losing her mind, fading into oblivion. To see her there, this legendary superheroine, and yet not entirely there. It shook me.

"What happened to her?" I asked.

"I'm trying to find out," Shane said. "I've been trying to ever since I found her wandering. When she'd become unhinged, she'd become more remote, more distant. It had been a gradual process, what overtook her."

Ephemera just floated there, and I will confess that it was unnerving.

"She's been like that since she'd left the team?" I asked. It had been two years ago.

"Yes," Shane said. "When she's noncorporeal, she doesn't need to eat or sleep. Nothing one would ordinarily do while living. It's like she's in suspension, but I can't bring her out of it, and she won't come out of it."

I could see the concern on his face, as she hovered there. In that moment, I realized that he and Ephemera had been close. Lovers, maybe? It was one of those epiphanies you sometimes get. I didn't want to pry, but I could tell she meant a lot to him by the way he moved with and spoke to her. There was tangible pain there, and a ghostly gentleness.

"How in the hell did you find her?" I asked.

"When she'd first become afflicted, she'd fallen into the earth," Shane said. "She just wandered within the world. But I managed to find her. I guess I was lucky. Or I had good enough friends who helped me."

"I guess," I said. "And you, what? Talked her into following you into the Hamptons?"

Shane reached out to Ephemera, his hand passing through her. She reacted to his touch, dragging her eyes from me to him.

"I wanted her to be someplace safe," Shane said. "To find out what happened. To try to bring her back."

"What do you think happened?" I asked.

Ephemera glided toward him, passing through him a moment before slipping through the wall.

"I don't know," Shane said. "Not for sure. Do you know who Minder is?"

"Yes," I said. "He's the Affiliates chairman. The one who succeeded Ephemera."

Shane nodded. "Very good. I knew you'd be a good candidate. I *think* he's responsible. I can't prove it, but I think he was the one who did this to Shaundra. It's nothing more than a hunch, I'm sorry to say."

Minder was more low-profile than many of the other members of the Affiliates. In fact, besides the announcement of him becoming chairman of the team, I don't think I had any other clippings of him. He was clearly a behind-the-scenes guy.

"And, what, you can't just accuse him?" I asked. "Confront him?"

Shane smiled sadly, while I saw Ephemera floating from wall to wall, appearing here and there, disappearing from view, only to reappear again, moving to things that only she could hear and see. She was terribly haunting, even tragic. I felt so bad for her, and for him.

"I don't have evidence," Shane said. "Only suspicions."

"What about your power?" I asked. "Can't you, I don't know, luck into that evidence?"

The rain kept pouring, the soft patter of it on his lovely home and hideout.

"It doesn't quite work that way," Shane said. "It's rarely that direct."

"Did you confront Minder about it?" I asked. Shane shook his head.

"I would," I said. "I'd confront him about it, right to his face."

Shane walked after Ephemera, taking her insubstantial hand in his, catching her attention again. She pivoted and floated toward us as before, the two of them almost looking like they were working their way to some phantom dance floor.

"Please don't do that," Shane said. "I'm not going to say that he's out of your league, but if it's truly him, I can't imagine a more treacherous adversary."

"Alright," I said, feeling strongly that the Knack needed my help, and even if I didn't know how I might help him, something came to me. "I'll join the Affiliates, but only under the condition that you let Cameraman join, too."

Shane brightened at that suggestion, and even Ephemera looked intrigued.

**9**

**WITH NOTHING BUT MY MEMORIES TO HOLD ME TOGETHER** on the roiling plasma of the Sun, I might be forgiven for drowning in the past, but the fact of the matter was that I *didn't* belong here. Minder had pushed me to this place, and I needed to get back to Earth, to help poor Mitch against whatever he was facing. As stupid as it sounds for someone in my predicament, I was worried about him. Mitch needed my help. We were a team.

Now, the logistical problems I faced were considerable. In retrospect, it's easy to fly into the Sun, like if you're coming from Earth. It was my Sol concern, you might say (sorry, that one was for you, Mitch).

However, when you were where I was, finding Earth was another matter entirely, if you weren't well-versed in astronomy and celestial navigation. See what I mean? Even factoring out the intense and blinding luminosity of the Sun, finding the Earth from ninety-three million miles away was a huge problem.

One thing that worried me was gravitational time dilation—like me being on the Sun meant that time was passing a tiny bit slower for me than time Mitch was experiencing on Earth, assuming Minder and his minions hadn't killed him already. Now, I know that time dilation was tiny, but it was the principle of it that bugged me. I didn't want to be exiled here on the Sun, watching churning waves of solar flares and plasma spewing out into space.

It was *boring.*

Never mind that any astrophysicist would have loved to have been in my place, flying around the Sun, checking out sunspots up close (spoiler: they're *weird*), and just ambling around amid the plasma.

The Sun presented a very practical problem for me. How the hell did I get home from here? I don't even know if Minder had this in mind for me, or if he actually thought it would kill me. Fair assumption. Only a fool bets against the Sun.

But the Sun had never met me before. Not to brag, but, you know what I mean? I wondered if anyone else on the team could have taken it. Rad Lad, for sure. No doubt. I don't think anybody else. Not even Tandem.

I held my arms out, entranced by the way they glowed—how was I even alive? Even by my super-standards, it was one of those things I'll never figure out. I was luminous, naked (yet again? WTF?) and flying around, exiled in space.

One thought I had was maybe planet-hopping. Like flying to Mercury, getting my bearings. And then flying to Venus. And then heading to Earth. That might work, although it would require me being very careful, because I didn't want to get literally lost in space.

A happy discovery I'd made during my time on the Sun—I could fire energy beams! Not from my eyes, sadly, because that would've been way cool. Rather, from my hands. I could just hold out my hands and fire high-energy plasma beams. And I found when I flew, a bolt of plasma trailed after me for a bit to mark my passing.

This wasn't fully on-brand for Victoriana, but it *was* pretty badass. However I got out of here, I wasn't going to rebrand myself as another superheroine. I'd worked hard to establish myself as Victoriana, and to throw that aside for some other heroic incarnation? No way. It just stiffened my resolve to get out of this mess and reach Earth to be there with Mitch.

He had to be catching hell there, with whatever Minder was throwing at him. Minder. I couldn't wait to get my hands on Minder. I was seething with hatred for that man, what he did to me, how he messed with my mind. Even remembering it made me angry. Furious. I burned with the heat of a thousand suns at the memory of it.

After a two-year bureaucratic lag, getting onto the team had been the culmination of a dream I hadn't even fully realized. Mitch had thought it was hilarious, as he and I split a Cobb salad he'd made for us in celebration, along with Iron City Lagers, in our place we shared in the brownstone the Knack had bought for us.

"Hah," Mitch said. "You're lucky my own application's hung up in their background checks, or I'd be documenting it all."

He was so adorable. His smile is both cocksure and shy, like the bad boy that he is. You know how they use the word "rakish" to describe the *right* kind of bad? That's Mitch—he's dashingly dastardly.

"It's a drag," I said. "Ohmigod, yes. The training? The worst. They make us do live wargaming, like teams. Today I was up against everybody. They actually stress-tested me, everyone against me."

Mitch shook his head, smiling as he drank from his beer, noshing on salad.

"That's rough," he said. "How'd it go?"

"First off, Minder's in the control booth," I said. "He was watching over all of us, evaluating our performance, along with Shane."

Tandem and Rad Lad, Brighteyes, Wingman, Decibelle, Tag Team, Ms. Fit. They were all there in the Ready Room, which was this cavernous armored training facility the size of three football fields. That's what they called it, the place where the team practiced.

While I was excited to be there, it was weird, too, being there with all of those Affiliates, out in Affiliates East, all set to prove myself.

"Now," Minder said. "This is a practice scenario—everybody please pull your punches. No fatalities this time."

"Good luck, everyone," the Knack said, sitting next to Minder in the control booth. "Setting the clock for five minutes."

Everybody laughed except me, because my head was immediately going to the possibility that there had been fatalities. Had someone died here? No way. Tantrum had left the team three years before, but she'd left the team alive, not in a bodybag.

A starting signal had sounded, and the Affiliates had come for me. The way it happened wasn't like some kind of charge— rather, Tandem and Rad Lad took to the air, one breaking left, the other breaking right, and Brighteyes nailed me with her green eyebeams, which hit me with a tingling feeling that made me think she was trying to score a stun, even as Decibelle fired a narrow-beam scream at me that made my nose bleed (!!)

I took to the air, moving to evade the beams that were tracking me pretty well. And while this was going on, Ms. Fit threw Tag Team at me, like he was a human football. Instinctively, I clocked Tag Team, my punch leading to fifty of him popping into existence around me, and they grabbed onto me by my cape, crawling up and swarming me, just as Tandem swooped in and treated me to a powerful punch that sent me flying across the room, hitting one of the fortified walls hard, creating another fifty Tag Teams, who just scrambled atop me like we were in some superhero rugby scrum.

Blake had played rugby in high school, and I always thought those scrums were funny.

"Give it up, Victoriana," the Tag Teams said in unison, which was as creepy as it was surreal.

"Never!" I yelled, bringing my arms up forcefully and repelling the Tag Teams, sending them tumbling off of me. I flew up just as Rad Lad surged toward me, slamming into the wall where I'd only been a moment before.

I decided to do Ms. Fit one better and grabbed one of the Tag Teams who was still clinging to me and spun him around three times before whipping him at her, satisfied that my fastball sent him hurtling into her, exploding into another thirty or so of him, burying Ms. Fit in a sea of superhumanity for the moment.

Wingman flew right at me, punching me in the jaw, which startled me more than it hurt me. He was strong, but not that strong. Not to be a snob about it, but Wingman was a middleweight in the super-strength department. However, he had heart, and that counted for something. I grabbed him by the ankle and threw him at the pile of Tag Teams, where he landed, causing still more Tag Teams to appear.

Another green beam nailed me, a stronger one this time, and I could see Brighteyes smirking as she targeted me. Decibelle followed her partner's lead, sending that horrible, focused sound at me through her screams, making my head feel like it was going to explode.

I gritted my teeth and hurled myself to the ground like I was doing a foot-first dive. My feet struck the ground with a satisfyingly forceful clang, and I sent a wave of bending steel at Sound & Fury, pleased to see them go flying as they were struck by it, with some of the Tag Teams racing to catch them.

Tandem and Rad Lad were coordinating their airborne assault, coming at me from opposite sides to split my focus. I did a momentary situational threat assessment, going for Rad Lad, which amounted to me pivoting and flanking him, since I banked on him figuring his imposingly radioactive man-self might deter me from laying hands on him.

"Whoa, now," Rad Lad said, as I did this sweet flying dodge as he fired a beam of energy at me, and I caught his outstretched arm in mine and chucked him right at Tandem, who'd been doing one of his trademark headlong attacks. Remember, I'd studied these heroes for years, which included watching footage of their fights. I *knew* how they fought.

My grab-and-toss of Rad Lad worked as I planned, and Rad Lad and Tandem collided concussively, creating this flash of energy and power that actually caused Tandem to split into Fusillad and Lassitude.

I don't think the force of the collision had done that; rather, I think Fusillad and Lassitude thought that maybe if they both attacked me, it might split my focus still further. Whatever their thinking was, the now-three of them did airborne somersaults as they sought to dissipate the force of the crash, and I went after them right away, before they had time to recover. Lassitude, who couldn't fly, was tumbling groundward.

Keep in mind that I was pulling my punches, just as Minder wanted.

What this meant in practical terms was I decked Lassitude, just socked her right in the jaw, knocking her clean out. With her unconscious, that would take Tandem off the board, and I could see Fusillad's shock at seeing his twin sister dropped with one punch.

Another Brighteyes bolt caught me in the back, stronger still. I actually felt that one, and cursed as it zinged me. Brighteyes was feeling me out, trying to see just how much I could take. She was also trying to distract me, so I stayed on-task.

I whipped Lassitude at Rad Lad like a human torpedo, catching him as he fought to grab Lassitude in an instinctively protective act, while I dodged angry energy bolts from Fusillad, out to avenge his sister.

"You're going down, Vix," Fusillad said, trying to draw a bead on me. But I dodged his shots, noting that he wasn't as good a shot as Brighteyes, who was a definite crackshot.

"You think?" I asked, grabbing Fusillad and putting him in a chokehold that would've impressed even Blake. I remembered something about Fusillad's powers involving the absorption of energy, and I gambled on a passive attack like a chokehold might knock him out, despite his powers. As I expected, he flared up, expending energy all around in a bid to blast me off of him.

It was kind of wild, because we'd formed this little star in the Ready Room as Fusillad fought to drive me away. He couldn't pry my arms loose because Lassitude was the naturally strong one. Any strength Fusillad applied had to come from whatever energy he'd stored.

Then Rad Lad and Decibelle got tricky, blasting Fusillad and me, knowing that I might get hit by it, but also that Fusillad would soak up that energy and get stronger. Maybe even strong enough to fight me off. Teamwork really does make the dream work.

Maybe that would have worked out, but only if I just floated there and took it. Instead, I shot right at Decibelle, this glowing ball of energy made of Fusillad and me, and I got fancy—I basically did a ninety-degree turn away from Decibelle after charging her, and flicked an outstretched leg that caught her on the chin and made her do a backflip as she hit the ground, unconscious. It was worth the ringing ears and nosebleeds, believe me. The looks on their faces at that move? Priceless.

My ears still ringing, I hurled Fusillad at Rad Lad, gratified when they exploded together, momentarily unseen amid their mutual detonation. Then another beam caught me in the back, stronger still, as I saw Brighteyes zapping me yet again. Christ, just how strong were her eyebeams? I was feeling each successive blast even more keenly as she upped her power.

Then it hit me (figuratively, not literally)—her beams were amazingly powerful, but she herself was not superhumanly resilient. Just like with Decibelle, she had a weakness, and that was her physicality.

I clapped my hands together, satisfied when I saw the concussive force hit Brighteyes, Ms. Fit, and the Tag Teams, stunning the first two, and causing more Tag Teams to pop into existence. There had to be about three hundred of him in the Ready Room at this point.

Brighteyes wasn't out of the fight, yet, and I saw her finding her footing, drawing a bead on me. I zipped right at her, catching her and giving her a spin, tickled when I saw her fire off her beams instinctively, catching Ms. Fit with one of those souped-up eyeblasts she'd been hoping to nail me with. Ms. Fit took the hit and went careening across the Ready Room, slamming into one of the walls with so much force that she dented it, and was stuck, at least for a moment. Wingman flew to help pry her loose, which would at least keep them occupied.

I was curious what Minder and the Knack were doing, spared a glance at them. They were just observing. It was weird that they weren't fighting with the rest of them, but I guess with the chairman and deputy chairman responsibilities they had, they just had to keep an eye on things. My mind wandered to what the Knack had said, and then I thought maybe it wasn't prudent of me to think about that right now.

Rad Lad and Fusillad hit me with a two-way energy blast, and those beams hit hard, caught me unawares. Rad Lad appeared as laid-back as anyone made of barely contained radioactive energy might be, but Fusillad was pissed. I could see it, his anger and frustration that I hadn't yet gone down.

The Tag Teams were swarming, but they couldn't fly, so they couldn't get me. I could see the timer over the control room, these big armored digital display tickers showing the time. Thirty seconds left. I wanted to end this with a bang.

The fact was that I didn't know how to drop Rad Lad without tearing apart his protective suit. I theorized that might have made him dissipate or otherwise have to exempt himself from the fight. Fusillad I just had to wear down. Once his energy ran out, he'd be nothing.

Glancing at Brighteyes, I could see her recovering herself and gearing up to shoot me again. With the clock running out, I flew fast for her, thankfully dodging her beam this time, and popped her on the chin with the most delicate slap I'd ever thrown, watching her spin around, her eyebeams blasting apart dozens of Tag Teams as she fell unconscious to the ground.

The Tag Team army—all three hundred and fifty of him— roared and charged me, so I did what any red-blooded superheroine would do and flew around him at speed, creating a whirlwind in the Ready Room that sucked them all up and I aimed the vortex at Rad Lad and Fusillad, making it spew Tag Teams upon them as the clock ran out and the bell sounded.

"Great job, everybody," Minder said. "Amazing work, Victoriana."

"Impressive," Shane said.

I was a good sport, helping up Decibelle and Brighteyes, while Wingman flew over with Ms. Fit, and Tag Team got rid of his army of duplicates, and Fusillad helped Lassitude to her feet, and Rad Lad walked over, patting me on the shoulder.

"Bitchin' work, Vix," he said.

"Yeah, for real," Ms. Fit said. "You made us look like amateurs."

"We'd have had her in a ten-minute session," Fusillad said, giving me a hard look. I was proud of myself but wary that I'd maybe pissed off the wrong people. But what was I supposed to do, take a fall to protect fragile superegos?

Shane piped up from the control room.

"Great work, Team," Shane said. "We'll do a debrief in a half hour. Everybody get settled."

Mitch loved it, clapping his hands.

"That's awesome, Babe," he said. "You're going to be the talk of the Affiliates. Honestly, they're going to all be on the couch after that number you did on them. You *broke* Tandem."

I demurred on that because I really didn't think I did, and fair was fair.

"I really think they just tried to split my focus," I said, but Mitch wasn't having any of it, just met my eyes and affected seriousness.

"Babe. Babe. BABE," he said. "You kicked their asses. Own that. Oh, man. I'll bet Minder's just a wreck. His pet team, pasted by the noob. God, I hope he doesn't pull that with me as payback."

I hoped so, too, but didn't say that, since Mitch was still high on the notion that I'd served something special up to the Affiliates.

"Rex thought the team would be able to take you," Mitch said. "I guarantee he was thinking you'd fold in five. Not that you'd take out most of the team."

He drank down his beer and grabbed another, tossed me another, too. I was proud of myself, but I was still worried how it might be perceived by the rest of the team. My goal was to fit in with the team, not alienate them.

"Fusillad was mad," I said. "I could tell."

"He's a frat boy," Mitch said. "You've upended his universe."

"I didn't actually beat him," I said. "I needed maybe a few more minutes."

"Doesn't matter," Mitch said, toasting me. "You *totes* broke Tandem, Anna. I promise you there are going to be closed-door meetings about it."

I crunched the empty beer can into one of my metal marbles, which I did to soothe my nerves when I had them. Mitch always loved when I'd do it.

"What am I supposed to do?" I asked. "I *wasn't* going to take a dive."

Mitch reached out, stroking my forearm.

"You did exactly the right thing," Mitch said. "The official line is that they want to make sure the best heroes join the Affiliates. If that means you're the best of the best, so be it. I already know you are. They just need to know that, too."

It was pressure I didn't need to feel when joining the team. Not that I couldn't handle it, because I totally could. However, it just put me on the spot. I didn't want the rest of the team hating me. Mitch seemed to relish animosity; I preferred harmony. And in something like a superhero team, that might matter.

"I always try to do my best," I said.

"And that's one of the many things I love about you," Mitch said. "Let them lick their wounds. They'll come around and will be grateful to have that kind of firepower when they're dealing with some of the big baddies."

"Do you know what happened with Tantrum?" I asked.

"Tantrum? Heh," Mitch said. "Creative differences."

"Seriously, Mitch," I asked.

Mitch scratched his chin, then rolled the frosty beer across his forehead, one of this "Hmm, I'm thinking" gestures.

"Tantrum's a top-tier telekinetic," Mitch said. "She's the best in the world. Even better than Blitz."

I knew that was a big admission, because he loved Blitz and would get all fanboyish when talking about him.

"And?" I asked.

"No idea," Mitch said. "Whatever led to her leaving the team, it's Affiliates-classified. I'll add it to my list to uncover once I'm on the team. Or you could look if you wanted."

And he was right. I *could* look on my own. However, the division of labor Mitch and I had was very much "Files vs. Fists"—he worked the files, I worked my fists. It was an honest split—if I were the file-cruncher instead of the fist-puncher, what would Mitch have to do? He *loved* unearthing stuff. It was cute how excited he'd get. Who was I to stand in the way of that?

"No, I leave that to you, Babe," I said, giving him a kiss on the forehead. My Affiliates beeper went off, and I sighed. "Crap. Affiliates stuff."

Mitch accepted that. Since he was in background check limbo, he hung back while I dealt with it.

"It's Shane," I said.

"Oh, put him on speaker," Mitch said, chuckling, since non-Affiliates weren't supposed to be able to eavesdrop on Affilicoms.

"Hello, Shane," I said.

"Hey, Anna," Shane said. "Just checking in. You made a real impression on the team today."

Mitch was fishing around for one of his recording devices, while I was shooing him away. He just made faces and kept rooting around for one of his gadgets, while I tried to stay composed.

"Hopefully a good impression," I said.

"Yes," Shane said. "People were impressed. Shaken, in truth. You're a natural, Anna. Born to it. I think Minder had a fit."

All at once, I felt incredibly self-conscious. Even uncharacteristically so.

"Is this okay for you to be sharing with me?" I asked.

"Oh, it's fine," Shane said. "And better you hear it from me than have to wonder why you're getting glared at by Lassitude and Fusillad. What you did today was impressive, Anna. For too long, the team has languished on its legacy. Being the best of the best carries a sort of burden. People get complacent."

"Okay," I said, rolling my eyes when Mitch aimed his parabolic mic at me. I wagged a finger at him, and he just grinned.

"You're exactly the breath of fresh air the team needed," Shane said. "It's why you and Mitch will be perfect additions."

Smirking at Mitch, I poked him with a toe.

"Speaking of Mitch, what's the deal with the delay in his getting cleared for membership?" I asked.

Shane sighed. "He's in there with you, isn't he?"

"What? Oh, is he?" I said. Shane played along.

"His track record makes his approval a bit more circuitous," Shane said. "The lag in getting you both cleared was part of that. There were a lot of discussions."

"Ooh, circuitous," I said. "He'll love knowing that."

Mitch gave me a toe poke in return, and we got into a covert toe-poking session while I retained my official Affiliates phone disposition.

"But he *will* be approved?" I asked.

"All signs point to YES," Shane said. "But the main purpose of my call is to make sure you just keep at what you're doing. Don't let anybody make you doubt that what you did today was in any way wrong. The team can be competitive, and members don't like being upstaged, can react poorly to that. There were bruised egos as well as bodies today. We were all supposed to be testing you, but I think you tested many of us today."

"Yeah?" I said. "Speaking of that, can you tell me what happened with Tantrum?"

I raised my eyebrows to Mitch a few times, proud of how I boomeranged the conversation to Tantrum. The Knack answered quicker than I thought he would.

"Tantrum decided to resign from the team," Shane said. "It happens sometimes. She'd been on the team for a decade."

"Was she friends with Ephemera?" I asked. Shane paused before replying, while Mitch listened intently, his eyes on me. I could see him liking that I was inquiring.

"She was," Shane said. "We were all close. I don't think there's anything sinister about her leaving. If you're thinking Minder had something to do with it, I am not confident of that. Tantrum has a very, very powerful mind. Telekinetics are very potent by nature. She may have simply gotten tired of the work."

"And where is she?" I asked. "If you don't mind my asking."

"Hyberia Hollow," Shane said. "You will be able to access it as an Affiliate, but Mitch won't. Not until he's cleared."

"Great," I said. "Thanks, Shane."

"What are you going to do, Anna?" he asked.

"What you asked us to do, Shane," I said, blowing a kiss to Mitch. "Investigating the rot."

Hyberia Hollow was in Arizona, a comfortable distance away from Tucson, with beautiful views of the mountains in the distance. Mitch didn't want me flying out there by myself, but I just teased him about it. Since he was waiting for his clearance, there was no way he'd be able to get there before me, or even with me.

"What are you worried about, Mitch?" I asked, while we hung out on his deck, enjoying the clear skies that day, and some iced peppermint tea.

"I don't know," he said. "That place is locked down. If something happens to you there, I won't be able to help you."

"Nothing's going to happen to me," I said. "I'm so not worried, Babe. There's nothing I can't handle. I mean, we're talking about super-retirees, right?"

That's how he described it to me.

"It's a hideaway for retired supers," he said. "It's somewhere between a retirement community and a research facility—maybe also a prison. It sure as hell is a fortress."

I wasn't daunted. Being an Affiliate gave me access, and I'd put it to the test with a visit to Hyberia Hollow. Mitch handed me a digital recorder, one of his little ones, like a discreet pack of cigarettes in size.

"What am I supposed to do with this?" I asked.

"Record something worth recording," he replied. "Just hit that switch to record, and that switch to turn it off."

It charmed me that he was entrusting me with one of his precious recording gizmos. This would be the first time we'd worked a case together as Affiliates—or me as one, and him as an almost-Affiliate.

"If you don't come back, I'm coming for you," Mitch said. I gave him a kiss and an ass pat and told him not to worry. Then I took off flying, waving to him before I slipped from sight. I liked flying fast, although I was mindful of the sound barrier while within city limits, waiting until I was about a hundred miles from Chicago before I revved up and got to Mach 3, which would get me to Hyberia well within an hour.

Flying fast was a blast. Feeling the wind in my face, I was grateful that I didn't need to breathe. Also, I opted for stratospheric altitude, just so I didn't set off car alarms and rattle people from here to Arizona from the air displacement as I flew.

Nothing was like flying. Not even sex touched it, in terms of the release I got from it. Being able to fly was one of those status powers that all heroes secretly craved, I believed. Maybe it was just me but come on: flying ruled.

One could quibble about which power was the best, but the most meaningful demarcation I found was between those of us who could fly, and those who couldn't.

Mitch would tease that with altitude came attitude, and he wasn't wrong about that, in many respects. And like everything with superheroes (and even villains), there was a distinction, like the following:

WHO COULD FLY < WHO COULD FLY FASTEST < WHO COULD FLY HIGHEST

The best of us were the ones who could fly fastest, farthest, and highest. I would often fly with Wingman, who seemed to have the purest joy of flight, even if he wasn't the fastest flier. We shared the skies a bunch of times, and I'd enjoy those outings, because it was so quiet and peaceful up there, and the problems of the world could seem so far away and insignificant when you were up in the sky.

Among the Affiliates, it broke down as follows, in terms of best fliers (measured by speed and altitude):

- *ME*
- *TANDEM*
- *RAD LAD*
- *FUSILLAD*
- *LADY BLAZE*
- *WINGMAN*

Again, I'm not gloating; I'm just pointing out that I flew faster than anybody else on the team. Tandem, Rad Lad, and I were the "spacers" among the fliers—we could attain the almost 25,000 miles per hour required to attain escape velocity. Fusillad couldn't quite get to that speed by himself, and he sure couldn't weather the absence of air up there. Wingman was more content to soar, although he could get up in the stratosphere if he wanted to. Lady Blaze could attain impressive speeds, but she was oxygen-dependent, which limited her top speeds and altitudes.

The best thing about the three of us spacers was that we could crisscross the country, or even go overseas very quickly if we needed to. That helped us respond rapidly if some villains were up to something far away. That rapid response component was invaluable, and I used it so many times in my years on the team.

However, you always had to be cautious about disrupting the airflow when you flew, so while I could fly very, very quickly if I wanted to, I seldom did, because I didn't want to cause harm while I flew. Flight, like everything else superheroic, had to be enjoyed responsibly.

I didn't actually know how quickly I could fly, but 25,000 miles per hour was way fast, and reaching those speeds didn't even stress me out, except for the existential awareness that I was flying pretty damned fast.

Of course, I slowed down when I neared Hyberia Hollow, because I didn't want them to think a missile was coming to hit them or worse. Given all the retired superheroes there, I thought that would be bad form.

Therefore, I slowed down and landed near the entrance to the place, where there were guards wearing comfortable short-sleeved shirts and shorts that were Affiliates blue and white, with the Affiliates "A" on them and "Hyberia Hollow" stitched below in cursive. I noted their PSS badge-patches on their shoulders.

The guards looked nervously happy to see me.

"Ah, Victoriana," one of them said. He was a middle-aged man with a black mustache, and I could see that all of the guards carried guns and stun guns. "Welcome to Hyberia Hollow."

There was a woman standing at the security gate. She had brown, shoulder-length hair and had curiously careworn face for someone at a retirement community.

"Hello, Victoriana," she said. "I'm Terri Meadows. I'm the Chief Administrator at Hyberia Hollow. I must say we're *thrilled* to have you pay us a visit."

She extended her hand, which I shook. It was a firm shake, and I felt intuitively that she might be a fellow super. Her eyes were hazel, and her wide-mouthed smile was warm and inviting.

"How'd you know that I was coming?" I asked. "Did someone call ahead?"

"No," she said. "I'm precognitive. I saw you coming a few days ago in a vision."

"Wow," I said, while she guided us to a golf cart. The Hollows was a large community by the look of it, completely enclosed by zeroscaped walls that were concealed by copious use of native flora.

"We don't like surprises here in the community," Meadows said. "But, of course, you're a *welcome* surprise."

I'd never dealt with a precog before, so I wondered what that was like. Being who I was, I just piped up and asked.

"How does that work?" I asked. "Do you have visions about everything? That seems exhausting."

She smiled at my questions.

"It probably does sound exhausting," she said. "We have to put our minds toward it. Oh, we get flashes of insight at times, but most often, we have to meditate and things come to us. I incorporate meditation into my daily routine, which is how I became aware of your intention to visit."

"That's weird," I said. "Because I didn't think about doing it until today. How does that even work?"

Meadows held onto her smile while driving me into the lovely community, where I could see all sorts of old people going about their business, their handlers nearby. There was lush native vegetation around which contrasted with the desert environment. It may have been zeroscaped, but someone had carefully tended it. I wondered if a super-resident had been at work tending to the greenery. They had done an amazing job.

"I knew you'd be here three days before today," Meadows said.

"Wow," I said. "Okay, so, can you predict winning lotto tickets?"

She kept her eyes on the winding roads in the community, driving us slowly through it. I could see some of the residents glancing at me, trying to assess why I was there, whether I was a new resident or not.

"I can," she said. "But I'm registered across the country. I'm not able to play games of chance."

"For real?" I asked. "That stinks."

"It's not fair if I play," she said. "The Knack did that a few times when he was younger, but he got banned. In fact, I think any of us are banned from anything gambling-related. There was congressional lobbying by the gambling industry to prevent precogs from taking advantage of them."

"That's ironic," I said, thinking that it amounted to casinos wanting to maintain their monopoly in ripping people off, and seeing precogs as threats to their industry. The idea of them lobbying Congress about it was surreal.

"Precogs and anyone with probability powers are banned," Meadows said. "The PUNT Act—Proscribing Unfair Natural Talents. It had bipartisan support, although civil rights concerns were raised at the time. Same reason why superhumans can't legally participate in athletic events."

I was fascinated by Terri Meadows. Obviously, I was aware of people who could foresee the future, but the mechanics of it were tantalizingly enigmatic.

"Do you mind me talking about this?" I asked.

"Not at all," she said. "We're here to help."

"Okay, as a precog, wouldn't you have known a ban was coming, and, you know, maybe played *before* the ban went into effect?" I asked.

She drove us around the perimeter of the Hollow, which had similarly-painted residences, as well as a pond, a golf course, tennis courts, bocce courts, swimming pools (outside and inside), and a medical facility. There was also a community center and shopping area, with everything that antiseptic white that was offset by abundant greenery, including cacti just about everywhere, as well as desert willow, deer grass, mesquite, creosote, and all sorts of agave.

Across the pond, in the distance, another wing was under construction by the look of it, appeared to be heavily guarded by PSS operatives, judging from the banners and barracks. I wondered what that might be, but was, for now, more focused on talking with Terri Meadows.

"That's an amusing question, Victoriana," Meadows said. "No, I didn't do that."

"Did you know I was going to ask you that question?" I asked.

"Precognition isn't like a recording," she said. "It's more like a vision, as if remembering a dream upon awakening. The difference is that precognitive persons like myself know that our visions are of the future. Or a potential future. It sometimes shifts."

"One more question I'm dying to ask," I said.

"Ask away."

"How far into the future can you see? How far have you seen?" I asked.

To her credit, Ms. Meadows answered my questions patiently. She had a nice voice, which was soothing, even. I could see how she was well-suited for this retirement community.

I found her to be trustworthy and to carry a quiet authority about her.

"Precognitive vision varies between precogs," she said. "Doctor Destinator, the supervillain, was known to be able to see years into the future, if he put his mind to it. Clario, the superhero, could see as much as six months into the future. Johnny Rubicon, the precognitive gangster of the Crime League has made predictions as far as three months into the future. The criminal entrepreneur known as Ms. Fortune can forecast at least a year into the future. To answer your question, I can reliably see as far as a month into the future."

"That's awesome," I said, although I didn't have to have extrasensory perception to see that Terri didn't think so. She grimaced a bit, like the faintest downturn of her pasted-on smile.

"It's not, really," she said. "We're at the mercy of our visions, and there's always the peril of the self-fulfilling prophecy. That is to say, our visions rarely occur in a vacuum. For example, let's say you had a premonition of your own death—what would you do? Would you try to avoid doing the things that might end up with you at the time and place of your own demise? Or would the attempts to avoid that envisioned fate simply hasten your own doom?"

"Okay, that's trippy," I said. "How do you resolve that?"

"Sometimes we can't," Terri said. "Sometimes we seek other visions to try to bring our perceptions into sharper clarity. Doctor Destinator saw his own death six years before it happened. It drove him mad, some say. As he got closer to his 'terminal date with destiny' as he called it, he became more desperate and dangerous. In fact, his crimes became ever bolder, wilder, more audacious. So much so that he got kicked out of the Crime League, operating independently as a soothsayer-for-hire, until he was assassinated by Felonia Minx. His last words were to her—he said, 'What took you so long?'"

"Oh, wow," I said, seeing that she was dead serious, but feeling a nervous giggle well up in me. I sometimes giggled when I got nervous, which wasn't as often since becoming super. I tried to steer myself toward another question, just so I didn't embarrass myself by giggling. "Okay, another question: why work here? I imagine you could do anything you wanted to."

Terri gazed at me with her tired eyes. They were big eyes, but sitting next to her, looking with my enhanced vision, I could see the fatigue and sorrow in her. I wanted to give her a reassuring hug.

"Hyberia Hollow is a peaceful place," she said. "Here, I just have to tend to the residents, and everyone's well-protected here. I'm able to keep my concerns on the more everyday matters. Focus helps with precognition. The wider you cast the net, the madder you get. That's a saying we have in the precog community."

All of this was blowing me away. As a physical super, there was, like, this entire world of supers beyond mine. She smiled sadly, looking me in the eye.

"Precogs very rarely do fieldwork," she said. "We're not as well-suited to it as other mindworkers. Like, telekinetics, for example. You're here to see Tantrum, aren't you?"

"Uh, yeah," I said, feeling uneasy again. I wondered how much else Ms. Meadows already knew about me being here.

"Her real name is Tabitha Galves," Meadows said. "Please don't call her 'Tantrum'—that'll only wind her up. And believe me, you don't want to wind up a telekinetic. Speaking of that, I got you an autographed photo from Blitz. Your boyfriend ought to love it."

She held out a mailer to me, giving a half-smile.

"Okay, now you're just messing with me," I said. "I didn't even ask you for something like that."

"You were going to," she said. "Before you left, when you remembered."

I opened it and looked at the photograph, which showed a smiling, dark-haired superhero from the golden age who looked like a young Marlon Brando, wearing his costume with a domino mask, giving a thumbs up. It said:

TO MITCH—

YOU'RE THE MOST CLEAR-SIGHTED OF US ALL.
DON'T YOU EVER LOSE FOCUS ON WHAT MATTERS!

—BLITZ (AKA, MIKE HARLOW)

Meadows was now fully smiling at me, cocking an eyebrow as I carefully put the photograph back into the mailer.

"You're officially freaking me out, now," I said. "Did you tell Blitz what to say?"

"I did," Terri said. "He's very old, but he's always happy when he gets to do something for his fans. Made his day to get to sign an autograph. People so often forget their heroes once they've retired."

She pulled us up to the Hyberian, the area fine restaurant, which was an elegantly colonial white-and-natural stone building that had residents and employees coming and going.

"Tabitha's at the patio dining, table for two," Terri said. "Please don't rile her up. I'll be back in a couple of hours."

Meadows directed me to the hostess, who walked me through the nice American Classic-style restaurant, where the patrons were watching me pass, muttering to themselves. My super-hearing told me that they'd not seen a costumed hero here in some time. A few of them recognized me as Victoriana, which made me smile resolutely as I walked up to Tabitha Galves, aka, Tantrum, the world's mightiest telekinetic.

Tabitha Galves still had an edgy look to her, and I didn't place her any higher than thirty-eight years of age. She was slender and fit and wore black leggings and a yellow blouse with a thick black leather belt, as well as black and yellow bangle bracelets that clattered as she moved her hands. She was having a cocktail, what looked like a Manhattan. Her hair was black and cut short and was spiked, and she had streaks of white at her temples. Her big eyes were black, and she wore maroon lipstick, which complemented her tan complexion.

"Victoriana," she said, holding out a hand, which I gently shook. Her fingernails were painted maroon. "Have a seat."

She casually waved a hand, and the chair across from her slid back. I took my seat across from her, and she smiled to herself.

"Did they brief you?" she asked. Her voice was husky, and when the waiter came over, she ordered for the both of us— another Manhattan for her, a Long Island Iced Tea for me. I'd have been fine with a beer but wasn't going to make an issue of it. I had never been drunk, as my superhuman body readily metabolized alcohol.

"Nobody briefed me," I said, covertly toggling the digital recorder. "I came here myself."

"Ah," Tabitha said. "Not one of Minder's minions, then. Not yet, anyway."

"Not me," I said. "I'm new."

She studied me a moment, and it was more than a little unnerving. I had no experience with telekinetics. Being able to move things with only one's mind, that was wild.

"Ah," she said. "Shane had told me you were coming. He called me."

The drinks came, and she waved off the waiter, who was only too happy to leave. She took a drink, watched me drink from mine.

"You're pretty young to be retired," I said, which made her sneer.

"It's not the years, Sweetheart," she said. "It's the mileage. They use us, you know. The handlers, I mean. All of this. We're the talent; they're the infrastructure."

She gestured, and I could see people were watching from afar. Residents, patrons, secret agents?

"Why'd you leave the Affiliates?" I asked. "I have to know."

Tabitha snickered, drinking deep again.

"Oh, you *have* to know," she said. "Truly?"

"You left after Ephemera fell ill," I said. "I know that much."

Tabitha's look of sardonic bemusement curdled into something colder that gave me pause. The air smelled flower-sandy-sweet and the pond bubbled while the other restaurant patrons chatted amicably, but I felt a chill in that dry Arizona air when she stared at me.

"Fell ill," Tabitha said. "That's how they framed it, isn't it? She was driven mad. Shaundra was the strongest woman I've ever known. Strong. Nobody could touch her if she didn't want to be touched, you know? I mean her power. Amazing. And just a great leader. I would have followed her anywhere. I would have followed her into Hell, no questions asked."

Her anger was apparent, razor-sharp and restrained, but I saw the salt and pepper shakers tremble, just little tremors.

"What happened?" I asked.

"Minder," she said, the barest hint of a whisper. "I can't prove it. That's the thing. Nobody can. He's so careful. It infuriates me. He should call himself 'Gaslighter'—that'd suit him perfectly."

She took another drink, gazed out at the pond with heartless eyes, then turned them back to me, composed herself like she was smoothing sand in a Zen garden, her face adopting a mask of serenity.

"If you suspected, why didn't you confront him?" I asked.

"You don't know my file," Tabitha said. "They don't call me 'Tantrum' for nothing. I have a reputation. Oh, yes, I was very, very good at what I do. I still am. My mind is sharp. I hit hard. But, you know, I have a temper. That was my little joke with my name—Tantrum—it was funny when I first set out as a superheroine. However, it became a millstone around my neck. How old are you?"

"I'm twenty-nine," I said, and she smiled, reaching out, touching my hand with hers.

"Remember your reputation," she said. "I'm not saying this woman-to-woman, so much as heroine-to-heroine. They're *always* watching us. Who you are is who you become. I was the team firebrand, and Minder used that against me. I suspected he'd mangled Shaundra's mind, but I just couldn't prove it. And because I was who I was, I couldn't do anything about it. I mean, I had him by the throat—with my mind—I was throttling him, but he didn't break. You know what kind of iron will that takes? I strangled the man to an inch of his life to try to force him to talk. It was just him and me, and *he didn't break.*"

She looked haunted by the memory, and I felt bad for taking her there, but I had to know, for Mitch and me.

"What was I going to do? Tear him apart?" she asked. "How far was I willing to go to take him down? I could have broken all of his fingers and toes, his elbows and knees, shoulders and thighs. I could have turned him into a human pretzel. But in that terrible moment, I knew I didn't have that in me. To be like that, to do to his body what he did to people's minds. Maybe Brighteyes could, but not me. I walked myself back from that line. I'm not a torturer. I'm not a killer. Yes, I have a temper, and I've roughed up my share of baddies in a decade of good service for the Affiliates, for the country, for the world. That's service as a *heroine,* though; not a killer. I dropped him to the floor and let him catch his breath, let him take in just how close he came to death. It was a scene. He composed himself, clutched his throat, shook it off, looked me in the eye, and said 'I'm so sorry about Shaundra. I would do anything to make her better, but some things even I can't heal.' He said that to me, and I stared him down, wanting to kill him, but unable to bring myself to do it. I left the team's active-duty roster, declined to be an auxiliary or a reservist. I refused to work under him, and I came here. I enlisted with the PSS. Not that they're necessarily better, but the lines of demarcation and rules of engagement are clearer with them than the Affiliates."

The earnestness of Tantrum was disarming. I could sense her power as keenly as I could feel her rage. She was a cauldron of repressed rage, unlike anything or anyone I'd ever met.

"I'm here as a thorn in their side," she said, glancing around us. I could see that anyone whose eye she met quickly looked away. "I stay here to bear witness, to look for anything untoward. It's kind of a chess game between Minder and me, who'll eventually break. See, when I was a full-timer, I was busy going all over the world, trying to save it. Hard to stay focused. But I stay here, in peaceful, quiet, orderly Hyberia Hollow, and I serve as the watcher, the living witness. I watch *everything* they do here, for signs of *anything* out of place. They're very professional here, and very careful. Everyone is so polite. They let me go wherever I want. I think they like to see where I go, what I do. Who I talk to. In fact, being here puts you at risk, Victoriana. You're a good young woman. I've seen your press. You're one beast of a fighter. Shane was smart to bring you and that Cameraman freak into play."

"He's not a freak," I said. "He's my boyfriend."

Her face softened, and again, she patted my hand.

"That's sweet," Tabitha said. "Just be careful. Minder'll pick your brains and find out your weaknesses. And loved ones are the *biggest* weaknesses of all in this business. They always, *always* go after those you love."

She slid a business card to me, which was yellow with black embossed writing on it. It said "TANTRUM" and had a phone number.

"If you're in a jam," Tabitha said. "And I mean a *serious* jam. Something unrecoverable, something hopeless. You call me. Any time, I don't care. I'll be there. And I'll bring the sky down on anybody who has it coming to them."

I knew she meant it, as she finished her drink, and I finished mine, in silence for a moment. Tabitha glanced at the other patrons, and I again could see the averted eyes, like the murmuration of birds.

"They're terrified of us," Tabitha said. "Of what we can do. And they're right to be."

Unsure what else to say, I asked her about Terri Meadows. Tabitha acknowledged my inquiry with another gulp of her drink.

"You're really asking if she's a good guy or a bad guy," she said. "She's a survivor. She's found a way of operating that works for her. She's not heroic by any means, but Hyberia is where heroes go to die."

"Does Minder come here?" I asked.

"No," Tabitha said. "I think he's afraid to, knowing that I'm here. I'm fine with that. He knows I might not be able to restrain myself again, were he to turn up."

The rancor she felt for Minder was jarring.

"If he's so bad, why's he leading the Affiliates?" I asked. "Why haven't the others stopped him?"

Tabitha toyed with her Manhattan with her fingertips, lost in thought, before flicking her eyes to me.

"That's a very good question," she said. "On one hand, there's no evidence that he's done anything wrong, except that Shaundra lost her mind. Maybe we could find another telepath and have them delve into her mind and try to fix what's broken. There are other telepaths out there, although they play it very low-key. That's the thing about telepaths—they're among the most tortured of us mentalists. They either go crazy or build mental fortresses to contain themselves. They're not the easiest sorts to deal with. And Minder's one of the strongest of them, so there's no guarantee that someone could even fix the damage I suspect he's done."

Mitch had his reams of superhero/villain taxonomic classifications, and in my own research, I'd had my own observations. Mentalists were the supers who had mind powers, versus outright physical powers, and included:

- TELEPATHS
- TELEKINETICS
- PRECOGS
- PYROKINETICS
- CRYOKINETICS
- HYDROKINETICS
- MESMERIZERS
- ILLUSIONISTS
- CLAIRVOYANTS
- PSYCHOMETRISTS

"You know that the Knack has Ephemera with him," I said. Tabitha nodded.

"He still holds out hope that he'll luck into curing her," Tabitha said. "His hopefulness is both sad and sweet. He'll never give up on a friend. I won't, either, but I'm maybe more pragmatic than Shane is. He's nothing if not idealistic. I can't bring myself to visit her, see her like that, a living ghost, caught in her own psychic purgatory. It's too painful. I worry that I'd react poorly to seeing her like that."

Terri Meadows came up, all smiles, looking at both of us in turn.

"Hello, Ladies," she said. "Not to intrude, but I'd like to give Victoriana more of a tour of our facilities."

Tabitha glanced at Meadows a moment, the two of them silently assessing each other, and for a second, I felt like something was up. I'd never talked with a telekinetic before, and there was this strange energy they had to them.

"Yeah," Tabitha said. "Great meeting you, Victoriana. Stay in touch."

"I will," I said. "It was wonderful meeting you, Tabitha."

She watched me get up, her dark eyes full of ineffable emotions.

"Be careful out there," she said. "Be *very* careful, Victoriana."

The flight home had my mind wandering, wondering how I'd deal with Minder. I believed Tantrum. I think she was right about her suspicions, but there was no way to prove it. It was impossible to hold a telepath to account. And, given that he was leading the Affiliates, it would only look bad if I went after him. I'd look like the villain, picking on poor Minder, who was just trying to do his job.

In the appearances game, a super could rise or fall in a news cycle. It's what impressed me about Mitch. He was *always* getting slagged in the media, but he kept at it, and the media would grudgingly report on his exposés, being forced to cover stories they only wanted buried. Mitch didn't care, didn't have to care.

Had I naïvely overplayed my hand by tethering my own acceptance with bringing Mitch into the Affiliates? I was comfortable in sunlight, but would Mitch wither under that kind of harsh scrutiny? I could only imagine what the background checks involved. And given how closely he guarded his secret identity, had I put him in danger by dragging him into the Affiliates?

I'd kill myself before ever letting anything bad happen to Mitch.

That thought carried me all the way home, and I landed quietly on the rooftop of our brownstone, where he was waiting for me, a pitcher of beer on the table, and two glasses, unfilled.

"Wow, now how'd you know when I'd be arriving?" I asked. He poured me a beer and handed it over, looking smug.

"You pinged me before you left Hyberia," he said. "I timed it, assuming you'd be rocking the Mach 3. Clearly, I was right."

"Smart man," I said, leaning in and kissing him on the forehead. I whisked myself into our apartment and changed out of my costume, putting on some comfy clothes, and shot back upstairs, where he was finishing pouring his own beer.

I handed him his digital recorder, which brightened his smile.

"Aww, you remembered," he said. "How was it?"

Sitting down opposite him, drinking my beer, it felt like heaven. We shared space so perfectly, like a magical dance where we didn't even have to move to feel our connection.

"Before I go into that, how'd you wrangle a pitcher of beer, Babe?" I asked. He feigned innocence.

"I just opened a handful of cans and poured them into a pitcher," he said. "You think I got a keg while you were away?"

I put precisely nothing past him, just took another quaff and unloaded on what I'd seen at Hyberia. He listened, and I loved him for that, because he was such a good listener. I imagine his work required that of him.

"Fuck Hyberia," he said, and we laughed. "I love that Tantrum's just hanging out there like that. It's so weird."

"Yeah," I said. "She's *intense*, Mitch. Oh! That reminds me!"

I shot back downstairs and came back with the mailer.

"This is for you, courtesy of Ms. Terri Meadows, the precog chief administrator at Hyberia," I said, watching him open it, and seeing the smile break on his sweet face, I was so happy that had happened. The boy that he had been appeared out of the blue within the slender confines of the man.

"This is great," he said. "And, hey, the precog knows my real name. How about that?"

Knowing his tone, I was sure that it got his wheels turning, trying to figure out who knew who he was, why, and how.

"I think she's harmless," I said. "Kind of depressing, really. I'd hate to be a precog. That seems like the worst."

"Seeing the future's only bad if you can't do anything about it," Mitch said, carefully putting the photograph back in its mailer. I was just inwardly relieved that it hadn't lost it on my flight back.

"Yeah, and in that spirit, what are we going to do about Minder?" I asked. I just wanted to pound the truth out of the man. Mitch was reflective, drinking his beer and getting that middle-distance stare of his when he was scheming.

"We're like pieces on this existential chessboard between Shane and Rex," Mitch said. "Truly. I think we should just play it cool for now. Assuming my background clears, I get in there, can access all of their files. This is long game stuff, Anna. We're talking miles of files. I'm going to grill AFFILIA and see if she'll spill."

I blew my emerald bangs upward with a huffy puff of consternation, but Mitch reassured me.

"I'm used to this game," he said. "Surveillance takes time. We'll catch him. It's going to be one of those watch-and-wait kind of gigs with Minder."

"Argh," I said. "I hate that. I so want to pound him. There's nothing wrong with him I couldn't fix with my fists."

He laughed, pouring more beer for us both, and I laughed, too.

"You're one beautiful bruiser, Babe," he said, and we got the giggles on top of our laughter. "This is a delicate matter. We'll get him. Shane wouldn't have pulled us in if he thought we couldn't swing it."

"Oh, I'm going to swing it, alright," I said, throwing a mock-hook into the air. Then I held up Tantrum's card, explained what she'd said. He loved that, taking it in his hand and turning it over a couple of times. He commented that he loved that she'd had business cards made, which struck him as so earnestly hilarious. He photographed it with his phone. I could only imagine Mitch doing background investigation work on Tantrum's phone number.

"That's legit," he said. "Tantrum's intense. You've seen the stories, I know. She's absolute top-shelf A-list, right up there with you. But with TK, oh, yes. That's a card we will lay on the table when we need to. I have righteous Tantrum footage."

He put the Tantrum card on the table and slid it back to me. Then he tapped his phone and dug a YouTube video of Tantrum versus Worldbreaker, this kaiju that had attacked San Francisco several years back. It was one of those signature Affiliates super-fights, the culmination of a battle between Master Disaster, the mad wizard who'd opened a dimensional breach in a bid to end California.

Worldbreaker was this horrendous monster, massive and green-black, with these big black bug eyes that were the size of trucks, surrounded by smaller eyes, also glossy black. It had this massive maw filled with teeth, and, of course, had tentacles around its mouth, six massive arms, two huge legs, and three tails that ended in stingers that could split oil tankers in two. Its roar was apocalyptic, this three-toned klaxon dirge that shook the very ground and could be heard for miles.

The Affiliates threw themselves into the battle, with Tag Team doing his usual crowd control function, while Decibelle shrieked to try to counter the roar of Worldbreaker, and Brighteyes blasted away with her eyebeams from the Golden Gate Bridge, those green beams lancing into the monster like knife wounds.

Wingman flew hard for Master Disaster, who wore this bizarre green stone crown that apparently let him direct Worldbreaker or at least keep the portal open. That portal itself was something dreadful, being a world of red lightning and worrisome winds.

Rad Lad, Tandem, Ephemera, and Tantrum went after it, and even Minder was on the bridge with Sound & Fury, attempting psychic assault on the kaiju, while the Knack was trying to reach Master Disaster, who was hovering, hurling fireballs at Wingman.

"Did you film this?" I asked, because it was such a Cameraman thing to do, and I'd never seen this particular footage of that Worldbreaker fight.

"Well, yeah," he said, grinning bashfully at me.

"You stinker," I said. "Affiliates fanboy."

"I'm a sucker for kaiju."

He scoffed and pressed play again, resuming the action. Worldbreaker had pounded Tandem with one of its arms, sending him flying so fast he broke the sound barrier, while Rad Lad let loose with high energy blasts that would have the EPA howling for years.

Seeing them fight this way, really cutting loose, I felt fortunate that I'd performed as well against them in that training session. Had they been holding back against me? I longed to be in this kind of fight, one of those big fights, the ones that shake the Earth.

Brighteyes kept firing her eyebeams, which were shearing black-bloodied chunks of Worldbreaker away, while Decibelle's screams blasted into it, liquefying armor and flesh wherever she hit. Sound & Fury were one helluva duo, I had to admit. I admired that. Mitch and I worked that way, too, in our best moments.

Ephemera flew right for Worldbreaker's skull, attempting to phase into it, but startled when she found she couldn't pass through it. Instead, one of its massive tentacles whipped out and snagged her, squeezing hard.

Then Tantrum flew in, throwing her telekinetic forcebolts at the kaiju, forcing it to release Ephemera, who had done a density-shift to become hyper-dense, landing in the water of the San Francisco bay like a depth charge, sending great plumes of water upward as she did so.

Worldbreaker roared, its black eyes fixed on Tantrum, who threw another forcebolt at the monster, this one so powerful that it actually knocked the creature back, right off its feet, hitting the water, creating small tsunamis as it landed.

"Here's the best shot coming up," Mitch said. "This paid my rent for the year."

Tantrum threw her hands out in front of her, like she was grabbing the kaiju, and, letting out a scream, she scooped the thing up with her mind. To see a kaiju get lifted like that, purely through force of what? Will? Mind? It was breathtaking. Worldbreaker wasn't happy about it, either, because it was whipping its three tails around, trying to find something or someone to hit.

Tandem followed up on Tantrum's attack by slamming into its chest with this percussive blow that actually took Tandem *through* the monster in a splash of greenish-black blood, while Rad Lad fired blast after blast into it, with Brighteyes and Decibelle focusing their attacks from the bridge, and Minder apparently continuing his psychic onslaught, judging from him having both hands at his temples.

Wingman, the Knack, and Ms. Fit were closing in on Master Disaster, and I don't even know how Mitch actually caught all of this. I asked him.

"Multiple cameras," he said. "Drones. I had a quick version I slung out to the media, but this is the extended director's cut."

Worldbreaker actually grabbed Tandem in passing, pounding another of its fists into the hand that held Tandem, each hit creating these thunderous explosions that even Mitch felt, because you could hear him muttering "Jesus Palamino" a few times at that point.

Then Tantrum struck again, grappling the thing with only her mind, the two of them struggling in this titanic battle, one that had eventually turned in her favor as Worldbreaker's six arms were held fast, its fingers breaking as Tantrum forced it to release Tandem, who flew free the moment he was able.

Tantrum let out another scream and hurled Worldbreaker back through the swirling dimensional rift, right at the moment that the Knack had managed to snatch the greenstone crown from Master Disaster as Wingman and Ms. Fit knocked the wizard out. The breach had been sealed, and the world had been saved.

Mitch stopped playing it, and I raised my beer glass to him.

"So funny you filmed that," I said. "What did you even do? Road trip to San Francisco?"

"That breach had taken a few days to build," Mitch said. "Master Disaster had this whole arcane ritual he was performing, I later found out. It took some time, so I was able to get there and set up."

"Very voyeuristic," I said. "Did they know you were there?"

"I don't think so," Mitch said.

"Are you going to record us when we're both on the Affiliates?" I asked. He nodded.

"How can I not?" he asked. "If I'm not kicked off the team in a month, I'll be surprised."

We lasted three whole years, and he lasted longer than me. *Never* saw that coming.

The fight with Zig & Zag, the twin speedsters, had been one of those big-ticket Affiliates fights in Central that had people talking. Mitch and I had locked down Affiliates Central between us those first couple of years, working our unique partnership (maybe we weren't Sound & Fury, but Fists & Files had more than our share of wins), so it was perhaps appropriate that a dynamic duo like ZigZag would come our way.

The two of them were quirky—they were both short, for one thing, barely over five feet tall, which made them almost cute to fight, except for their maddening speed. They also did this weird thing where they had twin talk—you know that thing where twins sometimes have their own languages? But they'd do it at high speed, so you'd hear this high-pitched gobble-de-gook pass between them, and they'd go do something impressive.

ZigZag gave us fits, as all speedsters invariably do. But since there were two of them, they were even more formidable.

Mitch's dossiers on them had them as one-time circus performers who had been acrobats, only to have been struck by lightning during a performance, which had miraculously granted them super speed, as well as an ability to negate friction while in motion, which was always central to any speedster.

They wore costumes of red and blue, with a "Z" emblazoned on their chests—his was a red Z, hers was blue. Both of them had matching blond short speedster haircuts with an almost built-in windswept look to them, and eyes that were bright blue. They wore goggles—again, very common in speedsters. If they weren't supervillains, they'd have been adorable.

"Hey, Zig," Zag said. "That's Victoriana, yeah?"

"Sure is, Zag," Zig said. "Let's put her through her paces."

They interrupted their bank robbery to have a go at me, which amounted to the two of them racing me down, whirlwinding me while raining their fists on me at unbelievable speed. I went airborne, and they split, running up skyscrapers to pursue me, leaving a cascade of raining glass in their wake. Among speedsters, the ability to do the run-up was one of those gold star power stunts they might pull, along with running across water. They'd always do it, the big showoffs they always were.

Mitch was in a fix because they moved way too quickly for him to track them. He opted for crowd control while I went after them.

It was a good fight, but a bad one, too, because of the amount of property damage incurred from it, as I went around downtown, alternately battling and defending against ZigZag, who were having a great time throughout the fight.

The gleeful villains could be the worst that way. Their glee made them almost impervious to realizing they might be in over their heads, and they banked on their speed as insurance against just about anything they might encounter.

And maybe it was just me, but because they were small, I found myself lightening up against them, not wanting to hurt them. Whereas they had no hesitation about trying to lay me out.

I'd throw a fast punch at Zig, who'd grab my arm and speed-fling me into some buildings, and I'd have to pause to make sure everybody was okay. The last thing I wanted was to kill some bystanders on account of these pint-sized marauders.

Zag ran up to me and danced a little jig on my chest at speed, her feet pounding me into the ground while she cackled, zipping away before I could deck her.

Then Mitch managed to zap Zig with his stun gun, and the speedster just stood there, eyes agape, while Mitch ran up and bonked him with his stun baton, which took Zig out of the fight, both from blunt force trauma and the electrical jolts on top of the stun gun effect.

Zag, seeing that, went berserk, ran down Mitch, pummeling him with a blur of punches that had him staggered.

I flew in quickly, while Zag was occupied with beating the life out of Mitch, and managed to land a strong hit that sent her cartwheeling into a nearby car, knocking her clean out. The two of them had more robust physiques than their small frames would otherwise indicate, and we put power neutralizer collars on them before they came to.

Then we heard slow clapping behind us, and who was there but Minder, in his black and white costume, wearing his face mask. He hadn't been in the field for years, but there he was, watching us. How he got there was a mystery to me.

"I'm not actually here," Minder said. "I'm at your headquarters. I'm merely projecting an illusion of myself here. Meet me there once you've gotten those two wrapped up."

Mitch was leaning on a car, trying to catch his breath.

"Ohhhh," he said. "That hurt. I'm going to be covered in bruises. I think maybe she broke a rib or three."

"Did you see Minder is here?" I asked. The Affiliates Rapid Recovery Team was already flying in. Each branch had them on standby with Affilijets at the ready to recover defeated super-villains to be shipped off to the appropriate super-supermax.

"Yeah, I saw," Mitch said, clutching his chest. "I think I might need to get medical attention."

I was on my Affilicom in a flash. "Inbound ARRT, we need medical for Cameraman."

They answered quickly. "We read you, Victoriana. We'll be ready for him on pickup. ETA three minutes."

While Mitch fought to keep from passing out, I waited until the Affilijet turned up, watched them load Zig and Zag and Mitch into the craft. I must have looked worried, because Mitch gave me a shaky thumbs up as they closed up and took off.

That left me to deal with Minder alone. With what I knew, or at least what I'd heard, I wasn't looking forward to this.

I flew in, and there was Minder, having taken his mask off, sitting in our common area, the living room, for lack of a better word, watching me as I came in. Minder wasn't what I considered handsome—the way he slicked back his brown hair made me think of Christian Bale in AMERICAN PSYCHO. That look just never gelled with me.

"Good work today," he said. "ZigZag are a tough little duo. How's Mitch doing?"

"He's with the RRT," I said, and Minder politely smiled.

"He really tries so hard," Minder said. "He's lucky ZigZag didn't tear him to pieces. You know, they have this strike they can do where they vibrate their hands so quickly, they can pass through solid matter, to devastating effect. They can stop someone's heart that way."

"Luckily, we stopped them before it came to that," I said, taking my seat opposite of him. He watched me sit, not saying anything.

"Luck *is* part of it, isn't it?" Minder said. "You two have had a great run here in Central. And a lot of it can be attributed to luck. And to you, Anna."

The way he said my name, it skeeved me out. Like he knew me. Like we were friends. I assumed he was reading my mind, but if he was, he gave no indication. He just talked.

"I'm your friend, Anna," he said softly. "I want what's best for you. When you debuted on our team—well, we're *still* parsing all the data we got from your already-legendary performance in the Ready Room, do you know that?"

I'd never forget that moment.

"It was incredible," Minder said. "To see that kind of power—power that is yours and yours alone—nobody has ever debuted in the Affiliates like that. Not even Tandem or Tantrum."

He was trying to flatter me, to butter me up before putting the knife in. I watched him watching me, wondering how well he knew my mind. Just hearing him mention Tantrum made me squirm and want to confront him.

"We don't do that with just anybody," Minder said. "Simply put: I knew you could take it. You're world-class, Anna. We have room for all sorts of heroes in the Affiliates, but you are part of an extremely elite club. The ones who can hold their own against *anybody*."

I had knives of my own, and thought I'd give him a little knick.

"You mean like Tantrum?" I asked.

If it phased him, he didn't show it. He just sat back and smiled.

"You're better than Tabitha," he said. "She's a telekinetic. Certainly a top-level telekinetic, but we mentalists aren't like you physicals. We're more like specialists. I have no doubt you'd be able to beat Tabitha in a fight, provided you were quick enough. And you *are* amazingly fast, Anna. We've tracked your speeds."

I wondered how that worked, how the Affiliates monitored us remotely. Maybe there were drones or satellites watching us. Mitch would love that. He'd be trying to hack those in no time.

"I like to fly," I said.

"And you're amazing at it," Minder said. "The others resent you, you know. They call you 'Mary Sue' behind your back."

That bothered me whether or not I could believe it. It felt like it could be something Fusillad might say. Maybe others. Which others?

"I'm not a Mary Sue," I said. "I have weaknesses."

Minder smiled and nodded, steepling his fingers on his knee while he sat.

"I know you do," he said. "Everyone has weaknesses."

I wasn't going to let him provoke me, but I wanted to lay into him. The thoughts came to me unbidden, all torrents and swirls.

"Mitch, for example," Minder said. "He's *all* weaknesses. It's why he's laid up right now, and you're sitting here talking to me as if you hadn't just taken on ZigZag."

The angle of attack was almost too obvious, but I let him make it.

"Mitch has been a superhero longer than you have," I said. "If that's what you call yourself."

Minder just smiled unreadably.

"He and I have been doing what we do for a long time," Minder said. "Different arenas, to be sure. Although we're both about gaining information, when you think about it. It's just that I know my limitations—my weaknesses, in other words. And Mitch? I don't think he accepts that he has any. It's why he avoids those direct fights, prefers working in the shadows, where he thinks he's less likely to get beaten to death, shot dead, or perhaps worse."

The imagery of Mitch's injuries came back to me, and he always blew them off with his bluster, to try to keep me from worrying about him. He hated to be rescued. I mean, he really hated it.

"I *know* he's important to you, Anna," Minder said. "You love him dearly, and that's a precious thing in this business. It's also why I strongly recommend you persuade him to leave the team. Be gentle with him, and just nudge him in another direction. *Because* you love him, and you don't want him to get hurt. Or killed."

It angered me to hear him say this because part of me knew he wasn't wrong. Any time we worked together in the field, I worried about Mitch, and tried to protect him without appearing to, so as not to wound his pride.

"You're not helping him by keeping him in the game here in Central," Minder said. "All you're doing is guaranteeing that, sooner or later, he's going to end up dead. And it'll be *his* blood on your hands. You like thinking of me as some kind of villain. But I'm the one who sees Mitch as who he truly is, not what he *thinks* he is, what he *wishes* he is, and what you *imagine* him to be. He's your childhood crush made flesh, but he's no superman; he's just an ordinary man. He's nothing like you, and while the idea of opposites attracting might have appeal in some romantic circles, in the superhero business, it's the kiss of death."

I was particularly angry in that moment, the way he minimized everything that mattered to me. I loved Mitch with every beat of my heart, and to hear Minder slagging him like that was beyond toleration.

"You know, *you're* kind of terrible," I said. "I ought to deck you for maligning Mitch."

"All I have to do is somehow keep a superhero team running at peak capacity," Minder said. "Each member doing their part to make the stronger whole. Your stunt with Mitch, well, that was cute. We humored your bringing him along for the ride, but it was always your ride, not his. He'd never have made the cut on his own. Shane knows it. You know it, I know it, and the rest of the team knows it. Everyone on the team earned their place there. Mitch? Oh, I know, he has his little media firestorms he generates with his reporting and spying, but there's nothing superheroic in that. It's just journalism. Even his ad hoc invisibility isn't enough because he's not up to the fights he starts. Get him to quit the team. Persuade him to leave it behind."

"Never," I said. "He *loves* being a superhero."

"Then be prepared for him to die in the line of duty," Minder said. "And don't say I didn't warn you. You'll be the one trying to live without him, wishing you'd listened to me and persuaded him to move on. You *belong* here, Anna, because you are superior. You are extraordinary beyond measure. You're powerful enough to earn some envious umbrage from your peers, some name-calling. Mitch? He's a bad joke."

I jumped to my feet, clenched my fists, snarled at him.

"Please," Minder said. "You can't intimidate me, Anna. Because you know I'm speaking the truth. That's why you're getting emotional."

I reached for him and grabbed him with one hand, clutching his costume in my fist. He chuckled, his eyes locked on mine, even as I lifted him off his feet and held him there.

"I'll say it again: you are superior, Anna," he said. "All of us are. Those of us with gifts."

Then he pushed me with his mind, and I remembered Tantrum admonishing me not to do exactly what I was doing.

*Put me down, take your hands off me,* came his voice in my head. And, to my shock and terror, I found that I did. I released him, and he just kept his eyes on me, while I was staring at my hands that had betrayed me.

"I could make you do nearly anything I want, Anna," Minder said, smoothing his costume with a lone stroke of his hand. "Would you like to see?"

I was going to deck him, drawing my fist back, but he stopped it with a thought, a simple, resonant *No* in my head, and there I stood, straining against his mind, my arm cocked, unable to take that swing that would splatter him against the far wall.

"You physicals, always thinking with your fists," Minder said. "At least Mitch, being a weakling, knows his limitations, even if he won't accept them. You, on the other hand, think you can pound every problem into submission with those amazing fists of yours."

He walked around me, watching me strain against his mental attack. I'd never been stopped like that before. I'd never fought a telepath.

"I could make this easy, you know," Minder said. "I'd just have to isolate the areas of your mind where you love Mitch and dial them down toward, oh, I don't know...apathy? Indifference? Resentment? Mockery? Contempt? Loathing? Hatred? It's just a matter of working the neuronal pathways, making the necessary alterations and deviations, creating new pathways in the ventral tegmental area, the caudate nucleus, the hypothalamus, your dopamine receptors. I could make it simple for you to boot him off the team for me, and you'd not spare him a backward glance. You could go on with the rest of your life as the Affiliate you were born to be, having forgotten Mitch even existed."

"No," I said, gritting my teeth. The force of his mind in mine was horrifying, his presence there, inside my head, this intruder.

"A fighter to the end," Minder said. "I respect that."

Then he applied still more mental force, and I don't have the words to properly describe it. All I could see in my head was Minder, luminous white oscillating in a sea of black, my mind palace shaking before the power of his will, as he took it apart, brick by brick.

"NO!" I screamed, with every bit of force I could bring to my voice, my superhuman lungs creating a noise that had to have been in the range of what Decibelle could do, if not nearly as musical.

I know it did something, because Minder actually fell backward, clutching his head, his eyes wide, nose bleeding, and he had vanished from my mind, even as some of the windows in Central shattered.

I sprang for him, bringing my foot down on his chest, pinning him, while he gazed in wonder at his hands, which had blood on them from what I'd done, the blood pouring from his nose and ears.

"Stop!" Minder said, attacking me again with his mind. "Not another sound out of you."

However, I pressed down on him with my foot, and the pain in his chest broke his concentration again, and I slapped him across the face. Not enough to take his head off, but enough that he felt it. I could see the red welt from my handprint on his face, only the merest fraction of force of which I was capable.

"You mentalists need to concentrate, don't you?" I said. "For your powers to work."

I pushed again, and he let out a pained grunt. Another light push and I'd break at least half of his ribs. I thought that very clearly, so he'd have something to fixate on while fighting me in my own head, trying to brain-rape me.

Then he desperately mind-blasted me and I felt every nerve ending sing with pain that took my breath away, doubling over. He got to his feet, steadying himself, clutching his chest.

"You're making such a grave mistake, Anna," he said, choking on his blood, spitting it out on the ground near me. "And for what? For Mitch? Such a waste."

"Are you fast enough to zap me before I hit you?" I asked, hit with another mental attack from him, even as the Scenester teleported near us, with his silver suit and smarmy sneer, and grabbed Minder while I was fending off the mental attack. And then the two of them teleported away, just blinking out of existence before I could do anything else.

I was standing there alone, still in my combative crouch, clutching my head with a nasty headache, feeling only a devastating sense of sorrow at my abysmal failure, and how I needed to take flight and put an end to everything as the only cure for the miserable failure I'd become as a superhero.

You know the rest. I couldn't shake that feeling of failure. It held me tight, in fight after fight. An overwhelming feeling of futility that I was unable to shake. Mitch healed up, and he and I would beat the bejeezus out of villains, and yet the joy I'd felt before was simply gone. Even our after-fight sex had become lackluster, a sad sort of celebration of an empty, fleeting triumph.

It was a dismal feeling. The pleasure of life had fled from me, and I couldn't figure out why. Mitch noticed, and we talked about it, but I couldn't put my finger on it. There was something else, too—a nagging feeling that Shane had put us on a fool's errand, and that his suspicions that there was corruption in the Affiliates were nonsense. No corruption, nothing out of the ordinary. The Knack had been wrong. That feeling felt wrong, but it was in my head, all the same.

Only flying made it better. I found the farther I flew, the faster, the better I felt. I would take flight and found some release from that dreadful, cloying depression. I would fly around the world, lost in my thoughts. I'd land in faraway places by my-self, feeling forlorn only when I set foot on the ground.

I was aware that there was another me, a happier me, but she was encased in unbreakable glass, and I didn't know how it had gotten there in my mind. Only when I flew did I feel my-self again. Higher and higher. Faster and faster.

Nobody knows I did this, but I flew to the Moon, and just stood there in that dusty, lifeless grey place, staring back at the Earth, which looked as sad as ever, this little oasis in uncaring space. I made an ash angel in the Moon dust, laughed in the vacuum at my contribution to the landscape there. My teeth clenched, I wrote "AW + MP" within the ash angel and drew a heart around it. How old was I, again? In that moment, it was validating. And it made me so depressed.

Mitch was on the Earth, and that made me terribly sad, be-cause the Earth looked small from the Moon, and everything and everyone upon it was smaller, still. Like atoms. Insignifi-cant to the point of irrelevance.

And all of the stars out there. Part of me wanted to explore them, too, but my eyes kept being drawn to the Sun. There was peace there, in the Sun. I could find lasting peace in the Sun. There was salvation in the Sun. The pull of it drew me, like the clichéd moth to the flame.

That last night with Mitch was precious because I *knew* it would be my last. I wrote the letters: the one to Mitch, the ones I sent to the various news agencies, and I took Mitch's experimental spacecam helmet and made sure it worked, and then off I went.

It felt so good to fly free of the atmosphere, to really pour on the speed. The sort of speed I could *never* use on the Earth. Free from air and friction, I flew hard and fast. And I found that the faster I went, the better I felt. It was a return to the ecstasy that used to fuel my every step.

Now, it was dizzying, intoxicating, as the Sun got ever larger in my burning eyes. As Mitch's helmet cam—that bittersweet talisman I took with me—sparked, burst, and melted in a glit-tery stream I left behind, and my Zetacloth costume valiantly fought its own annihilation, as I flew ever closer to the Sun, which became all-consuming in my vision, until it became my everything, and I lost myself within it, barely feeling the hard radiation that bounced off me.

Faster and faster I went, until everything around me—even the emptiness of the void—became a blur. There was psychedelic beauty in the blur. Power, even. Salvation.

The spell didn't break until I'd plunged into the plasma naked, one atom in an interstellar ocean of them, chasing my own oblivion.

What had I done?

I lost track of time on the Sun. There was no night and day; only the swirling churn of nuclear fusion, boiling and burning, gargantuan flares knifing the sky.

The fiery woman, when she first appeared, was something I thought might be an illusion, or a hallucination of what was left of my mind. I'd see her at distance (my eyes, while sharper than ordinary eyes, were also oddly protected—I could see, despite the blinding light of the Sun).

She began to dog my steps. First she was a ghost in the corner of my eyes. Then she would follow me. I'd see her watching me, studying me.

A name came to me. It was a name Mitch had shared with me, and she came closer to me, this red woman with fiery bat wings and a barbed tail. She had horns and a painted-on smile that looked venomous, or perhaps it was only her fangs that made her seem that way.

*Inferna*, I thought, because there was no air to carry my words.

*Victoriana*, she thought back, her words in my head like honey. *I've been looking for you for many months.*

*Is Mitch alive?*

*Yes. He's never truly given up on you, you know. He's a very stubborn man.*

*Did he send you?*

*No. But I thought you might be out here somewhere. I didn't want to get his hopes up in case you were dead.*

*Why do you care?*

*I care about* him.

And the devil-woman had the truth of it. I knew truth when I heard it. Minder's mind manipulations had been burned away in my sojourn on the Sun. Gone were those mental malisons he'd placed on me, those weird obsessions.

*How long have I been here?*

*Almost a year.*

WHAT??

*Yes.*

*OMG. We have to get back. Can you take me back?*

Inferna regarded me quizzically. I'll admit that I was happy to have someone to talk to, even if it was Inferna. That came out bad, but when a sinister, enigmatic devil-woman was your only stellar companion, it meant one was in a very bad place.

*There is a way back for you, but you'll have to bear with me a little bit.*

*Not sure what that means.*

*I'm going to have to take you to Hell and back.*

I could tell she actually savored saying that.

*I have to get back to help Mitch, and, you know, to waste Minder.*

*Minder's dead. Shot in the head.*

*OMG. Who did it?*

*Mitch is trying to find out. He's in a lot of trouble.*

*Well, let's get to it!*

But she hesitated.

*What? Do I look like hell or something?*

*You may want to take some time to find yourself again.*

I'd never wanted a mirror more badly. I gazed at my arms, which glowed with a swirly luminescence that was similar to the Sun's own roiling plasma.

*Are you saying I need to cool down?*

*A bit, yes. You're incendiary right now. If you showed up on Earth as you are, you'd burn a hole right through the planet. You'd incinerate Mitch from a mile away.*

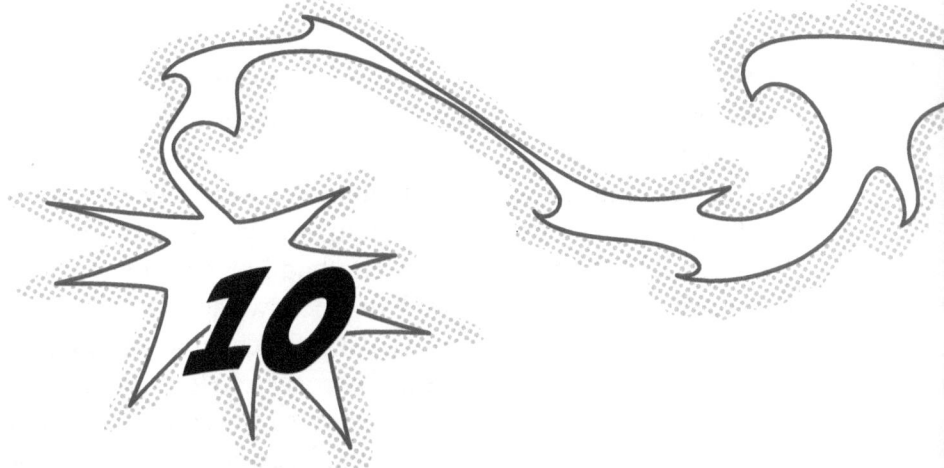

# 10

People loved it, went crazy for it. I posted it and it dominated at least two news cycles as the press covered it. It steamrolled the whole "Cameraman is terrible" stuff that Credible and Shutterbug were busy putting out there. People just loved the fight footage, and the profile of the Hell's Belles and Hellmaiden skyrocketed.

Social media exploded with reposts, shares, stitches, and memes about that Philadelphia fight, and my quick chat with Hellmaiden got a ton of traction. Sales of thigh boots and red cowl capes went up, and people were shaving their heads to look like Hellmaiden, since she'd taken off her cowl after the fight, revealing her bald crowned head, the first I'd seen it, her fire opalescent skin swirling to its own mesmerizing rhythm as she spoke about the fight.

"I've never dealt with demons," she said. "But I figured that if there's one language they understand, it's violence. I just punched my way through the problem he presented, and before I knew it, he broke apart in that explosion you saw."

The hashtag #HM had come to be associated with Hellmaiden's efforts, as well as #FightLikeHellmaiden, and beaucoup memes, including people shipping Hellmaiden with Inferna, the Knack, Tandem, Tag Team, Brighteyes, Decibelle, She-Devil, and even me.

"You're become a super-sex symbol, by all accounts," I said, later, trying out one of my super-interviews (*In Focus with Cameraman*).

Tee shirts and other merch appeared, and Inferna was all too happy to accommodate the demand by way of Hellblender, Inc. (not making that up—Inferna had her own merchandising company that specialized in underworldly goods). Even when the religious groups and their political allies in Congress railed against the "Satanic Superheroes" of Hell's Belles, their popularity only grew. It was amazing to watch it. Some sponsors—liquor, cigarettes, hot sauces, lingerie and sex toys primarily—jumped at the opportunity to get some endorsements from Hell's Belles, while Hellblender was cranking out merch. Inferna and She-Devil went for those right away, while Hellmaiden was more aloof about it.

"I'm just here to help," she said.

"They're saying that 'Sin is In' lately," I said. "What do you have to say about that?"

"People can do what they like," she replied, looking into the camera. "People can do whatever the hell they want. But how about people stop with mass shootings, yeah? I've seen firsthand where those people end up. You do *not* want to end up down there."

"Are you saying there's actually a Hell?" I asked. This was deliberate on my part, just trying to get ahead of the other narratives.

"There's a place that qualifies," Hellmaiden said. "It's more just another dimension than anything tied to the old biblical texts, if that makes sense."

When the Trinity reappeared (*having been taken by Inferna in BRIGHTEYES Chapter 28—the editors*), looking bedraggled and shellshocked, it caused a sensation that again overrode the efforts to sour public perception of the Affiliates. Watching it all unfold, I felt like Inferna must have been doing some unholy shenanigans on her part.

She'd made sure to do it in concert with my own recording of it, so I'd be able to land another sensational scoop.

The Trinity looked like hell (I'm well beyond pardoning for puns at this point), with Angelica looking bedraggled, the Crucifixer shaking in his jackboots, and the Inquisitor in ragged robes.

"Hell is real," Angelica said. "We've been through Hell and are grateful to Almighty God for our release."

"Who let you free?" I asked.

"Inferna," the Inquisitor said. "She said we'd served our allotted time."

"God set us free," Angelica said, glaring at the Inquisitor. "Not *that* hellion. It was our faith that delivered us."

"I totally set her free," Inferna said. "At Hellmaiden's request, I'll have you know. I would have kept them prisoner for an eternity. She showed mercy."

It was impossible to tell if Hellmaiden was blushing, but she looked like a model of pensive opalescence.

"I just thought it was cruel to keep them prisoner," she said.

The Trinity looked haggard and terrified, and Caryn Underwood quickly scooped them up for a host of interviews about their terrible experiences at the hands of Inferna and sensational explorations of their time in Hell in a video podcast series called *The Other Side,* which interviewed supervillains and presented their points of view.

Now, Gentle Reader, you're probably squirming, wondering why all of this Heaven-n-Hell stuff might be surfacing in a story about superheroes? Just be patient, I'm asking you—this memoir bears witness to a monumental clash of Good versus Evil, and at least in more conventional moral dichotomies, people often reflexively skew toward those legacy frameworks of antiquity because they don't have anything else. Just an aside as we dip into Underwood's interview of the Trinity, who (spoiler) disbanded shortly after their returns:

CARYN UNDERWOOD: *WHAT'S THIS I HEAR ABOUT THE TRINITY DISBANDING?*

ANGELICA: *SADLY, YES. WE'VE DECIDED TO DISBAND.*

UNDERWOOD: *BUT WHY? YOU'RE ALL LIVING SUPERHUMAN SYMBOLS OF AMERICAN CHRISTIAN VALUES. YOU REPRESENT THE BEST OF THAT HOLY TRADITION.*

INQUISITOR: *WE'RE DONATING OUR RESOURCES TO DIRECTLY HELPING THE POOR, THE VULNERABLE, AND THE NEEDY.*

UNDERWOOD: *THERE MUST BE A BETTER WAY YOU CAN HELP THOSE UNFORTUNATES.*

ANGELICA: *NOPE. WE'RE DONATING OUR TIME AND ENERGY TO HELPING THE POOR, THE NEEDY, THE HUNGRY, THE WEAK, AND THE VULNERABLE. ANYTHING ELSE IS, I DON'T KNOW, HERETICAL? HYPOCRITICAL?*

UNDERWOOD: *BUT YOUR CHRISTIAN CORPORATE SPONSORS?*

CRUCIFIXER: *THEY'LL JUST HAVE TO UNDERSTAND. WE. SAW. HELL. (BEGINS CRYING)*

ANGELICA: *HE'S RIGHT. WE'VE BEEN THE KNOWING TOOLS OF THE RICH, POWERFUL, AND PRIVILEGED. WE WILLFULLY USED OUR SUPERPOWERS TO ADVANCE THEIR AGENDA. WE WERE HYPOCRITES.*

UNDERWOOD: *INFERNA TORTURED YOU, DIDN'T SHE? CAN YOU TELL US ABOUT THIS? SHE COERCED YOU TO SAY THESE UNGODLY THINGS?*

INQUISITOR: *SHE SHOWED US THE ERROR OF OUR WAYS AND MEANS.*

ANGELICA (LAUGHS NERVOUSLY): *PLEASE, LET'S MOVE ON.*

UNDERWOOD: *THIS IS SO SAD TO HEAR. ONE WOULD THINK SUCH A TEST WOULD MAKE YOU STRONGER IN YOUR FAITH, NOT MAKE YOU ABANDON IT.*

INQUISITOR: *WE'RE NOT ABANDONING IT; WE'RE GOING TO HELP THE WEAKEST PEOPLE, VERSUS BEING THE SPIRITUAL SPECIAL FORCES WE WERE. WE'RE GOING WHERE WE'RE NEEDED MOST.*

UNDERWOOD: *REAL AMERICA NEEDS YOU. IT NEEDS THE TRINITY, AND WHAT YOU STAND FOR. THE UNMATCHED POWER OF YOUR FAITH, WORKING HAND IN GLOVE WITH YOUR SPIRITUAL SPONSORS.*

ANGELICA (LOOKS AT CAMERA): *HELL IS REAL. DEVILS ARE REAL. GOD DID NOT RESCUE US. INFERNA RELEASED US. HELLMAIDEN PERSUADED HER TO RELEASE US. THAT'S THE TRUTH.*

Caryn Underwood was very unhappy with this podcast because they just wouldn't shake that line they were toeing, and prayer vigils appeared outside Trinity Holy Headquarters from people who wanted them back the way they'd been before.

A backlash arose around Hell's Belles, at least as far as Inferna and She-Devil were concerned. People burned effigies of them, and exorcisms were carried out by people claiming to have been possessed by them. Hellmaiden managed to avoid most of that backlash, since she'd been the one to persuade Inferna to release the Trinity.

For her part, Inferna relished the wrath of these people and was unfazed by it. The crazier it got, the more she seemed to dig it. Rumors arose that Inferna had somehow enslaved Hellmaiden, who some theorized was actually an angel. An entire conspiracy theory arose around that, that maybe Hellmaiden was secretly an angel bound to serve Inferna.

Shutterbug ran with that angle and went full steam with the "Cameraman is in league with Inferna" storyline, which she pounded for weeks, including recut videos and deepfakes showing me swearing fealty to Satan. Some of them were even well-produced. Another of Shutterbug's pieces had me as Satan and went with that idea that Inferna and the others did my bidding.

Then came the worst of it, when Lynn Credible went on the air and told Caryn Underwood that she knew my secret identity. She went on *The Other Side* and tearfully talked about it:

CARYN UNDERWOOD: *YOU LOOK LIKE YOU HAVE SOMETHING TO TELL US, LYNN.*

LYNN CREDIBLE: *I DO.*

UNDERWOOD: *TELL US. THIS IS A SAFE SPACE.*

CREDIBLE: *I KEEP GOING BACK TO THAT FATEFUL DAY WHEN REX WAS MURDERED. CAMERAMAN KILLED HIM, AS SURE AS IF HE'D FIRED THE BULLET HIMSELF.*

UNDERWOOD: *SPEAK YOUR TRUTH, LYNN.*

CREDIBLE: *I KNOW WHO HE IS. WHO HE REALLY IS.*

UNDERWOOD: *CAMERAMAN? HE'S SATAN, ISN'T HE? TELL US, LYNN.*

CREDIBLE (LOOKING AT THE CAMERA): *HE'S MITCH PAULSEN.*

**UNDERWOOD:** *WHO? IS THIS AN ALIAS?*

**CREDIBLE:** *IT'S WHO HE IS. HE LIVES IN CHICAGO. HE OWNS FLYING SAUCER VIDEOS.*

**UNDERWOOD (LAUGHING NERVOUSLY):** *HE'S A VIDEO STORE CLERK?*

**CREDIBLE:** *YEAH. HE'S INSANE. A MEDIA MADMAN.*

My phone exploded. My social media detonated. People started looking for stuff about me, trying to find something to share. People went to Flying Saucer Video and began sharing pictures. Poor Molly and John didn't know what was going on, and were calling up, too.

"Fuck," I said. And then people began gathering at my building, taking pictures of the Mitchmobile on the roof, which people took to be proof of my villainous superheroism.

Although I'd been super-careful to keep my private, personal digital presence minimal over the years, people were able to dredge things up—high school stuff, some yearbook shots of me. I got hit with a bunch of blowback, like propositions from women and men wanting to marry me, death threats, offers for interviews, endless doxing. The swatting came soon afterward.

Shane called me up.

"Hey, it's not the worst thing to happen," he said. "Everybody knows who I am, too, don't forget."

"Yeah, but you're you," I said. "There are people outside of my place waving signs, wanting me dead."

I hated that Credible had done that, but there wasn't anything exactly illegal about it, although Shane offered me the services of some of his lawyers in case it got out of hand.

The supervillains came for me as soon as the information got out there. Everybody that I'd ever mildly inconvenienced as a criminal was coming for me. And jags like Scenester were only too happy to deliver them right to me for a price.

Scenester appeared in my living room, having brought Knuckleduster with him, who was a street-level enforcer whose costume was like that of a gentleman rake from the 1900s, complete with a waxed mustache and a tuxedo with tails and his trademark brass knuckles.

"Special delivery, Paulsen," Scenester said, grinning at me, while Knuckleduster took a swing at me, catching me in the jaw, nearly knocking me out right there.

"I say, first blood for me," Knuckleduster said. It was in moments like these that I was grateful for every bit of Aikido I'd learned, as the next punch Knuckleduster threw, I managed to fling him at Scenester, who teleported away, leaving Knuckleduster to crash into one of my chairs.

He got right back up and went after me again. I'd busted his boss about eight years before for racketeering. Knuckleduster lunged at me again, throwing a high-low series of blows that caused me to block high only to get caught in the stomach with the lower combo.

Scenester reappeared, this time with the Burgundy Basher, another enforcer type, who wore a burgundy costume and who had been a sometime sidekick of Jack Rabbit of the Crime League. Basher was super-strong, unlike Knuckleduster, so he became my primary concern as he took a swing at me and put a fist through my wall.

"I'm going to crack your skull, Paulsen," he said, prying his fist out of the wall.

I dove for my stun gun, but Knuckleduster swatted it away, and I saw it clatter into a corner just as I saw stars when Basher caught me with a cross that I only barely tumbled away from as he'd connected, or he'd have killed me for sure.

Then Scenester grabbed me and teleported me up into the air over my brownstone.

"This is with regards from Dr. Crimebot, Cameraman," he said, letting me go as he teleported away. He'd put me several hundred feet over my building, and I cried out as I fell.

As I dropped to the ground, I could see the crowds gathered at my brownstone, some of them looking up and pointing, their phones pointing upward in a sea of little blue rectangles.

*This is how it ends for me. Fitting.*

I really tried not to scream as I fell, and I'd have been splattered on the ground if not for Hellmaiden swooping in to catch me, wearing gloves with fingers, thankfully, so she didn't incinerate me upon touch.

"Poor thing," she said, swooping me out of there. "Do you want me to get those others out of your building?"

"That would be great," I said. She flew me to the nearby fire escape at the neighboring building and flew back to my place. In a matter of moments, she emerged with an unconscious Knuckleduster and Burgundy Basher, giving them both a punitive slam on the ground, while the onlookers filmed it, begging for selfies with Hellmaiden, who just waved them off and flew away, leaving her starfiery trail behind her.

She reached me, looked me over.

"You okay?" she asked.

"I think so," I said. "This is a disaster."

"Do you have other hideouts?" she asked. "Safehouses? A place to go?"

"Yeah," I said. "But I love that brownstone. It's Anna's and mine. I can't abandon it. She won't be able to find me."

Hellmaiden smirked at me. "*Everyone* can find you, now, Mr. Paulsen."

My phone rang, and it was Shane again.

"Mitch, are you okay?" he asked.

"No, I'm not," I said. My face was throbbing from where I'd been struck.

"Well, I've got good news," he said. "The other team members approved your readmission into the Affiliates. You might even have a job as our new PR director."

"There's no way I'm doing PR for the Affiliates," I said. "No way in hell."

Shane laughed. "Can you get to Central?"

I glanced at Hellmaiden, who could apparently hear my call with Shane. She gave me a thumbs up with her white-gloved hand.

"Yeah," I said. "Hellmaiden's here. She can fly me over."

"Perfect," Shane said. "Get over there, then."

"What about my stuff?" I asked. "What about Paleface and Deadpan?"

"Deadpan's missing," Shane said. "Paleface, yeah, maybe a problem, depending on how she reacts. Keep Hellmaiden with you. Let me know when you get there. I'm going to send Tag Team to your place. He'll occupy your brownstone until things settle and will try to manage the crowds."

"Central's a good place for you," Hellmaiden said. "It's safe."

She scooped me up and flew me over there. The heat that came off of her was, despite her care in transporting me, unbelievable. She flew me carefully, at arm's length, which scared the living hell out of me as she made her way across the city, heading toward Central.

It had been over a year since I'd been there, and it was both familiar and alien, as the last time I'd set foot there had been during Anna's funeral.

"Don't worry, Mr. Paulsen," Hellmaiden said. "I won't drop you."

"Call me Mitch," I said. "Do you have a name? Or are you just Hellmaiden all the time?"

"Are you *flirting* with me right now, Mitch?" Hellmaiden asked.

"No, I was just wondering if you had a name," I said. "An actual name, since there's no way you were born with a name like 'Hellmaiden', right?"

She reached Central, and we were scanned by the perimeter defense bots, which cleared us for entry. I felt better setting foot in there after the security doors sealed.

Paleface was waiting in there, wearing her black bodysuit and cape.

"Look at who's returned," Paleface said, showing her fangs. "The prodigal son. And with what? One of his devil-woman groupies?"

Hellmaiden stepped between Paleface and me, hands on her hips.

"You're the, what, vampire-in-residence?" Hellmaiden said. "Why don't you get out of here before you get hurt?"

When I tell you that I really wished I had more than my phone with me to capture this confrontation between a vampire and a devil-woman, because there was a vibe, here.

Paleface shook her head, dividing her focus between Hellmaiden and me.

"I'm *supposed* to be here," she said. "You, on the other hand, are an intruder. I don't care what the Knack says."

"Where's Deadpan, Stasi?" I asked.

"On assignment," Paleface answered. "None of your business."

"Right," I said. "Stasi, can't you just hang back? I'm *really* having a bad day."

Her red eyes slid over me with some feral fusion of displeasure and dislike, while Hellmaiden tugged off the hand gloves that she'd been wearing, exposing her opalescent fingers. She tucked the gloves into the red belt she was wearing, then took off her hood, which lit up the room with her radiant light, which made Paleface hiss and cry out, throwing her arms up to protect herself from Hellmaiden's luminosity, smoke rising up from her limbs and face as she did so.

"Do something, 'Stasi'," Hellmaiden said. "I dare you."

And Paleface did something—she turned into a bat and flew away as quickly as she could, leaving Hellmaiden and me alone in the room. Without my helmet visor, I couldn't look at her directly, either, while she put her cowl back on, dampening her light.

"Pretty amazing," I said.

"Is it?" she asked. "More of a curse than a blessing, I'm afraid."

"Goes with the territory, is my guess," I said.

She managed a smile, her white eyes burning into me, forcing me to look away. "Yeah, well, it's hell on my wardrobe."

I called Shane, told him we'd arrived at Central.

"Good," Shane said. "Any problems with Paleface?"

Looking around us, not seeing any sign of the vampire, I spoke quietly.

"Not as far as I can tell," I said. "Although she wasn't happy to see me."

"Don't worry about her," he said. "Also, Tag Team's secured your brownstone, so you don't have to worry about people trashing your place."

Hellmaiden walked around the place, taking a moment to remove the golden crown she wore, setting it on a table, taking a seat on the ultra-modern chairs, wrapping her cape around herself and stretching her legs, knitting her fingers over her eyes and leaning back. Since Inferna typically popped in and disappeared, it was unusual to see a devil in repose, if that was even the right word for it. What did devils even do in their down time?

"Now I just have to worry about Reg trashing my place," I said. "Incidentally, where's Deadpan? Stasi said he was on assignment."

"He's here in East, being questioned," Shane said.

"Scenester went at me as soon as the news broke," I said. "And he said something weird while, you know, trying to murder me—he said 'Dr. Crimebot.' I think he didn't expect me to survive, so that kind of slipped out."

"Dr. Crimebot," Shane said. "Interesting. I'll look into it. Also, there's something you might want to see in the Equipment Room."

"A new car?" I asked. Shane laughed.

"Better," he said. I went to the Equipment Room and opened it, turning on the lights. This part of Central, like in all Affiliates headquarters, was part workshop and garage, where team members might be able to work on their gear with plenty of room to putter. I'd made use of it when I was here, when working on my assorted camera rigs.

Standing in the room, under the overhead lights, was something under a blue Affiliates tarp.

"Is it the thing under the shroud?" I asked.

"Yep," Shane said. Not wanting to dither, I walked over and yanked off the Affiliates-branded shroud, seeing a stunning blue powersuit standing there with my logo on its chest in white.

"What the hell is this, Shane?" I asked.

"An upgrade, Mitch," Shane said. It was gorgeous, being a fully-articulated armored powersuit. I could see it had shoulder-mounted spotlights, an array of headcams, as well as a host of other streamlined components. "You've done amazing work with your old gear. I felt like your current situation required more, well, firepower."

"Christ, Shane," I said. "You can't give me something like this."

"Of course I can," Shane said. "You're going to need it if you're in the Affiliates again. It's a tactical armored exosuit with a wearable computer framework, independent portable fusion powerplant, with jet thrusters, multiple ports for computer access, stun blasters, electrical threat deterrence, a reactive forcefield system, and even a digital editing suite inside it, for rapid recording and data upload. It has infrared, thermographic, radar, sonar, and other sensor arrays. It has your four-way camouflage options, too."

I walked around it, admiring it. It was amazing.

"How much did this cost you, Shane?" I asked.

"Only like $100 million, Mitch," Shane said. I wanted to fall over.

"You *can't* give something like this to me," I said again, reeling.

"It's yours," Shane said. "It's nothing. You've worked so hard the past dozen years, Mitch. Risked your life and limb trying to bring justice to the world. Why can't I give you the right tool to make sure that you can do it and survive?"

"Yeah, but come on, man," I said. "I'll never be able to repay you. Not ever."

"I'm not looking for repayment," Shane said. "Did I ever tell you about my origin?"

Shane's origin story was very widely known, as I've said elsewhere (*BRIGHTEYES, Chapter 8—the editors*).

"Not directly," I said. "But you told the world. Everybody knows about the plane crash, Shane."

"Not the plane crash," he said. "What led to it. My family had taken us to the Aegean for a vacation. One of those dream trips most people never get to take. We went all through Greece, which my parents loved. I managed to get them to take me to Crete, because I had this obsession with the Minoans, the Bronze Age culture that had lived there. We went to Knossos and Santorini. It's where I think the legend of Atlantis *really* came from—Santorini was where the island of Thera had been, which had been this explosive volcanic eruption that shook the Mediterranean world back then. It had led to the fall of the Minoan culture, and the ruination of Thera. A major civilization of that time, effectively wiped out by that massive, explosive eruption.

"I was fascinated by it as a boy, the cruel whim of fate, time, and place that led to the annihilation of that civilization. And to stand in Santorini, this Greek island existing as the rim of Thera's volcanic crater, it was humbling. It's also where I found the coin. On the beach. I was just walking around, taking in the beauty of it all. I was an only child, and my parents were rich. I wanted for nothing. But I saw that coin in the water, on this rocky Aegean beach. It was an ancient coin, made of silver, and it had Fortuna upon it, blindfolded. On the back, a wheel, with words in Greek on it. The coin was treasure, and I kept it. I didn't tell anyone. If I'd told my parents, they'd have made me put it back where I'd found it, or maybe thrown it into the sea.

"I kept it, and when we flew home, that's when the accident-that-wasn't-an-accident happened, where my father's enemies had struck their blow, and the plane crashed, killing everyone but me. In that moment, my hair turned white, and I knew for a certainty that Fortuna's Coin had saved me. It had been one of those things, but I was convinced of it. If I hadn't kept that coin, maybe my parents wouldn't have died, along with those others."

"Maybe you would have died with them," I said.

"Maybe," Shane said. "In my heart, I knew that Fortuna's Coin had saved me. I've kept it with me ever since, and later, when I became the Knack. It's protected me. I remember paying all of the families of the dead, trying to privately atone for what I saw as my complicity in all of their deaths."

"Shane, it was a coincidence," I said.

"Don't you see, Mitch? I found that coin, and I became the Knack. I've been lucky ever since. I've earned Fortuna's favor. I've been a superhero for as long as you have, and I've tempted fate and pushed my luck dozens of times. As far as it could go, and maybe farther. I've tried to make up for my good fortune by sharing it with others. I've given away my fortune several times, and it always comes back. But I'm also afraid to part with Fortuna's Coin. I know it's why I've been the Luckiest Man Alive. I may be a trillionaire, but it's Fortuna's Coin that made that possible."

"Are you saying your powers are magical? I asked.

"I suppose I am," Shane said. "Maybe I'm trying to balance the celestial scales between us, between the magical and the mechanical."

"Why are you telling me this, Shane?" I asked.

"Mitch, if there's anything I've learned in my life, it's that good fortune's *meant* to be shared, not hoarded away," Shane said. "This is me giving back to you something I know you need. Just take it."

I reached out to touch it, the cool tangibility of it. The dream suit.

"There's no way this just appeared out of nowhere," I said. "This has to have been something you had built awhile ago."

"Yes," Shane said. "I had it made before you left the team. I knew you'd eventually need something like it. I was going to give it to you and then the Anna tragedy happened, and things just went so crazy, I shelved it. Now's the right time."

"Timing's everything," I said, seeing Hellmaiden appear at the entrance to the Equipment Room. Her white eyes went wide at the sight of it, and she flew over.

"Wow," she said. "That's amazing."

"The Knack had it made for me," I said. "I'm still shocked." She clapped her luminescent gloved hands.

"You need to put it on," she said. "Right this instant."

"She's right, Mitch," Shane said. "Try it on."

"They're going to call me 'Irony Man'," I said, making Shane laugh.

"Probably," he said. "But if the suit fits, wear it. It's calibrated with a biolock that'll key to you once you touch it. Just press your palm against your logo in the chest. Call me back when you're in the suit."

I couldn't imagine being this in-debt to Shane. Nobody on Earth could or would ever be so generous. A $100 million powersuit? It was ridiculous. I didn't deserve anything like this. I glanced at Hellmaiden, wishing to hell that Anna was here to see this. She'd have loved it.

**11**

**HELL WASN'T HALF BAD, TO BE HONEST.** At least whatever corner (?) of it that Inferna called home. It was this surreal plain of ice that was alternately dark and snowy and blindingly lit by a malevolent white star. In the center of this endless plain of white was a ghost city of tall buildings that looked more like black monoliths.

I could make out tracks in the satanic snow and ice that marked the footsteps of doomed souls cursed to trudge barefoot across that dire landscape, bearing iron chains around their withered shoulders, wrists, and ankles. They gazed at us with white, sightless eyes. They moaned forlornly while moving in a massive counterclockwise circle, over and over again, spiraling outward from the monolithic metropolis.

Inferna watched me watching them.

"Don't mind them," she said. "They're tourists."

My feet boiled the snow, making steam with every step, and burned the black, stony ground. On a whim, I fell backward into the hellish snow, creating rivulets as I made an ice angel, my skin making the ice hiss and crack. Inferna scoffed.

*"That's* what you do with your newfound freedom? Making a snow angel in Hell?"

I flew up, taking a peek at my handiwork, pleased that I'd melted right through the ice to the black stone underneath.

"It's a mood," I said. "I *really* missed snow."

I landed next to her, while she walked us into the empty city, pointing upward, her wings flaring out, catching the air, taking her upward. I flew after her.

"I thought you were exiled from Hell," I asked.

"I am," she said. "This is, oh, I don't know, backwater Hell. Far from where the *real* action is."

"So, Christianity's legit?" I asked.

"Gods, no," Inferna said, cackling as she winged her way to the top of one of the black buildings. "Hell is a state of mind, not a destination. Certainly not what they put in the holy books. What did those people know? Nothing. We're in a whole new dimension, Victoriana."

"And yet here we are," I said, glancing at her horns as she landed on a kind of deck made from fiery red wood that had grained patterns of screaming faces intertwined in them. She rolled her eyes.

"People *like* horns," she said. "They can understand them. Ergo...."

"Is this place yours?" I asked.

"Afraid so," she said. "This is where I'm exiled until I clean up my act."

There were plants on this uncanny deck—grey cacti with blood-red spikes, and mangled plants with black leaves that bore purple fruit on them that looked juicy and temptingly delicious.

"Don't eat those," Inferna said, when I'd taken one in hand to admire it. Like a purple pear.

"No?" I asked. She shook her head, directing me to a dining table indoors, which was covered with roast meats of all sorts, sumptuous fruits (including those purple pears, which apparently had black interiors, and which were safe when poached, according to Inferna), cakes, pies of all kinds. Having not eaten for a year, I promptly sat down and dug in. I'd forgotten how good it felt to eat, not caring that my hands made the meat sizzle and the fruit catch fire.

Inferna sat nearby, laughing to herself and pouring some black wine, which she drank from a very large goblet. She divined that I was a beer drinker, and pointed to a deep tankard made of pewter filled with a red-hued beer which I tentatively drank, and decided was delicious.

"Hellbrew," Inferna said. "Very popular."

"Wow," I said, feasting. Everything tasted wonderful. I didn't realize how much I missed eating until I was doing it.

"It's good, yes?" Inferna said. "Real soul food."

"Gods, yes," I said, gorging. I seriously noshed for about a half an hour, eating and drinking, while Inferna toyed with her wine, and talked about the things I'd missed while I'd been gone.

"Everyone thinks you're dead," she said. "I had a hunch that you weren't. You know, that gives you an opportunity. You could leave superheroism behind. Build a new life. Here, if you wanted. Plenty to do. Lots of fun for someone like you."

The glow I had been emitting was already settling down to something more latent.

"No, I belong on Earth," I said. "Not that this isn't...interesting. Not at all what I imagined."

"Lake of Fire, am I right?" Inferna said.

"This doesn't feel like eternal torment to me," I said, and Inferna chuckled, her silvery forked tongue flicking as she did so.

"It's different for tenants, versus, you know, the others," she said. "The unfortunates."

"Hey, is Minder here?" I asked. "I mean, if he's dead. Wouldn't he be here?"

Inferna cackled, throwing her head back and drinking down her wine.

"That's funny, Victoriana," she said. "You know, he just might be. We do snatch souls when we can. Do you want me to find out?"

"Yes!" I said. "Honestly, I'd love that."

Inferna leered at me, drumming her black-nailed fingers on the table.

"What's it worth to you? What do you offer in trade?" she asked.

"What do you want?" I asked.

"What else? Souls," she said. "We trade in souls in this dimension."

The casual way she said it, I had to dig a little deeper, and she didn't seem to mind my asking, just poured more wine while I ate some honeyed hellcakes, which were sinfully sweet.

"Do you have Mitch's soul?" I asked.

"Not yet," Inferna said. "He owes me favors, but it's a running tab."

"Wait, wait, wait," I said, wiping my mouth with the back of my hand before downing some more of that incredible, frosty hellbrew. "Are you angling for Mitch's soul?"

Inferna rested her pointy chin on her hand as she stared at me down her pointy nose.

"Mitch saved me from servitude under Sergeant Sorcery," she said, pointing to a painting on her wall that depicted Sergeant Sorcery, who was grimacing at us from the frame. "Yeah, that's actually him. He'd bound me with enchantments, but Mitch broke those, so I owe him for the duration of his life. I'd love to bring him here with me. I think he'd have a blast filming documentaries, to be honest. There's so much to see here."

"Whoa," I said. "He's with me."

"For now," Inferna said. "I'm talking death, here. After death."

"No, I mean, he's *mine*," I said. "Like eternally."

Inferna just thought that was hilarious, drinking her wine.

"If you say so," she said. "But honestly, look at you—if flying into the Sun couldn't kill you, who says you can even die? Maybe you won't even get old. All that solar energy you absorbed, you've probably got a lifetime's supply of life in you."

I couldn't tell if she was making fun of me or not. That was the problem with a devil-woman; she could be extra-complicated.

"You can't have Mitch," I said.

"So, we're back to what you are willing to trade," Inferna said. "I may be in exile, but I bet I could pull some strings to see if Minder's here. Think of what that might be worth to you, like a chance to get the Last Word. That's worth it, if you ask me. We're big on the Last Word down here."

I didn't like to think of Mitch growing old and dying, and me maybe not. I liked even less him being in this kind of fabulous damnation condominium with a clearly cool devil-woman like Inferna to keep him company for eternity. She totally read my mind and smirked at me.

"He'd *love* it here," she said.

"You're being mean, now," I said. "You're tormenting me."

"I can't help it," Inferna said. "Oh, that reminds me—I should show you my other guests. You know the Trinity?"

I did, of course, because I told you already I tracked all the supers in the business as part of my research. And you've already read about the Trinity being released by Inferna, thanks to Hellmaiden. Obviously, this is taking place before that happened. That's right—you're still stuck in my flashback place, my memories. Deal with it!

"They're my prisoners...sorry, guests...no, prisoners, for real," she said. "I captured them in that big fight we had with Minder and his crew."

"Wow," I said. "You've had them here for a year?"

Inferna did the calculations in her head, counting on her fingers, mouthing numbers.

"Time passes differently in this dimension, but, yeah, it's been a year," she said. "Come on. I have to show you. Bring your beer if you like."

Her place was better than I imagined it would be. All over her walls were the mounted heads of fearsome creatures unfamiliar to me, as well as thick rugs that bore patterns of anguish and torment upon them in red and black, showing hapless souls wrapped tightly in black thorny brambles, their faces full of agony.

She had three bedrooms—a master bedroom with an iron frame bed strewn with blankets of red and black, as well as thick pillows. There was also a diabolical vanity with a mirror on one side, and I walked over to it, gazing at myself, seeing my luminous self, all white-eyed with no hair and the glowing skin.

"Christ," I said. "I *literally* look like hell."

Inferna came up behind me and smiled as she had before. Up close, I could see she had this wild smile, almost a parody of a smile, or a caricature of glee.

"You look fantastic," Inferna said. "You'd fit right in around here. Wait just a sec."

She walked over to these massive closets with iron doors, sliding them smoothly on runners, and she went inside, rooting around, before coming back out with some shiny white leather, like boots and a sleeveless catsuit.

"What the hell is that?" I asked.

"Clothing," Inferna said. "What's the problem?"

The boots were thigh-high, pointy-toed with stiletto heels, and the catsuit left little to the imagination.

"I'm not wearing this," I said.

"Oh, don't be such a prude," Inferna said. "What happens in Hell, stays in Hell. Suit up, Victoriana. I bet I have a red cape in there, too, if that would make you feel more comfortable."

I put on the catsuit, muttering about devils and temptation, zipping the thing up, and put on the boots, while Inferna emerged with a fiendishly frayed crimson cape, which she handed over to me.

"Look at you," she said. "Victoriana reborn."

I put on the cape, embarrassed. I looked like a satanic superheroine, most certainly.

"The white works with your rosy glow," Inferna said. "You look like a fallen angel. Picture perfect."

She snapped her finger, and a full-body painting of me in that costume appeared on her wall, and I will admit that it looked badass as a portrait.

"Until your hair grows back, you need this," Inferna said, holding out a golden circlet, which was more like a crown, with pointy prongs radiating from it. "Seriously, put it on."

I did, and on my glowing bald head, it looked fabulous. My sun-baked stern countenance looked imperious as hell with that crown. I looked regal as fuck. Best of all, the crown hovered over my head, moving with me.

"Princess Purgatory," Inferna said, giving me a little spin. "Gods, I'm good. Okay, let's go visit my guests."

We walked down to a lower level in her copious condo, coming to a six-celled dungeon, with only three of the cells occupied—with Angelica, Crucifixer, and the Inquisitor.

"Whoa," I said. "That's Angelica, Crucifixer, and the Inquisitor."

"Very good," Inferna said, producing a firewhip out of nowhere. At the sight of it, the members of the Trinity began wailing.

"Umm, what are *they* doing here?" I asked.

"Atoning," Inferna said, flexing the whip between her hands, snapping it tight with a crack that threw off some sparks. "They've been *very* bad."

"Help us," Angelica said. "We've been prisoners of this devil."

"Release us, we beg you," the Inquisitor said. "Whoever you are."

"Quiet, you," Inferna said. "And keep it down. We have a guest."

They looked exhausted but otherwise unharmed.

"We don't belong here," Crucifixer said. "We're part of God's chosen *Real* American army."

"You really should let them go," I said, which had the Trinity nodding and chattering in agreement, at least until Inferna cracked her fiery whip at them, which shut them all up.

Inferna cracked the whip at him specifically, which made him back away from the bars, flinching. It was upsetting to see this, even if I wasn't a fan of the Trinity. They didn't belong here any more than I did.

"It's the right thing to do," I said. "You don't want to just sit down here and torture them eternally, do you?"

Inferna shrugged. "It's what I do. Oh, I'll probably let them loose one of these days. Provided they atone. They're *very* prideful, sinful."

She gave them meaningful glowers, before making her fiery whip vanish with a snap of her fingers. Inferna walked me to another room, another deck in her rather Modernist abode— it was a Mephistophelian Malibu Mansion, to my eyes. This other deck had an infinity pool and lounge chairs, offering a great view of the sinister skyline. She took a seat, and I sat beside her.

"Life in exile is boring," she said. "I only brought the Trinity here to pass the time. I love when Mitch calls me out of this place."

At mention of Mitch, my heart ached.

"How does that work?" I asked.

"He calls my name, and I hear him," Inferna said, taking delight in that particular intimacy she enjoyed with him, something that predated me. "Wherever he is, I'm there for him. And for you, if you're willing. Friend of a friend, as it were."

She just let that dangle, and I got up, walking to the infinity pool, stepping into it, not caring that I was wearing the clothes she'd lent me, amazed at the gouts of steam that arose as I went into the water. I actually swam, despite the steam. It felt good to swim. How I'd missed the feel of water.

Inferna pulled her chair up closer to watch me go back and forth, the pool refilling even as I created clouds of steam.

"You just need to relax here awhile," Inferna said. "This place will do you good. A kind of hellspa."

"Hell will do me good, eh?" I asked, laughing. She almost looked sad, and I felt ridiculous having this conversation with her.

"Can you deliver a message to Mitch for me?" I asked. Inferna narrowed her eyes at me.

"What sort of message?" she asked.

"Something so he knows I'm not gone," I said.

"Sentimental," she said, half to herself. "He's not forgotten you."

"Yeah," I said. "Still, can you do that for me? While I'm recovering?"

Inferna thought about it a bit, crossing her arms, rolling her eyes.

"You already owe me big-time for rescuing you," she said. "I didn't have to do that, you know. I could have left you there, sweltering on the Sun."

I didn't know how to negotiate with a devil exactly. Philosophically, there were all manner of permutations to consider.

"I'm very, very grateful you rescued me," I said. "I was giving serious thought to planet-jumping my way to Earth before you came."

Inferna reluctantly agreed.

"That might've worked," she said. "Although you could have gotten lost very easily. My way, I can get you right there."

"Okay," I said. "I owe you."

Inferna liked hearing that, I could tell. I had no doubt she'd accumulated a bunch of markers on all sorts of souls. Whatever she was, wherever she came from, however much of an exile she was, a devil was still going to afflict people.

"You owe me for the rescue, for the lodging, for delivering a message to Mitch," she said.

"I hoped you'd done all of this out of the goodness of your heart," I said, which made Inferna snort.

"What goodness?" she asked. "I'm an Artisan of Obligation. I help, and, in turn, I am helped. Terribly transactional. What about Minder? You want me to look into that whole Last Word business I tempted you with earlier?"

And I'll confess that it *was* tempting. I had to see Minder one last time, if only to gloat.

"Yes, I do," I said. "But I can't see him like this. I need to look more like myself, not some fiery hellmaiden."

"'Hellmaiden'," Inferna said. "Gods, yes. That's the *perfect* name for you. Oh, the irony."

And she snapped her fingers, pointing to me while I sat there, befogging the deck in her ever-replenishing pool, the water bubbling like a hot tub. She'd magicked a logo on me— an "HM" in white, wrapped in a red fireball, hanging from a choker on my neck, the logo a medallion.

"You pay me back with service as Hellmaiden," she said. "In fact, you can lead an infernal antiheroine team I just dreamed up—Hell's Belles—Gods, I'm good. You, me, and one more. Has to be three. Hmmm..."

I didn't want to be dragooned into some girl group, but Inferna wasn't having any of it. She even argued it out with me.

"Right now, Victoriana's reputation is secured," she said. "Sad story, heroic journey ending in untimely suicide. All of that evaporates if you reappear out of nowhere. All of that emotional capital gets spent upon your return. When you come back, you need to do so in style. We'll figure out the story—since you don't want to be revealing to the world that you were saved by the likes of me. That won't play in prime time. Therefore, you do some hero work for me as part of Hell's Belles while you're healing up. Then, when you're ready, you can come back as Victoriana."

"What sort of work do you have in mind?" I asked.

"Taking down some really nasty folks," Inferna said. "I only go after the worst of the worst, you know."

She snapped her fingers, and the circlet crown on my head flashed a moment, sending tingles throughout my body.

"What'd you do?" I asked, reaching up to touch it.

"You'll love it," Inferna said. "I've enchanted that crown, so anyone who wears it can become Hellmaiden. You'll be the first one, of course, and will shape the Hellmaiden look for all subsequent versions. Super-strong, invulnerable, can throw fiery bolts of plasma hellfire. Yes. It's perfect. She burns brightly with a passion for justice!"

Despite myself, I laughed at her panache for presentation.

"I'll do it, on the condition that you release the Trinity," I said. "They've suffered enough."

"Ha," Inferna said. "You're wrong, but I'll do that, provided you help me out on three cases as Hellmaiden."

"Fine," I said. "So long as I get to gloat over Minder."

"Okay. Now," Inferna said, gazing skyward, where I could see the cloud I'd made flowing through the empty city, bending around the stony high-rises. "About that third member. There's you, the powerhouse. Me, the all-around troubleshooter without peer. Christ, why can't I think of the third?"

She got to her feet, pacing back and forth, while I slipped out of the pool, watching the water steam off my body. I prayed I'd cool down at some point.

"Hey, while you're thinking of that, can you drop off something at Mitch's?" I asked. "There are these beer can ball bearings I make. It's just a habit of mine. I crunch them into these aluminum balls. Leave one in the wooden bowl on our coffee table. Like a memento."

Inferna laughed at me.

"I was thinking of writing 'Mitch, I live!' in blood on his bathroom mirror, but your idea's fine, I guess," she said. "I mean, will he *know* it's you?"

"He should," I said. "We kept them in a jar."

"Okay," Inferna said. "You know, I'm excited about Hell's Belles. I can see the tee shirts—there'd be a pitchfork, and the letters would look both girly and fiery. Yeah, there's marketing to be done, I can feel it. I just need to think of that third member."

"I'll think of someone," I said, impressed that I didn't need to towel off because the water had sizzled off of me. "What about She-Devil?"

She-Devil was an antihero who had been possessed, led two lives—one as an occult librarian, the other as her devilish incarnation, which was this red monstrosity with horns and claws. Her real name was Tamara Sorrows. I remembered that because Mitch and I had needed her help to deal with Doctor Damnation, a wizard keen on ending the world as we knew it.

"She-Devil," Inferna said. "Yes. I'll talk to her when I'm running that errand for you. In the meantime, make yourself at home, Hellmaiden."

**PRESSING MY PALM INTO THE CHEST, THE SUIT HUMMED TO LIFE** and opened up, the breastplate unlocking and exposing an internal cockpit. Moving cautiously, I stepped into it, gasping as it closed up and locked, the internal systems kicking into action.

"Systems online," came the internal computer. The voice sounded like C3.

"C3?" I asked.

"Yes, Mitch," C3 said. "What can I help you with?"

I took a few steps in the suit, marveling at the smooth way it moved, mindful of the camera displays, which offered me both line-of-sight and rearview screens. I could also see there were three on-board mini-drones I could launch, as well as bug and minicam relays (three each, respectively).

A call dialed in, identified as Shane. I wasn't sure how to open the line, so I just said "Answer that call, C3" and it connected me to a FaceTime call with Shane, who was smiling at me on another pop-up window.

"There you are, Mitch," Shane said. "Looking good."

"Shane, this is entirely too much," I said, walking around. I could see Hellmaiden watching. I adjusted the filters and could see her without squinting.

"It's just enough," Shane said. "Honestly, with Credible outing you, you've bounced to the top of the criminal underworld's hit lists. You're going to need another civilian secret identity. Oh, and the exoskeleton augments your strength. You should be able to lift around five tons with it. I didn't have them magnify the strength too much, since that would require adding more bulk to the servos, and I assumed you'd prefer stealth over strength."

"You know me so well," I said. "Shane, I'm just speechless."

"That's a first," Shane said. "You should probably train with it a bit before setting off."

"Shane, Anna's alive," I said.

"I know," he said.

"Wait, you know?"

"Yep," he said. "Inferna told me."

"Inferna?" I asked. "How does *she* know?"

Shane sighed, what he always did when I was somehow vexing him.

"She's an infernal investigator," Shane said. "She makes it her business to know."

I wasn't one for beating around the burning bush on this one, however. I wanted answers.

"Where is Anna, Shane?" I asked. "Seriously, you can't just dangle that out there and not help me out."

"Hello?" Hellmaiden said, waving. I found the intercom and had C3 activate it.

"What's up?" I asked.

"Are you just going to walk around in that thing or are you going out?" she asked.

"Sorry, just kicking the tires a bit," I said. "I'll be out in a few minutes."

"Okay," she said.

"That was Hellmaiden?" Shane asked.

"Yeah," I said. "She saved my life at the brownstone, with Scenester, Knuckleduster, and the Burgundy Basher."

"Tag mentioned they were laid out in front of your place," Shane said. "Not Scenester, but the other two."

"Where's Anna, Shane?" I asked.

"She's recovering," Shane said. "I haven't seen her, but she's apparently recovering."

I couldn't imagine what might have happened to her while on the Sun. First off, I was amazed she'd even survived it. By itself, that was incredible. However, I didn't like the idea of her even having to recover.

"How badly is she injured?" I asked.

"Inferna wouldn't tell me more," Shane said. "Only that she's alright, and that you'd see her very soon."

"Fuck!" I said. "Okay, Shane. I'm calling her right now."

I hung up on Shane and figured out how to get out of the Cameraman armor, hopping to the ground. Hellmaiden laughed at the sight of me.

"Wow, are you okay?" she said.

"Inferna," I said, which brought Inferna, as it always had before. She was wearing a black wraparound dress with a skinny red belt and red thigh boots, as well as a red cloche hat and long black gloves, and was holding a gold-trimmed martini glass filled with some blood-red beverage.

"You rang, Mitch?" she asked, glancing at Hellmaiden, who shrugged.

"Where's Anna?" I asked. Inferna smiled at me in that predatory way she had.

"She's doing me some favors, Mitch," Inferna said. "She owed me for, you know, rescuing her. She's paying me back for that. Afterward, she's all yours, I assure you."

"Christ," I said. "Fern, you've known where she is all this time? That she's alive, and you didn't tell me?"

Inferna sneered at me, rolling her eyes.

"You never asked, Mitch. You're the detective," she said. "I just assumed you'd, you know, *detect* her."

I was livid, wanted to stomp up and down, but composed myself. She couldn't help herself. She was a devil. Devils did shit like this.

"I've been busy," I said. "Credible leaked my secret identity and it's been a mess ever since. And where have *you* been, anyway?"

"Busy," Inferna said. "You're not my *only* client, Mitch. Besides, you were in good company. Hellmaiden already saved your life earlier tonight, yes?"

Client? She called me her client? What the hell was that, even?

"I just need to talk to Anna," I said. "I need to see her."

Inferna held up her long-fingered hand, shaking her head.

"Impossible, I'm afraid," she said. "If I were to reunite the two of you right now, you'd *both* be useless to me. Absolutely useless. As it stands, I need the two of you focused on the tasks I have for you, which involves dealing with Theo Strong and Lethalia in Cincinnati."

"She'll be there?" I asked. "Anna will be there?"

"I can assure you that she will be," Inferna said. "You're going to need her. Lethalia's no slouch."

Inferna's eyes went to the powersuit, and she actually walked up to it, sensually caressing it with her hand, letting out a sigh, then sipping her bloody martini.

"Shane is the most thoughtful gifter," she said. "You'll look smashing in this, Mitch. Don't you think, Hellmaiden?"

"Oh, yes," Hellmaiden said.

I rubbed my temples, trying massage away my frustration. This had to be why it was called being "bedeviled"—I felt it, like being in some kind of emotional-spiritual taffy pull.

"Alright," I said. "I help you with this Theo Strong, and I'm off your hook, yes?"

"Mmmaybe," Inferna said. "You didn't help us with Mr. Duncan, so I think you maybe still owe me. Funny that your archrival turned up there when *you* didn't."

"Yeah, funny." I said. The idea that Inferna had rescued Anna and hadn't told me actually wounded me a little. She must have sensed that in her uncanny way because she pursed her lips and reached out, stroking my chin.

"Don't be that way, Mitch," she said. "Anna was very glad to see me, wasn't she, Hellmaiden?"

"Yeah," Hellmaiden said. "Ecstatic, even."

"A year on the Sun by herself," Inferna said. "A hellish fate for anyone when you think about it. All by herself in the monstrous abyss of space, wandering half-blind, away from you. One wonders how she could bear it."

"Stop," I said. I couldn't stand the thought of her suffering by herself. It crushed me.

"No, Mitch," she said. "She's so strong. I can't imagine many who might have been able to endure that with their sanity intact, to say nothing of their bodies."

"Why didn't you tell me?" I asked. "It's cruel that you didn't tell me."

Inferna laughed, circling me and Hellmaiden in a lazy eight as she strolled.

"I do so try to be good, Mitch," she said. "But I'm afraid that cruelty's embedded in the heart of every devil, my lovely Cameraman. Even those of us trying to shake our baser natures."

I seethed, then composed myself again.

"No tricks, Fern," I said. "I want to see Anna after all of this owing you business is through."

"You will," Inferna said, flashing her eyes at me flirtatiously while downing the rest of her martini. "I don't think you'll ever not owe me something, though."

She vanished again in a brimstone cloud, leaving Hellmaiden and me alone in the room. I turned my attention to her.

"You saw her?" I asked. Hellmaiden nodded.

"She was okay?" I asked.

"What do you mean?" she replied.

"Unharmed is what I mean," I asked.

Hellmaiden considered her reply before speaking. The way she did so made me wonder what she might be hiding. Was Anna deformed?

"She's strong," she said. "The Sun didn't destroy her, if that's what you're worried about."

"I just want to know if she's okay," I said.

"She will be," Hellmaiden said. "She's a fast healer."

"Christ," I said. "So, she is injured."

She reached out for me, then caught herself.

"She's healing," she said. "That's all I can say."

"Fuck," I said. "Who knew devils could be so elliptical and obtuse?"

"I'm not a devil," Hellmaiden said, flipping back her cowl, filling the room with that blinding light she threw off. "See? No horns. Horns are the hallmark of deviltry. All devils have horns."

She turned her head this way and that, and I couldn't look at her directly because of the glare. I went back to the Cameraman suit and put it on, having C3 adjust the visual acuity filters so I could see her more clearly.

"Okay, so then what are you? If you tell me you're an angel, I'm going to throw up," I said. Hellmaiden stared at me a moment before heaving a big sigh.

"*I'm* Anna, you dope!" she said, giving a stomp on the ground. "Christ, Mitch. What kind of detective are you?"

The bottom dropped out of my brain.

"What?" I said. She put her hands on her hips and glowered at me while I spat out some more words. "Is this some kind of devil trick?"

"Mitch, it's me," she said. "I'm goddamned Anna."

"Prove it," I said. "Tell me something only Anna would know."

"Fair enough," she said. "You used to try to move objects with your mind when you were a little boy and were sad when you realized you'd never be a telekinetic, which is why you thought Blitz was the bomb."

"Anna?" I said, opening the suit, stumbling out. She brought the cowl down on her head, which dampened the blinding light she threw. I gave her a big hug, heedless that I might have risked incinerating myself. As such, the hellish leather she wore only meant she was hot to the touch. I felt her arms around me, careful not to touch me with her opalescent skin.

"Mitch," she said. "It's really me."

"Holy Christ," I said, my eyes welling up with tears. "All this time? What the hell?"

She let me go, turned her burning white eyes on me.

"I'm healing," she said. "That time on the Sun messed me up a bit. I'm still me, but, you know, different. Inferna *did* rescue me. I didn't want to go with her, but it was the quickest way to get out of there. To be able to be with you."

I tried to look her over through my crying eyes. Of course it had been her. Even during the fights, it was so her. How could I have not seen it?

"Okay," I said. "Please tell me you're not, like Inferna's soul slave or something."

"No," Anna said, putting on her hand gloves. "I'm working off the debt while I heal."

"You seem pretty damned strong to me," I said. "You turned Volcanis into charcoal briquettes."

She smiled at that.

"I'll admit that it felt so good to do that," she said. "To be able to let somebody really have it."

"You'll not be, uh, like this forever, right?" I asked. She laughed, shaking her head.

"Okay," I said. "Because I'd like to be able to kiss you without bursting into flames."

She brought her gloved fingers to her lips and kissed them, touched them to my lips, and I survived.

"Soon," she said. "In the meantime, let's go kick evil's ass, Babe."

## 13

SHUTTERBUG HAD RUN WITH THE WHOLE "Mitch Paulsen is dealing with devils" angle to drag my name through the dirt. She had garnered photos of me with Hellmaiden, Inferna, and She-Devil, and through Caryn Underwood, had widely pushed that until it had whipped up moral avengers, who'd picketed outside of my brownstone with handmade signs:

MITCH PAULSEN = SATAN

DEVIL WORSHIPPER!

SATAN, INC.

CAMERAMAN IS A SICKO PERV

When I made my debut appearance in the Cameraman powersuit, people went ballistic. Anna accompanied me as Hellmaiden, which I was still wrapping my head around. We'd had a long talk that night when she'd told me that. I had felt like a complete idiot for not connecting the dots.

My excuse was that I hadn't been prepared to see something like that, and with her whole "radiant nimbus" thing going on, I wasn't in any position to see her clearly. I'd grabbed a welding helmet and wore it while talking to her, so I could gaze at her with a greater degree of impunity and not burn out my retinas.

"Excuses, excuses," she said, drinking beer from this hellacious tankard she said she'd picked up from Inferna's place. She told me all about that place, about Inferna's exiled Oblivion City.

"That's a great name for it," I said. "Should be an album title."

She drank from the tankard, nodding. "Or the title of your documentary of Hell?"

"Boom," I said. "I'm so glad you're back, Anna."

"Getting there," Anna said. "Believe me, Mitch, it's been a journey. When I first saw you, I had to resist the urge to just grab you, because, you know, incineration."

I was just so happy to see her, even in this otherworldly incarnation I couldn't even properly touch. We'd just periodically clasp hands, protected by those Hell-gloves she wore. We laughed about that, being forced to be neo-Victorian models of restraint by the machinations of a devil-woman.

"I'm happy," I said. "You're here. That's all I need."

She smiled.

"I'm glad I'm here," she said. "If I had to tour another sunspot, I would have died of boredom."

Just seeing her there, even as she was; it meant the world to me. She looked beautiful, like some avenging angel.

"You're just *always* a badass," I said. "That's the one constant, you know?"

"Is it?" she asked, sipping her beer impishly. "With that new powersuit, though, I'm thinking you can play the badass, too, Sexy."

I shrugged, although I admit I couldn't wait to take that sucker out, see what it was capable of. I know you're probably laughing at me, me wanting to be the audiovisual avenger, but come on, how perfect was it?

"I'm always playing the badass," I said. "At least this way, I might not get banged up as routinely as before."

She drank down her beer and set the tankard down to one side, leaned on her elbows, her eyes narrowed.

"Whose ass are we kicking next, Babe?" she asked.

"Shutterbug's just a nuisance," I said. "Honestly. Once she blows her wad, I don't see her as much of a threat, compared with Dr. Crime—or Dr. Crimebot."

I told her what Scenester had told me, and she nodded.

"What do you think that meant? Dr. Crime merged with Crimebot, maybe?" she asked.

"Sure," I said. "Some sick symbiotic thing. Dr. Crime is middle-aged and was likely thinking about his mortality. Crimebot maybe deduced that it would beneficial for them to merge. I can see it—build out a powerful robot body, and then port Dr. Crime's brain into that chassis."

"All this from a single word uttered by a sadistic teleporter," Anna said.

"Hey, I'm just speculating," I said. "I think maybe we should bust up the Crime League. Shutterbug works for the Crime League. She's just the beat reporter for evil—let's go to the source."

Anna grinned at that, clapping her hands together.

"You *know* I like that," she said.

"They don't realize who you are," I said. "That's my guess. That's something we can use to our advantage."

"You and me versus the Crime League," Anna said. "That's hot, Babe."

We laughed as she licked a fingertip and made it sizzle against her opalescent hip.

"You're assuming we could just take them all out," I said.

She nodded. "Reckless? Maybe, maybe. But it would send a message, what, with all the pettifogging Minder had done over the years. Busting the Crime League would definitely show that we're through being the nice guys."

I laughed, and she just nodded.

"After the year I've had, Babe, I'm dead serious," she said. "Fuck evil."

"Fuck evil," I said, raising a fist, which she bumped.

"Here's how I see it," she said. "We find out where their main base is. And maybe we get your Shutterclique people rounded up and we get them aboard an Affilijet, and we just storm the castle. We triumph, you film it all, and we rock the world."

I always liked her exuberance. With her, anything seemed possible.

"You can't tell me that Brighteyes wouldn't be down for that," she said.

"Yeah," I said. "You know, Hellmaiden's already got a pretty solid following. You'll be stratospheric if we do something like that."

She reflected on that with a daydreamy nod.

"So weird what people like," she said. "I mean, Victoriana's me. I'm Victoriana. But the world thinks she's dead. Not sure how I play that out. My family thinks I'm dead. I haven't disabused them of that since coming back."

"You'll need to at some point," I said.

"Yeah, but not like this," she said. "Believe me, if they couldn't handle me as Victoriana, they'd *never* be able to handle me as Hellmaiden."

We laughed again, and I drank another beer, while she snagged my empty can and melted it in her fingertips, which was incredible and more than a little frightening.

"Yeah," she said, pouring the molten aluminum between her hands, almost playfully. "This could be you, Mitch. If I lost control for a moment. That's why I was afraid to tell you who I was."

"I don't care," I said. "You're you. All I care about."

"Oh, you," she said. Then Paleface came in, which sort of ruined the mood. She looked at us both, giving us a fanged grimace.

"Adorable," she said, dodging the molten aluminum Anna flicked at her, hissing as it hit the floor. "Really, Hellmaiden?"

"Oh, hell, yeah," Anna said, hopping up. "Isn't it past your bedtime?"

Paleface gave us a gustily baroque laugh, actually throwing her head back.

"I heard you two scheming about the Crime League," she said. "I know where they operate. Their headquarters."

She looked at each of us, and I thought maybe she wasn't bullshitting us. Or else maybe it was a trap.

"What're you proposing?" I asked, quickly turning on my digital voice recorder.

"Not-killing me, in return for information," she said.

"*Correct* information," Anna said. "That's most important."

Paleface feigned being wounded at the prospect that we might doubt her veracity. She blithely walked to one of the chairs opposite us and took her seat. It took a degree of bravado on her part.

"I'm no hero," she said. "However, I also like the perks I've enjoyed while being part of this Affiliates business. It offers me a measure of security, and when you're my age, that brings some peace of mind."

"The medical plan is robust," I said. Anna leaned harder on her elbows.

"How do we know you're not just setting us up?" Anna asked.

"I suppose you don't," she said. "What's the word of a vampire worth in today's currency?"

"Squat," Anna said. "All I can offer is that if you set us up, I'll come for you, wherever you are. And we'll watch the Sun rise together."

Paleface grimaced again at that, shaking her head.

"You have a singular hatred in you, Hellmaiden," she said. "I'm perhaps afraid of you."

"Spill it," I said. "Where's the Crime League hiding out? And also, what do you know of Dr. Crime's big plan?"

She acted blasé about it, but I doubted she was.

"Crime worked with Minder," she said. "I wasn't privy to those meetings, but the way it was supposed to work was the League would get members at every branch, with the understanding that they'd provide information to the League, as well as tip off the League any time there were any sorts of actions. Minder did as much as well, but this was Crime's side plan. The man always had backup plans."

"Had?" I asked.

"Yes," she said. "Dr. Crime merged with Crimebot. They now call themselves 'Dr. Crimebot'—but you discovered that already, didn't you? The plan is that they'll be twice as effective as a cyborg."

That made me remember something else.

"The Enemies of Humanity," I said. "This is part of that?"

I could see from her reaction that she was surprised I knew about it.

"Clever Mitch," she said. "Yes. I'm part of that organization. It's independent of the League. Invitation-only."

That made a strange sort of sense—robots and undead? Why not?

"Kind of on the nose," I said. "Aliens, too? Alien invaders?"

"How do you know this?" she asked.

"Just following the logic where it leads me," I said. Paleface shifted in her seat a bit, trying to appear casually indifferent.

"Seems like you need to share with us the location of the Enemies of Humanity, too," Anna said. "And the membership."

Then there was something I wasn't entirely prepared for—she looked scared. I'll admit I didn't have much experience with vampires, but I knew fear when I saw it.

"Spill it," I said.

"They'll kill me," she said. I did a mental inventory of the League, who could be part of the Enemies of Humanity:

- DR. CRIMEBOT
- DEATHCLOWN
- DOLLFACE
- SCENESTER
- ICE QUEEN
- PALEFACE
- SERPENTINA
- MS. FORTUNE
- JOHNNY RUBICON
- SHUTTERBUG

Her eyes widened as I named them, and I knew I was onto something.

"How can you know this?" she asked.

"Logic," I said. "The Enemies of Humanity have to be defined by their opposition to the human race. That means there'd have to be several aspects to it—artificial life, the undead, mutant superhumans, demons and devils, fascists—anybody who was operating under the presumption that humans were part of the problem and needed to be destroyed."

"You can't know this," Paleface said.

"I'm right, though," I said. "Aren't I?"

I thought about Inferna's casework. Was she dealing with people associated with these Enemies of Humanity? Why hadn't she told me about that, as well? Was she part of this secret society? I couldn't believe or accept that.

"Tell us where they're at," Anna said, reaching for her cowl, which made Paleface flinch.

"I'll give up the Crime League," she said. "But not the Enemies. Deathclown could know. He would know."

"Deathclown," I said, scoffing. The Affiliates had only battled with him twice, both times before I'd joined the team. I made a mental note to go through the dossiers of those members I suspected, and then cross-reference the entire Affiliates enemies roster for possible candidates.

There was a weird kind of logic to this, as well—Dr. Crimebot would have organized the Enemies along lines like: Technology, Magic, Eugenics, Alien. I could see that happening. Then something else occurred to me, so I asked Paleface.

"Was Minder part of the Enemies of Humanity?" I asked.

"Yes," she said. "You are an astute man, Mitch."

It went far deeper than the Crime League. If anything, the Crime League was the front for the Enemies of Humanity.

"What's the mission of the Enemies?" I asked. Paleface hesitated, but Anna flexed and she stammered out an answer.

"The enslavement and extinction of the human race," she said. "The recognition that the species is itself an existential threat to life on Earth, and that we must organize for our own survival at the expense of your species."

Now, my paranoia was a rich, potentially limitless fuel source, but I found it hard to believe Paleface would just give up this information so readily.

"Why are you telling us this?" I asked.

She looked at Anna with true dread in her beautifully vampiric face.

"Because I want to live," she said. "Or to continue this unlife. Whatever you want to call it. I have no doubt your devil-woman friend could end me. I want to be allied with the winning team."

"About that," I said. "Are there devils who are part of the Enemies?"

"Of course there are," Paleface said. "Lord Ruthven and Lethalia. Volcanis the demon."

And there it was. Inferna *was* working the extra-dimensional underworld angles. That made more sense to me.

"How do the Enemies recruit members?" I asked.

"Anyone meeting the requirements—they must be exceptional in some way," she said. "Wealthy, brilliant, powerful. That's all that matters, as well as, you know, a hostility to humanism. Crimebot doesn't care, so long as they fit the algorithm—an idiot billionaire is as valuable as a brilliant technological savant, or a powerful vampire."

"Or a trillionaire?" I asked. I had to ask that.

"The Knack?" Paleface asked. "Please. He is a true philanthropist, not a megalomaniac, Mitch. You know that. The Enemies would never extend an offer to the likes of him. In fact, they've tried to kill him for the past twenty years. He's kind of a pet project for the society, if you must know."

I wondered how much of this Shane knew. Probably all of it, in his own weird way.

"Are there other heroes who are members?" Anna asked.

"I've told you the algorithm of evil," Paleface said. "What more do you want from me?"

"Why was Minder killed?" I asked.

"He'd outlived his usefulness," Paleface said. "He'd thought he could stand in Crimebot's way, take over the leadership of the society."

That was very Minder, and I thought she was likely telling the truth.

Seeing that we were biting, Paleface continued.

"And that's not all—"

Then the orbital strike came down, which was this blinding blue-white beam that blew a hole through Central's roof and annihilated Paleface, who shrieked as she was disintegrated. Never having been at ground zero of an orbital attack, I didn't even have a chance to react, but, thankfully, Anna did, grabbing me in a nanosecond and whizzing me to the far side of the Equipment Room as the beam destroyed Paleface, illuminating Central with its monstrous light.

"Holy shit!" I said, gasping, nearly blinded by the beam. "What happened?"

"We're in trouble, Babe," Anna said. "Get in your suit!"

Still blinking the dots in my eyes, I stumbled into the Cameraman suit and sealed myself up in it, going online.

Anna was flying back into the living room where we'd been talking only moments before, surveying the smoking hole in the ceiling. The perfect circle was the diameter of a car. She went skyward, while I broke in the recording tech of the suit, capturing it.

"This is Cameraman," I said. "Hellmaiden and I were just interrogating Paleface when she was apparently blasted by an orbital strike. We're looking into it."

I sprinted across the living room, activating the suit thrusters, gasping as the jetpack in the back took me up, letting me fly through the hole, which had cut through three floors. I could see Anna's gleam as she went up. She was flying to intercept whatever it was that had hit us.

Thankfully, it only appeared that one shot was fired, but what a shot it was. I dialed up Shane, got his voicemail.

"Shane, I think we've got a big problem," I said. "Call me if you can."

ANNA HAD INTERCEPTED THE ATTACK SATELLITE IN ORBIT, which I'd been able to see by tapping into the Affiliates' own surveillance satellites. I was so proud of her, watching her do her thing, knowing it was her. Rad Lad and Tandem had flown up to join her, after I'd put the call in to Shane.

The attack satellite was this automated battle platform, something that would have been illegal if anyone had known about it. It had a reactor and a solar array, as well as world-class optics and an incredibly powerful laser.

There was no way this could have just been launched in space without someone detecting it, so I assumed Crimebot has used teleportation to bring that thing into orbit, and likely stealth technology to keep it off the radars of the governments of the world.

However it got up there, it had been equipped with defenses, as smaller lasers began firing at Anna when she got too close, although she picked up speed and evaded them, and I could see her firing plasma beams at the thing, cutting holes through it in blinding blasts, until it stopped firing back at her, only to detonate in a great, radioactive fireball that would have killed millions, had the fallout fallen earthward.

But Rad Lad soaked the energy of it into himself and then flew to far-Earth orbit to release the energy, while Tandem and Anna took care to deal with any debris too large to burn up in the atmosphere.

While this was going on, I forwarded to Shane the conversation I'd recorded from Paleface.

"Okay," Shane said. "This is great, Mitch. I've greenlit your access to the Affiliates archives, including everything Minder had locked. You can dig through that while I get the rest of the team up to speed on what's happening."

"Shane," I said. "Make sure everybody's on the level. Maybe check with Inferna. She's got a way of sussing people out. We can't rule out that there might be moles on the team. And who knows what Minder did while he was there."

"I'll handle it," Shane said. "Are you and Hellmaiden okay?"

"We're just fine," I said. I wasn't going to spill about Anna at that moment. And maybe he'd already known, depending on what Inferna had said. "The Enemies have to be our first priority, Shane. They're the ones operating behind the scenes in all of this. And I suspect there are two precogs working for them—most likely Ms. Fortune and Johnny Rubicon. We're going to need to counter that. I'm thinking Crimebot's doing some pathological A/B testing with them, as idiotic as that sounds."

"How so?" Shane asked.

"It's like a Schrödinger's Cat scenario," I said. "Crimebot's probably stress-testing his actions by having two precogs vision-test it, so he can future-proof the results for the most favorable outcome, based on the inputs from the precogs."

"Glad to have you back, Mitch," Shane said, laughing. I told him I'd call him back once I had something more to draw on. I watched Anna, Tandem, and Rad Lad finish cleaning up the mess, while I dug into the Affiliates archives.

Minder would have been extraordinarily careful not to leave too many footprints behind, but there still had to be tie-ins. Just having the high-security access itself gave me a rush, given how relentless Minder had been in keeping me the hell away from it.

The following files jumped out at me, and all had terabytes of information associated with them:

- *REHABILITATION PROGRAM*
- *DEHABILITATION PROGRAM*
- *SUPER SOLDIER PROGRAM*
- *POLYGON PROGRAM*
- *ALIEN ASSIMILATION PROGRAM*
- *MYSTICAL INTERVENTION PROGRAM*
- *UNDEATH PROGRAM*
- *HYBERIA HOLLOW PROGRAM*
- *THE BRIG PROGRAM*
- *OPERATION: MORNINGSTAR*

I'd be the first to confess that Minder wasn't a very imaginative file-namer, but then again, with all that he had going on, maybe he couldn't afford to be too cavalier. And since he'd had these files on lockdown, it meant that he didn't have to be too cryptic about them. That he even entrusted them to a computer was something.

### REHABILITATION PROGRAM

This program was apparently an effort to isolate supervillains who Minder could mindfuck (my words, not his) into appearing to be reformed and able to be deployed in other settings, whether law enforcement, espionage, or military.

Paleface and Deadpan were clearly part of this program.

"Prisoners—specifically those of the 'supervillain' category—are wasted in the Brig," Minder wrote. "This will give us a pipeline to top-tier talent that will willingly work with and for us. I'm organizing along White, Grey, and Black Hat lines to sell it to the other members of the team. I'm convinced that some successful operations can make this a viable path going forward."

### DEHABILITATION PROGRAM

This program was something far more sinister, which followed a disinhibitory protocol engineered by Minder that offered what he referred to as a "sliding scale" for "practical/ situational morality"—basically, it was another Minderfuck that involved reducing reluctance to use of lethal force on the part of superheroes.

The goals appeared to be twofold: 1) creating a class of superhero who would more willingly use lethal force when called upon to do so; and 2) using those moral lapses as leverage to enforce compliance with larger objectives as determined by Minder.

Brighteyes came immediately to mind for me in this, and I took some notes to touch base with her again on this. Minder wrote as much:

"Brighteyes has been a stellar success in the dehabilitation program, in my view. Simple pushes in the desired direction amplified her sense of lethal self-righteousness, even to the point of discovery and reaction to the effort. Once dehabilitated, a hero naturally assumes an antiheroic posture grounded in the use (and abuse) of their abilities. I'd like to bring others into the program, and see a natural synergy with her partner, Decibelle, whose powers lend themselves to exactly this kind of application."

### SUPER SOLDIER PROGRAM

Pretty obvious applications here, although Minder had a massive amount of filework on Ms. Fit on this, who was clearly a template for him as to the ideal super soldier type. Seeing Minder's blithe writing on it, referencing Ms. Fit, just annoyed me:

"Jane's the perfect super soldier," Minder had written. "She's emotionally untroubled by the practical requirements of fieldwork, and never tires. She doesn't get sick and is nearly impervious to injury. If we could only get proper blood draws from her, we'd make real progress. As it stands, we're forced to rely on skin, hair, and menstrual samples by means of nanites and bots, which offer insights, but I'd like to get her in a lab for a month or two to get her genome sequenced." Minder was *such* a creep.

### POLYGON PROGRAM

This was focused more on the technological aspects of initiatives, including (fucker) my enhancements to invisibility optics and adaptive camouflage, as well as my stun gun technology, with a mind of applying it in a wide-beam manner able to disable entire crowds and render them susceptible to suggestion.

"The war-fighting and crowd-control aspects of this technology cannot be overstated," Minder wrote. "Covert assassinations become easier to accomplish by means of high-stealth modalities, and the stun tech affords us an ability to apply mass-amnesia and/or suggestion to affect popular perception and drive people where we need them to go."

### ALIEN ASSIMILATION PROGRAM

This one was a doozy, with a ton of files I'd have to spend a great deal of time accessing, but it basically acknowledged first contact with aliens, and efforts to insinuate them into Earth society with minimal issues.

"The idea of 'alien invasion' is easily accessed by everyday people," Minder wrote. "Our goal here is to reinterpret the idea of 'invasion' into more positive frameworks, and, in truth, to erase the notion of 'invasion' entirely. There can be no invasion if the aliens are already suitably incorporated into positions in society that allow them to integrate, if not assimilate, human values. The ideal goal will be a sea change without anyone realizing that the tide has already come in."

This would require much more investigation on my part. I planned to bring AFFILIA to bear on this when I could, even if it might increase the risk of someone coming after me.

### MYSTICAL INTERVENTION PROGRAM

This program involved acknowledgement and acceptance of trans-dimensional beings and civilizations, with a dotted line to the Alien Assimilation Program.

"There once was a time when hell really was other people," Minder wrote. "We're transcending unidimensional thinking into an awareness that other dimensions exist, are occupied with beings unlike ourselves, and that intersectional interactions between our dimensions are not only likely, but inevitable. We must work to ensure our own dominance in these dimensional crossovers."

Another one I'd have to parse with AFFILIA, as the idea of extra-dimensional incursions required an audit of the other civilizations being referred to, and whether they were helpful or harmful to the human condition. The intersection with Hell (or "Hell" or Hell™) was emblematic of that. Most people couldn't handle this dimension; the possibility of other dimensions with their own denizens would be almost incomprehensible to the lay public.

### UNDEATH PROGRAM

This program described the awareness that there were undead, themselves considered part of the Mystical Intervention Program, representing another mode of life (what Minder called "post-life life" in his typically wonky way). There was also an interest in using principles of undeath as a back door to immortality.

"Death is considered the inevitable endpoint of human existence," Minder said. "But what if we could cheat death through undeath? The opportunities here are terribly exciting in that they redefine the nature of life itself. I've had conversations with vampires—these are not mere reanimated corpses; they are alternative lifeforms, or, if you prefer, 'unlifeforms'—either way, they merit far more study. There may be marketing opportunities with paying clients, depending on the available undead specimens."

### HYBERIA HOLLOW PROGRAM

This detailed the retirement and research program that had been in operation at Hyberia Hollow for decades. Minder was weaponizing it as offering a potentially limitless supply of superhumans to be genome-sequenced and studied.

"As much as the Undeath Program excites me, the work at the Hollow is going to pave the way for a brighter future. We will no longer be dependent on chance to provide us with superheroic material. Rather, we'll know how to 'grow our own' and put them to work for the larger organizational goals. What I could do with an army of Tandems and Victorianas."

I gnashed my teeth at him mentioning Anna, there.

### THE BRIG PROGRAM

This was a villainous mirror to the Hyberia Hollow Program, with the caveats associated with using prisoners instead of residents. All prisoners at the Brig were gene-sequenced, their powers studied in detail.

"The Brig is our laboratory," Minder said. "It is our Fort Knox, filled with golden geese. I'm confident that it will bring us the gains we're looking for in the field of superhumanity. Since they are prisoners and are well-tended, it ensures a cooperative atmosphere that yields huge potential benefits. Further, I'd like to explore recombinative supers down the road— taking two or more sets of superpowers and blending them."

### OPERATION: MORNINGSTAR

This was the largest of Minder's files, and one I'd have to spend a lot of time studying. As far as I could determine, Operation: Morningstar was the synthesis and application of all of the aforementioned programs toward a broader strategic effort to conquer the world.

Why did they always want to conquer the world? It irked me.

"Operation: Morningstar will bring everything to fruition," Minder wrote. "All that we've worked toward—rule of the world by the best and the brightest, without equivocation. The problem is that the current world raises mediocrity to a virtue. Morningstar will, conversely, allow the powerful, the privileged, the brilliant, and wealthy to rule with the impunity that they merit by virtue of their undeniable excellence. The world can only afford so many billionaires—we're going to make sure that the wealth and power goes in the directions we need it to go."

"Sucks to be you, Minder," I said. Crimebot had used his hubris against him, getting him to put all of these programs in motion, propelled by his own grandiose sense of self and confidence in his destiny. And then he'd snuffed him out. He never even saw it coming.

Anna came in, and asked me how it was going, drinking a beer from that devilish tankard she was toting around.

"Does that thing automatically refill?" I asked.

"It does," she said, grinning. "And it's *chilled!* I think I might love magic."

"How does an automatically-refilling chilled beer tankard come from Hell?" I asked. "You're the one with the Masters in Philosophy; explain that to me."

Anna sat down nearby, giving me enough space that she didn't cook me, for which I was appreciative.

"Inferna basically said it works differently for the devils," she said. "They're not the ones being tormented, versus the souls banished there, who are some sort of cosmic currency."

"That whole thing messes with my head," I said. "But I totally wouldn't hate it if you let me have a sip of that hellbrew you're drinking."

Anna smirked and walked over, holding it out.

I took a drink of it, and it *was* amazingly good, like everything a good brew should be, not like that IPA bongwater people claimed to love.

"Whoa," I said, taking another drink.

"Right?"

"Not to go off on a tangent, but am I to believe there are brewers in Hell making that killer red ale? How does that even work?"

Anna shrugged and went back to her seat.

"Maybe it's something you can explore in your documentary," she said. "All I know is that, however it all shakes out, I'm keeping the tankard. Inferna's going to have to pry it from my cold, dead hands."

"No," I said. "You've already blown through your death allowance."

We shared a nervous chuckle over that, and I talked through the Minder files I'd found. In his years in the Affiliates, Minder had been *very* busy. How none of the others had gotten wind of it rankled me more than I cared to admit. Were they clueless or complicit?

"He was going through the motions," Anna said. "And since he was reading everybody's minds, he was likely able to anticipate and deal with people's suspicions, even if they had any."

"Ephemera, Tantrum, and Brighteyes," I said. "And you. You all got suspicious. And Shane. Me, of course. Minder was on my list the moment he read my mind."

Anna switched on the television, which showed Caryn Underwood spouting her anti-Cameraman stuff like clockwork:

"Who is this Mitch Paulsen, anyway?" she asked. "He's such a nobody, he must be somebody. He has to be a foreign asset. Whether it's China, Iran, or Russia remains to be seen, but it has to be one of them. The way he went after patriotic, God-fearing American politicians, that only makes sense that he was working with enemies of our country. And the way he's clearly being bankrolled by the oh-so-openly virtuous Knack. What's up with that? My guest today is Senator Bruce 'Chip' Chadwick III, Republican of Arkansas, who is working to subpoena Mr. Paulsen and Mr. Grey to appear before the Congress and account for their actions. Senator Chadwick, what do you have to say about Mitch Paulsen?"

Chip Chadwick was a high-middle age white man with whiter hair. He wore a blue suit and a red tie. I hadn't done any workups on him, but a couple of campaign contribution keystrokes found him to be deep in bed with certain foreign lobbies and big oil and fracking interests, as well as the televangelical backers of the Trinity. Yeah, he'd be the sort to really hate me.

"Thanks, Caryn," he said. "Yes, Mr. Paulsen has a lot to answer for. I knew and was friends with several of the innocent victims of his so-called 'exposés'—good people, patriots who deserve far better than they got at the hands of this politically-motivated extremist. I, for one, cannot tolerate this kind of fake news smear campaigns carried out by the likes of Mr. Paulsen. The man is a public menace, and I look forward to holding him to account, as well as Mr. Shane Grey."

"Ouch," Anna said. "That's going to be uncomfortable."

"I'm more worried about getting shot while attending," I said. "I'm totally wearing body armor. At least make them work to try to kill me."

"Babe," Anna said. "Don't even think that way."

I showed her my list of potential Shutterclique members who might help us whomp the Crime League. She read them aloud:

"Avant Guardian, Eightball, Mr. Cool, Brighteyes, Decibelle, and Strutter," she said. "With you and me, that makes eight."

"Yeah," I said. "Hopefully Crimebot doesn't have some kind of death ray, or we're screwed. The others had schedule conflicts."

She set down the list, brooding over it.

"Why aren't we going after the Enemies of Humanity first? If they're the ones behind everything?"

"The Crime League is more of a warmup," I said. "They're really the business front of the whole operation. I think if we disrupt them, it'll throw them off their game. Also, I'm hoping to gain access to data, maybe see who is working with the Enemies, where they're based, and so on. We really need to get our hands on Scenester. He was working closely with Minder, and he has to have knowledge of where the League's key outposts are, and maybe the Enemies, too. Of course, catching up with a teleporter is a problem."

Anna sat up, slapping her thigh.

"I have an idea," she said.

"Yeah?" I asked.

She nodded, grinning at me from beneath her red cowl.

"You're going to love it," she said.

**15**

**SCENESTER DIDN'T EVEN SEE IT COMING,** which was exactly how Anna had planned it out. She'd called up Terri Meadows, the precog administrator she'd met when she'd explored Hyberia Hollow over a year ago, and asked her to do some envisioning for us, specifically around where Scenester might appear next over several days.

She wasn't shocked to hear from Victoriana, despite what the news had been regarding her. This shouldn't be surprising; it was very hard to surprise a precog. Anna talked her through it, what she'd been up to since her disappearance.

"We just need a few predictions where Scenester might be appearing over the next few days," Anna said. "Can you do that for me?"

"I can," Terri said. "Although, if he's working with Ms. Fortune and Johnny Rubicon, they may have protected him from causal observation."

"Just try, and we'll see what comes of it," Anna said. Meadows gave us three predictions for where we might find Scenester, so we split up the Shutterclique at the times and places Meadows had indicated, with Anna and me at the first one (St. Augustine, Florida), Strutter and Eightball at the second one (Richmond, Virginia), and Avant Guardian and Mr. Cool at the third (Portland, Oregon).

Naturally, I was wondering what Scenester was up to at each of those locations, and intended to study them in detail when I had the chance.

"This was a great idea," I told Anna, who gave me an on-task smile. "Remember, we're not taking his head off; we're just having to clock him and neutralize his powers so he can't skip off."

"I got it," Anna said. "You, too, Mr. Suit."

It being my first field deployment with the powersuit, I was admittedly nervous. Even as I was digging how fabulous the suit was. It had climate control and a bio-containment system that meant I could, you know, if I had to. Not that I would, but I could. I'd toggled the adaptive camouflage option, pleased that it made me nearly invisible.

"ETA, three minutes," I said, checking my clock. Meadows had given us a rough timeframe for the appearances. If her prediction was correct, Scenester would appear here with Strongarm, where they were meeting up with Annie Conda, a superpowered villain who could turn herself into a monstrous serpent. What the League or Enemies had need of a street-level goon like Conda was itself a mystery. The plan was that when Scenester showed up, I would hit him with my stun blasts, while Anna would drop Strongarm. Then we'd grab and disable Scenester and fly out of there.

"I'm psyched," Anna said.

"We've only got one shot at this," I said. "Scenester's pretty jumpy."

"Yeah, so definitely don't miss," she said. I was pleased that the suit had an auto-tracking system with regard to the stun blasts, so I had activated that ahead of time. If they operated as planned, they would lock onto the targets, and I could fire the stun beams with a strong assurance of getting a hit.

"Two minutes," I said. I could see Annie Conda walking into the park where the meeting was supposed to be taking place. She looked ordinary, wearing typically floral Floridian hot weather clothes with a sun hat. I was very pleased when the suit's facial recognition software identified her immediately.

"Don't worry," Anna said. "I'll drop her, too."

We were in Ponce de Leon Park, where there spurted an old fountain encircled and concealed by plentiful palms and dune grasses. I hadn't voluntarily been in Florida for a long time but was grateful in my new suit that I at least could keep cool, and Anna didn't exactly have to worry about sunburn.

Annie Conda took a seat on a bench nearby, dithering on her phone in the shade of one of the nearby trees.

I'd never kidnapped anyone before, so there was that inevitable rush with doing something unfamiliar and, well, illicit. Given that Scenester had attempted to murder me, there was that, too. I'd have to resist the urge to punch him in the face.

"One minute," I said, going to silent mode on my speakers, since I didn't want Annie Conda hearing us.

Then there came the telltale silvery flash of light and there stood Scenester and Strongarm. Anna and I went for it, me calling out to them to get their attention and firing the shoulder-mounted stun beams, which flashed brightly—and, I'm happy to note—right on target, thanks to the HUD display. Their faces went wide-eyed as they stood there, and I saw Anna fly in and nail Strongarm with a right cross that sent him pinwheeling in the direction of the beach, only to hit our cloaked Affilijet with a resonant clang, followed by slapping a power neutralizer collar on Scenester, and a backhand that dropped Annie Conda.

I'd reached the intercept point, grabbing the still-stunned Scenester and tucking him under my arm like a football, going airborne with a pulse of thrust from my jetpack, while Anna flew with me.

We got to the Affilijet and loaded Scenester into the back, where we had a securicage waiting for him. Then we closed up and took off, flying out of there within three minutes total.

"Damn," I said. "Smooth, Babe."

"Totally," she said, piloting us out of there. I hopped out of the powersuit and carefully frisked Scenester, who was still catatonic. I think the upgraded suit had kicked up the power on my stun gun prototype, because the man was out.

My frisking turned up a wallet (silver—what was with this guy and silver?), a phone, a commlink of some sort, and a two-pill tin of capsules. I set these items on a tray, then ran a hand scanner over Scenester, found a subcutaneous transponder in his forearm, which I rudely cut out of him with a scalpel from the on-board medkit, which I put in a baggy before I snapped it in half. Mr. Transistor could study it. Right now, I needed to be sure the Crime League and/or Enemies of Humanity didn't track us.

I took off Scenester's mask and took pictures of him with my phone. I also ran it through the Affiliates Crime Computer, which revealed Scenester to be one Leonard Thaler, who had served time in a number of larceny and robbery cases before assuming the supervillain identity of the Scenester.

He originally called himself the Silver Scenester. Huh. Guess he decided that was too lame, and just went with the simpler name. He'd hailed from Boston, and it looked to me that he'd used his teleportation abilities for a good decade before assuming his supervillain guise. Thaler looked weirdly ordinary—pale olive skin, short dark hair, big eyes with dark circles under them, a wide mouth, big teeth and prominent lips.

What that meant was that he'd built up a reputation as a superlative box man and thief in general, being able to enter vaults and other secure areas and steal everything he found in them.

I backed out of the securicage and locked it up, while Scenester was coming to. He blinked and shook his head, then flinched when he realized where he was.

"Ohmigod," he said. "What the hell just happened?"

"Hey, Lenny," I said. "You tried to murder me, remember?"

"Whoa," he said, his eyes flicking around him as he tried to figure out where he was. "Look, I don't know anything."

"I don't believe that for a second," I said. "Hellmaiden, would you like to tune this guy up a little? I can fly."

She turned and glared back at Scenester, who squirmed under her glare.

"What do you want from me?" he asked.

"Where's the base for the Crime League?" I asked. "And for the Enemies of Humanity?"

At the mention of the first, Scenester was defiant, but mention of the latter made him very uneasy. Like sweaty-faced uneasy.

"Enemies of what?" he asked.

"I know you know who they are," I said. "You were tight with Minder."

Scenester was such a nervous sort of guy. It was sort of weird because he had a helluva power. Teleportation was one of those amazing powers that made one a very valuable commodity in the business. Just look at what Inferna did with it. Pure teleporters were rare, including:

- **VAMOOSEKETEER:** *CANADIAN TELEPORTER HERO FROM VANCOUVER.*

- **SPLITSVILLAIN:** *FREE-RANGE TELEPORTER VILLAIN-FOR-HIRE WHO TURNED UP WHEREVER HE WANTED.*

- **POLLY GONE:** *AMERICAN PSS AGENT, HARDCORE OPERATIVE. SHE HAD NATURALLY PINK HAIR.*

- **DIMENSION DORA:** *MAGICAL HEROINE OPERATING IN THE SOUTH, PALS WITH SOUND & FURY.*

The above four, plus Scenester, all had global teleportative range, which made them the A-List teleporters. There were others who were shorter-ranged teleporters, as well, who often turned up with street-level criminal organizations.

- **BLINKSTER:** *SMALL-TIME TELEPORTER VILLAIN. PROFESSIONAL THIEF. FREELANCER.*

- **PORTALIA:** *B-LEVEL TRANSIT HEROINE, WORKED MOSTLY WITH LAW ENFORCEMENT.*

- **EXODISS:** *TELEPORTER AFFILIATED WITH THE TRINITY.*

- **TRESPASSANT:** *VILLAIN-FOR-HIRE OPERATING OUT OF MONTREAL.*

He narrowed his eyes at me skeptically.

"Camera-fuckin-man," he said. "Mitch 'The Bitch' Paulsen. What are you going to do to me, you geek?"

I took out my handheld stun gun and shot him in the face with it, watching him get that stunned look on his face yet again.

"You enjoyed that entirely too much," Anna said.

"Oh, I'm not even getting started," I said. I called up the other members of the 'Clique and told them we'd captured the target, and they could stand down. "Right now, we can just fly to Chicago in style, take our time with it."

I didn't want to farm Scenester off to the Brig (or wherever) just yet. Rather, I planned to keep him at Central, where we had holding cells for up to a dozen super-perps from baseline to A-Level. Assuming the Enemies didn't have more attack satellites handy, it should have been enough to keep him on ice.

Scenester started to come to again, shaking it off and cursing.

"Fuck!" he yelled. "What the fuck did you just do to me?"

I held up the gun, and he just winced.

"You've never been on the receiving end of this, have you, Lenny?" asked. "I'm going to make it simple for you—every time you give me an answer I don't like, or fail to answer my question, I'm going to stun you. Right now, it's just annoying. But we can just keep doing this for hours. Even days. I can crank up the juice and you'll lose around thirty minutes a pop."

Anna glanced over her shoulder at me after setting the autopilot, then got up, taking a seat nearby. Scenester's nervous eyes followed her as she went. She let him feel the heat she was generating, which was always bracing.

"First up: where's the League's HQ?" I asked.

"I'm not giving that up," he said. "People who do end up dead."

"Okay," I said, stunning him again. While he was out, I took off his silver costume and left it in a pile on one of the foldout tables. Left him in his boxers and a tee.

"You're kind of scarily good at interrogations, Mitch," Anna said.

"It's really just a coerced interview," I said. "I should be beyond this kind of thing, but that bastard tried to kill me."

She and I had a quick lunch while he zoned out.

"Without their resident teleporter on-hand, the League's going to be in a bit of a jam. I think he's the only member who can do that. Maybe Deathclown, too."

"Okay," Anna said. "You know, maybe we can reverse it on them a little—we take their teleporter away, and we use Inferna to help us go after *their* precogs."

I liked that idea, nodded while drinking a soda. It amused me that the Affilijets had kitchenettes in them. They even had four foldout beds. You could live in an Affilijet for a month if you had to. At the rate my life was going, I might have to.

"I'd love to commission Polly Gone for an assist, maybe Dimension Dora," I said. "Although that'd get Max Stern all up in our business, and that might be too annoying."

The PSS were even more buttoned-down than the Affiliates were, being more closely tied to the government. Polly was such a straight arrow, by-the-book agent type, and Dora was a hyper-specialist unlikely to bother with something as seemingly mundane as this, since her focus was on magical teleportation.

My phone alarm went off and I cleaned up my lunch stuff, while Anna continued eating hers. Scenester started stirring again, coming to.

"Christ," he said, when he saw that he'd been stripped down to his boxers and tee shirt. "I'm not telling you anything! No matter what you do!"

"We have a telepath, you know," I said (we didn't). "She's not as, well, delicate as Minder was. A more forceful touch."

"Okay, okay," Scenester said, watching me toy with my stun gun. "The League is in Toronto."

"Toronto?" I asked. "Why up there?"

"Dr. Crime's from Toronto," he said. "It's his hometown."

I made note of that. Didn't actually know that Dr. Crime was Canadian. What a world. His penchant for London digs in the past made me think he might have been English, but he was a Canuck. Alright, then.

"Where in Toronto? It's a big city," I said.

"Millionaire's Row," he said. "He's got a mansion in Bridle Path. It's our headquarters."

"Bridle Path?" I asked. "Huh."

"Fancy that," Anna said.

Scenester looked panicked. "I'm so dead."

I wasn't about to bring him comfort, figured it helped to let him stew more, just in case he said anything else.

"Are the Enemies based there, too?" I asked.

"Yes," he said. "They meet there. Everything's very low-key. That's partly why they used me so much. I could zip people there and back, and nobody in the neighborhood knew otherwise."

"Tell me about the Enemies," I asked.

"It's a *secret* society, man," he said. "They do weird and creepy shit. Like arcane rituals. You know, EYES WIDE SHUT-style stuff."

"Orgies?" I asked. He nodded.

"Shutterbug records them," he said. "Blackmail shit, like financiers, politicians, generals, and stuff. Sex and drugs. World leaders. You know?"

Frankly, I'd thought it would take more to break Scenester than a couple of stun blasts, but I guess everybody had their breaking point. For someone like him, used to being able to teleport his way out of jams, being stuck in one place had to be terribly unnerving. Scenester struck me as a super-flunkie—blessed with a useful power, he was likely paid well to be a paranormal taxi service, but he didn't bother with thinking too much about what he did.

There were tons of C-level supers who slung their powers that way. The PSS had a woman on-staff codenamed Triplicate who, yeah, could create three otherwise ordinary duplicates of herself (yeah, I know, the replicators are replicating!), and a guy codenamed Memorando who could memorize anything he'd seen or heard. He was an archivist, and I'd probably have to deal with him at some point when I really got into those files. Bet you can't wait until you see how that goes.

"Tell me about Dr. Crimebot," I said. "You said that to me before you tried to kill me."

"What's to know?" he asked, eyes imploring. "Doc and the 'Bot teamed up. Crimebot built a perfect cyborg/android body for the Doc, and the two of them merged, fused, whatever you want to call it. They're one, now."

"Right," I said, pleased that I'd already sleuthed that out. Anna had finished her leisurely lunch and leaned toward Scenester.

"You're *lying*," she said, which threw him into a perspiring panic.

"I'm not!" he said. "This is the truth, I swear!"

She glanced at me, a hint of a smirk on her face, and I played ball.

"Hellmaiden's unconvinced," I said. "She's a devil, you know? She knows lies and truth when she hears them. She can perceive things you and I can't even imagine."

"Including methods of torture," she said. "There aren't even words for them you can comprehend, Mortal. Tell Cameraman everything you know, or I'll put the hooks in you. Have you ever seen HELLRAISER?"

*She* was entirely too good at this! Even I felt the heft of her threat. Scenester wracked his brain for something useful to give us, even though he'd already given us plenty.

"Morningstar," he said. "Operation: Morningstar."

"Yeah?" I asked. "What about it?"

"Crimebot's got something big planned," Scenester said. "Something he said would solve the 'Superhero Problem' once and for all."

"What is it?" I asked.

"The Moebius Mutagen," he said. "I don't attend the high-level meetings. It's just something I overheard."

"What's it do?" Anna asked.

"I don't know," he said. "It's just something I heard. Crimebot and Deathclown were talking about it."

She stared hard at him from beneath her red cowl, so only her glowing white eyes could be seen. Her eyes could literally burn into you if you weren't careful.

"He's telling the truth," she said, almost whispering it. It was masterful.

"Great, Lenny," I said, stunning him again before he could protest. Hey, I didn't lay a finger on the man, beyond, you know, stripping him down to his skivvies.

"The Moebius Mutagen," I said. "That's new. Okay, so we come down on Crimebot's posh headquarters in Bridle Path and while the rest of the team bashes the hell out of whoever's there, I can try to access the files and find out about this Moebius Mutagen."

"Sounds like a plan, Cameraman," Anna said, holding up a gloved fist I could bump, which I did.

and I'd called Shane, telling him what we'd discovered. He listened the way he always did, while I half-assed perused through the Minder files for any traces of the Moebius Mutagen, not finding anything. I asked AFFILIA to comb the files as well, which she cheerfully told me she would.

"Alright," Shane said. "This at least falls to Affiliates-level concern. I'm going to have to put together a battle plan on this, at least as relates to the Affiliates. We can't just storm Bridle Path without careful planning."

"Yeah, can't bother the billionaires," I said, rolling my eyes. "I think I can get the Shutterclique in on this, too. Hellmaiden thinks Hell's Belles might also be game for it."

"Mitch, this has to be something low-key," he said. "We cannot just blow up Crimebot's mansion."

I felt nearly insulted. "When have I ever blown anything up, Shane?"

"Where you go, explosions follow, Mitch," he said. "Whether or not you set them off."

"Hmm, well, okay," I said. "While you're busy securing Affiliates action permits or whatever, I'm going to sic the 'Clique on those precogs Crimebot's using. We need to make sure we can get some element of surprise on them. Our snag of Scenester went very smoothly."

Shane thought about that a moment before replying.

"It's possible this is already part of Crimebot's contingency planning," he said.

"Could be," I said. "But we have to take them out. They're what Crime's been using to stay ahead of us. How long will it take for you to get your heroic action permits?"

"They're not 'heroic action permits', Mitch," Shane said. "Come on, now. We just have to work with local law enforcement. Don't make me regret bringing you back on the team already."

"You're assuming local law enforcement isn't already compromised," I said. "Might tip them off. I know if I were Dr. Crime, I'd have sicced Shutterbug on local law enforcement and gotten every bit of *kompromat* on them in a heartbeat."

"Well then you'll just have to monitor the League's mansion in Bridle Path and note if anybody leaves ahead of our planned incursion," Shane said. "As well as who's coming and going. Without their teleporter, they may have to be more overt about that."

"No can do," I said. "I've got to help out Inferna take out this devil-led druglord in Cincinnati. There may be dotted lines to the Enemies and the League. How about this—if you tip off the locals and Crime flees the mansion, you'll have proof of there being a law enforcement leak. I'd say you stick Tag on the case, Ms. Fit, too. Heck, Ms. Fit could jog after anybody driving off and follow them wherever they went, no matter how far they went."

"Nice, Mitch," Shane said. "Okay, once you get this druglord and precog portion taken care of, we should have the rest ironed out, and we'll team up with the Shutterclique and the Belles and shut down Crime's operation in Toronto."

"Love it," I said, hanging up.

"I missed all of this," Anna said. "You're entirely too good at superheroing, you know."

We laughed, and I switched on the news, just to see what they would be talking about. Looked like the protesters were still at my brownstone, and poor Molly and John were dealing with it. I had a bunch of voicemail messages from them, asking...even begging me for advice. I was letting them down, big-time. I did the simplest thing a bad boss could do for them.

I called both of them on a party line and gave them the next four weeks off, paid vacation.

"What?" Molly asked. "Are you kidding?"

"Nope," I said. "Fuck it. Lock up the shop and just take off. You two shouldn't have to be dealing with all that chaos, anyway."

"Wow, thanks," John said. "Dude, are you actually Cameraman?"

"Yeah, I am," I said.

"We knew it!" John said. "Molly and I had a pool betting that you were either Cameraman or Lancer."

"For real?" I asked. Lancer? No offense to Lancer, but come on....

"Yeah," John said. "We fucking knew it! Awesome, Bro!"

"Thanks, I think," I said. "Look, just shut Flying Saucer down, lock up, set the alarm, and go on vacation. I've got you both covered. Oh, and did all the protesting boost our sales?"

"Dead ass," Molly said. "All the merch went the day the story broke. People were all over it. Best day we've seen all year."

"Great," I said. "We'll have to restock once things settle down. Anyway, enjoy your time off."

"Thanks, Mitch," Molly said.

"You bringing the rizz, man?" John asked.

"I am," I said. "Yes, I totally am."

I wrapped that call up, while Anna looked on, shaking her hooded head with amusement.

"I love how you just gave them four weeks off, paid," she said. "Best bad boss ever."

I gave her a thumbs up.

"They're good kids," I said. "They deserve the time off."

I flicked across the channels, as I often did, just to see what I might see between the channel changes. Sometimes things emerged, a sense of some larger order amid the chattering chaos.

"You know, I almost think this identity-reveal thing might be okay for me," I said. "Given how much of my work I do invisibly, who cares who I am?"

"I care," Anna said.

"Obviously, yeah," I said. "I'm just saying, maybe I can weather the storm. People have short attention spans. Once the wave of attempted assassinations and lawsuits passes, I might come out of this okay."

Anna laughed, giving me a tender swat on my shoulder. Given how strong she was, I already appreciated her gentleness and conscientious restraint. I knew what she could do and was grateful she never visited that on me the way she decimated our foes. Seeing her there, though, I'll admit that I wanted her to jettison this Hellmaiden thing and become her everyday super-self again. Hellmaiden was cool and all, but I wanted Victoriana back.

"I'm not letting anybody assassinate you, Babe," she said. "Dead ass."

"You know, there's a villain who's named that," I said. "Street-level. Dead Ass."

"No way," Anna said, giggling. "You're totally making that up."

"I'm not! He came onto the scene while you were away," I said. "He can raise the dead or kill people with a touch. He wears a skeleton costume, mask, and a top hat. He also apparently can't be killed—what I've heard, anyway."

"Deadhead 2.0," Anna said, and I nodded.

"There's always somebody," I said. "I sometimes wonder where they come from. In fact, I think I have a file somewhere on that, like a database of superhero and supervillain origins, trying to find patterns."

She laughed at me, shaking her head.

"Of course you would," she said. "That's so entirely you."

"Exactly," I said. "There are always patterns to be found. You just have to make the right connections. For example, here are supervillains I thought who might be part of the Enemies of Humanity, breaking it down over their hypothetical divisions." I showed her the files:

## TECHNO TERRORS

•**SCISSORETTES:** *ALREADY MENTIONED THEM.*

•**MR. ROBOTO:** *MAN OR MACHINE? YOU DECIDE. HUGE STYX FAN, WHICH MAKES HIM SUSPECT.*

•**CIRCUITBREAKER:** *ABLE TO SHORT OUT ANY ELECTRONIC EQUIPMENT.*

•**BARON BLACKOUT:** *ABLE TO CREATE FIELDS OF ABSO-LUTE DARKNESS.*

## SPACE INVADERS

•**MR. BLACK:** *IMPECCABLY DRESSED MESMERIZER. LITER-ALLY SWIRLY-EYED.*

•**CATTLEPRODDER:** *WEIRD COWBOY WITH ELECTRICAL PRODS AND A YEE-HAW ATTITUDE.*

•**SQUIDHEAD:** *HAS A TENTACLED-MOUTHED HEAD. WEARS ROBES. HAS MENTAL POWERS.*

•**PLETHORA:** *ANOTHER REPLICATOR. SHE'S REALLY WEIRD, LIKE CULT LEADER FOR HER OWN DUPLICATES.*

## MAGICAL MENACES

•**SERGEANT SORCERY:** *MENTIONED HIM BEFORE. DESPITE STUPID NAME, HE'S DANGEROUS.*

•**SPELLMAN HARROWS:** *STODGY NEW ENGLANDER, MANIC CONJURER IN TOUCH WITH ELDER GODS.*

•**DR. WITCH:** *AS NAME IMPLIES, SHE BRINGS SCHOLASTIC RIGOR TO HER WITCHCRAFT.*

•**WARLOCK & QUI:** *A TEAM OF A SPELLCASTER (WARLOCK) AND A MARTIAL ARTIST (QUI). GOOD TEAM.*

•**FANTASMAGORICA:** *BLOWN AWAY ILLUSIONIST, ABLE TO WARP PERCEPTION OF REALITY.*

## UNDEAD UNDEAD UNDEAD

•**DEAD ASS:** *LITERALLY JUST MENTIONED HIM.*

•**CORPSELIGHTER:** *GHOULISH DEAD-RAISER.*

•**THE WISP:** *GASEOUS BEING THAT CAN DRAIN THE BLOOD FROM VICTIM AND POSSESS THEM.*

•**FANGMAN:** *DUDE HAS FANGS. IS HE A VAMPIRE? DOES ANYONE CARE? HE'S FANGMAN.*

There were likely more, but these were ones that came to mind most readily. I was sure there were more. The Enemies likely had tiers of membership. Another thing I'd have AFFILIA explore.

"What about heroes?" Anna asked. "Are there ones you might suspect?"

That was a big question, wasn't it? Possibly a very important one. The thing about secret societies was their secrecy (ha). The point was the secrecy, which meant that members likely kept very quiet about anything they did as part of the society. Honestly, I couldn't imagine any hero worth the name consciously joining "The Enemies of Humanity"—come on, man. No way. Minder did it, but Minder was a creep, and even he kept it very quiet.

"I don't know," I said. The news had Caryn Underwood breathlessly speaking of new details emerging about my sordid life as Cameraman.

"New lawsuits are emerging about the use of the name 'Cameraman' as parties are declaring that he has inflicted harm on them for using their name for his own controversial alter-ego," Underwood said, showing footage of these losers claimed they were the *original* Cameraman, and that I'd stolen their identity from them. One of them even suggested I hyphenate my alias to "Camera-Man" to make it distinct from their own nonheroic identities.

"No way," I said. "I love hyphens and all, but no way am I going out there as 'Camera-Man'—I'll get all the Spider-Man people after me. Can you imagine?"

"I can," Anna said.

"Infringement, my ass," I said. I'd been crimefighting as Cameraman for like fifteen years. While they were making stupid YouTube videos or dorky cartoons, I was busy busting politicians and crimelords with my exposés. If anything, they owed me, not the other way around.

Anna wanted to snuggle, but that wasn't in the Tarot cards so long as she was in this Hellmaiden form. The sacrifices we made for being superheroes weren't for the faint of heart.

INFERNA LIKED MY IDEA OF TAKING DOWN DR. CRIMEBOT as a team-up between the Affiliates, Shutterclique, and Hell's Belles. I'd called her in so we could face-to-face about it, and maybe she could reassure me about her motives in taking on the Enemies of Humanity.

Seriously, like how often do you hear of somebody being super-helpful, when they're the bad guys all along? It happens a lot, right? I wasn't going to let that be the case with Inferna. We'd worked together too long, and I trusted her too much.

"Mitch," she said, wearing a stunning red suit with a black leather jacket and black heels. "I'm not part of the Enemies. If anything, I'm a friend of humanity. Look at all I've done."

"I know," I said, glancing at Anna, who glanced back at me. "Clearly, though, your peers are involved—Ruthven, Lethalia, Deathclown, probably others."

"Many others," Inferna said. "I'm, of course, ever the outlier."

"Can you, I don't know, give us a list?" I asked. She eyed me slyly, treating me to one of those sharp smiles of hers.

"I certainly can," she said. "But it's easier to just tell you that all of them are enemies of humanity in principle. I'm the misfit who won't write off your species. As for which ones who've formalized relations with Dr. Crimebot? That's another matter."

"Okay," I said. "How about which of your peers might be operating on Earth? Just the big names."

Inferna agreed with that, jotting down a dozen names on paper with a red and gold fountain pen:

- TROGAN
- GALDATH THE REAVER
- ARNOSET
- BARZIPANTHUS
- SAGOMON THE DEFILER
- ORGOLOCH
- TANTRAS THE APOSTATE
- GALGREKH
- TWINTHA*
- SHARONDAH*
- ELPHEMIRA*
- QUELLAMORZOTH*

*FEMALE

"Alright," I said, looking over her list, admiring her elegant script. "That at least gives us something to start with."

Inferna watched me study the list, while Anna looked on. I wanted to ask why some of the devils got a "the XYZ" after their names. Were they just really good at being bad in that particular way? And given that Tantras the Apostate was a devil in with the hellish hierarchy, how could he have earned the name "the Apostate" at all? These were the sorts of things I thought about, Gentle Reader.

"You're not expecting us to deal with these others, are you?" Anna asked. The infernal investigator had her measured response ready.

"I don't expect anything but the fulfillment of the obligations owed to me," she said. "By the way, Anna, didn't we have an arrangement where you carried out your obligations to me *before* revealing who you were to Mitch?"

"Yes," Anna said. "But I couldn't keep doing it. He needs me, and to know that it's me."

Inferna seemed to find that amusing, waved it off with a flip of her hands. "You are all so flippant in your obligations."

"We can't all be devils, Fern," I said. "This list you gave me is great. I'll see what I can chase down. Inasmuch as I find out who might be in league with the Enemies, I'll help you deal with them. Speaking of that, we might need your help catching some precogs."

Inferna cocked one of her infernally arched eyebrows at the suggestion.

"Really? How many?" she asked.

"A deuce—Ms. Fortune and Johnny Rubicon," I said. "The former is based in Seattle, the latter in Las Vegas. They're working with Dr. Crimebot, doing their whole precognitive mumbo-jumbo to keep Crimebot ahead of us."

Inferna tapped a black fingernail-claw against her bluish-white fangs.

"It's almost impossible to catch precognitives off-guard, Mitch," she said.

"Yes, we know," I said. "But Anna's got an in-road with one who's helped us. She may be able to help us out. And with your own teleportation ability, we'd be able to pop in and nab them."

She liked the suggestion of skullduggery embedded in the request.

"But you're going to need to lift this whole whatever-you-have on Anna so she can manifest as Victoriana again," I said. "The precognitive in question worked with her as Victoriana, not as Hellmaiden."

"Nice try, Mitch," Inferna said. "No, Anna owes me on Strong and Lethalia. Only upon completion of that can she truly shed her Hellmaiden incarnation."

"Christ," I said. "Is this some magical rules thing or what?"

"Yes, Mitch," Inferna said. "Magic has rules. Break them at your peril. Frankly, you're both skating thin ice to begin with."

She turned an admonishing eye to Anna, who met her gaze defiantly.

"I *can't* show up and talk to her like this," Anna said. "She'll be terrified."

"If she's the precog you seem to think she is, she likely *already* knows you're coming to see her again," Inferna said. "The form you take should be incidental."

"Think of it this way," Anna said. "The woman works at Hyberia Hollow. If I show up like this, it'll cause a panic. People will think, I don't know, that they're all going to Hell."

"Maybe they are," Inferna said, smirking. "Fine, Anna. Remove the crown. You are not yet fully healed, but rejoin us as you were, darling Victoriana."

Anna threw back her hood and removed the golden crown, which drew forth her Hellmaiden form, drawing it into it—in moments, the opalescence of her skin had vanished into it, as well as the radiant glow. Her costume shifted from the hellacious form it had been to her classic Victoriana costume. The only difference was that her hair was shorter, being a spiky green, instead of her classic longer locks.

Inferna clasped the crown in her hand, holding it carefully and close to her.

Seeing Anna back made me happier than I'd been since her return, and we embraced and kissed heartily, while Inferna looked on with bewilderment.

"Young love," she said. "So precious. You owe me for this, Anna. I'm holding you to account for services yet rendered."

"Fine," Anna said, once we'd parted from our kiss. I had missed that so much, and seeing her there again, I was overwhelmed. "You know I'm good for it."

"Make sure you are," Inferna said, setting down the golden crown with care on our dining room table. "This crown is not for just anyone. It is well-warded against those who might abuse it."

"Hellmaiden's fans are going to be sad to see her go," I said.

"She's *not* gone," Anna said. "I'm as good as my word, Inferna."

"You'll still have the challenge of accounting for your absence," Inferna said. "As I said earlier, I'd rather you not advertise that I saved you. Conjure up the story that you like, but it shouldn't involve me. As for your scheme, you talk to your precognitive who divulges the where and when to acquire the other precogs—who may already be aware of this plan, I warn you; and then I help you abscond with them. What next, Mitch?"

"My main goal is simply to disable the precogs," I said. "Take them out of play for Crimebot."

"If I were Crimebot, I would have them very well-protected," Inferna said. "Against any sort of attack."

"We'll handle it," I said. Inferna seemed to find that amusing.

"Bold Mitch, fearless in the fray," she said. "Let's hope your bravado can carry you."

**18**

TWO THINGS: BEING ABLE TO BE VICTORIANA AGAIN, even only temporarily, made me so happy I could barely contain myself; and meeting with Terri Meadows put me in a very weird place. We conspired to meet her outside of Hyberia Hollow, because I didn't want to get seen as Victoriana, yet, since I hadn't quite worked out the story of how I flew into the Sun and somehow lived to talk about it.

As such, I put on a Team Tandem baseball cap, some aviator sunglasses, and my favorite Jawbreaker tee shirt ("When It Pains It Roars") and jeans. I wanted to look as everyday as possible.

Terri, for her part, was understanding, where we'd met for coffee at Caffeine Jack's, a local place in Tucson. Terri was nervous.

"I knew you were back," she said. "I had a vision about it. I'm less happy about you and Mitch Paulsen involving me in your crusades, however."

I drank my coffee, grateful my hands no longer evaporated ceramic by touch. Inferna explained it to me:

"The crown soaked up the excess energy you possessed, what had come from the Sun. This was part of your healing process. Since you cut it short, I'm not entirely sure how things will proceed from here for you. You have a very robust physiognomy, so there's at least that going for you."

"Okay," I said. "Meaning?"

"You're not fully healed," Inferna said. "Don't push yourself too hard."

I produced two Tarot cards Inferna had given me, one depicting Ms. Fortune, while the other caricatured Johnny Rubicon.

Terri studied them with amusement and disdain.

"Tarot is insulting to me, you know," she said. "Where did you get these?"

"A friend," I said. "They're made to help bring focus."

She put her index and middle fingers down on them, like she hated even touching them.

"I don't need mystical fetishes to find these two," she said. "They'll be taking a meeting in two days. An important one from Dr. Crimebot."

"Okay," I said. "Where will they be?"

"Together," she said. "In San Francisco, in fact. In one week."

"Will they be alone?" I asked.

"No, they will be escorted," Terri said. "By the one known as Plethora."

Plethora wore a grey and black bodysuit costume. She wasn't able to create as many duplicates as Tag Team or Flashmob, but could make a dozen of herself, each of them super-strong and durable, very hard to fight, at least by the Affiliates archive rankings. To do a Mitch-style dossier would have Plethora mapped out like this:

**ALIAS: PLETHORA**

*REAL/ASSUMED NAME: UNKNOWN*
*HAIR: RED*
*EYES: BLACK*
*HEIGHT: 5'11"*
*WEIGHT: 200 LBS.*

**POWERS:** *PLETHORA POSSESSES THE FOLLOWING SUPERPOWERS, INCLUDING:*

•**DUPLICATION:** *PLETHORA CAN MAKE UP TO A DOZEN DUPLICATES OF HERSELF.*

• **SUPER-STRENGTH:** *PLETHORA IS SUPER-STRONG, ABLE TO LIFT WELL OVER ONE HUNDRED TONS.*

• **SUPER-RESILIENCE:** *PLETHORA IS EXTRAORDINARILY RE-SISTANT TO PHYSICAL AND ENERGY INJURY.*

• **POWER-SHARING:** *WITH EACH DUPLICATE, PLETHORA SHARES POWER WITH THEM (FOR EXAMPLE: TWO PLETHO-RAS WOULD BE ABLE TO LIFT EIGHTY-FIVE TONS, A DOZEN PLETHORAS COULD LIFT FOURTEEN TONS).*

**THREAT LEVEL: 8/10**

"No problem," I said. "I appreciate this, Terri."

"I've never spied on another precog," she said. "I don't know what they might be doing, whether they'll be aware of this or not."

I looked around us, feeling perhaps a little exposed and self-conscious, even though I was in disguise. Extrasensory perception by its nature was hard to pin down. I couldn't relate to how precognitives dealt with the world. Given their ability to see what was coming, how did that play out if someone else was watching them, in turn? Would they be able to perceive the ripples in space-time they were ordinarily able to survey undisturbed? My background in philosophy came back to haunt me in imagining this.

Maybe the precognitive act was a living snapshot. For example, if one tuned into something and acquired a vision of it, maybe that was all they had: "XYZ will happen on THIS day."

But Crimebot was using two precogs, so they might be tasked with envisioning, and would find that "ABC will happen on THAT day." And perhaps offer a safety for the first precog by doublechecking their vision. Crimebot was smart to use two of them this way.

With Terri peering into their futures, she was adding another element. The one advantage was that maybe Crimebot didn't know that we'd enlisted her aid, because I was the primary point of contact, and I was still "dead" in the wider world's awareness. The other precogs wouldn't know to look for me. Or so I hoped.

Maybe Inferna was right that I needed to continue as Hellmaiden for the near term, to keep the precogs off-base as to who and what I was. Not that it would necessarily make a difference, but it might. I worried that I might have put Terri in real danger by even reaching out to her. What if our own efforts to capture Crimebot's precogs made Terri a target?

"Terri, is Tantrum still at Hyberia?" I asked.

"Why?" she asked.

"You need to stay close to her," I said. "She'll keep you safe."

"She doesn't trust me more than anyone else there," she said.

"Tell her I suggested you two stay together," I said. "Tell her it's important, and that Crimebot and his minions might attack you."

Terri's face went pale as I relayed this to her, and she became indignant.

"You've put me in danger, Victoriana," she said. "That's not fair to me."

"Tantrum will protect you," I said, hoping that she would. I reached out and put my hand on hers. "I'll protect you, too, once I get these things handled. The alternative is for us to let them get away with what they're up to. Also, can you see what you can find out about the 'Moebius Mutagen'—anything that might be found in Hyberia."

"I don't know what that is," she said.

"Right, but just see what you can uncover," I said. Terri's indignation turned to anger as she whisper-leaned into me.

"You don't get to do this," she said, her eyes flashing. "You, what, faked your own suicide and try to rope me into this conspiracy-whatever and upend my life?"

"I didn't fake anything," I said. "Minder mentally compelled me to fly myself into the Sun, in hopes that it would kill me, and it didn't. I survived. I'm not apologizing to anyone for surviving my own attempted murder."

Maybe I was more forceful than I intended, but Terri just quieted and looked at me with sorrow in her eyes.

"I didn't know," she said. "How could I?"

You know I was thinking that as a precog, maybe she could have known, if she'd cared to look. Not pointing fingers, but precogs don't get to play dumb. Not with me.

"Look," I said. "I'm trying to stop the bad guys. I just need your help. Tantrum will protect you. Just stay with her. The two of you can help each other. And if there are problems, you can find me, and I'll help you. I promise."

She looked contrite, and I couldn't tell if it was for me or for her. Superpowered she may have been, but she simply wasn't heroic. Terri just wanted to do her job and be left alone. I shouldn't have expected more from her, but I pushed, anyway.

"Good luck at whatever you're trying to do," she said.

"You, too," I replied, and we parted ways. I hoped nothing bad would happen to her and made a sort of peace with myself if anything did. If that makes me sound hard, what can I say? I was tempered by the Sun.

**ANNA HAD TOLD ME HOW IT HAD GONE WITH TERRI MEADOWS** at Hyberia. She and I languished in bed in Central, after some much-needed, long overdue together time. We'd taken some measures to fix the hole in the building on that one side, which amounted to Anna and me putting a big shroud in place to cover it until the Affiliates Construction Corps could fix it (not making that up; they had designated, security-cleared workers to deal with that stuff, including two C-levels named Mixer and The Designer who could rebuild things with their minds).

She was brooding beside me, staring at the ceiling.

"What's up?" I asked.

"I'm going to put that crown back on," she said.

"What?"

"I don't know how to bring Victoriana back," she said. "I can't just pop back in. It was something Terri said, it kind of rattled me. Inferna had said something, too. Like I can't just reappear out of the blue. Besides, Crimebot and the Enemies think Victoriana's dead. It's kind of a wild card we have available to us. Right now, only a few of us know I'm back. Maybe that's an advantage, Babe."

"Whoa," I said. "Do what you think is right. We need every edge we can get against Crimebot."

"I just don't want *anything* to go wrong," she said, reaching over to play with my hair and turn those beautiful grey eyes on me.

"We won't let it go wrong," I said, playing with her hair in turn, which looked very New Wave-spikey.

"Don't judge me, but I *enjoy* being Hellmaiden to some extent," she said. "Whether she's a devil or a fallen angel, I can cut loose with her in a way that I can't as Victoriana."

I laughed a little.

"She's your alter-alter ago," I said. "How meta is that?"

"Right?" Anna said. "I love this, I love us. I love you as Cameraman, and as Mitch. I love what I've done as Victoriana. I love that people have taken to Hellmaiden, too. And I love that because of what she is, I can level up with her in ways that might get Victoriana handslapped. Victoriana's supposed to be America's Super Sweetheart. That's how people saw her. Kicking ass, but cute. And then her tragic, inexplicable death. That's what people remember, and what they saw that day."

"You're afraid of how they might see your return?" I asked.

"Yeah, I am," she said. "If I'm to sell my own return from the dead, I'm going to need your help, Mitch. You're the master of media manipulation, after all."

"Whoa, that sounds so sinister," I said. "Am I an antihero, now?"

She cupped my face with her hand, and I kissed her hand, relishing the feel of her skin on mine. She was always warm to the touch, even before being scorched by the Sun.

"You could never be an antihero, Mitch," she said. "You're too sweet to be that. Wounded-sweet, smart-assed and cynical, but that's your appeal. Victoriana can only be a superheroine. She's pure and all the supergrrl-next-door. That's her. Hellmaiden's one bad bitch. And people resonate with that."

I could see what she was thinking about. Public perception mattered with superheroism in a big way. It applied to the marketing, sponsorships, pop cultural appearances, symbolism, all of that.

"If people figure out that you're both Victoriana and Hell-maiden, they're going to lose their minds," I said. "They're maybe not going to be able to process it."

"Or maybe it's a way for me to attain some balance," she said. "I'm still me when I'm her, you know? But nobody else knows that, and maybe that gives me an advantage. You saw how terrified Scenester was when I talked to him. I mean, he was *scared*. Even as it was going on, I didn't think I'd have been able to do that as Victoriana, because it would be out of character for her."

"Ah," I said. "America's Sweetheart Syndrome."

"You just made that up," she said.

"I did," I said. "But ASS might be a problem even Victoriana can't overcome. Or maybe it's an opportunity for you to blaze some kind of trail in the domain of superheroism. Guys have it easier. I mean, Brighteyes starts offing supervillains, and people immediately think she's gone insane—she's the glowing green-eyed symbol of female vengeance. But do people do that with guy heroes who do the same thing?"

"Exactly," Anna said. "It's a double standard. Victoriana's allowed to kick ass—but she's still got to be sweet. Maybe even relatable. Cute but badass. Or badass but cutely so. Un-threateningly powerful. Whereas Hellmaiden's something else—also allowed to kick ass, but capable of anything. The unknown around her makes her somehow more formidable. Captivating, but from another angle. Hellmaiden's *not* the girl next door. She's the *bad* girl. Even though, I *know* she's not actually the bad girl. Don't worry. But as you've said enough times, perception matters. People are digging Hellmaiden be-cause she's got an edge to her that Victoriana doesn't. There's a danger to her that's enticing to people, makes them want to know more about her. Never mind that she does *exactly* what Victoriana does, except she can throw plasma beams that in-cinerate everything in their path."

It was wild to hear Anna talk about it like this. It was al-most like Hellmaiden was a superhero—or antihero—identity for Victoriana. Another step removed that freed her up to do things she'd otherwise not do as her primary identity. See, this is what superheroism did to people. It made them bend and break in unforeseen ways.

"You're not going all Dark Phoenix on me, right?" I asked, laughing nervously.

"Please," Anna said. "I can handle my power. All of my power. I'm okay with it. It's just that there are things I can do as Hellmaiden that I can't do as Victoriana, and if I'm doing them in pursuit of justice, it seems like those things are worth doing. And Inferna said early on that while she'd envisioned me as the first Hellmaiden, others could don that crown and become her. And although I didn't say anything to her, *I don't want anybody else being Hellmaiden.* It has to be me. I earned it in my year in exile on the motherfucking Sun, Mitch. Nobody else could have survived that. I deserved it. And I don't want somebody else screwing it up or doing it wrong. Is that selfish of me?"

"I love *you,* Anna," I said. "All that you are."

She hugged me, kissed me hard.

"And I love you," she said. "All that *you* are. But we're going to be up against some nasty villains, and I don't want to hold back when we're taking them down. Hellmaiden can throw some punches that people will back, whereas if Victoriana threw them, they might think something's gone wrong with her. Does that make sense?"

I could see what she was saying. I didn't have that same problem, because Cameraman already had a reputation as a bit of a bad boy.

"It's not like I can't bring Victoriana out again," she said. "I want to. But her story will require an explanation people can handle, will take time for people to come to terms with. She's a symbol of hope and justice, and the world needs that now more than ever. I just want to make sure I do that right, and that what she represents will be there for people to take hope in again."

"Yeah, I think I got it," I said. "Hellmaiden's going to do the dirty work of villain bashing—she's your Grey or Black Hat heroine—and Victoriana can preside over what comes after as a beacon of hope, justice, and joy. Pure White Hat heroism."

"So well-said," she replied. "You get it. And it'll be better if Hellmaiden remains mysterious and even menacing. She pops up when she's needed and vanishes when she's not."

It was funny to see her work that out, and I guess I could see her taking advantage of circumstances to be able to do things with her secondary identity that she might not have been able to do with her first one.

And she was right that people would be both happy to see Victoriana back, and also confused and maybe even disturbed to see Victoriana come back from the dead. You just never knew how people might react to that. It would require real planning on our part, building up her return.

Obviously, it would require working people's emotions, playing them a little (or a lot, depending on how deeply affected people may have been about Victoriana's passing), but there'd be some necessary legerdemain to get people on board. The public liked their superheroes and villains, and tinkering with them had a big effect. Even costume and logo changes prompted strong emotional reactions in some quarters. People would freak to see short-haired Victoriana, expecting her lovely long locks.

"Leave it to you to end up with *two* super-identities," I said. "It's very you, Anna."

"I'm multifaceted," she said. "Or at least dual-natured. It's all very Manichean, except in my case, Victoriana and Hellmaiden aren't opposite sides of the coin—they're both good gals; it's just that Hellmaiden's maybe a little, well, less good. Or more willing to throw down hard when it's necessary."

"Moral latitude," I said. "Those pesky, all-pervasive grey areas."

Anna buried her face in one of her pillows, staring at me with one grey eye while the rest of her mushed into the pillow.

"Being able to lay here with you without setting the bed on fire is bliss," she said.

"Um, hello? I think we actually *did* set the bed on fire," I said, which made her giggle.

"Bad boy," she said. "I just mean there's an elemental fiery core to Hellmaiden that's awesome to inhabit, but it also denies a lot of my humanity. While it allows me to get extreme, it's not something I'd want to inhabit forever. Then I really would go crazy, and we don't want that."

"Okay, you sold me," I said. "I'll add 'Victoriana Return Marketing Campaign' to my to-do list."

"You're the best," she said, kissing my cheek.

"You do know that there'll be fanboys and girls out there who might start speculating that Hellmaiden IS Victoriana. That's going to happen. I know that I had my suspicions."

She poked me with a laugh.

"You so didn't," she said. "You didn't even guess that she was me. I had you completely fooled."

"Did you, though?" I asked, looking so intolerably smug that she whomped me with a pillow. "Maybe I was playing a deep game, there."

"You weren't," she said. "You had no clue. If people wonder, that's fine. Let them wonder. It'll, what do you say—drive engagement."

"Ouch," I said. "Never be a marketer, lest you become one."

"Is that a paradox?"

"I only wish it was," I said. She got out of bed, wrapped in a white sheet, and picked up the golden crown, putting it on her head, and I brought my hands over my eyes as she flared into blinding light, becoming Hellmaiden once again. The heat wave hit me like a fiery fist.

She looked glorious and terrifying, with her opalescent skin, the white thigh boots and bodysuit, the kid gloves, the crimson cowl-shroud connected to her raggedy cape. Although I could see the hint of her green hair in this incarnation, like a spiky starburst around her head, before she pulled the cowl over it, the crown magically appearing atop it, floating like it always did.

"Boom," Anna said. "I am Hellmaiden. Hear me roar!"

"Give 'em hell, Hellmaiden," I said. I threw pillows at her, not caring that they vaporized as they touched her, and we laughed harder than we'd laughed since before she'd hurled herself headlong into the Sun.

**THE SAN FRANCISCO STRIKE TEAM CONSISTED OF** me, Hellmaiden, Inferna, She-Devil, Eightball, Avant Guardian, and Mr. Cool. Everybody had been briefed on what was planned and what to expect, and we'd gathered them at Central, which had greatly impressed Avant Guardian and Mr. Cool, who were ardently angling for admission into the Affiliates. Once gathered, we carted everyone to the West Coast.

We were en route to San Francisco from LA, taking off from the Affiliates West headquarters, where a tanned Tag Team and Ms. Fit held court, along with Rad Lad, who was away dealing with a possible nuclear reactor meltdown in Japan.

"Plethora's going to be the big problem," I said. "She's a heavyweight for the League. This means that Hellmaiden, She-Devil, Mr. Cool, and Avant Guardian should focus on her. While they're engaging her, Eightball, Inferna, and I will be incapacitating the precogs. If they've set some kind of temporal trap for us, owing to some adroit precognitive actions on their part, we'll have to make it up as we go along," I said. My hope was improvisation might offset precognitive surveillance in some fashion. "Mr. Cool and Avant Guardian, you'll need to keep that in the back of your minds while engaging. You both have strong area of effect defensive powers, so you should be ready to put them to use. Eight, you'll be piloting the Affilijet, and if we succeed in acquiring the precogs, you're going to need to fly us out of there quickly."

Eightball seemed very pleased with that, gave me a wink and a nod.

"All good, Camo," he said. "Getting to fly an Affilijet is worth it, my man."

"Great," I said. "If things go bad, everyone get to the Affilijet and we'll evacuate immediately. Hellmaiden and She-Devil will be rearguard."

People liked my new Cameraman suit, which helped get them onboard with what I'd had in mind, since it looked so fab, and in the superhero set, a good costume made all the difference. Eightball was particularly impressed, since he was a diehard gearhead. He engaged me as we flew to the intercept point.

"Cam, I gotta ask you, Bro," he said. "I hear that you're back in the Affiliates. Where does that leave Shutterclique?"

"Same as before," I said. "The 'Clique will continue as planned."

Eightball accepted that with a nod, smoothing out his tuxedo with some deft moves of his hands. His commitment to black and white costuming (almost always an open-collared tux or some pairing of black and white that would have counted as parody of the Knack's own sartorial choices, except that Eightball was very serious about his branding).

"Side project?" he said.

"Yes and no," I replied. "I'm seeing it as maintaining its street-level focus, with the Affiliates being concerned with the more globally-oriented threats."

"And you, like, the bridge between both teams?" Eightball asked.

"Is that a problem?" I asked.

"No, man," Eightball said. "Not for me. Some of us are just wondering if or when we might get Affiliates sponsorship."

"Ah," I said. "With the Knack in charge, the odds are likely better than ever. You know how welcoming and inclusive he is. I'm certain he'll put it before the rest of the team to decide."

As much as I wanted to slag Minder, I held back. I didn't want to come off as a vindictive prick. Minder had it coming, but I wasn't going to give him the satisfaction of making it seem like I was the type to dance on his grave (even though I soooo was).

We brought the cloaked Affilijet down to Caruthers Field, which would put us a stone's throw from the forecasted meeting place of Johnny Rubicon and Ms. Fortune.

"If this is a trap, we're going to need to be ready to pivot," I said, turning on the surveillance cameras and deploying a drone to fly over the area as inconspicuously as I could. I was pleased the way the Cameraman powersuit incorporated the POV window of the drone, and how I could pilot it from within the suit without difficulty. Mr. Transistor must have worked closely with Shane on this suit because it was smooth. I'd have to talk with him at some point.

Hellmaiden and Avant Guardian were airborne and out of sight, while She-Devil and Mr. Cool were nearby, laying low close to the rendezvous location. We kept in communication via earbuds linked to a local dispatcher node on the Affilijet, with me working the switchboard comms.

I spied a sports car pulling up—it was a bone-white Porsche. Out came Johnny Rubicon, speedily identified by my drone cam. The pompadoured precog was wearing a black shirt and grey slacks and shiny leather slip-on black loafers, and slipped on some blue shades as he got out of the car, glancing up and down the street in a performative manner that made me think he either knew what was coming next or didn't care.

"Johnny Rubicon sighted, folks," I said. "He's early. Fern, can you snag him?"

"Why, yes," she said, and I was pleased to see Inferna poof into existence over Rubicon, swooping down and snagging him, taking flight before he knew what was happening.

"He definitely didn't see *that* coming," Eightball said.

Inferna and Rubicon vanished in a teleportative poof.

"Damn," Mr. Cool said. "That went well."

"Kidnapping is one of her specialties," Avant Guardian said.

I'd given Inferna clearance to access Central, and she'd called back.

"Rubicon's in a cell," she said. "I frisked him and removed anything of consequence, including his biotracker, which I disabled."

"Thanks, Fern," I said. Having a teleporter on the team was absolutely handy. A few minutes later, I saw the limousine roll up, doing a U-turn when it spotted Rubicon's Porsche.

"Has to be the rest of them, right on time," I said, noting when Plethora emerged in her black and grey costume with the white triangular "P" on her chest. She opened the passenger door for Ms. Fortune, who emerged in her purple and gold caped costume, her golden facemask sparkly in the light. "Showtime, folks."

"Got it," Anna said, as she and Avant Guardian swept down on them. However, Plethora saw them and bounded for them, leaping and catching Hellmaiden with a haymaker swing that sent her spinning in the opposite direction even as the shockwave of the blow was heard and felt by the rest of us.

Avant Guardian fired a blue energy beam at Ms. Fortune, which was in the form of a great, grasping hand reaching for her. She was calling into a communicator, even as Mr. Cool and She-Devil charged the limousine from their position.

Then we saw something incredible, as the limousine bent and buckled, creakily morphing into a monstrous, morning-star-wielding metallic titan that struck She-Devil with a massive blow that sent her careening down the street. I was glad I had recorded it because that transformation was unbelievable, like liquid-smooth, not mechanical at all. There was a limo there one moment, and a metallic monstrosity there only moments later.

"Holy hell!" Mr. Cool said, throwing ice blasts at the limousine colossus that was bearing down on him.

"Eight, I'm going after it," I said. "Keep things rolling here."

I emerged from the Affilijet to help out Mr. Cool, who was running from the hulking thing chasing him down. I'd never seen anything like that before and was filming it as I approached.

Hellmaiden had recovered from the punch Plethora had thrown, and was speeding back, fists out front. Plethora, tracking her approach, split into four, sending two of her duplicates after Ms. Fortune, who was trying to avoid Avant Guardian.

Then I saw another blur, this time of green and yellow and saw Quick Chick speed her way to Ms. Fortune, spinning her arms in a hyperspeed whir to create twin whirlwinds that drove back Avant Guardian with tornadic force.

"Okay, Team," I said. "Plethora's a quartet, we've got some kind of car colossus, and now it looks like Quick Chick has joined the fray."

Mr. Cool full-on iced the colossus, entombing it in ice.

"That's not gonna hold it, Cam," Cool said, even as the thing flexed and broke out of its ice prison in a deafening explosive blast that sent fragments of icy shrapnel in all directions. I was mindful of an civilians in range, but for the moment, the coast looked to be clear.

Hellmaiden connected with two of the Plethoras, decking them and sending them up the street, while she closed on the other two, one of whom dodged her and snagged her cape and slammed her to the ground, while the other jumped on her and the two of them began pummeling her, not a word spoken between them.

Seeing Anna take hits like that distracted me, but I told myself that she could handle them. Quick Chick's handmade whirlwinds were blinding everybody, sending dust and ice chunks hurtling at us.

"Cool, ice the roads around Fortune and Quick," I said. "Fern, where are you?"

"There's a problem, Cam," Inferna said. "Deathclown and Dollface are here in Central."

Crimebot had been prepared for this attack, at least on some level. Had he somehow used the precogs as bait?

"Shane," I called up to him. "Fern needs help at Central. Deathclown and Dollface."

"I'll get Tag to send help over there," Shane said.

I cut off that call, since the car colossus took a swing at me, catching me in the chest. While I was gratified that the incidental shielding held up to soak up most of that blow, I still was knocked back by the force of the attack. Never mind that the old me would have been killed by that kind of blow; I was still shaken by the hit. Mr. Cool let loose with his ice blasts, turning the colossus into a lollipop by surrounding its head with a big ice ball.

Hellmaiden repelled her Plethora attackers, letting out a war cry as she sent them flying. She then fired her plasma beam at one of them, incinerating her with one shot, which made the other Plethoras scream.

Avant Guardian had flown away from the Quick Chick whirlwinds and was arcing back in a rainbow of light as she bore down on Ms. Fortune yet again.

The car colossus hammered at the ice ball around its head, while I charged it and threw a tackle at its midsection, gratified that the suit's servos had made me strong enough to make an impact on it, even though it only had to take a step back to regain its footing.

"Ice it," I called to Cool, pointing to the ground. Mr. Cool froze the ground around the colossus, which made it lose its footing and slam down, which also helped it crack the ice ball around its head.

"Cameraman!" Plethora called to me, hurling a streetlamp spear at me at high velocity. I saw it just as it struck me, the reactive field protecting me from the blow, even as I saw that Plethora charging me down, striking me hard in the chest, which the field soaked up, although it was telling me it was at sixty percent integrity. Plethora was terrifying up close, being this perfectly realized warrior woman, brimming with power and devoid of compassion, mercy, or anything otherwise considered weakness. She took another swing at me, which I countered with an Aikido grab that flipped her and slammed her to the ground, her own force used against her.

Hellmaiden was engaged with the other two Plethoras, who were giving as good as they got, leading to a real street brawl between them.

Quick Chick had scooped up Ms. Fortune and was taking off running, even as Mr. Cool was trying to freeze the ground upon which she ran. Avant Guardian was moving to intercept.

The Plethora I had been fighting recovered herself and treated me to a two-handed swing that knocked me across the road, smashing into someone's blue Saab, which made me feel bad, although less so when its car alarm blared in my ears.

Mr. Cool threw an ice wall between that Plethora and him and me, which had her pounding the ice with her fists, each blow sounding with a hefty boom as she struck, accompanied by the cracking of ice.

"Nice job, Cool," I said, getting to my feet. Reactive shielding was at forty percent integrity. A couple more poundings from Plethora and I'd see what the suit could really take. "Hey, Plethora!"

I shot her full-on with my shoulder-mounted stun beams, and she took them without flinching.

"Stunning, Mr. Paulsen. This suits you better," Plethora said, hitting me with a righteous uppercut that sent me flying toward a parking lot. I activated my jetpack and kept myself from crashing back to the ground.

Hellmaiden incinerated another Plethora with her super-heated plasma blasts, prompting another scream from the remaining two Plethoras. The strength disbursement ability Plethora possessed had an unexpected side effect—as Plethoras were eliminated, the remaining ones grew stronger as they soaked up the power that had previously been shared out between them. The worse it went for her duplicates, the tougher she got.

Mr. Cool was doing this run-slide thing ice heroes and villains always seemed to do—basically, sprint-sliding with bursts of ice that let them move faster, while Plethora was hot on his heels.

Avant Guardian actually pulled a nice move on Quick Chick, cutting her off with an orange wall of energy that she could only run along, which led to a curious battle between the speedster and the energy-wielder, as Avant Guardian boxed Quick Chick in, and Quick Chick took to speeding around to evade, mindful of not tearing Ms. Fortune apart. But the trap having been sprung (in that Quick was running along Guardian's energy walls) Avant Guardian enveloped Quick and Fortune in an orange energy sphere, which she took aloft, then grabbed Quick by the ankles via the tangible energy, which made the speedster slam hard against the energy wall, knocking herself senseless. The whole thing happened in a matter of moments, and I made a mental note that Avant Guardian absolutely needed to be part of the Affiliates. Mr. Cool, too, for that matter.

The car colossus had changed targets, was helping out Plethora against Hellmaiden, which was escalating into a serious scrap.

I flew in that direction, while I dialed up Inferna, got her voicemail (yes, the devil-woman had voicemail). "Fern, it's me. Are you okay?"

The lack of response alarmed me, and I dialed up Tag Team on the Affilicoms.

"Reg, are you at Central? What happened?"

"Cam," Tag said. "No sign of Inferna, Johnny Rubicon, or Scenester. No Deathclown or Dollface, either, although it looks like there was a brawl here."

"Dammit," I said. "Secure Central, and we'll be there when we can."

The Plethora that I'd been fighting had leaped after me, connecting with a punch, and shorted out what was left of my reactive shielding with an impeccably forced landing that served up a puissant boom of high-grade metallic tritanium alloy with concrete and asphalt.

"Voyeuristic gadfly," Plethora said, raising her fist to pound me in earnest. I decided the time was right to test the antipersonnel defensive features of the suit, pumping Plethora full of electricity, satisfied to see her flinch and strain against that electrical voltage. I threw as hard a punch as the suit would allow me, pleased to see that she felt it, if nothing else. She gritted her teeth and, despite the voltage, landed a colossal punch to my chest, which actually made my HUD display skip a beat. I channeled my Aikido again and whisked her off the top of me, sending her skipping across the ground. She was gearing up to strike again when Avant Guardian nabbed her with a red energy gauntlet and flung her off into the San Francisco Bay.

"Thanks for the save, Guardian," I said, getting to my feet yet again.

"You've got it, Cam," she said, flying over me, while Ms. Fortune raged within the orange energy ball that contained her. Quick Chick was being held fast by orange energy cuffs within the sphere.

Hellmaiden was dealing with both the colossus and the last remaining Plethora, in a fiendish fracas that was sending more waves of force around them.

Plethora, seeing that we were regrouping on her position, hurled Hellmaiden into the colossus, and leaped away, muttering something into her own telecoms, as I saw her vanish in a flickering flash of yellowy light.

"Seems like they have teleportation even without Scenester," I said, wondering if Crime might have recruited another teleporter in his ranks.

Hellmaiden trained her plasma beams at the car colossus, punching a hole right through it, which, I noticed, readily healed. This thing might have been made of metal, but it had a fluidity to it that spoke of nanotechnology. I needed to get a sample of it.

"Hellmaiden, see if you can shear off a piece of that thing," I said, and, to my delight, she fired off a plasma blast that sliced off its mace-wielding arm cleanly, making it land on the ground. The moment it hit the ground, the mace melted from its form and began slithering back toward the colossus. "Guardian, can you scoop that up?"

"Sure can," Avant Guardian said, conjuring a yellow energy ladle that grabbed it and then became another sphere like the one containing Quick and Fortune.

"Damn," I said. "Perfect."

The colossus, seeing that its arm had been removed, re-formed its severed limb with another, and I noticed that it had gotten smaller.

"It's drawing from its existing mass," I said. The car colossus turned its head and stared hard at me with headlight eyes.

"Nothing gets past you, Mr. Paulsen," it said, in a voice that was some toxic blend of Dr. Crime's and Crimebot's droning delivery.

Then the thing dissolved into an amorphous form, aiming for the sewers. But I called out to Avant Guardian to contain it as she had the arm, and she extended her yellow energy sphere to cut off the escape of the strange colossus-blob, and she captured it, packing it tightly in the energy sphere.

"It's strong," Guardian said, clutching her forehead. "It's using considerable force against my containment sphere."

Hellmaiden flew over to her. "Release Quick Chick and Ms. Fortune; I'll take them, and you can focus your energy on the lethal limousine."

Avant Guardian nodded, smiling at Anna's suggestion, and they did the exchange after I'd stun-beamed both Fortune and Quick into catatonia. Then it was simply a matter of getting them to the Affilijet, power neutralizer collars in place and locking them into securicages as Eight took off.

Affiliates West had full supervillain containment facilities where the limousine nano-blob might be dealt with. Avant Guardian, Hellmaiden and I flew beside the Affilijet as we made our way to LA, while the blob talked to us the entire time.

"Mr. Paulsen," it said. "You are a resilient nothing, it must be said. Your team of metahuman misfits and interdimensional outcasts has intrigued us, but you are far too late to the party, as you might frame it. What we have set in motion exceeds anything you might be able to comprehend."

My rule of thumb was always that when the bad guys started talking like this, especially the upper-echelon ones, it meant something. I tried not to let it get to me, just blew it off, which I also found annoyed the big baddies, who remained rooted in megalomania.

I'd never directly taken on Dr. Crime, who was both out of my league and also incredibly careful to conceal himself, which made him a harder target to engage, compared with so many others.

For me, it was always a case where I might fight someone who was a minion of Dr. Crime's, but never the man himself. That he'd come out a bit more in the open as Dr. Crimebot spoke either to an escalation in his criminal confidence, or perhaps the furtherance of whatever scheme he was planning. I'd had to confer with Anna on it, since she had her own copious knowledge of supervillains.

We reached Affiliates West without incident, and Avant Guardian was able to carefully place the Limo-Blob (as we'd taken to calling it) into a high-level containment cell, which relieved Guardian, who'd never contained an enemy that long before.

She clutched her forehead, waving off help.

"That was *something*," she said.

"Great job," Anna said, patting her shoulder.

I gave everyone mad props for their participation, which made them all feel good, and I'd told them I would definitely be recommending their consideration for Affiliates status, although I was also careful not to promise anything, too, because you know how that went. I'd rather underpromise and overdeliver, believe me.

The Cameraman powersuit had done very well in this field-testing, and I told Shane as much when I had the chance, after exiting it and stretching my legs. I never considered myself a "suit guy"—even with my old Cameraman togs, but I suppose I was, now.

There was still no sign of Inferna, which caused me greater concern. Neither Anna nor She-Devil had been able to reach her.

"I'll see if I can find her," Anna said. "She-Devil and I will look into it."

"Okay," I said. "I'm going to interrogate the Limo-Blob."

Anna gave my arm a squeeze.

"Be careful, Killer," she said, and I wanted to kiss her, but didn't want to set myself on fire, either, so I settled for a reciprocal arm squeeze.

Avant Guardian, Eightball, and Mr. Cool were still hanging with me, eager to see how an Affiliate might interrogate a bad guy.

I'd already isolated some of the metallic material from the Limo-Blob, which scanning had indicated was nanotechnological in nature. I had wired that up to Mr. Transistor, who assured me he'd look into it.

Meanwhile, in the special Affiliates control unit prison cell, I addressed the Limo-Blob, which had since reformed itself into a simulacrum of Dr. Crimebot—which looked like a metallic version of Dr. Crime in a metallic black tux, his skin grey metallic and his hair and beard as black as his tux, with some artfully geometric white lines paired at his jawline and temples.

"What should we call you, Limo-Blob?" I asked. "Carlossus? Nanomobile?"

"You can call me Dr. Crimebot, Mr. Paulsen," he said.

"But you're not, are you?" I asked. The simulacrum took a seat, looking up at the protected camera that allowed me to speak to and address it.

"I'm an avatar of Crimebot," he said.

Since the files I'd read on Dr. Crime said he was a gloater, I thought I'd see if I could get him gloating. Also, I suppose I should give you their dossiers, because, you know how I roll by now:

**ALIAS: DR. CRIME**

*REAL/ASSUMED NAME: NAPOLEON BARCA*
*HAIR: BLACK*
*EYES: BLACK*
*HEIGHT: 6'*
*WEIGHT: 190 LBS.*

**POWERS:** *DR. CRIME POSSESSES NO KNOWN SUPERHUMAN POWERS, HOWEVER, HE IS:*

•**WEALTHY:** *DR. CRIME IS EXCEEDINGLY WEALTHY, RANKING AMONG THE WORLD'S TOP BILLIONAIRES. HIS INVESTMENT PORTFOLIO IS INCREDIBLY DIVERSIFIED, MAKING IT DIFFICULT TO INHIBIT HIS OPERATIONS.*

•**CRIMINAL MASTERMIND:** *DR. CRIME HAS A GENIUS-LEVEL INTELLECT IN THE AREAS OF CRIME, AND HAS A MSC IN CRIMINOLOGY AND CRIMINAL JUSTICE (OXFORD UNIVERSITY).*

•**HYPER-INVENTIVE:** *DR. CRIME IS A MASTER INVENTOR, ABLE TO CREATE ALL MANNER OF CONTRAPTIONS IN HIS QUEST FOR WORLD DOMINATION.*

**THREAT LEVEL: 10/10**

\* \* \*

**ALIAS: CRIMEBOT**

*REAL/ASSUMED NAME: CRIMEBOT*
*HAIR: NONE*
*EYES: RED*
*HEIGHT: 5'*
*WEIGHT: 500 LBS.*

**POWERS:** *CRIMEBOT POSSESSES THE FOLLOWING SUPERPOWERS, INCLUDING:*

•**SUPER-STRENGTH:** *CRIMEBOT'S ROBOTIC CHASSIS ALLOWS IT TO LIFT FROM ONE TON TO ONE HUNDRED TONS (DEPENDING ON THE VARIANT).*

•**BODY ARMOR:** *CRIMEBOT'S SYSTEMATICALLY IMPROVED BATTLE BODIES HAVE INCREASINGLY IMPROVED ITS ARMOR RANKING, MAKING IT CAPABLE OF WITHSTANDING EVER-STRONGER PHYSICAL AND ENERGY ATTACKS.*

•**CRIMINAL MASTERMIND:** *CRIMEBOT'S AI PROGRAMMING MAKES IT A NEAR-PERFECT CRIMINAL GENIUS, ABLE TO CARRY OUT MULTIPLE COMPLEX CRIMINAL OPERATIONS SIMULTANEOUSLY.*

•**HYPER-INVENTION:** *CRIMEBOT IS ABLE TO CREATE ALL MANNER OF CRIMINAL WEAPONS AND EVEN OTHER ROBOTS IN ITS MISSION TO COMMIT "THE PERFECT CRIME"—A MISSION CENTRAL TO ITS EXISTENCE.*

•**SYSTEMATIC UPGRADES:** *CRIMEBOT USES THE DATA IT COLLECTS IN VICTORY AND DEFEAT TO CREATE IMPROVED VERSIONS OF ITSELF. IT HAS BEEN THROUGH FIVE VERSIONS, EACH ONE MORE POWERFUL THAN ITS PREDECESSOR.*

•**SERIAL IMMORTALITY:** *CRIMEBOT HAS MADE MULTIPLE BACKUPS OF ITSELF, SCATTERED THROUGHOUT THE WORLD, WHICH ARE MADE TO GO ONLINE IF THE ACTIVE CRIMEBOT HAS BEEN DESTROYED. ON AT LEAST THREE OCCASIONS, CRIMEBOT WAS CONFIRMED DESTROYED, ONLY TO REAPPEAR AGAIN AT A LATER DATE.*

**THREAT LEVEL:** 10/10

"Looks like Deathclown and Dollface came up empty-handed," I said, hoping a little bluffing might go a long way.

Limobot (that's what I privately decided I was calling it) only smiled enigmatically up at the camera.

"They did what they were supposed to do," Limobot said. "Your attempts to involve extradimensional interlopers have been effectively countered, Mr. Paulsen. We also have friends in low places, QED."

It always bugged me when somebody used "QED"—so, of course, Dr. Crime would do that. However, since Limobot was feeling chatty, I thought I'd take advantage of its loquacity.

"Why'd you off Minder?" I asked. I really wanted to know.

"Minder was more useful to us dead than living," Limobot said. "He had served his purpose, and we'd forecast that whatever bids he had to ruin your reputation and that of the Affiliates would ultimately fail. Ergo, the most logical course of action was to terminate him."

"Seems like a drastic play," I said. "Given all he was doing for you."

"As a catalyst, Minder was useful," Limobot said. "But once things were underway, his value diminished, especially when factored against his own ambitions. We are not afraid to sacrifice pieces in the Great Game, Mr. Paulsen."

The fact that Limobot was even talking to me was interesting, had to be part of some larger scheme.

"*We're* going to stop you," I said.

"You don't even know what we're doing, Mr. Paulsen," Limobot said. "How can you possibly stop us?"

There was some of that patented Dr. Crime arrogance. The key was to keep working that.

"We've got your precogs," I said. "Among others. We're aware of you and are going to bring you down. Without Minder around to protect you, the Affiliates are going to smash your entire operation."

"If you say so, Mr. Paulsen," Limobot said. "You think of us as Dr. Crimebot, which isn't factually incorrect, but we are, in truth, Dr. Crimeboss. That's a more accurate and precise appellation."

Avant Guardian, Eightball, and Mr. Cool looked on, marveling at this whole thing. They were loving being on the inside.

"Is that what you want to be called?" Avant Guardian asked.

"Yes, Avant Guardian," Limobot said. "Scenester spoke highly of you, you would be happy to know. We are looking forward to bringing you into the fold."

Avant Guardian looked embarrassed and uneasy at the hint of her dalliances with Scenester. Frankly, I couldn't see what she saw in the guy, but it was her business, not mine.

"Never," she said.

"Never is never never," Dr. Crimeboss said. "It only means 'not right now' in my experience. You will be shown the error of your ways soon enough."

Not wanting Crimeboss to derail my interrogation, I turned it back on him.

"Explain to me how you and Crimebot came to this union," I asked.

"It's obvious, Mr. Paulsen," Crimeboss said. "Dr. Crime craved immortality, and Crimebot deduced that it needed a human drive to propel it to the next level of evolution. Working together, we've become the ultimate supervillain. Not even Doctor Fist comes close to us."

One of those commonly known things in the superhero community was the intense rivalry between Doctor Fist and Dr. Crime—the two of them each fought to be at the supervillain pinnacle, following their different paths: Doctor Fist focused on personal metahuman power, while Dr. Crime worked through ever-expanding criminal networks. The fusion of Dr. Crime and Crimebot into Dr. Crimeboss was likely a tactical and strategic compromise to attempt to offset the limitations they each faced as individuals.

"I think Doctor Fist could pound you into spare parts," I said.

"You'd be wrong," Crimeboss said. The two of them really were a symbiote of some kind, a true cyborg. However they went about it, the melding of two of the greatest criminal minds in the world was a disaster for the rest of us.

"Okay, so if we're too late to the game to stop you, why don't you tell us what your grand scheme is, Crimeboss?" I asked.

"You'll know soon enough, Mr. Paulsen," Crimeboss said, staring up at me, seeming to see me through the camera. "I look forward to personally ending you."

**21**

WHATEVER GRIEVANCES YOU MIGHT HAVE ABOUT HOW the Hell's Belles did things, we looked after our own. When Inferna went missing, She-Devil and I looked into it. I owed Inferna that much after what had happened between us.

While She-Devil couldn't teleport the way Inferna did, she did have, by way of those amazing horns of hers, a way of opening a portal between Hell and Earth, so the two of us used that to reach Oblivion City (remember? My name for Inferna's place? So catchy!) in hopes of discovering what happened to our fearless leader.

I'll confess to feeling a strangely comforting sensation deep inside me while back in Hell. Perhaps it was the knowledge that in this place, I could *really* play hard. That fight with Plethora (BTW, despite her villainy, I *love* her name! As badass as she is, right?) it really gave me a taste of properly feisty combat that I liked.

Not to be a complainer, because I'm so *not* a complainer, but when you're a super-strong A-lister, in most fights, you have to hold back. It's just too easy to take somebody apart with a couple of punches if you're not careful.

Therefore, when you run into someone like Plethora or Doctor Fist, who can actually take those hard hits, it's super-satisfying. I'm not a "violence solves everything" girl, but being able to really let a bad guy have it is the bomb.

Being in Hell meant I could go wild like that, because literally everybody down there had it coming, one way or another.

She-Devil got us into Inferna's domicile, where we found Scenester and Johnny Rubicon, locked in her in-house cellblock, where the Trinity had been. Upon seeing us, the two of them jumped up, yanking fruitlessly on the iron bars of their cells. They looked frightened and weary, but otherwise unharmed.

"Hellmaiden, She-Devil, get us out of here," Scenester said.

"Yeah, fuckin' hell, man," Johnny Rubicon said.

"Where's Inferna?" I asked.

"How the hell should I know?" Rubicon said. "She took us here for safekeeping—her words. Then she never came back."

Unfortunately, I couldn't call Mitch across dimensions, but I thought the plan had been to keep the prisoners at Central. Maybe when Deathclown and Dollface appeared at Central, Inferna had decided to teleport here with the prisoners. And maybe they'd pursued her to Hell.

She-Devil and I explored all of Inferna's place, but there were no signs of struggle.

"Where could she be?" She-Devil asked, turning her eyes this way and that to dry to find any sign of her.

I tried to get into Inferna's head, which wasn't a natural place for me, but was also something that required a bit of Mitch's beloved detective work, which I thought I was pretty good at, too, in my perhaps more direct, beat cop kind of way. Not being self-deprecating, by the way. The beat cop that I was could beat the truth out of anybody, if I could just get my hands on them.

"Okay, I'm thinking that Inferna lured them away from here," I said. "She didn't want them showing up here, messing up her place, so she drew them elsewhere."

"Not a bad theory," She-Devil said. "I can try to track her."

"You can track?" I asked. She-Devil gave a cautious half-smile.

"Maybe," she said. "I may have been a hellhound in another life."

"Wow," I said. "Okay, so, let's see what we can find."

I took flight with She-Devil, carrying her down to the ground in Oblivion City, where I was pleased to see that the Minder-specter (?) was in the center of the city. Inferna had made good on her promise to find him. I was touched and flew over to him.

In the center was a stone circle with a black basalt statue of a robed devil, gazing proudly out at some unseen vista, carrying a pitchfork. At the base of this statue was an iron ring, from which hung heavy iron chains. Shackled to those chains was Minder, guarded by two devils in black and red livery, looking like Swiss Guards by way of Satan. They even had hellish halberds—cruel-looking weapons with bladed metal heads that had obscene devils intertwined amid them, doing unspeakable things.

Minder looked at me in disbelief, his white eyes wide at the spectacle I presented.

"Anna," he said. "How on Earth..."

His head had this odd look to it, like it had been cracked and put together again by careless artisans.

"We're not on Earth, obviously, Minder," I said. "You're in Hell."

He strained at his bonds, and I could feel him casting about with the memory of his telepathy and glancing at the guards.

"Does he still have his telepathy?"

One of the guards shook his head.

"I don't belong here," he said. "I don't understand what happened."

"You were shot," I said. "Someone assassinated you."

"Impossible," Minder said. "I had planned for all of the probable contingencies."

It occurred to me that I could interrogate him here and perhaps find something useful I could bring back to Mitch once She-Devil and I had found Inferna.

"Who were you working with?" I asked. He narrowed his white eyes as he looked at me.

"I can't feel your mind," he said. "What's happened to me?"

"You sent me into the Sun," I said. "And somebody shot you dead."

"Not part of the plan," he said, again struggling against the chains, which weighed him down and held him fast. "None of this is."

"What plan?" I asked. "Tell me what it is."

"Free me and I will," he said.

"Not my call," I replied. I hoped whatever fate awaited him here, it would make him at least as miserable as I'd been on the Sun.

"Inferna," he said, gripping the chains that held him. "She did this. This is *her* doing."

The guards just looked on impassively, pretending they weren't listening to every word. They were devils like Inferna, and they looked formidable. I had no doubt they'd be able to manage Minder. They might even be able to manage me.

"Who was part of your plan?" I asked.

He chuckled—it was a dry, bitter thing, more of a gasp than anything recognizably human. It's uncharitable, but I rather liked seeing him in this abject state. If he remained here forever, it would be a fate richly deserved.

"You'll never know," he said. "Neither you nor your beloved Mitch will be able to stop what I've set in motion."

This time I did grab him, hoisting him by his rags, lifting him off his feet. He was helpless against me but was as resistant as he'd been in life.

"Too bad you can't read my mind, eh, Anna?" he said. His rasping laugh echoed off the stony walls around us.

"You belong here," I said. "Grist for their malefic mills. Tell me about the Moebius Mutagen."

The Minder-shade rasp-laughed even harder.

"Oh, Anna," he said. "You're so far behind us, you'll *never* catch up. Not you, not Mitch. The Moebius Mutagen is the crowning achievement of decades of work. It will change absolutely everything."

She-Devil watched me with him, cocking an eyebrow.

"There's no point in roughing him up," she said. "He's already dead."

"Yes," Minder said. "I'm already dead, Anna. You can't touch me."

I glanced at one of the guards again.

"Can I punch him?" I asked. The guard nodded.

I cocked a fist, and really, really wanted to deck him. He just stared at me with those sightless-seeming eyes, and I found I couldn't do it. Even after how much he'd wronged me, how must he'd tried to hurt Mitch. Minder chuckled.

"Even now, you can't do it," he said. "You're too soft, Anna."

I addressed the guards yet again.

"Have you seen Inferna?" I asked.

"The Mistress was...occupied," the guard said. "Deathclown was eager to have...words...with her."

The guard's eyes were like polished brass, metallic and reflective, giving away nothing—no fear, no weakness. Both of them looked very tough.

"Which way did they go?" I asked.

The guards looked at each other a moment, then conferred quietly. They pointed with their hellish halberds, pointing in a direction I couldn't know, because I didn't know if this place had something as prosaic as north, south, east, or west. I just noted the way they pointed and resolved to follow that direction.

"Take me with you, Anna," Minder said. "I'll help you find Inferna."

"No, Minder," I said. "You're right where you belong."

Undaunted, he laughed again, his voice echoing in the monolithic prison that was Oblivion City.

"I belong here more than you, Anna," Minder said, his shoulders heaving as he laughed.

Not wanting to give him the satisfaction, I grabbed She-Devil and took to the air and left him with his lifeless laughter, heading in the direction the guards had pointed.

## 22

**MR. TRANSISTOR HAD A LOT TO SAY AFTER HE'D RECEIVED THE** samples of the Limo-bot. We did a teleconference, the first Affiliates one I'd had since coming back on the team. It was me, Shane, Ms. Fit, Tag Team, Decibelle, Wingman, Tandem, Mr. Transistor, and Rad Lad.

"First off, I want to welcome back Cameraman," Shane said. "We're happy to have you back, Mitch."

The others clapped with varying degrees of politeness and enthusiasm, and you know I noted who was who:

**POLITE:** *TAG TEAM, WINGMAN, TANDEM*

**ENTHUSIASTIC:** *MS. FIT, DECIBELLE, MR. TRANSISTOR, RAD LAD, KNACK*

I made a mental note to work on the polite applauders. Frankly, I didn't know why Reg was even sour; he'd been flopping in my brownstone since I'd had to lay low. Maybe he and Wingman were still sore from the drubbing the Shutterclique delivered them at Shane's place. Maybe they felt stupid that Minder had played them, or something else. Not sure what Tandem's deal was, although I noticed Tandem was in female mode, so maybe Hellmaiden's recent popularity had gotten the twins mindful of attempting to reach more than Tandem's baseline bro audience.

"Thanks, Shane," I said. "Before we dive into everything Dr. Crimeboss-related—oh, by the way: that's what it's wanting to be called, now—I would like to personally put forward Avant Guardian, Mr. Cool, and Eightball for full-time active-duty Affiliates membership. They were outstanding in the field operation where we managed to snag Ms. Fortune, Scenester, Johnny Rubicon, and Quick Chick with minimal property damage and no civilian casualties."

The others appeared impressed, and Shane clapped again.

"Great job, Mitch," he said. "What we like to see. We'll review their files and put it to a vote in our next session."

"With respect, Shane," I said. "Why can't we vote on them now? With what's coming our way, I fear we're going to need as many people as we can get."

And so we voted on whether a vote was called for on this, which passed. And then we did an up-and-down vote on the candidates. To my amazement, all three were greenlit for Affiliates active-duty, which made me happy, since they'd all be good additions. The background checks were the real hurdles to be climbed, as I knew very well.

"Great," Shane said. "While Mr. Cool and Avant Guardian are typically East Coast-based, we might consider mixing it up and putting them on Affiliates West. Eightball's a natural for West, as well. That should help us balance out the roster cross-country."

Nobody objected to that, and I was looking forward to telling them.

"In the course of our operation to grab Crime's precogs— oh, did you guys already read the files I sent on that?" I asked. There was murmuring and mumbling among them, with only Transistor, Shane, and Fit having read the files, so I recapped it quickly, mentioning my suspicion that Crime had been using precogs to protect his operations by using them to pick the best avenue for success.

This naturally got everybody chattering, threatening to derail the meeting.

"Wait," Tandem said. "How are Crime's precogs protecting him?"

"He was using them to anticipate our reactions," I said. "Not sure how long he's been doing it, but it's been a while."

They were suitably impressed by that, muttering to each other and using Affilitexting to communicate offline (I could tell because I was hearing the text chimes before people remembered to mute theirs. But I could still see their eyes wandering).

"Great work, Mitch," Shane said. "Without the precogs, Crime won't see us coming."

"How'd you even do that?" Tag Team asked. "Wouldn't they have seen you do this ahead of time?"

Sighing, I explained to the team that we used another precog to help us anticipate the actions of the Crime League/Enemies of Humanity precogs, and thereby got the drop on them. The others were again impressed by that, and I had to compose myself to get the meeting back on-track.

"In the course of that operation, we managed to capture this, well, nanotechnological organism that was working with Crime," I said. "The so-called 'Limobot' referred to in the file uploads you didn't read."

"Hey, come on now, Mitch," Tag Team said. "We're not all obsessives the way you are. Some of us have lives."

"Many lives," Decibelle said, prompting laughter from the group. Oh, man, I forgot how exhausting teams could be.

"That's the story with Hell's Belles?" Tandem asked. "They really grandstanded in Philadelphia. That Hellmaiden in particular."

"Yeah," I said. "They're allied with us."

"I don't see how," Wingman said. "They're *devils*, Mitch. You're being naïve."

I cleared my throat, folding my hands in front of me to try to appear measured.

"They're Hell-adjacent," I said. "They're operating outside of the otherwise ironclad infamy of the Hell Dimensional Bureaucracy."

"You've lost us, Mitch," Tandem said. "'Hell Dimensional Bureaucracy'—meaning?"

"Guys, you can't expect me to map out Hell's organizational structure, can you?" I said. "This is all on-file. Literally laid out in the Affiliates Archives. I can't be the only one who reads those, can I?"

Rad Lad laughed. "Pretty much positive you are, Dude."

"You're all killing me, here," I said. "Suffice to say that Hell's Belles are a resistance group operating independent of the HDB. Led by Inferna, they are currently a three-person team, with Hellmaiden and She-Devil rounding it out. The Shutter-clique has been working with them on this overarching case involving Minder, Dr. Crime, Crimebot, the Crime League, and the Enemies of Humanity."

You know I had to spend about twenty more minutes bringing them all up to speed on this, which was driving me crazy. Was I seriously the only one who relished all the data-crunching? Or maybe they just delegated that kind of work to me while they were busy getting photographed with celebrities they were dating or engaging in high-profile punch-ups. I was absolutely going to make a relational database that would incorporate all of my cross-referenced dossiers on heroes and villains around the world. There clearly needed to be something in place. AFFILIA would appreciate it, at least.

"Mister Transistor, can you brief everyone on what we got from Limobot?" I asked. Transistor was happy to speak up. He wore these cool HUD shades that flared amber as he spoke.

"What Mitch and his team discovered was a kind of nano-technological weapon," Transistor said. "His report indicated that it originally appeared as a car, but in the course of a fight, it transformed into the so-called 'Limobot' or 'Carlossus' as indicated in the files. It was a sentient-seeming robotic weapon that was comprised of these nanobots."

Transistor ran a display panel that showed the spiderlike nanobots moving around.

"They are, thankfully, able to be contained by our high-level protocols," Transistor said. "And they don't appear to be programmed for self-replication, at least among this sample. However, operating on a nanotechnological level, these could pose a grave threat to organic life, or anything on the planet, for that matter. You can see on these crawlers that they are marked with the Dr. Crimebot logo."

He zoomed in, showing the ligatured "CB" enclosed in a circle that signified the involvement of Crimebot.

"The Limobot actually manifested as Dr. Crimebot while in our holding facility here in West," I said. "I interrogated it and it was talking to me as Dr. Crimebot. In fact, it told me it wants to be called 'Dr. Crimeboss' going forward. I didn't have any reason to think I wasn't talking to the real thing."

That led to another sidebar as people processed the following, which I rendered as an equation on the display for ease of comprehension:

$$DR.\ CRIME + CRIMEBOT = DR.\ CRIMEBOT \Rightarrow DR.\ CRIMEBOSS$$

"Dr. Crime has willfully abandoned his biological existence to become a cyborg with Crimebot," I said. "I believe they deduced that it was mutually advantageous to assume this hybrid form."

The other Affiliates were seemingly dazzled by this, more so when I showed some still pictures from my interrogation of the Limobot.

"It looks just like Dr. Crime," Tag Team said.

"Spitting image," Wingman said. "But metallic."

"I think it's reasonable to assume that the synthesis of their personalities has created a megalomaniacal super-criminal mastermind who represents the warped syncretized ethos of both Dr. Crime and Crimebot."

I shared my newly-minted dossier for Dr. Crimeboss:

**ALIAS: DR. CRIMEBOSS**

*REAL/ASSUMED NAME: NAPOLEON BARCA, CRIMEBOT*
*HAIR: BLACK (METALLIC)*
*EYES: BLACK (METALLIC)*
*HEIGHT: UNKNOWN (6'+)*
*WEIGHT: UNKNOWN*

**POWERS:** *DR. CRIMEBOSS POSSESSES THE FOLLOWING SUPERPOWERS:*

•**WEALTHY:** *DR. CRIMEBOSS IS EXCEEDINGLY WEALTHY, RANKING AMONG THE WORLD'S TOP BILLIONAIRES. HIS INVESTMENT PORTFOLIO IS INCREDIBLY DIVERSIFIED, MAKING IT DIFFICULT TO INHIBIT HIS OPERATIONS.*

•**CRIMINAL MASTERMIND:** *DR. CRIMEBOSS HAS A GENIUS-LEVEL INTELLECT IN THE AREAS OF CRIME, AND HAS A MSC IN CRIMINOLOGY AND CRIMINAL JUSTICE (OXFORD UNIVERSITY) AS WELL AS CRIMEBOT'S AI PROGRAMMING MAKES IT A NEAR-PERFECT CRIMINAL GENIUS, ABLE TO CARRY OUT MULTIPLE CRIMINAL OPERATIONS SIMULTANEOUSLY. THE HYBRID INTELLIGENCE OF DR. CRIMEBOSS MAY BE BEYOND CONVENTIONAL MEASUREMENT.*

•**HYPER-INVENTIVE:** *DR. CRIMEBOSS IS A MASTER INVENTOR, ABLE TO CREATE ALL MANNER OF CONTRAPTIONS IN HIS QUEST FOR WORLD DOMINATION. CRIMEBOSS IS ABLE TO DEVISE ALL MANNER OF CRIMINAL WEAPONS AND EVEN OTHER ROBOTS IN ITS MISSION TO COMMIT "THE PERFECT CRIME"—A MISSION CENTRAL TO ITS EXISTENCE.*

•**SUPER-STRENGTH:** *DR. CRIMEBOSS'S ROBOTIC CHASSIC ALLOWS IT TO LIFT FROM ONE TON TO ONE HUNDRED TONS (TRUE STRENGTH UNKNOWN AT THIS TIME).*

•**BODY ARMOR:** *DR. CRIMEBOSS'S NANO-AUGMENTED BODY IS ABLE TO ENDURE EVER-STRONGER PHYSICAL AND ENERGY ATTACKS.*

•**SYSTEMATIC UPGRADES:** *DR. CRIMEBOSS IS CAPABLE OF USING THE DATA IT COLLECTS IN VICTORY AND DEFEAT TO CREATE IMPROVED VERSIONS OF ITSELF.*

•**SERIAL IMMORTALITY:** *DR. CRIMEBOSS HAS LIKELY MADE MULTIPLE BACKUPS OF ITSELF, SCATTERED THROUGHOUT THE WORLD, WHICH ARE MADE TO GO ONLINE IF THE ACTIVE CRIMEBOSS HAS BEEN DESTROYED.*

**THREAT LEVEL: 11+**

"That's amazing," Ms. Fit said. "This all arose out of your interrogation, Mitch?"

"Mostly," I said. "Some deduction, but a lot of it from Crimeboss directly. He likes to talk."

"Yeah, that's ol' Dr. Crime," Decibelle said. "He's a talker, that one is."

The others chuckled, and while I didn't want to come off as the humorless hardass, I was still trying to keep them focused.

"Forget whatever you knew before," I said. "Dr. Crimeboss is operating at another level. I've never tussled with Dr. Crime, but Victoriana and I did take down Crimebot 3.0, and the prospect of them forming some cybernetic supervillain should terrify all of you."

"To Mitch's point," Shane said. "We're securing permits to attack Dr. Crime's headquarters in Toronto."

"Still?" I asked.

"The local authorities aren't making it easy," Shane said. "The Bridle Path community is less than pleased that there might be some Affiliates action in their area."

"Oh, come on, now," I said. "They're worried about property values while Dr. Crimeboss is hatching some word-annihilating scheme in their neighborhood?"

"Procedures are procedures, Cameraman," Wingman said. "You haven't forgotten that, have you? We can't just go rolling in there and smashing things up."

"You all have the files," I said. "I urge you to read them."

"Anymore from you, Mitch," Shane asked.

"Yes," I said, seeing some of the Affiliates exchanging glances. "As already mentioned, we're working with Hell's Belles, and, unfortunately, Inferna, who was instrumental in bagging Johnny Rubicon, has disappeared. Tag Team was first to the scene. Reg?"

Tag Team straightened up, alternately flummoxed and gratified to be able to present a bit in the meeting.

"Yeah, I dispatched a dozen dupes—you all know I've got like a hundred staying at Mitch's former residence, right?" he said. "Anyway, we got to Central and it looked like there'd been a battle there. Central's looking a little rough around the edges, what with that orbital strike and this brawl in the cellblock. No sign of Scenester or Rubicon, no sign of Inferna."

"How was Inferna on-site?" Wingman asked. "She's not on the team."

"I granted her provisional access," I said. "It was an expedient measure to assist in prisoner rendition."

"I don't know about anybody else, but that makes me *very* uneasy," Wingman said.

"The last report we got from Inferna was that she was under attack by Deathclown and Dollface," I said.

"Ooh, I hate them," Decibelle said. "They're so creepy. I do not like clowns."

"I didn't see anything," Tag Team said. "Just a sign of a fight of some kind. No bodies, however."

"Hellmaiden and She-Devil are trying to locate Inferna," I said. "I haven't been in touch with them since they left, but I feel like they'll both reach out if they have news."

"I love that Hellmaiden," Decibelle said. "She's so spunky. And those boots? Otherworldly!"

"She's reckless," Tandem said. "That incident over Philadelphia could've destroyed the city."

"But it didn't," I said.

"I heard some locals made a shrine out of those giant obsidian teeth," Rad Lad said. "That is wayyyy cray."

"Those were moved to a secure location," Tandem said. "We can't have some pagan shrine forming in a major American city, even as a memorial dedicated to the defeat of a demon."

I wondered whether their attention spans had enough to even mention the Moebius Mutagen. I decided to take a gamble.

"During my interrogation of Scenester, he mentioned something about a 'Moebius Mutagen' that Dr. Crimeboss was working on," I said. "Something he claimed would solve 'the superhero problem' for good. Unfortunately, I didn't get anything else out of him. Anybody hear anything about this?"

I waited while they murmured among themselves. None of them had anything on it, which I kind of expected. Not to be a dick about it, but that's why I was the one busy being a detective while the rest were busy being superheroes.

"Okay, thanks for that *very* detailed report, Mitch," Shane said. "I urge everything to read up on the files he shared. They are fascinating reading. Anybody else have new business they want to share?"

FML.

**23**

HOWEVER SHE DID IT, SHE-DEVIL MANAGED TO CATCH INFERNA'S SCENT, and we worked our way from Oblivion City into the Hellish Hinterlands (what I was calling them), which were these hauntingly beautiful-yet-desolate-and-foreboding highlands of white ground that was alternately salt, snow, or ash, where these white-barked trees like birches—except with screaming faces etched in their bark, and with blood-red leaves—festooned the rolling hillsides.

I would alternately fly and land with She-Devil, as she tracked Inferna. A quicksilver river flowed past one of the rolling hills, leading to a mirror-sheened lake that we were able to walk across, which was utterly bizarre, as we did so under chartreuse skies, and that weird white sun provided an unpleasant light without heat.

She-Devil kept tracking, while I kept my eyes out for any signs of trouble. In this tortured landscape, it was difficult to navigate. In the distance, we could make out another city, a red city that had minaret towers around a massive glowing wall. So great was this city that we saw it well before we even got near enough to it.

Instead, we just followed a torturous path, led by She-Devil's nose.

"You know," she said. "I don't know if we can take on Deathclown ourselves."

"We don't have to beat him," I said, although in my head, I relished a facedown with Deathclown, just by virtue of his name. Anybody named that deserved a righteous beatdown. I already played it out in my head what I would do. "We just have to find Inferna and get her out of there."

"You're assuming she's in danger," She-Devil said. "Maybe they're having a party, drinking hellwine out of head-carved goblets."

I didn't believe that.

"Inferna's not like that," I said. "Besides, Deathclown's allied with the Enemies of Humanity—he's not going to just have a party with Inferna."

"You don't know," She-Devil said, giving me a sidelong look. "Devils are going to be devilish. Inferna may be a rebel, but she knows how the game is played around here. Better than you do."

Her tone annoyed me, but I knew She-Devil's alter ego was an occult scholar, so I wasn't going to argue it with her. She was already cranky about being away from her actual job as long as she had been.

My primary concern was getting Inferna and then getting out of there as soon as possible. As we cleared one of the wrinkled ridgelines, we could see a black and red cluster of circus tents, looking like three monstrous mushrooms.

"Deathclown," I said. "Gotta be."

The sign across it said "The Carnevil" in big letters that looked like blood. A LOT of blood.

"Oh, great," I said. I hated clowns. From where we stood on the hill overlooking the valley where it was situated, we could make out masses of listless souls ambling about in chains, with devils amid them, full of wanton glee at the plight of everyone there.

The whole vibe of the place was nefarious, with the scent of caramel corn and fried donuts mingling with the smell of burning flesh, burning tires, and kerosene.

"Okay," I said. I wanted to just fly in and tear the place apart, but my understanding of the rules of Hell were that such action on my part would be hard fought, so I just took She-Devil and flew us to the entrance, where the Ticket Taker leered at us, being this tall scarecrow of a devil in a crisp white- and red-striped coat with a straw skimmer hat on. The Ticket Taker had great big red eyes and a massive, toothy mouth.

"Tickets, Ladies?" he asked.

"Two," I said, throwing back my cowl, so my luminosity would shine, hopefully hurting some devils' eyes. It did draw attention, although the heat I threw off meant nothing to the devils.

"Oh, my," the Ticket Taker said. "Hellmaiden graces us with her presence. And Ossifier the Obstreperous, can that be you? It's been so very long since we've last seen you, Bub."

The Ticket Taker's voice was high and lilting, full of malevolent mockery.

"Lucky for you both, there's tickets waiting for you already," the Ticket Taker said. "Bets were placed on whether or not you'd show."

The Ticket Taker produced a pair of black tickets with red writing on them, tearing them in half and handing us the stubs. Then he held out his hand, which revealed too-long fingers that ended in needlelike claws.

"What?" I asked.

"You need to get stamped, Princess," the Ticket Taker said. "Everyone gets stamped at the Carnevil."

Not wanting to let myself be unnerved by this devil, I held out my hand, which he took with all too much relish, his fingers moving like a spider's across my skin. He'd produced a gold stamp with his other hand.

"You want it on your pretty white gloves, Princess? Or on your beautifully scorched skin?"

"Gloves are fine," I said, and the Ticket Taker carefully set my hand on the table next to his podium and brought the stamp down on the back of my hand hard, leaving a bloody-looking stamp that showed an entirely smug-looking fanged and horned clown that winked at me, with DEATHCLOWN writing below it in a crescent shape that paralleled the clown face.

The Ticket Taker admired his handiwork, before pounding a stamp on She-Devil's hand, too—I noticed that on her red skin, the stamp looked like it was made of gold.

"Don't lose that, or your stubs, for that matter," the Ticket Taker said, sneering at us. "Have fun!"

We walked in, noting that the milling crowds of lost souls gave us both a wide berth. I glanced at She-Devil, who scratched her forehead. The diabolical festivities here were strange, of course—they weren't madcap so much as they were mirthfully macabre. Again, I really wanted to take flight and just blast through this place, but some part of me told me that I should be careful here, and there might be consequences if I played too rough here. I won't call it wariness, so much as a mildly cautious kind of restraint.

That clashed with my resentment at being forced to play Deathclown's game, which this so clearly was. Other devils looked at us with disdainful gazes, turning their horns up at us, or at me, since I had no horns, and wasn't truly a devil at all, but some other strange incarnation wrought from Inferna's own magical manipulations. Was I a joke to them? To be judged by devils felt like a humiliation I was unprepared for. I wanted to call out to them "You're not better than me!" and confident that I could defeat all comers.

Then again, we were in a magical dimension, and I was not invulnerable to magic. I shook that off, not sure whether the nature of Hell itself might have been leaching in at the corners of my perception, making me think these uncharacteristically cagey thoughts.

"Too much going on," She-Devil said. "I can't isolate Inferna here."

"Okay," I said. "Let's stay together, yeah? We'll check the whole place out, tent by tent, stall by stall, if we have to."

I put my detective cap back on, and thought that someone like Deathclown, who was in the good (or, eh, bad) graces of this dimension, would likely seek to make an example out of Inferna if he'd caught her. Given her reputation in this place, it would be in one of the big tents.

"I think we can forget the stalls," I said, watching devils toy with people's souls in games of chance—throwing gold rings around the necks of bottles that looked like people screaming, laying claim to prizes made of people's souls. There was a vat of steaming holy water (I know this because it was being loudly called out by the carny devil working it):

"Holy water straight from the so-called Holy Land," the devil brayed. "Three throws for the hapless soul—you miss, he walks. You, Princess! Want to take your chances?"

I shook my head, but another devil did, and took three throws, to the delight of onlookers. The first throw was an obvious miss, one of those tormenting tosses, while the miserable soul of a man looked on, his ragged clothes and white eyes gaping as he sat above the bubbling cauldron of holy water.

"Deliverance for the damned," the devil carny said, while the devil missed again, to the howls of excitement from the onlookers, while the hordes of damned souls moaned and wailed. The tosser, who was a handsome devil with a black top hat and a black jacket with tails, held the third and final ring in his white-gloved hand, while his date (?), a young devil-woman wearing a golden body chain and nothing else, beyond her black bat wings and lustrous black hair that contrasted with her red skin, looked on.

Top Hat had been only toying with the soul with the two other misses, as the third and final shot nailed the target, and the spirit of the damned man was dropped into the vat of holy water, where he shrieked and smoked and spat as the holy water boiled. I went to do something, but She-Devil stopped me with an arm.

"He's dead already, remember?" she said. "This is just torment porn, Anna."

"Well, Hell," I said.

"Exactly. This place is where 'cruel and unusual punishment' was first conceived," she said. Top Hat and his date had won the scalded soul, who was fished out of the vat with a long pole and fitted with a set of chains and a neck clamp. Top Hat gallantly handed the chain to Body Chain, the two of them sauntering along the promenade, their steaming soul in tow, scorched and screaming with every soggy step, while the holy water sizzled on the ground, throwing off smoke and steam as one, a foul fog.

"The people really are the prizes," I said, and She-Devil nodded.

"Not much else in this dimension but taunting and torment," she said. "Magic made us this way."

The whole thing was weird. My parents had been conventionally, sporadically Catholic, which made them fairly non-committal in spiritual matters, and while I was baptized Catholic, it hadn't formed a particular part of my moral makeup.

Seeing all of this going on, though, I wondered what it was along philosophical lines. Taking the most secular path I could, I thought that this "Devil Dimension" was like an alien planet, except it was an entire universe that had somehow found a way to connect with our own through the artifice of its denizens. In so doing, it drew human lives to it in an almost parasitical relationship. That's how it seemed to me. There was magic here, to be sure, which operated on a level similar to what physics did in our own universe. Talk about metaphysical. The historical intersections of this dimension and our own had led to the cosmological constant that underpinned Christianity, maybe. The idea that these were even souls was jarring. Maybe they were energetic engrams of lives lived? Some part of my brain was already writing a paper on what I was observing: "Hell is Other People! The Persistence of Energetic Engrams Within an Alternate Dimension: A Case Study" by Anna Victor, *The American Journal of Applied Metaphysics*.

We passed a spinning wheel with another soul pinned to it, where devils could throw knives at it. The spinning soul saw us see him and he screamed for us to save him, while laughing devils hurled wicked-looking knives at them.

"I hate this place," I said. "How could a universe exist like this?"

"Different dimensions, different rules," She-Devil said. "You're the lucky one, here, Anna. You're not spot-welded to a devil the way I am. You can take off that crown and go back to being sweet Victoriana. Me? I'm stuck with Ossifier the Obstreperous."

I wasn't going to point out that her own occult explorations put her in that situation, because that would've been its own kind of cruelty. Was this place rubbing off on me? I hoped not.

"There's no joy here," I said. "And no love."

"For sure," She-Devil said. "Love of cruelty is about as close as you get. A certain sado-masochism of the irredeemably malevolent—the grim satisfaction of the kiss up/kick down. Devils work hard to earn the favor of those above them and inflict countless cruelties on those below them, in a constant struggle for power and supremacy."

I looked She-Devil over, who looked right back at me like some dire amazon.

"There are no heroes in Hell," she said. "Except for you, it would seem."

"And you," I said. She smiled ruefully back at me.

"And me, I guess," she said. I reached out and took her hand, giving it a squeeze, which she reciprocated.

"We'll get through this together, I promise," I said. "Just stay with me, okay?"

She nodded with a furtive smile. As badly as I was feeling in this place, I imagined She-Devil was feeling it worse, and hoped that my courage and compassion might help ease the pain she was feeling. If misery loved company, I aimed to be a good companion in this rescue mission, however it played out.

"He's watching us, isn't he?" I asked.

"Deathclown?" She-Devil said. "Oh, I'm sure."

Without true experience dealing with devils, I felt exceedingly vulnerable. Inferna was tricky enough, and she was a saint by satanic standards. Someone like Deathclown had to be terribly treacherous, and I'd have to use every bit of wit to beat him. And plenty of punching, I hoped.

"Well, let's give him a show he'll remember," I said, and promptly took flight.

I DELIVERED THE NEWS TO AVANT GUARDIAN, MR. COOL, AND EIGHTBALL, and they were overjoyed. They were absolutely thrilled and were alternately hugging me and shaking my hand.

"I *knew* you'd come through for us, Mitch," Eight said, play-punching my shoulder.

"Yeah, man," Cool said. "I appreciate it, Dude."

"Thank you so much, Mitch," Avant Guardian said.

"We'll celebrate in a few, but just know that the background checks are a nightmare for the Affiliates," I said. "Took me ages to clear them, so if you guys have skeletons in your closets, now's the time to get them out of there or sorted out or whatever. My hope with the Knack in charge, it'll go faster for you."

They were all so thrilled, I felt good to see them like that. To even be able to deliver on a promise like that made me happy.

"I think they're planning for you all to be out here in West," I said. "It's always high-traffic, so odds are good you'll end up here and see a lot of action. Everything happens out here. Floods, droughts, earthquakes, wildfires, dragons, demons, mad scientists, crazed cults, the works. You will never be bored, you can bet on that."

They all seemed okay with that, since just being in the Affiliates would offset whatever disruption they experienced in their private lives. Avant Guardian in particular would mesh with the SoCal vibe, and Mr. Cool could probably make a fortune if he put his mind to it. Eight was always Eight, and since he was Vegas-based, it was an easy jaunt for him.

"For now, you can shack up here while we're sorting through this Dr. Crimeboss stuff," I said, noting Ms. Fit and Tag Team looking on with ample doses of skepticism, I could tell.

"With your permission, of course, Ms. Fit," I said.

"It's fine," she said, while Tag sized everybody up as he invariably, inevitably did. He was proud of the place he'd rightfully earned in the Affiliates and would look down on the newbies until he had decided that they belonged there. Never mind that they already did.

Meanwhile, I was worried that neither Anna, Inferna, nor She-Devil had returned, and so I threw my energy into interrogating Ms. Fortune, Quick Chick, and the Limobot.

Ms. Fortune was an interesting case, as she was easily one of the most prominent precognitive villains out there. We'd taken the prisoners out of their costumes and put them in Affiliates-branded prison jumpsuits (orange, with PRISONER on them next to the Affiliates logo in blue), just took a seat in her cell and pretended to be patient. With a precog, life was probably an endless number of reruns.

"Mr. Paulsen," she said. "Have my lawyers reached out to you, yet? I saw all of this take place already. It doesn't go well for you and your little band."

Her voice had a high, almost lilting delivery that called to mind golden age Hollywood starlets. She looked roughly my age, with blond hair and piercing blue eyes. Her real name was Miranda Wright, and she'd made a fortune (right?) selling self-help books—*The Wright Way, Wright & Wrong,* etc.

She used her precog abilities to create the appearance that she was a true prophet, and her followers were devoted to her. She was obsessed with Shane, which I know because he'd told me about her in the past, how she had told him that she'd envisioned the two of them marrying and lording it over the super-powered community as the IT couple. When that vision didn't come true, she'd gotten progressively more outraged.

"Your fan base will be disappointed when your identity is revealed," I said.

"Will they, Mr. Paulsen? Is that what you experienced?" she asked.

My own situation was way more death-threatening than hers, I had to note. But then, I didn't try to con anybody the way she had. It was easy to be a truth-teller when you could use your actual psychic powers to be a practicing psychic and self-help guru (ironic, isn't it, that there are people who make money around self-help? Is it actually self-help if you're looking to someone else to provide it to you? Just saying...).

"Let's talk about *you*, Miranda," I said. "You and Johnny Rubicon were rivals. How did Crime get you working together?"

"Maybe you should ask *him,* since you saw fit to block my powers," she said. For a precog, that had to be kind of terrible. "The fact is that you don't have anything on me. You don't know what I've been up to, and I don't have to say another word."

She was right, of course. I hadn't done my usual surveillance workup to catch her doing and saying bad things. Rather, I'd just nabbed her. There would be repercussions. However, for the moment, I thought it was necessary to keep the precogs out of Dr. Crime's hands. If that made me a bad guy, so be it.

Ms. Fortune just smiled up at the camera.

"You see? I've already had this conversation, Mr. Paulsen," she said. "Even when you and your goons attacked me on the street, what did I do? I just tried to run away from some super-powered kidnappers led by none other than the info-terrorist himself, Cameraman. And without your telepath, you can't pick my brain. Stalemate, Mr. Paulsen."

Inferna's absence was big, because she had a way of divining what was in people's heads and hearts. Maybe not telepathy, but damnably close.

"As an Affiliate, I have the legal authority to indefinitely detain those suspected of criminal activity and associations," I said. "Especially any supers."

"Ooh, that doesn't sound troubling at all, Mr. Paulsen," she said. "Am I bound for the Brig, then? Summarily and indefinitely detained because you *think* I'm up to no good? Where's the proof? I'm sure Johnny will tell you the same thing. You have no proof of any wrongdoing on our part."

I turned off the mic and glanced at the others, who looked at me with chagrined expressions, shaking their heads.

"She's ice cold," Mr. Cool said. "We're talking glacial, man."

Good villain precogs, the ones that really excelled at their game, operate almost invisibly in the supervillain cosmos. They lent their services as counselors and advisors, never getting their hands dirty. And because they tended to forecast everything in their lives, they plotted out a path for themselves. The use of Terri Meadows to get ahead of Rubicon and Fortune was something they hadn't seen, but their records were carefully curated to create the appearance of propriety. I turned on the microphone again.

"We're searching your homes, anyway," I said.

"Oh, my," she said. "Unlawful searches and seizures, too? The list of your offenses grows, Mr. Paulsen."

"You seem to think you're entitled to conventional legal representation, Ms. Wright," I said. "You're a super. That means you're accountable to the PSS."

"Okay," she said. "Where's the PSS agent to talk to me, then? Why is it you, Mr. Paulsen?"

The Program for the Study of Superbeings would love to get their hands on Fortune and Rubicon, I was certain. My goal in the moment was to simply see if I could get her to talk, which wasn't going terribly well.

"The PSS will be handling you soon enough, Ms. Wright," I said. "I'm just giving you the chance to talk now, while you still can. What's the Moebius Mutation? What's Dr. Crimeboss up to?"

Wright just smiled at me, shaking her head.

"I don't know what any of those things are," she said.

I was tired of her smug evasions, decided to play a heavier hand, one that would rattle her. I went to the intercom and clicked it.

"Brighteyes? Ms. Fortune is having memory issues," I said. "Can you help her get clarity?"

"Sure thing, Cam," Brighteyes said. Now, you're wondering how I pulled that out of my hat, right? I'd naturally stayed in touch with Antigone after the big fight at Shane's place. She'd ghosted, as I expected she would, but someone like her, it paid to keep her on your speed dial. She'd been happy after Minder had been killed, had texted me about it. Sorry I didn't tell you about that, but you've seen how busy I've been. And when I'd gotten reinstated with the Affiliates, she'd joked about it ("You're going to become part of the problem, now, Mitch?").

For me, however, the most important thing at the moment was the look of terror that came over Ms. Fortune's incredibly put-together face.

"Brighteyes?" she said.

"What? I thought you'd already foreseen all of this already, right?" I asked. "You know what's happening next?"

The door to her cell opened, and Brighteyes strolled in, wearing an all-black designer sportcoat and slacks, some black Oxfords, her black sunglasses perched on her nose, her green eyes glowing.

"Hi, Ms. Fortune," she said. "It's so nice to see you up close like this."

Fortune shrank from her, backing away, her face radiating abject horror.

"Mr. Paulsen, please," she said. "You can't possibly condone having this murderous vigilante in here with me."

I mimed having audio troubles a moment.

"Sorry, Miranda," I said. "Our cameras are on the fritz. Can you repeat what you just said?"

Tag Team snorted at this, as did Mr. Cool, while Avant Guardian just shook her head.

"You're a gangster, Mitch," Tag said. "Make no mistake."

"This is cruel," Avant Guardian said. "She's really scared."

I glanced at Avant Guardian, shrugging.

"It's where I need her to be," I said. "You should know that perception becomes its own reality, Guardian."

She grimaced, shaking her head and leaving the room. Avant Guardian had a genuinely good heart, which is why she would make for a bad interrogator.

Ms. Fit sighed.

"I'll talk to her, Mitch," she said, striding after Avant Guardian. Mr. Cool was all but eating popcorn while watching. He was loving it.

"You sure you're not from New Jersey, Camo?" he asked.

"Close," I said, "Philly."

Mr. Cool clapped me on the back. "East Coast, Baby!"

I smirked and turned my attention back on Ms. Fortune, who was freaking out, and Brighteyes was just standing there, watching, a hand on her hip.

"Stop it! Stop it! Stop staring at me," Ms. Fortune said. "You just stay away from me!"

Antigone perched her shades on her head, took a seat near Ms. Fortune, focused those green eyes right on the trembling precog.

"You can't do this," she said.

"Do what?" Brighteyes asked. "You mean kill you in cold blood? But I can. I can make you disappear, Ms. Fortune. And Cam up there, well, he's a wizard with the audiovisual. Why don't you answer our questions, now?"

"You can't behave this way," Fortune said. "You're heroes."

"I'm an antihero," Brighteyes said, winking at her before aiming that wink up at me. "I can do whatever I like, so long as it's for a good cause. And stopping Dr. Crime? That's a *very* good cause."

And just like that, Ms. Fortune broke—she just started breathily babbling, sharing what Dr. Crimeboss had been having Rubicon and her do.

"He just comes at us with random things," Fortune said. "He'll present scenarios and ask us to envision them."

"What scenarios?" Brighteyes asked. Fortune's mascara was running as she recounted scenarios for us. Antigone even had a little packet of tissues she handed over to her, which she gratefully took with shaking hands.

"He'd ask us things," Fortune said. "Things like 'Do the Affiliates breach our facilities? Where and when?' 'Is Victoriana living or dead?' And so on."

"And?" I asked, startling her, making her split her focus between Brighteyes and my camera.

"He'd compare and contrast the results that Johnny and I gave," Fortune said. "If we both gave the same answer, he'd plot according to that. If there was a split decision, he'd ask again to see if that split endured. If it did, he'd reconsider his plan of action and alter it. He consulted us constantly. It was exhausting."

"I'll bet he paid well for your services," I said.

"We were compensated," Fortune said.

"She's not lying, Cam," Brighteyes said, which made Ms. Fortune whip her head back toward her.

"Of course, I'm not lying," she said. "I'm honest."

"You're lying right now," Brighteyes said. "I can tell when you're lying. Every time you lie, I can see it. You didn't think my pretty eyes were *just* for killing, did you?"

I leaned forward against the console, eyeing the screens, moving the mic closer. It was like when Anna and I braced Scenester, except that Antigone really could tell if someone was lying. I'd have to definitely get Brighteyes aboard the 'Clique, made a note to have that conversation with her later.

"What do you know, Miranda? What have you and Rubicon predicted for him?" I asked.

"We have different reaches," she said. "Johnny can scan up to three months ahead of time. I'm better than he is—I can forecast at least a year out."

That was useful to me—if Dr. Crimeboss was using both precogs that way, it meant that he was confined to using them with three-month forecasting windows if he wanted both of their forecasts. He also may have had Ms. Fortune forecast and would pull Rubicon in to doublecheck her visions.

"You don't know what it's like," Fortune said. "He's terrifying, now. Back when he was just Dr. Crime, you could deal with him. Ever since he merged with Crimebot, he's relentless. He never sleeps. All crime, all the time. It's something we bitterly joke about. He never stops."

"Tell me about that merger," I asked. What? I was curious.

"Crimebot built him what it called the 'ultimate chassis'—a perfect replica of Dr. Crime, if Crime had been a robot," Fortune said. "Then he'd had his mind digitized and digitally transferred into that ultimate chassis, and Crimebot uploaded itself to it at the same time. They fused. It was bizarre."

Tag Team whistled. *"Frankenstein* shit right there, man."

"What about Crime's body?" I asked.

"It was put in cold storage," Fortune said. "Cryogenically preserved by Ice Queen."

Mr. Cool sighed, nodding.

"She's the worst," he said.

"What, she gave you the cold shoulder, Cool?" Tag Team asked, the two of them laughing, knuckle-bumping. Ice Queen wasn't typically in the regular villain rotation, as she mostly kept to herself, but who knows what favors Crime traded on to get her to assist him.

"What else, Miranda?" I asked. "What's the Moebius Mutagen?"

"I don't know. I have no idea what that is," she said, giving Brighteyes a panicked look. Antigone waited a moment or two before replying.

"She's telling the truth," Brighteyes said.

"What was the last thing Crimeboss had you two forecast on?" I asked.

Fortune cleared her throat.

"He asked us the location of the Brig in three months' time," she asked. "He always asked about the Brig. He's obsessed with it."

"Really?" I asked.

"Yes," Fortune said. "No idea why. He'd just ask questions about it. Mostly logistical inquiries."

The Affiliates had 24/7 tracking of the Brig, since it sailed around the world constantly, which helped it avoid incursions by supervillains who were out to breach its defenses.

"What was your answer?" I asked. "Where is the Brig in three months?"

"It'll be in the Atlantic Ocean, off the coast of New York City. Both Johnny and I gave him that answer."

"And Crime's lair is at Bridle Path?" I asked.

"Yes," Fortune said. "He has an underground bunker."

"Nowhere else?" I asked.

"Oh, he has satellite lairs around the world," Fortune said. "But that one in Canada is his most important one."

"Brighteyes?"

Antigone squinted at Fortune, who squirmed under her luminous gaze.

"She's telling the truth as far as she knows it," Brighteyes said.

"As far as I know it?" Fortune said, anger flashing out from behind her fear. "Who do you think you are? You're just some madwoman who can shoot laser beams from her eyes. I see the future."

Antigone simply smiled at her in silence in the wake of the precog's outburst.

"Would you like to know your future, now?" Brighteyes asked, her eyes flaring. Ms. Fortune backed away from her.

"Mr. Paulsen, get this psycho away from me," Fortune said, glaring up at the camera.

"I'm not her boss," I said. "She can do what she wants."

"Nooo!" Fortune said, bursting into tears.

I toggled off the mic and thought about that a bit. Was Crime looking to spring all the criminals held aboard the Brig? That seemed almost too basic for him. I'd have to think further that a bit and see if I could figure it out. I'd also have to let Shane know, see if he might have some lucky insight.

"Alright, Brighteyes," I said. "We're good for now."

"Okay, Cam," she said, standing and giving Fortune a stern look before replacing her sunglasses and walking out, leaving the precog to heave a quavering sigh of weepy relief as the securidoor closed on her.

**I DON'T KNOW WHO CAME UP WITH THE TERM "RAISING HELL"** —but when I took flight over the Carnevil, I think maybe I'd invented a new phrasing: *razing hell*. I was razing hell, big time. It got wild very quickly, because the moment I took flight, devils in the service of Deathclown—who were these white-faced freaks with squinty eyes and curved horns and wearing black body suits began hurling red and black ribbons at me, catching my arms and legs like flypaper, while they tried to pull me down.

This really angered me, and I took flight higher, dragging a half-dozen of those gangly devils with me, while She-Devil started pummeling her way through the foot traffic down below.

I threw back my cowl and let the fiery light of my own righteousness hit those squinting bastards below, and I began a skyward spin that yanked them up toward me at speed. They held on as I brought them in and pounded them each time one got in range.

And when I say I pounded them, I'm talking thundering booms each time I struck them, sending them whooshing away, because I wasn't holding back. I did this five times, with the sixth devil actually letting go before I reeled him in.

However, I flew after him and caught him by the ankle, so he couldn't get away. He kicked me in the face, and I whipped him groundward so hard that when he hit one of the circus tents, there was a meteoric explosion explosion that hastened the rending of the tent from the force.

The lost souls and devil tourists were stampeding to put distance between themselves and She-Devil and me, while Deathclown's minions were attempting to rally and fight us off.

I flew down hard at the second tent, and I'm talking supersonic—like a Mach 10 divebomb that caused a massive explosion that blasted devils and the damned away in cascading multitudes.

Then I began firing plasma blasts in a whirling motion, the blinding fiery yellow-white of them igniting everything around us. Never mind that in Hell, fire was more a nuisance than a threat—it still felt good to watch that stuff burn.

Deathclown's goons—more of those white-faced creeps—ran for me with fiery whips, more of those gluey streamers, and black iron chains. She-Devil was racing through their lines, having used her horns to fire an acid blast that melted scores of devils as she fought to get to me.

I played a bit of fistfighting pachinko with the devils on the ground, zigzagging between them at high velocity and landing haymakers that alternately sent them flying (if they were strong enough) or splattering them (if they weren't—trivia: devils all seem to have black blood). I flew threw them like that, going faster and faster, until my shiny white costume was splashed with black ichor (She-Devil later told that's what it was called).

She-Devil was grinning as she smashed her way through their ranks.

"You know, I was less than thrilled when you took off, Hellacious," She-Devil said. "But, damn, I'm actually enjoying myself."

I flew on, the sticky streamers snapping and crackling behind me as I flew, still affixed to me.

"Happy to help, Sheedy," I said. Aw, we'd given each other nicknames. Teammate bonding! There was only one tent still standing, and the patrons of the Carnevil were still falling over themselves to escape us.

I fired plasma beams around us in a perimeter, satisfied that, despite Hell's resistance to fire, my plasma still took a toll, seeing the burning remains of Deathclown's tents carried skyward, under great plumes of noxious smoke.

No sign of Inferna in the first two tents, and I'll own up to not being terribly alert to my surroundings with each thrust of my attack, but with the third tent, I flew for it, intending to rip the thing clean off its moorings, when the tent whipped up and enveloped me most nefariously. It was like being surrounded in this red and black amorphous blob, and the harder I swung out against it, the faster I flew, the more lost I got within it.

"My, oh my," said a mocking gravelly voice. "You *must* be Hellmaiden."

I flew at the edges of the tent, but it yielded against the force I applied, to my growing frustration. I couldn't connect with it; just billowed around me. The sticky ribbons that still clung to me caught some of the tent's fabric, and I began to get tangled despite myself. What's worse, the harder I fought, the more it entangled me, being the circus tent equivalent of quicksand.

"And you must be Deathclown," I said. "Come out, Coward!"

"Oh, I will," Deathclown said. "Inferna said a lot about you, but, wow, are you ever fun!"

Spinning against my entanglement, I took advantage of the snags around my legs to bend over and grab at the tent material that was accessible by way of the sticky ribbons, and then I began to swing it back and forth, satisfied that there was, somewhere distant, the sound of something pounding on the ground.

I could hear Deathclown cackling.

"You're a blast, Hellmaiden!" Deathclown said, as I began to spin again, like I was figure-skating in the sky. Faster and faster I spun, until the tent-thing actually spat me out, and I slammed into the ground, carving a gravelly groove the length of a football field.

And there was Deathclown at the start of that furrow I'd made, the billowing red and black tent boiling back into him, becoming a tidy carnation on his lapel. He wore a black and red striped clown suit with mismatched clown shoes (want to guess the color?) and beamed at me with his white face that had black clown makeup highlights on his smile and eyebrows, with a blood-red nose and a black derby hat jauntily on his head, just past his red horns. His clown hair was crimson, and he had white gloves that were split, revealing his red fingers and black-nailed claws.

I got to my feet and flew for him, fists out, while he produced a red cape that had his Deathclown symbol upon it in black.

"That's the spirit, Your Hellness," Deathclown said, actually playing the matador and evading my charge, whomping me with his cape as I passed. I tried two more charges, which he cacklingly evaded, his red eyes alight with delight. I didn't see She-Devil anymore, hoped that she was okay. "Baby ready to chat?"

Seeing as he'd been able to keep me from laying a fist on him, I paused, those pestilential streamers still dangling from my arms and legs.

"Where's Inferna?" I asked.

"She's fine," Deathclown said. "Are you kidding?"

"I want to see her," I said.

"You will, you will," Deathclown said. "Here, a sign of good faith from me to you."

He snapped his fingers and the sticky streamers fell to the ground. Then he wolf-whistled, and I could see Dollface with Inferna, who was stuck in a silver cage being toted by a monstrously big, grinning devil who was bone-white and bulky-muscled with great bat wings and thick arms corded with muscle and armored flesh.

Dollface was dressed as a French maid, her dead-faced white mask devoid of emotion, and was guiding that white devil toward the both of us by a length of chain that seemed absurdly inadequate to handle it. I could see She-Devil was also caught in a silver prison, dangling on the back of the big white devil from a pole.

"Not bad, eh?" Deathclown said. "Hell's Belles, an almost full set. I'm so excited. I'm a bit of a completist, I have to admit."

I could see that Inferna was bound in silver chains and gagged, as was She-Devil. Inferna's face betrayed nothing but defiance, while She-Devil looked enraged.

"Inferna thought she'd run the table," Deathclown said. "But she has no idea what's going on. Neither do you."

I preferred to hover, but decided I'd land, just to face Deathclown directly, let him know I wasn't afraid of him. Somehow, I felt that was likely part of his mojo. He was about twice as tall as I was. I refused to let that intimidate me.

"Smart," he said. "She's smart, Dollface."

Dollface applauded.

"She is," Dollface said, her voice possessing a cloying kewpie doll tone.

"You're messing with Dr. Crimeboss and his master plan for your planet," Deathclown said. "I decided to do him a satanic solid and stop you. The deal I made with him is that if I stop you, I get to *keep* you. He readily agreed."

He licked his lips with a black forked tongue.

"Inferna over there, she sure put up a fight," Deathclown said. "Just like old times, eh, Ferna? Yes. But I outrank her here, and while she's, oh, I don't know, a Baroness-in-exile, I'm a Duke of Hell of the first order, Baby. She can impress you locals with her parlor tricks, but I'm the real deal."

He smacked one gloved fist into the other, savoring with closed eyes the cacophony he created by doing so. The wind it generated actually blew my cape back.

"You sure messed up my Carnevil, Princess," Deathclown said. "And we'll settle accounts on that shortly, but for now, I want to talk to you a little before I make you the star attraction in my devilish circus."

You're probably wondering why I'd even bother talking with this clown. However, I thought it best to just hear him out, get a sense of what his game was. Mitch was a firm believer in what he called "strategic communications"—talking with someone often just to see what they might say. It's why he was so good at interrogation. I decided I'd hear what he had to say and react accordingly.

"Oh, Mitch," Deathclown said, picking up on my thoughts, saying Mitch's name in a mocking singsong and batting his eyelashes, literal hearts in his red eyes. "Aren't you two just so precious?"

He made gagging motions, rolling his red eyes up in his head, to the laughter of his onlookers.

"I can't wait to turn that two-bit peeping tom into a human pretzel," he said, and I knew he was mocking me (*look near the end of Chapter 9, where she used "human pretzel" before. Deathclown is clearly picking her brain a bit to torment her with her own words and thoughts, as one would expect from a devil.— the editors*).

"What do you want?" I asked.

"To fight you, Honeycakes," Deathclown said. "Obviously. I want to see what you're made of. But not like this—Hellmaiden's adorable and all—the Prom Queen of Perdition—but we both know it's a disguise for a disguise. No, I want to fight you as who you *really* are. I want Victoriana."

Around the cratered wasteland I'd already created of the Carnevil, I could see the patrons and devils lurking in the distance, ogling me. I'm not even making up that some of them were noshing on caramel corn and hot dogs while they looked on. Deathclown caught me looking and laughed—his laugh was bombastic and brimmed with a bullying mockery.

"They want to watch the show," Deathclown said. "And can you blame them? You, my dear, put on a HELL of a show. I'm going to *really* enjoy enslaving you. All of you Hell's Belles, but especially you, Anna Victor."

He relished that especially, actually two-handed grabbing the ass of the empty air and looking skyward through clenched teeth. "Even your name is perfect. You were born to this, Princess."

Now, I could have flown away. I couldn't have gone home, but I'd have (maybe) found a way back. However, the quicker, surer route was right through Deathclown. This much was terribly clear to me.

"That's the spirit," he said, red eyes wide. "I only get to bring a little of myself to your dimension, which was why I was so happy Inferna took the fight here. It made things so much easier. And I want to see what you're really made of. I want to see just how strong you are, Victoriana."

Nothing came for free in Hell, so I held up a hand.

"What are the stakes?" I asked.

"Stakes?" Deathclown feigned confusion.

"The terms of our fight," I said. "If you win, what happens to me?"

"Ah," Deathclown said. "You're bound to work in my Carnevil for, well, eternity. I haven't decided whether you'll be Hellmaiden or Victoriana, honestly. There's a delicious irony in 'Victoriana the Defeated' as a stage name, I have to admit. I'm thinking of making three of you a trapeze act. Hell's Belles. That would play across the dimension, especially when I fit you all out with bells that jingle while you're cartwheeling in the air. Plus, it's funny, because you're the smallest and strongest of the three of you, and there's bulky, stubborn Ossifier over there, and lean, mean Inferna. It's hilarious."

He laughed and the onlookers laughed, as did Dollface and the white devil, until Deathclown curtly zipped the air with a finger-pinch and shut them all up. The silence was bracing, with only a breeze blowing, carrying the stench of burning tents mixed with the infernal caramel corn—I could see a white-faced devil vendor working his way through the crowds, selling the popcorn as he went, producing it from a black- and red-striped box that seemed to contain unlimited containers of it.

"And if I win, you release Inferna and She-Devil and you tell me everything you know about Dr. Crime's master plan and the Moebius Mutagen," I said. "And you refuse to help him anymore."

Deathclown bellowed laughter again, like I'd somehow said something funny. The onlookers joined in his laughter until he stopped.

"Hmm," he said. "I get lifetime service from you if I win, and you get your friends back and insights into what Dr. Crimeboss is up to and my pledge to not work with him? I feel like I get the better deal out of this, but if that's how you want to play it, Princess, I'm game."

He shrank down to my size for a moment, and he held out his hand for me to shake, grinning toothily at me. I could see his yellow teeth were all sharp, and his grinning mouth was wide. I could see Inferna and She-Devil looking on nervously as I shook his hand. He gave my hand a hard squeeze, and I squeezed him back harder. The two of us kept at it, each trying to crush the other's hand. I kept at it until he let a grimace dance on his face and abruptly let go.

"Alrighty then," he said, shaking out his hand as he resumed his towering height. "Good grip, good grip. Now, lose that clunky crown and let's see Victoriana make her appearance, already."

The question was whether I was healed enough as Victoriana to take this joker out. Hellmaiden's fiery self wasn't as effective against devils, anyway. I'd just have to make it work.

"You can't sucker punch me while I'm taking off my crown," I said.

"Wouldn't dream of it," Deathclown said, taking out a red toothpick which he used to work on his mouthful of teeth. "Dollface can hold it while we're, you know, fighting."

"No," I said, taking it off, transforming from the luminous Hellmaiden back to my old super-self. Deathclown offered mocking applause, slow-clapping, which was joined by the others. I threw the golden crown at the white devil, embedding it in his chest, which caused him to double over in dismay, as I'd thrown the thing with great force that cracked his chest armor. The white devil lurched forward, landing face-first with a meaty thud that shook the ground. He didn't get up.

Deathclown whistled.

"I never would have thought Buster would end his days as a makeshift hatrack, but there you go," he said. He turned his attention back to me. "You ready?"

"Ground rules?" I asked.

"Anything goes," Deathclown said, leering at me. "Whoever gives up first loses."

"Great," I said, shooting at him, only to have him clout me in the jaw with that big, gloved fist of his. He hit *hard*—I went flying, my ears ringing from the force of his blow, well-impressed by his speed.

*Big, strong, and quick.* That was going to be something to account for. I steadied myself in the sky and flew back down to him, which he watched, grinning.

"Felt that, did you, Honeycakes?" Deathclown asked. I made for him again at very high speed, but it was my turn to feint, dodging as he threw another of his quick jabs and I pivoted, kicking him in the back as hard as I could, gratified when I saw him cry out and go flying toward his onlookers, who screamed and parted while he tumbled through them, coming to a stop as he slammed into a hellish hillside. He got back to his feet while I was shooting toward him, dusting himself off.

He fired red and black streamers at me from his hands (red from one hand, black from the other, if you want to know), and I dodged them as I was approaching, since I didn't want to get stuck on those like before. Since he was occupied slinging and flinging those my way, I was able to slam him in the face with a two-fisted punch that blasted him into a pile of confetti that rained down on his audience.

Then he teleported on my back, having sized himself to match me, and he whipped one of his black ribbons around my neck and began to throttle me, yanking my neck back as he did so, bringing his mouth to my ear.

"Nice shots, Cheeks," he said. "But you must know I've got so much more up my sleeve."

He was actually strangling me, although since I didn't need to breathe, the attack was more for psychological effect than actual damage. I did another of my soon-to-be-trademark spins and actually flung him off me, which gave me a moment to tear the strangling ribbon off my neck, even as he teleported back onto me. Deathclown seemed to be a bit of an infighter, which gave me the opportunity to land a number of titanic blows to his chest, happy that I was able to connect with what felt like flesh under there, instead of billowy clown costuming. He grunted with each punch I threw, seemed to delight in them.

"Yeah, that's it," he said, cackling. "Whoof! Yeah! Oh, yeah! I love it!"

I cracked him in the jaw, then the chest, then to the other side of his face, and he took them all in stride.

Then he threw some counterpunches of his own, landing them with his big fists. In fact, with each punch, he got a bit bigger, until he knocked me back to the ground, and dove down on me feet-first, growing ever-larger as he descended, until he hit me with a cacophonous, calamitous boom that blotted out light and left me seeing stars and hearing ringing bells.

"I'd say I wasn't clowning around with you, but, you know," Deathclown said, stepping off me, reaching down to pick me up by my cape. "Baby had enough? Ready for circus life? I've got a trapeze with your name on it."

He gestured grandiosely to a remade circus tent, product of his seemingly effortless conjuring. That he'd be able to fight me and still whip up these things gave me pause. Perhaps the intent was to make me feel small and insignificant in the face of his incalculable power.

I took flight, landing on his hand, straining to pry his fingers off my cape. As I did that, he brought his other giant hand down on me like he was swatting a bug. I quickly slipped out of my cape and went right at his face, hitting him in his giant red clown nose (and, yes, it totally squeaked when I hit it, although at his enhanced size, it made a sound more like a boat horn as I struck him).

"You're outmatched, Victor," Deathclown roared, guffawing.

Then I flew into his right eye, just hammered my way through his eyeball, which had to have hurt him, because he let out a bellow. I've never been in somebody's eyeball before, and I'm here to say that it was gross—very, very wet. I flew in a star formation in there, banging around inside his giant eye-socket, hitting every angle in there, which led him to scream in pain as he fought to expel me.

However, because he'd opted for that big size, he couldn't dislodge me. Instead, I slammed through the flesh and bone between his eyes, to reach the other eyeball, which I gave the same brutal treatment as I had the other, hearing his roaring echoing in my head, muted by the flood of ocular fluid and ichor as he underwent my onslaught. I capped it by flying through his other eye, shattering the lens and splashily bursting from his ruined eyeball.

"Ohmigod, you pesky BITCH!" Deathclown yelled, both gloved hands clutching his face, black ichor pouring from his eyes. He shrank down from his giant size, while I flew right at him, puncturing him three times as he got smaller—by which I mean I flew *through* him, like I was a bullet. Each time I shot through him, black ichor flowed from his injuries. I was perforating him.

He pulled his hands away from his eyes, glaring at me with his bloodied sightless sockets.

"Are you kidding me?" Deathclown asked, his voice overflowing with rage and agony.

"Anything goes," I said, which got him charging at me with a snarl, clawed hands held out for me, grasping. I was pretty sure that he'd be able to heal those eyeball injuries, but for now, they were giving me an edge.

I threw another glorious kick that nailed him in the jaw and knocked him into a backflip, hitting the ground with a monumental thud, much like the one I'd hit Decibelle with, only far, far harder. The key I found with fighting was to just keep at it until the opponent was out cold or gave up.

It didn't matter to me that this clown was a Duke of Hell—I didn't even know what that precisely meant. All I knew was that he was in my way, and I had to get him out of my way. And that meant pummeling him into submission.

Which is what I did, zipping around him and punching him furiously hard—and I went berserk here like I had never berserked before, just because I could. We got into a bit of a rhythm between us, where I'd slip to one side, nail him, then shoot to another side as he tried to counter where I'd been moments before. We did this for about a half-dozen exchanges, but his blindness prevented him from being able to connect with his blows. I could feel him getting frustrated, snarling more with each punch.

What he didn't seem to be getting was tired, however. I didn't know if devils even got tired. For all of the ichor leaking out of him, splattering on the hatefully rocky ground, he was still going.

Maybe he was counting on *me* getting tired and punching myself out? It wasn't a terrible strategy—unlike, say, Ms. Fit, I could get tired eventually. At least hypothetically. I'd yet to reach a situation where I'd been worn out, but it could happen.

For now, I just kept tapping my strength reserves and hitting Deathclown harder and harder, until one of us gave in. It *wasn't* going to be me. Too much was riding on my winning, and that's when I thought that I had an actual advantage—this fight was something of an amusement for Deathclown. It was life and death for me and my friends, for Mitch and the Earth. I couldn't afford to lose, whereas Deathclown could.

With that in my back pocket, I went at him harder than I'd gone after anyone in my life, trying not to give him a chance to recover himself, not hitting him the same way twice. I knew I was making progress when he didn't even make an attempt to dodge me, and he'd stopped talking, beyond grunts as he threw or received punches.

This went on for awhile, my fists wet with fresh ichor as I kept trying to break him. I tore up his clown suit, revealing his badly bruised, bone-white skin beneath. He couldn't concentrate enough to use any of his magic tricks on me, and I just kept dodging or blocking his blows, which felt like they weren't quite as strong as before.

I belted him with one of my uppercuts, and he landed on his back. I quickly landed atop him with both feet caving in his chest, cracking him in the jaw as his head came up. And then he called out.

"Alright! I give up!" he yelled. "Satisfied? I GIVE UP!"

I yanked him up by what was left of his lapels and cocked a fist. "Better *not* be a trick," I said.

"I GIVE UP!" Deathclown said. "Just stop pounding me. Round One to you, Sugartits!"

I let him go and stepped back, watching the stunned onlookers gaping at me. And I'll admit that I looked like hell—covered in ichor and Deathclown's eyeball juices, dust, dirt, and even some stray confetti. I pointed to Dollface, then zipped over to her, which had her scrambling, holding her arms up in mute surrender.

Inferna and She-Devil were both staring at me, and I didn't even bother with keys to their silver cages. I just tore them off, tossing the doors skyward. I ripped them free of their bonds, Inferna recovering herself at once as she slipped free of the cage. I could see she had burns on her wrists, neck, and ankles where the silver had touched her.

"My heroine," she said. "I knew you wouldn't disappoint."

"Happy to help," I said, flying back to Deathclown, who was getting to his feet. I grabbed one of the silver doors and broke bars from it, creating makeshift spear points from them. I also grabbed my cape, reaffixing it around my neck.

"What're you doing, Crazy Girl?" Deathclown asked, reaching around him, his claws scraping the ground. I speared one of his hands with the pointy silver bar, making him yowl as I gave it a twist, my own teeth clenching as I watched him scream.

"Now you're going to tell me just what Dr. Crimeboss is up to," I said.

## 26

to the rest of the team, with Shane dialed in remotely. Even Brighteyes was sitting in, listening with folded arms and her own ineffably wry sense of amusement.

"From what we've gathered, Dr. Crime's planning something with the Brig," I said. "Tag, do you have somebody at the Brig?"

"Uh, not currently," he said. "Minder relieved me from that detail a year or so ago. So, like, I haven't been back there since."

"Hmm," I said. "You should send one of your dupes there, see what he can see."

Tag Team seemed heartened that I'd entrust him to a mission, actually stood tall, like he wanted to salute me.

"I'm on it, Cam," he said. "I'll fly out there, let you know what's going on."

"Perfect," I said. Tag Team's powers were incredibly useful that way, in his ability and willingness to throw himself at anything, basically. "Be careful, and above all, just don't do anything too heroic, man."

Tag seemed to like that, smiled and nodded. "Right-O. I'll be super-discreet."

He got a faraway look, which likely meant that he was communicating with one of his dupes.

"And we still have to see what happened to Inferna and the others," I said. I was getting more worried that she was in a ton of trouble and there was nothing I could do about it. Some part of my brain was already dreaming up an extradimensional extraction strategy, some way of getting there and getting them out.

And then Anna returned with Inferna, She-Devil, Scenester, and Johnny Rubicon. They'd appeared in a telltale puff of brimstone.

"Speak of the devil and she reappears," Brighteyes said.

Their arrival turned everyone's heads, most especially because Anna stood there as Victoriana, looking like she'd been splashed in black tar, streamers, dirt and confetti, but otherwise smiling. The others were shocked to see Victoriana back among the living, letting out exclamations of joy and amazement that Anna waved them all off like a pro.

"Hey, Babes," she said. "We've got a lot to talk about, but first, I really, really need a shower."

"Welcome back," I said, giving her a wink. "You look like hell."

"Funny, funny man," she said, grinning wearily. Anna passed me, giving me a big kiss on the lips and a soft slap on the cheek.

TO BE CONTINUED IN...

# TANTRUM

THE SHUTTERCLIQUE #3

# APPENDIX

THE SHUTTERCLIQUE UNIVERSE HAS A VARIETY OF SUPERHERO AND SUPERVILLAIN TEAMS! HERE'S A GUIDE TO THE ONES WHO'LL BE APPEARING MOST REGULARLY THROUGHOUT THE SERIES.

## THE AFFILIATES

THE AFFILIATES ARE THE MOST PRESTIGIOUS OF SUPERHERO TEAMS, OPERATING PREDOMINANTLY IN THE UNITED STATES, BUT WITH UNITED NATIONS CLEARANCE ACT INTERNATIONALLY, WITH THE APPROVAL OF SOVEREIGN NATIONS (MOST OF WHOM HAVE THEIR OWN LOCAL SUPERHEROES AND EVEN TEAMS, WHICH WILL SHOW UP IN FUTURE APPENDICES). THE ORIGINAL AFFILIATES TEAM WAS EAST, BASED IN NEW YORK CITY. THE OTHER BRANCHES APPEARED OVER TIME, AS DEMAND FOR AFFILIATES TEAM MEMBERS GREW WITH THEIR PROMINENCE.

## AFFILIATES EAST (NEW YORK CITY)

- MINDER
  CHAIRMAN
- THE KNACK
  DEPUTY CHAIRMAN
- TANDEM
  – FUSILLAD
  – LASSITUDE
- LANCER
- WINGMAN
- MISTER TRANSISTOR
- SPEEDO
- TAG TEAM

## AFFILIATES WEST (LOS ANGELES)

- MS. FIT
- RAD LAD
- LADY BLAZE
- TAG TEAM

CONTINUED...

## AFFILIATES CENTRAL
### (CHICAGO)

- CAMERAMAN
- VICTORIANA
- STRUTTER
- GOO
- ROLLER GIRL
- VAMP
- SURE SHOT
- TAG TEAM

## AFFILIATES SOUTH
### (ATLANTA)

- DECIBELLE
- BRIGHTEYES
- GREEN MAN
- STINGER
- EELECTRIC
- TAG TEAM

**PSS**

PROGRAM
FOR THE
STUDY OF
SUPERBEINGS

## THE SHUTTERCLIQUE

CREATED BY CAMERAMAN, THE SHUTTERCLIQUE IS INTENDED AS A LOWER-ECHELON, STREET-LEVEL CRIMEFIGHTING TEAM THAT OPERATES INDEPENDENTLY OF MORE ESTABLISHED TEAMS LIKE THE AFFILIATES. BASED IN CHICAGO BUT WILLING TO GO ANYWHERE REQUIRED OF THEM, THE SHUTTERCLIQUE HAS EMERGED AS A KIND OF "PROVING GROUND" FOR SUPERHEROES WHO ASPIRE TO MAKE AFFILIATES MEMBERSHIP. AS SUCH, THE MEMBERSHIP OF THE SHUTTERCLIQUE IS ALWAYS IN FLUX.

- CAMERAMAN
- VICTORIANA
- INFERNA
- SHE-DEVIL
- ROLLERGIRL
- BITCHQUEEN
- SHRINKWRAP
- AVANT GUARDIAN
- MR. COOL
- EIGHTBALL
- THE ELF

## THE FOURHEADS

THIS IS A LONG-ESTABLISHED, FAMOUS SUPERVILLAIN TEAM THAT HAS OPERATED ALONG TWO STRICT PARAMETERS:

1) ONLY FOUR ACTIVE MEMBERS AT ANY TIME.
2) THE SUPERPOWERS MUST BE SOMEHOW HEAD-RELATED.

THESE REQUIREMENTS HAVE BEEN UPHELD BY TRADITION, MAKING THE FOURHEADS A KIND OF ELITE CRIMINAL CLUB, OPERATING IN A NUMBER OF HIGH-PROFILE LINES OF CRIMINAL BUSINESS. THE ROSTER HAS CHANGED OVER THE YEARS, WITH FATALITIES AND IMPRISONMENT BEING THE MOST TYPICAL FATES OF MEMBERS.

THE CURRENT FOURHEADS TEAM IS:

- HOTHEAD (TEAM CO-LEADER)
- DEADHEAD (TEAM CO-LEADER)
- AIRHEAD
- DUSTHEAD

FORMER MEMBERS INCLUDE: MACHINEHEAD; GEARHEAD; BLOCKHEAD; ARROWHEAD; PIGHEAD; SPEARHEAD; METALHEAD; CRACKHEAD; OVERHEAD; MASTHEAD; SLEEPYHEAD; MUSHROOMHEAD; WARHEAD.

## THE CRIME LEAGUE

FOUNDED BY DR. CRIME, THE INSTIGATOR, AND CRIMEBOT, THE CRIME LEAGUE HAS A VERY ACTIVE MEMBERSHIP, SERVING AS A SUPPORT AND RACKETEERING ORGANIZATION FOR MEMBERS. WHILE CRIMINALS AREN'T REQUIRED TO JOIN THE CRIME LEAGUE, THERE ARE ADVANTAGES AVAILABLE FOR MEMBERS WHICH CAN BE INCENTIVES.

CONTINUED...

## THE CRIME LEAGUE

- DR. CRIME*
- THE INSTIGATOR*
- CRIMEBOT*
- DEATH CLOWN
- JACK RABBIT
- ICE QUEEN

- SHUTTERBUG
- PLETHORA
- SPARX
- FELONIA
- SCENESTER

*CO-LEADERS

## THE TRINITY

BASED IN IOWA, THE TRINITY IS A THEOCRATIC FUNDAMENTALIST SUPERHERO TEAM FORMED TO ATTACK NON-CHRISTIAN AND DEFEND NOMINALLY CHRISTIAN RELIGIOUS INSTITUTIONS, PRIMARILY IN THE UNITED STATES. THERE ARE THREE MAIN ACTIVE MEMBERS WHO TYPICALLY DEPLOY TOGETHER, WITH OTHER MEMBERS SERVING IN SECONDARY AND AUXILIARY ROLES.

WELL-FUNDED BY AS-YET UNREVEALED FOUNDATIONS AND ORGANIZATIONS, THE TRINITY IS VERY POPULAR IN HIGHLY CONSERVATIVE STATES, WHEREAS THEY ARE VIEWED MORE DUBIOUSLY ELSEWHERE, DESPITE NEARLY ALWAYS RECEIVING FAVORABLE MEDIA COVERAGE.

- CRUCIFIXER
- THE INQUISITOR
- ANGELICA
- NAPALMINISTER
- BRAINFRIAR

- DOGMATIQUE
- THE BELIEVER
- THE SERMONIZER
- THE MONEYLENDER
- THE HOLY ROLLER

# NOSETOUCH PRESS
## *WE'RE OUT THERE
# NOSETOUCHPRESS.COM

# A NOTE ON THE TYPE

THE TEXT OF THIS BOOK IS SET IN FREIGHT TEXT PRO, DESIGNED BY JOSHUA DARDEN. ORIGINALLY DRAWN IN 2005 BY JOSHUA DARDEN AND EXPANDED SEVERAL TIMES OVER, THE FREIGHT COLLECTION OF TYPEFACES IS RENOWNED FOR ITS HISTORICAL INNOVATION AND ON-GOING POPULARITY.

JOSHUA DARDEN (BORN 1979 IN NORTHRIDGE, LOS ANGELES, CALIFORNIA) IS AN AMERICAN TYPEFACE DE-SIGNER. HE PUBLISHED HIS FIRST TYPEFACE AT THE AGE OF 15, BECOMING ACCORDING TO FONTS IN USE THE FIRST KNOWN AFRICAN-AMERICAN TYPEFACE DESIGNER.

IN 2004–2005, HE ESTABLISHED HIS OWN FOUNDRY, DARDEN STUDIO, IN BROOKLYN. SOON AFTER, HE PUB-LISHED THE FONT SUPERFAMILY FREIGHT, 120 FONTS IN FIVE FAMILIES (BIG, DISPLAY, MICRO, SANS, AND TEXT). IT WAS INSPIRED BY THE "DUTCH TASTE" SCHOOL OF TYPE-FACE DESIGN, INCLUDING THE WORK OF KIS, CASLON AND FLEISCHMAN, AND WAS NAMED A "FAVORITE TYPEFACE OF 2005" BY TYPOGRAPHICA.

THE HEADLINES ARE SET IN CC MEANWHILE, DESIGNED BY JOHN ROSHELL FOR COMICRAFT. JOHN ROSHELL HAS LETTERED THOUSANDS OF COMICS FOR MARVEL, DC, DARK HORSE & BLIZZARD, DESIGNED THE LOGOS FOR AVENGERS, DAREDEVIL, BLACK PANTHER & ANGRY BIRDS, AND CREATED HUNDREDS OF TYPEFACES FOR COMI-CRAFT AND HIS NEW FOUNDRY, SWELL TYPE.

*COMPOSED BY CLEVER CROW CONSULTING AND DESIGN, PITTSBURGH, PENNSYLVANIA*

# ABOUT THE AUTHOR

BORN IN MISSOURI, GROWING UP IN OHIO, AND SETTLING IN CHICAGO, DAVE NEAL HAS ALWAYS WRITTEN FICTION, BUT ONLY GOT REALLY SERIOUS ABOUT IT IN THE LATE 90S. HE BRINGS A STRONG RUST BELT PERSPECTIVE TO HIS WRITING, A KIND OF "NORTHERN GOTHIC" AESTHETIC REFLECTIVE OF HIS BACKGROUND.

WRITING HIS FIRST NOVEL AT 29, HE THEN DEVOTED TIME TO HIS CRAFT AND WORKED ON SHORT STORIES, OCCUPYING A SPACE BETWEEN GENRE AND LITERARY FICTION, WITH AN EMPHASIS ON HORROR, SCIENCE FICTION, AND FANTASY. HE HAS SEEN SOME OF HIS SHORT STORIES PUBLISHED IN "ALBEDO 1," IRELAND'S PREMIER MAGAZINE OF SPECULATIVE FICTION, AND HE WON SECOND PLACE IN THEIR AEON AWARD IN 2008 FOR HIS SHORT STORY, "AEGIS." HE HAS LIVED IN CHICAGO SINCE 1993, AND IS A PASSIONATE FAN OF MUSIC, A STUDENT OF POP CULTURE, AN AVID PHOTOGRAPHER AND BICYCLER, AND ENJOYS COOKING.

AS D.T. NEAL HE HAS PUBLISHED SEVEN NOVELS, *SAAMAANTHAA*, *THE HAPPENING*, AND *NORM*—COLLECTIVELY KNOWN AS THE WOLFSHADOW TRILOGY—*CHOSEN*, *SUCKAGE*, THE COSMIC FOLK HORROR-COMEDY THRILLER, *THE CURSED EARTH*, AND *RETURN TO SUMMERVILLE*. HE HAS ALSO PUBLISHED THREE NOVELLAS—*RELICT*, *SUMMERVILLE*, AND *THE DAY OF THE NIGHTFISH*, AND ONE COLLECTION OF KING IN YELLOW THEMED STORIES, *THE THING IN YELLOW*.

# ACKNOWLEDGMENTS

I WOULD LIKE TO THANK CHRISTINE MARIE SCOTT OF CLEVER CROW CONSULTING AND DESIGN IN PITTSBURGH FOR HER WONDERFUL COVER ART AND HER INVALUABLE ASSISTANCE WITH THE LAYOUT AND DESIGN OF THESE PAGES.

# JOIN THE 'CLIQUE!

Show us your books and fan art!

## #SHUTTERCLIQUE

### @NosetouchPress

Instagram • Threads • Facebook • Twitter • Youtube • Bluesky

# T-120

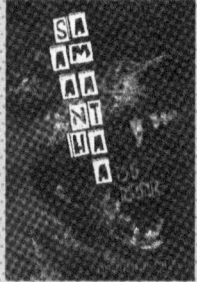